Do Earth-Dogs-Space-Alien Mutants Walk Among Us?

Halfway to Earth, something happened.

Instead of the silky ears of a Golden Retriever, Angel has ear tubes. It's not what he'd hoped for but their phenomenal hearing power might be an asset in his search for home and family.

The Night Dogs, the homeless strays, welcome this strange new breed into their pack. Their leader is Boss, a fearsome Rottweiler. Boss's first concern is his human companion, his Old Friend. His second concern is the pack, the other homeless strays. Someone has to maintain order and that someone is Boss!

The Day Dogs have homes and families. Lester is a favorite. A big, handsome Standard Poodle with fabulous hair, he reluctantly serves as the Show-Dog-Style-Model for Francine, the dog groomer. For his mother, Lucy, he feigns interest in the Top Show Dog Champion Crown.

Lester's favorite feature is his huge nose. It's not Poodle but it's powerful! Today: Hair-do model! Tomorrow: Crime-Sniffing Police-Poodle!

Will Angel's ear-tubes ever grow fur? Will Lester run away to pursue his own dreams?

A chance meeting with Boss changes everything...

Do Earth-Dog-Space-Alien Mutants Walk Among Us? © 2014 by Rose O'Connor. All rights reserved. First published as an ebook in 2014 by Rose O'Connor.

ISBN Number 978-0-9906903-8-2.

Photographs courtesy of Kevin R. Tobin
and Adrian R. Hyman.

Book Design by Maggie Oren
Meet the Cast – Photos sourced from Shutterstock

Artwork by Michael Capozzola:
Real Dogs Like Howling at the Moon (cover)
Ben and Jerry Find the Dog Park
The Doggie-Do-Right Day Care Center
We Have to Keep Him! (Randy, Boss and Angel)
Lester's Worst Hair Day Ever
Angel Risks It All
Old Friend
Busy Angel

Author's Notes and Acknowledgements

This story began its life as a musical comedy for the stage.

Novels are different from plays. The dogs can tell us more of their stories. The humans, Old Friend, Day Care Guy and Bob play much larger roles in the novel. Other humans created themselves for the novel: Francine the Dog Groomer, the Bus Driver and his Cousin, the Cop and his Nephew, and the many different owners of the Day Dogs.

I'd like to thank my sister, Anne Petersen, the original Lucy onstage, Nellie Cravens, director of Silver Moon Theatre who was brave enough to take it on, and to

J. Althea for music arrangements, cast training and performance. The actors in the original production brought their characters to sparkling life and I thank them all, along with Lisa, Kim E, Laura J (the seventh Jerry) and all of Silver Moon's supporters. Thanks also to Paula Martin, Kevin Tobin, Mary Marchetti and Tim Molinari, Ceil Muller, Mike Scott, Steve and Janice Kushman, Brenda and Lauren Marshall, Pam Freeman, Ray Kerr, Brian Hudgens, Mike Capozzola, Maggie Oren and to everyone else for the support offered to get this thing done, on to the stage and now on to your reading list. Special thanks to Terry O'Connor who brought me the Cammie-Dog Border Collie pup and trained her into the wonderful creature that she was. One fun note for me is that Randy, the Border Collie, although not the star of the show, had more singing time than any other character.

I hope you'll enjoy the story! As I used to say about the musical, "You'll laugh, you'll cry, you'll go home happy!"

The next page is the back cover of the Silver Moon Theatre production of "Dogs! It's the Musical" performance program.

Rose O'Connor

MEET THE CAST

Angel – Golden Retriever

Bailiff – Welsh Corgi

Ben – English Sheepdog

Boss – Rottweiler

Fifi – Shih Tzu

Jerry – Pit Bull

Lester – Standard Poodle

Lili – Bichon Frise

Lucy – Toy Poodle

Melinda – Irish Setter

Mimi – French Bulldog

Papillion – Papillion

Randy – Border Collie

Rufahlo – Doberman Pinscher

Spotty – Springer Spaniel

Table of Contents

Chapter One

Free, Not Free and Free with Strings Attached

A full moon was rising. All the dogs looked up.

Some howled, others considered it. The rest quietly noted its presence and turned back to their own dog business.

Bam!

When the heavy front door slammed shut like that, the walls of the small house shivered and so did Ben.

Stomp! Stomp! Stomp!

The windows jittered in their rotting frames as heavy boots pounded the floor.

"Where's that dog?" the Man roared. His huge "angry-man" voice pierced the walls from two rooms away.

"This can't be good," Ben thought. As the terror built, Ben reminded himself not to pee on the floor. That would only make things worse.

"Where's that dog?" The Man was closer now. Ben's sensitive nose twitched at the new smell flowing in from under the closed door. That sweet sour smell meant trouble. It meant the Man was angry and looking for a fight. Having found none, or worse, having lost one, he'd come home to punish Ben.

"Lousy guard dog," he'd say." Too friendly! Let's people get too close!"

Whatever he had going on in that trailer out back, his "science experiments" he called it, the Man did not want anyone near. As a guard dog gig, it was pretty easy. They were far away from other neighbors and the Man was a mean-tempered cuss. Very few people came around except the Man's few friends, other mean-tempered men like himself. Ben wondered why these men came around at all. None of them seemed to like each other. Ben suspected they weren't very good scientists either, as small fires kept igniting in the trailer. Panic would ensue as the men put out the fires, then they would yell at each other. Invariably, when the other men went home, the Man would find some excuse to give Ben a beating.

"You bark too much!" he'd yell, swinging his belt. "Well, what am I supposed to do when a fire breaks out," Ben would think as he dodged the blows. "I'm supposed to summon help, aren't I?"

Or, he would say "You eat too much!" which was a laugh and a half. If someone gave Ben a pet, which no one did these days, they would feel bones rattling just under his fur. The Man remembered to feed him only once in a while, grumbling all the time about the expense and the bother and the waste.

"Where's that ugly dog?" the voice roared.

Now that hurt.

They watched TV sometimes, the Man in the chair snoring, Ben hiding behind the chair to sneak a look. Dogs on TV were always pretty but their lives were different. Why couldn't the Man see that if he fed Ben nice food, like the dogs on TV were fed, his English Sheepdog coat could be as glossy as theirs? Or if he got a bath now and then, his coat would be clean instead of caked with mud and dulled with dust? If he got brushed now and then, it would be silky and smooth, not tangled up with knots. The Man didn't seem to understand any of this. He seemed to think Ben was ugly on purpose.

"Where's that dog?" The roar came from just behind the door. Ben hid behind the chair, knowing this would buy him only a few seconds. "Still, a few seconds of not getting beat up," he thought, "better than nothing."

Oh, if only some Angel from Heaven would come down to intervene! Ben had seen things like that on TV. A beautiful Angel could come down to Earth and lift Ben away on a cloud of glory, straight up to Heaven!

"Oh, wait," Ben thought. "If I was in Heaven, then I'd be dead. Don't want that," he thought. "But please, Mr. or Mrs. Angel! Please do something!"

Bam! The door to the back porch, Ben's room, slammed open.

"Where's that…"

Ka-Boom!

The huge noise came from right outside. Ben looked through the screen door and saw the ball of fire and smoke rising from what was left of the trailer.

"No!" the Man shouted. Clearly, he had forgotten all about Ben. He hit the screen door so hard he knocked it off its hinges then got all tangled up with it as he fell onto the porch. He got up and careened toward the burning trailer. Ben shook off the shock of it all and looked at the empty doorway.

"Thank you, Mr. or Mrs. Angel!" He bolted through the door, down the broken steps, through the weedy yard, then up and over the low bit of fence, the part that had been crushed when the Man forgot where the gate was and rammed it with his truck.

As he jumped, another loud boom sounded from behind. A blast of hot air lifted him higher and he sailed through the air like a bird. He rolled a bit when he landed but ended up on his feet. As he shook his legs to see if they were all there and all right, he saw the Man's hat flutter to the ground a short distance away. Then one of his boots. Then bits of the trailer, glowing red and steaming in the wet grass. He didn't need to see more.

"Thank you, Mr. or Mrs. Angel!" He ran away as hard and as fast as he could.

When Lester used his "Yes, Mother" face, he could often postpone whatever argument was brewing for at least a couple of minutes. He fixed his handsome features in a very serious pose. Nodding his head every now and then signified agreement with whatever she was saying. Nodding slowly gave the impression of careful consideration of her words. It also kept his top knot poodle poof still, which was much less irritating than having it flop around like a half-filled water balloon. The ear pompoms were bad enough, swinging back and forth like fluffy pendulums. He tried his best to ignore them.

He fixed his gaze on the middle distance. He felt this added gravity and complexity to his expression. It also meant he could gaze right over his mother's head and out the window.

She was so tiny, his mother, Lucy. A fully pedigreed, pure-bred Toy Poodle, how had she produced a pure bred Standard Poodle as a son? "She lied to me about Dad," Lester thought for the thousandth time.

He loved her, of course he did, but she had plans for him that he simply didn't share or care about. When he tried to tell her this, she talked and cried and argued. It was better to admit nothing, avoid the subject altogether.

"Surely, Lester, you can see my point!" she was saying. He nodded slowly, pompoms swinging and she was off again, the little bow on her poof top twitching with exasperation as her jaws snapped and flapped.

Lester tightened his face to look even more serious. He nodded slowly. Out the window, off in the middle distance, a fireball shot into the air, collapsed on itself and spewed clouds of smoke into the evening sky.

Lester's pupils dilated with excitement. "The Wild Places!" he thought, and suppressed a shiver of thrill.

Spotty knew all about the Wild Places beyond the edge of the nice, neat town where they played together at the Dog Park. They didn't talk too much about it, since it seemed a sad subject for Spotty, but Lester knew his friend was a Night Dog, a stray, no home, no family. Always hungry, Spotty devoured whatever biscuit or treat Lester managed to smuggle out in the collar pocket that was supposed to hold his poop bags. The food smuggling meant Lester never had any poop bags, a fact that confounded the Day Care Guy, who was nice enough but not really on the ball, in Lester's opinion.

Spotty's talk of Wild Places filled Lester with indescribable hopes and yearnings. Adventure! Life was out there! You could run through open fields, splash through mud, chase cats or rabbits, or whatever, without a care. Never mind that your carefully sculpted poof would go all flat, muddy and dread-locked, your coat would get ripped and ragged, torn by branches or encounters with wild creatures! Life was out there! Adventure! Spotty knew all about it! Spotty, who was always hungry and sometimes quite sick but still, he was free! Free! Spotty never had to sit still to have his hair and nails done. He wasn't combed out or sprayed with chemicals for a glossy shine. "He'd sit still if there was food involved but a Springer Spaniel has no poof to spray," Lester thought. "What would be the point? Still, Spotty would do anything for food...."

There were other Night Dogs and they were a pack, better than nothing, but Spotty had once had a family. Lester knew Spotty yearned for all the things Lester would leave behind in an instant, if Adventure ever called his name.

"We should trade places," Lester thought, a sudden purpose filling his mind and altering his calm but serious "Yes, Mother" face. "Please Mr. or Mrs. Angel," he thought. "Let us trade places. I would not be lonely! Adventure would be my Friend, Danger my mortal enemy! Danger! I'd hunt it down, I'd rip its pant leg......"

"And you'll have to have your hair done tomorrow! Again!" Lucy spluttered. "The Dog Show is two days away and look at you! No more of that low-life Spotty!

No more rolling in mud! If you're ever going to be the Top Show Dog Champion, you have to focus!"

"I don't want to be the Top Show Dog Champion, Mother." Lester spoke in a trancelike monotone.

"What?" Lucy shrieked.

"And I hate this haircut!" Lester reached over her head. "Where's those clippers?"

"Oh, no!" Lucy blocked and tossed him as well as any Rottweiler. "Not again! Not the clippers again! What's wrong with you?"

The other dogs boarding in the Doggie Do Right Day Care Center watched this familiar scene, transfixed by the drama

13

unfolding before their eyes. How would it play out this time? Would Lester prevail, get control of the clippers, give himself a buzz cut and break his mother's heart? Or would Lucy, biting and snapping and, one had to admit, fighting rather dirty for such a fancy little dog, would she win again and bring her son to heel?

They growled. They struggled. The clippers buzzed on and off as each one fought for control. In the end, as usual, the Day Care Guy noticed the ruckus, took the clippers away and sent the two dogs to their pillows. He sniffed the air.

"Is that smoke?"

He looked out the window and saw flames in the distance. "OK," he said. "Waaaaaay over there. No worries." He put the clippers away and all the dogs went back to minding their own business.

When the first boom rattled the trees, Old Friend flinched and sat up. After a second, he closed his eyes and sank back to the ground. Relieved, Boss rearranged the dirty coat and tattered blanket to cover his human again. Concerned, he noted that although his Old Friend had gone back to sleep, he muttered and mumbled and seemed ready to jump again.

"What's wrong with him?" asked Bailiff.

"Nightmares" said Boss. "Explosions like that make him remember."

"Remember what?" asked Bailiff.

"Things he needs to forget," said Boss. "Oh, Mr. or Mrs. Angel," Boss thought to himself. "Please help him forget those bad times, those bad places. Please make him well again!"

Bailiff cocked his big bat ears. "What kind of..." he started. Before he could finish, the second boom cut him off. Both dogs flinched. Old Friend sat bolt upright and opened his mouth as if to scream.

"Quick!" said Boss, "start licking!" Boss was tall enough to lick his left cheek. Bailiff stood on his hind legs to reach the right.

"Oh! Oh! Oh!" Old Friend moaned and shivered but the soothing film of dog spit applied by their vigorous licking calmed him down. After a minute, Old Friend shook his head, finally fully awake.

"Oh! I'm here! I'm here! Not there! I'm here and we're safe! Thank you, Boss, my baby boy. What would I do without you? And your little friend here, what a cute fella, how is it you don't have a home?"

"I don't want to talk about it," Bailiff hung his head.

"Well, you can stay with us. It's cold out here but the trees keep the wind out of our little circle. Lucky me! Two dogs to keep me warm! Do I smell smoke? I think I do…but it seems far away. Let's go back to sleep, my baby boys."

Old Friend settled back down on his ratty scarf pillow, covered his head with the broad brimmed hat and was snoring again in an instant. Boss arranged the coat and the blanket to cover him and snuggled up close.

"I smell smoke too," he said. "Will you go see what it is?"

Having just been invited to snuggle up to a nice warm human, Bailiff didn't want to go anywhere. But when a big, strong Rottweiler tells a little Welsh Corgi to go do something, it was generally in the best interest to go do it. Besides, big, bad-looking Boss wandering around the Dog Park at night would frighten people. When people got frightened, bad things could happen. No, it was safer and the better idea all around for Boss to stay here. People saw him with the human, the one he called his Old Friend and left them alone.

Tiny little Bailiff could skulk through the bushes unseen, make his way to the high ground and try to see what was what. "Look at me!" thought Bailiff, "I have a job! An important and necessary thing to do! And when I report back, they'll be pleased and proud of me and let me snuggle closer to get warm. That will be very nice."

From the top of the high ground, Bailiff could see smoke rising

15

in the far distance. Flames still flickered but streams of water were beating them down. "All good," he thought.

By the time he got back, both Boss and his Old Friend were fast asleep. "I'll tell them tomorrow," Bailiff decided. "I'll give a full report."

Boss lay at his Old Friend's back, his head resting on the old man's waist, his paw slung over his legs. Slowly and carefully, Bailiff snuggled himself against the old man's stomach. The old man stirred a little and put his arm around Bailiff. "This is so nice," thought Bailiff. "Please Mr. or Mrs. Angel," he thought. "Please let me stay here with them!" He snuggled closer and drifted off to sleep.

Chapter Two

Heaven Can Be Boring

Most angels in Heaven were quite content to be there. Not many planned trips to Earth any time soon, in spite of the white noise of constant prayers sent their way. Sorting out the prayers, that was His department. Angels took orders, when He gave them, which was rare. In the absence of any direct order, they were free to float about, enjoying the harp music and thinking their own thoughts, if any occurred, which was also rare.

Angel had only one thought. It played over and over in his mind, effectively drowning out the harp music. He enjoyed this thought, he nurtured and loved this thought.

"If I keep this thought first and foremost in my mind," he reasoned, "someday soon, the thought will become reality." That sort of thing could happen. He had read all about it on the Ethereal dot net site. It was called "The Secret". "Although," he told himself," anything posted on the Ethereal dot net site won't be much of a secret after that. Never mind, think the thought some more."

So, he sat waiting, thinking the same thought over and over. His seat was the last in a row of empty cloud poof chairs set up under a sign that read "Reincarnation Project! Volunteers needed!"

He'd been here for seven days now. Other angels had already received their assignments and moved on. The first would be a hog. "Oooooo! Mud! Slop!" he exclaimed, spinning like a top from the joy of it all. The second would be a frog. "Lovely!" he said. "Must practice for that! Ribit! Ribit! Does that sound right?" he asked and then was gone.

Angel was still here. Had they forgotten his assignment or, worse, decided against sending him at all?

Another angel floated by. His beatific face seemed puzzled as he read the sign and looked at Angel sitting there. Angel gave a weak little wave, just for politeness' sake. The other angel shrugged as if to say, "Well, it takes all kinds, doesn't it?" He beamed beatifically once again and floated away.

If Angel's head had been a physical thing, it would be hurting by now from the effort of thinking his thought. What could be taking so long? Little cobwebs of despair formed around his halo. Brushing them away, he renewed his hopes and focused on his one thought.

Just then, a Busy and Important Angel floated up to the row of poofy chairs. Nothing says Busy and Important better than two rows of wings, one stacked upon the other and pointing upward dramatically. As if this weren't enough, he wore a Bluetooth and carried a clipboard! He mumbled something into the Bluetooth and flipped a few pages.

"Here we go!" Angel thought. "This must be it!"

The Busy Angel flipped a few more pages, seemed puzzled, then spun around to float away.

"Wait!" called Angel, "Wait!"

The Busy Angel turned and looked him over. "Not very impressive," he thought.

"What?" he thundered.

"Has He made a decision?" Angel asked meekly, his tiny wings flittering.

Busy Angel consulted his clipboard. His stern face relaxed.

"Oh, yes", he smiled. "Sorry, I'm a little distracted. Just heard the most wonderful concert on Cloud Nine! Harp music! Perfection! Aaaaaaaaaah, yes! So hard to concentrate when that heavenly music is playing!"

"It's playing all the time," said the trembling, cob-webby disgrace to all things holy.

"Which is why I'm so distracted!" Busy Angel sniffed. "All right, let's see here..."

He flipped a few pages. "Ah!" he exclaimed. He looked at the page, puzzled again.

"Look at that. You're going to be a slug...wait, is that right? I'm having trouble reading this."

His voice dropped to a whisper.

"His handwriting is awful! Can't read it, even when it's big and hanging on the wall!" He startled himself with this admission. "Look who I'm talking to," he thought.

He pulled his face back into the stern expression. "Can you see that? Hmmmmm, slug. Seems an odd choice." he said. "Even for you."

Angel stared at the page, shock turning to disbelief, then utter despair.

And then, his precious thought, treasured and nurtured for so long, changed to an idea.

"No," he said brightly. "That's not it. See, the cursive s actually connects to L. The u here is actually an o that hasn't been closed properly. Such a Busy Being, has to write very quickly, no wonder it comes out a bit slap-dash."

Busy Angel was shocked by this impertinence. Such a thing to say about Him! But then remembering his own recent lapse in judgment, shamefacedly, he found he couldn't disagree.

"Look," the impertinent little thing continued in that bright, hopeful voice. "I'll just close the u and connect the dangling s and the L and there! That's better! You can read that now, can't you?"

"Oh, yes! Clear as day. That makes more sense." Busy Angel extended his hand slowly and ceremoniously. He fanned his two-tiered wings and said in a loud, Busy and Important voice, "And now, in the name of all that's holy, I pronounce you.........Dog!"

"Yes!" Angel squeaked. If his eyes were physical things, and very soon they would be, oh how they would cry for joy! He leapt from his cloudy perch, waved to Busy Angel, and made a belly flopping dive toward Earth.

Busy Angel smiled a bit as he floated off to his next assignment. "Takes all kinds, doesn't it?" he asked himself and flapped his two-tiered wings.

Heaven is not far from Earth and Angel was there in no time at all. When he got there he still had just enough angel left to manage a fairly soft landing. As he shook himself and checked himself to see if all the parts were there and working, he heard a soft hissing sound. With a pop and then a plop, the last of his little wings molted away and fell to the ground. After a second, they disappeared in a cloud of steam.

"I'm a Dog!" he whispered to himself. "I'm a Dog! No, wait, am I? Really?" He twisted and strained to look at as much of himself as he could see.

"I must see myself!" he thought. "But how?"

He remembered a story about a god from another religion. The god had looked into a pond and saw his reflection there.

"A pond!" Angel decided. "I must find a pond!"

He ran around the grassy land searching for a pond, a puddle, a little stream, anything!

"I must be careful," he cautioned himself. "That god saw himself, fell in love and never moved again! He watched himself all day. Not very useful. A dog must be useful. No matter how pleased I may be with myself, I shall count to ten and look away!"

He came to the edge of the field. A smooth stone surface stretched a few feet beyond its edge and then changed to a smooth dark surface. Angel decided that grass was better. He would stay on the grass.

Still looking for puddles, he was distracted by a movement in the far distance. He recognized the flicker of flames and plumes of smoke.

"Is that Hell?" he thought. "Is Hell really here on Earth?" He saw streams of water beating down the flames. Water! There would be puddles! But the flames and the water were far away and he couldn't see much grass in between.

He wondered what to do next. His eyes settled on a tall shiny object nearby. The object was a slender pillar with a bowl on top. Water dribbled out of the bowl! Puddles!

20

He approached cautiously. Near to the object was another pillar, a very tall pillar with a lighted top. "Like a moon on a stick!" he thought. After some experimentation, he found if he placed his head between the moon on the stick and the puddle on the ground, he could see his reflection.

And, oh, what glory there was in that reflection! He was gorgeous! "A very handsome fellow, if I do say so myself! Look at those ears!"

Remembering his cautious plan, he counted very slowly to ten. Then, because he was so unexpectedly and wonderfully handsome, he allowed himself another count to ten.

"Silky, red-gold hair, one, fine legs, two, nice snout, three, full flapping tail, four, dark soulful eyes, five…" and on he counted til ten.

"That's it! That's enough!" He willed himself away.

He started to say a prayer of thanks. Then, remembering his manipulation of the Almighty's will, decided he'd better not.

"Best to lay low," he thought, "and not call attention to myself."

Instead of a prayer, he decided to review the whole situation and express gratitude. He made a list of everything he could remember from Ethereal dot net.

"I get to jump on beds and sofas," he thought, "and roll in mud upon my back…

I get to pee on shrubs and bushes.…I can pee!" His heart filled with a somewhat evil glee. "Angel's can't!" he thought smugly. "And, if I knew just what one looked like, I would try to chase a cat!" He grinned from softly-folded, silky-haired ear to ear. "Whoo-hoo!" he yipped. "I'm a dog!" He flipped his tail back and forth.

Finally, because prayer was a familiar format, he forgot about not calling attention to himself. He raised his eyes to the billion stars and, quite tunefully, as if singing along with the now inaudible harp music, he howled.

"I'm a dog!" His howl was soft and soulful. "Thank you, God!"

he said sincerely.

"Iiiiiiiiiiiiiiiiii'm aaaaaaaaaaa dooooooooooooooog!" he howled at the smiling moon.

Chapter Three

No, You're Not

Nothing says angry like a Busy and Important Angel's two tiers of wing feathers sticking straight out like porcupine quills. Navigating flight is difficult with feathers in the angry position and Busy Angel's landing was bumpy and graceless, making him angrier still. He watched the golden puppy's joyous romp and allowed himself some rather sinfully happy anticipation of the pain he was about to inflict.

After a few seconds, he felt his feathers relax as his anger melted away.

"Such an engaging little creature", he thought. "Such a poor angel. Pathetic, really. But here he is, a lovely dog!"

Watching the happy puppy dance and sing and howl and wag its tail, he found he felt quite bad about the job he had to do.

"Don't look at the eyes," he instructed himself. "Puppy eyes can hypnotize and make one do stupid things, like give them more treats when they're already too fat. No! I must be strong and implacable. He got the better of me once and it can't happen again. Oh, look, he's thanking God, quite commendable and yet it makes my job all the more sad and difficult…oh, pull yourself together!" He admonished himself in that stern voice he used to frighten the Cherubim. "Don't look at the eyes and get this done!"

Angel howled his final line with all the bravado and brio of a still hopeful but fading opera star.

"Iiiiiiiiiiiii'm…..aaaaaaaaaaaaaaaa………dooooooooooooog!"

Busy waited 'til the last note of Angel's song had drifted up to the clouds.

"No………………… youuuuuuuuuuuuuuuuuu're……………… noooooooooooooooot!"

Busy sang the same notes as Angel's final line. "Why did I do that?" he thought. He didn't know. It just came out that way and now he felt bad. The job he had to do was bad enough without being mean.

"Look at the little thing. Not the eyes! Not the eyes! Look at the other parts! Look at him, frightened out of his wits. And just a moment ago, he was so happy. Oh, this is too hard! What is he doing? Good Lord, he's peed on himself!"

Indeed, Angel was now standing in a puddle and appeared to be wheezing.

"Hrrrk! Haahk! How do you do this? I did it just a second ago! Hrrrrrk!"

Angel gave up trying to howl and settled for a squeak.

"Help!"

"What do you mean?" boomed Busy Angel.

"Sir! I mean, Sir! Can I help you Sir?" Angel rattled, "What are you doing here, Sir?"

The right half of Busy's angel brain admired the little pup. "A physical brain and its limitations. A body…gravity…and the little spirit took all that on," he pondered.

Then the left side of his brain remembered the brimstone.

"You're a mendacious, manipulative, mutt! " Busy Angel boomed.

"A mutt?" the little pup asked. "I had parents? Did you know them?"

"You were supposed to be a slug!" he boomed in response. "Busy Being, bad handwriting! You did this on purpose! I had to dodge a lot of brimstone when He found out!"

"Didn't He already know it?" Angel puzzled. "He knows all things…."

"Of course He knows all things!" Busy spluttered. "But not all things at the same time!" he faltered. "Some things are sequential!"

He paused and breathed deeply, gathering strength. He finished in strong voice.

"And you're going to be a slug!"

A strong finish, only one crack in the voice. Too bad it was when I said 'slug'", he thought.

"No! This is right." The little thing spoke with surprising conviction. "I'm sure this is right!"

"Brimstone," Busy thought to himself. "Remember the brimstone and don't look at the eyes!"

"To be a dog is a privilege!" he boomed but felt the effort. This was not good.

"A reward!" He soldiered on. "Not a reincarnation experiment! A slug is a reincarnation experiment!"

He floated swiftly to the little pup's side. "You're a slug! That's it! Gimme those ears!"

Angel felt a pop and a plop. Something left his head and something new was put in its place.

"There!" said Busy Angel. "And now, in the name of all that's holy, I declare you...a slug!"

Angel closed his eyes and cringed. He felt nothing. He couldn't stand the terror. He opened his eyes and peered at his belly through his front legs.

He still had legs! Slugs didn't have legs!

He saw the beautiful red-gold hair floating in the breeze. He wagged his tail and the silken fronds swayed to and fro.

"Ummmmmm..." he said. "I'm still a dog."

Busy Angel smacked his forehead.

"Earth! Evolution! Fine! It will take a few days. But a slug you will be!"

Angel gazed sadly at his altered state. The beautiful red-gold, silk-covered ears he had seen in the puddle were gone. A pair of gooey looking slug tentacles bobbled in their place.

Angel's sorrow turned to anger and anger to will. His newfound will banished all fear.

He looked calmly at Busy Angel.

Busy made the mistake of looking directly into the still limpid and powerfully hypnotic puppy eyes.

"I'm a Dog," Angel said in a strong clear voice. "A Dog!" he continued. "With an ear-cropping job gone terribly wrong but, still, a Dog!"

Flustered by the puppy eyes and the little thing's new fearlessness, Busy relied on the tried and true: the Busy and Important.

He swelled his specter to lofty heights, towering over the little pup, who didn't run or tremble. Unnerved, Busy got busy.

"You don't just ...get to be a dog!" He boomed.

The puppy sat still and stared him down.

Willing himself not to choke, or to fly away too fast, Busy continued.

"You have to earn it!" he boomed, as haughtily and impressively as he could.

With a final mighty effort, he finished.

"I'll be watching!" he hissed.

As slowly as he could manage, trying desperately to appear nonchalant, he floated away. As distance increased, his composure returned. His wing feathers relaxed. He forced himself not to look back at the strange new creature, this strong-willed little thing who no longer feared him.

Angel sat motionless. He stared straight up til the specter melted into the darkness. "I'm a Dog!" he said. "I am!"

Except for the twinkling stars, the sky was empty now. Angel relaxed. He positioned himself between the moon-on-a-stick and his puddle mirror and gazed at his reflection. His spirits sagged. "No danger of falling too much in love with this," he thought. He looked...so very odd! The silly, slimy tentacles bobbed back and forth. "Oooo," he sighed, feeling very bad. After a second, he realized the tentacles were moving because he made them move, just as he could make his tail move when he wanted. As ears, they seemed to function quite well. "That's got to be good," he thought, cheering up a little. They weren't pretty but as he moved them all around, he realized he could point them in any direction and hear quite clearly. He noticed the sound of crunching leaves behind him but remained too self-absorbed to turn around. He saw himself again in the puddle. "Ooooo," he sighed, spirits sagging to new lows. "Stop it!" he bossed himself. "They're fine hearing instruments any dog would be lucky to have! If you don't like how they look, look away! Value what you have and avoid the sins of narcissism and envy! You're a dog and whatever they look like, they're excellent ears and very powerful!

The leaf crunching was quite loud now.

"Don't be staring at yourself, you're a dog and must find ways to be useful! Back away from the puddle! Back away...."

Angel stepped back from the disturbing reflection, praising his strange ears for their strength and ability. The leaf crunching was deafening now.

"Oooof!" squeaked something. "Oooof!" Angel squeaked back. The leaf crunching stopped, replaced by the ooof ooof bang sounds of something tumbling down the slope. He heard a small splash and turned to see what happened. His turn around completed, he could now see what had happened. Backing away from his reflection, he'd bumped into another creature. The impact had sent the creature tumbling down the hill. It splashed to rest right in the middle of the puddle of his piddle of fear.

"Oh! I'm so sorry!" Angel exclaimed, rushing forward.

"You!" the creature said. Angel stopped in his tracks. "I'm so sorry!" he said. "May I..." He found he couldn't say any more. A thrill he'd never experienced shivered through the body he'd never had before. This creature was ...another dog!

It looked nothing like him. It was small and round with very big eyes. Its tail was a silly curlique on top of its rump. Its coat was short and smooth and the color of French champagne, not that he really knew what that was, but the words popped into his head and sounded right. On top of its head were two magnificent, expressive bat-like ears. They moved like radar shields scanning the sky. Right now, they were pressed back flat. Where had this creature come from? What was it doing here? Angel's ideas on the subject were limited. He tried his best.

"Are you an angel?" he asked and noted a change in the creature's demeanor.

The creature seemed stunned. He moved forward to offer a paw of support to move away from the piddle puddle.

"How DARE you!" the creature growled.

"Good Lord! It's a girl!"

Unable to stop himself, Angel snuck a not too subtle peek between his legs.

"And I'm a boy! I'm a boy dog! And this is a girl!"

"Ahem!" he coughed and tried again. "Are you an angel?" he asked. "Do I see wings?" He offered his paw.

"How dare you bump me?" the girl shouted. "How dare you touch me at all? Who do you think you are? You do not touch Mimi! No one touches Mimi unless Bob says so! Or maybe I like you. But I don't! I don't even know you! Don't even try to smell me! I fight you! Yes, Mimi will fight! Or bark til you're deaf! Arf arf! Deaf, I say! Try to frighten me and I'll rip you to shreds like one of Bob's silk ties!"

Angel was shocked. He panted with fear. How could such a small creature hold so much anger?

"Oh no!" he thought. "She's going to explode!"

The little dog's face had shriveled to a terrifying grimace.

"She's gonna blow!"

Angel braced himself. A fine spray of pee-scented water hit his face. The little dog had not exploded after all. She shook her little body violently from head to toe, sending an explosion of spray floating into the air in all directions.

"Whew!" Angel thought. He looked at the angry little face and panicked.

"Oh no! She's going to shout again!"

Without really knowing why he did it, Angel flopped on his back, curled his legs in the air, and showed the girl-dog his belly.

"That's better," she said. "You may get up. Now, who are you?"

"A name!" he thought. "I need a name! What's my name? Think, dog, think!"

"What? You don't know your own name?" the girl shouted, stomping her paws.

"I do! I do!" he stammered. "Angel! Yes, that's it, that's my name, I'm Angel!"

"Sure you are," she snapped. "Don't even try to smell me! Where are you from?"

"Ummmm," Angel paused. Thinking seemed to be easier, although it still made his head hurt. He felt confident the answer would come.

"I've been here all my life." A tiny note of triumph crept into his voice. He'd given two good answers and hadn't lied once!

"Well, then," said the girl. "Maybe you can tell me where "here" is? What is this place? Where are we?"

"Uh oh," Angel thought. "Stall! No! Abandon ship! No! Change course, change course....surprise her!"

"Well," he tried very hard to do his best impression of Busy Angel. "Who are you, anyway? And who is Bob?"

The little dog's eyes bugged out.

"Her eyes!" he thought. "They're going to explode!"

He braced himself and started to shut his eyes but caught a glimpse of her face. It had changed. It was still haughty but did he detect a very small hint of amusement? He opened his eyes again. She was almost-smiling. It was a pitying look but Angel sensed this was better than most of the alternatives.

"I am Mimi," she declared. Her smile was lovely but her eyes said, "And don't you forget it!"

"I won't!" Angel promised himself.

"I am the Bulldog," she said. "French."

She batted her eyes and waited for the usual ooos and ahs. None came.

"And you are, I think, the Golden Retriever?"

The other dog's face was blank. He seemed to be waiting for more information.

"And Bob is my Friend," she said. Another moment of silence passed.

"My Friend!" she said loudly into Angel's blank face. "You know! My owner!"

"Think, dog, think!" Angel tried to sort this out. "This is what, three, four times now, how many times am I going to have to think in a day? I'm a dog! Must...focus..."

"Your pack leader!" The note of triumph was now quite clear. Overwhelmed with joy at this new success, Angel stretched his neck and stared at the moon. It was shining just over the top of the moon-on-a-stick.

"Yes," she said. "Sometimes I let him think so...."

Why did she sound so sad? Angel sneaked a sideways glance. Sensing no threat, he slowly turned his head to look at her. Her head was down, her ears cocked asymmetrically.

"Oh dear!," Angel cast frantically about for some distraction.

"Look! There's a sign!"

She looked up.

"It says 'Dog Park'" he finished.

Some of her former spark returned.

"I can see it is a Dog Park!" she snapped. "But where is this dog park? What city? What town? What zip code?"

"I know!" said Angel. "Earth!"

He bucked around a step or two. He couldn't help himself. "Gosh, I'm clever!" he howled to himself.

"But WHERE on earth?" the little dog shouted. She stomped her paws. Angel was glad to see this. She seemed herself again.

"Look!" he said, pointing his ears. "More dogs!"

"Oh good!" said Mimi, turning to look. "Maybe one of them will know where on earth we are!"

Mimi's eyes bugged out again. A pack of dogs was moving toward them. "This is well after bedtime," she thought. "Why are they here?"

Mimi was a dog park regular and no shy puppy in any group of dogs. "But where are their Friends?" she thought. All the dogs Mimi held court with at the dog park had their Friends nearby to control them. Sometimes Mimi took advantage of this. She smiled to herself. Yes, it was evil but it was also fun! "It's so hard being good all of the time," she thought to herself. "So who are these bozos?" She stared at the dark shapes lumbering toward them. "And who do I have to help me? Mr. Stare-at-the-Moon? Fine! Bring it on!" She stomped her front paws, one, two, one, two, in anticipation.

"She looks like herself again," Angel thought. "She must be feeling better."

Ben and Jerry Find the Dog Park

Chapter Four

Do Earth-Dog-Space-Alien Mutants Walk Among Us?

"Look! Two more dogs!" said Ben.

"Yeah," said Jerry. "Wait! The bigger one. Is that a dog? What're those things on its head?"

"Less talking, more walking!" the Border Collie snapped and nipped at Ben's heel.

"Hey!" said Ben, "I'm a sheepdog, not a sheep!"

"Move it along!" said the bossy Border Collie.

"What a strange night," Ben thought.

When the trailer exploded, he made his escape from the Angry Man.

"That's a good thing," he thought.

He ran and ran and ran, until he collided with Jerry, who had been sprinting just as hard in a cross direction. They tumbled over each other and landed in a heap. After some growling and posturing, they decided they were ok and could be friends.

Ben hadn't met many other dogs in his life. The Pit Bulls he had met were mean and scary. Jerry wasn't mean at all.

"Not scary, either," Ben thought. "He thinks he's scaring everyone else but he's the one who's scared! Kind of girlie for a Pit Bull." Still, a girlie Pit Bull was preferable to a snarling, jaw-snapping, scary one any day. Ben liked Jerry already and they'd only been together for an hour or so.

Jerry's head hung with shame when he told Ben he had run away.

"You did?" Ben exclaimed. "I ran away too!" That seemed to make Jerry feel better.

"I know it's wrong," Jerry had explained, "but I was so lonely! No one pet me, or played with me, or even talked to me. Just 'sit

33

here, guard the warehouse'..."

"Me, too!" said Ben. "Only mine was a trailer."

"It was big and cold and silent. Nothing to see but hundreds and hundreds of boxes! Nothing to do but look at them. I was so lonely!" Jerry started to cry.

"I'm a people dog, really I am," he cried. "But people don't like me! I must be no good."

"Correction," Ben said. "Those people were no good! And mine was no good either! Look at us! We're good dogs! And we're not there anymore. We're here and we're together! Where should we go now? I'm kind of hungry..."

The trailer and the warehouse were in the wild places on the distant edge of town. Following instinct, they moved away from all the bad memories there. Suddenly, their paws hit smoothly paved streets. Ben and Jerry pranced proudly down the sidewalks. They walked side by side, each one imagining a walk with some new Friend with treats in his or her pocket.

There were houses with pretty front yards. Small dogs in front yards rushed to their fences and barked. Ben and Jerry held their heads high and continued walking.

"No barking," said Ben.

"No talking at all," said Jerry.

"No touching."

"And no eye contact."

"It's ok, little dogs, we're just passing by," said Ben.

"We have no interest in your yard," said Jerry, although he was very interested, especially when the yard was littered with toys.

"Look at all those trees!" Ben pointed ahead. "Let's go there!"

They crossed the first line of trees and stopped to look around. A vast lawn stretched before them, sloping down from the crest where they stood, swooping up again into small hills at the edges of the lawn. Clumps of shrubs, small plots of flowers, groups of trees accented the lawn's surface. There was a sand pit for digging and - could they believe their eyes? - a play structure! Hurdles to leap, loops to jump through, tubes to traverse and toys! There were toys just lying on the ground!

"A ball!" Jerry yelped. "I found a ball!"

"Mmmmmph, squeak!" Ben chewed the squeak toy he had found. It smelled of peanut butter. He blissed out.

And that's when the Border Collie found them.

"'Ello, 'ello, 'ello, what have we here?"

The Border Collie had come up from behind.

"Drop the toys, gentlemen, they don't belong to you."

"But there's no one else here," said Jerry.

"Mmmmmph, squeak!" said Ben.

"First you meet the Boss," said the Border Collie. "If he says you can stay with us, then you can play with the toys."

The Border Collie looked them up and down. He shook his head. "I wouldn't worry about it, mates. In fact, bring the toys. You're shoe-ins, if I ever saw a pair. Bailiff!"

A little blonde Corgi appeared from under a clump of shrubs and ran to the Border Collie's side.

"Are we ready?" asked the Border Collie.

"Yes," Bailiff replied. "But, Randy, did you notice? There's two more up by the leaky drinking fountain."

"I see them," said Randy. "Two here and two more, four dogs found their way here in one night! What is this, Christmas week?"

"No," said Bailiff. "Christmas week was when Spotty arrived. That was a full moon or two ago. This is just...I don't know."

"And look at the ears on the bigger one!" Randy said. "Are they Dogs at all?" He cocked his head to one side. His eyes narrowed to slits.

"Or" he spoke softly. "Could this be the proof the world has waited for?"

His eyes opened wide as he spoke.

"Proof!" he exclaimed, as if preaching to a large congregation. "Proof of the space aliens' frequent visits to Earth to mate with local species? Could this finally be the Earth-Dog-Space-Alien Mutant that has been foretold?" His whole body shivered.

Bailiff sighed. "That's an ear-cropping job gone terribly wrong," he said. "There's no such thing as the Earth-Dog-Space-Alien Mutant, Randy! You made that up to scare the sheep!"

"Don't talk about my sheep!" Randy yelped. His eyes grew misty and he hung his head. Ben and Jerry stopped chewing their toys and stared at him. What was this about? Then the Border Collie chuckled.

"I used to tell the little wooly ones that they were the Earth-Dog-Space-Alien Mutants!" He laughed and wiped his eyes. "That really got them going!"

"And why you would want to get them going right before their bedtime is a mystery to me," said Bailiff. "Boss is waiting."

"All right, all right," Randy tried to stop laughing. After a few seconds he took a deep breath and said, "All right, mates, bring the toys, let's go get these other two and get down to Night Court."

"Night Court?" Jerry yelped.

"I didn't do it!" Ben was frightened. "I didn't do anything!"

"Then you have nothing to worry about, do you?" said Randy. "Unless YOU are the REAL Earth-Dog-Space-Alien Mutant!" He collapsed again, giggling, snorting and coughing. He sat, stretched his front legs out and wrapped his paws around his head.

His whole body shook with silent laughter. Ben and Jerry looked at each other.

"Randy!" Bailiff barked. "Boss is waiting!"

"All right, all right!" Randy wheezed and snapped to all fours again. "Come on, you two, nothing to worry about. I'll be your lawyer and I'll see you right."

Ben and Jerry looked at each other again. The Border Collie nipped their heels and the group started up the slope, Ben and Jerry leading, Bailiff following and Randy, still stifling snorts of laughter, bringing up the rear.

When the four dogs reached the two dogs, the six dogs sat silently for a moment, staring at each other.

"Good Lord!" said Randy. "You really are the Earth-Dog-Space-Alien Mutant! It's really true!"

"What?" Angel asked. "Me? What?"

"Are you from space?" Randy asked sternly.

"Sort of..." Angel answered meekly.

"I knew it!" Randy exclaimed.

"You know nothing," Bailiff sniffed. "What happened to your head?" he asked Angel.

"Leave him alone!" Mimi snapped. "Can't you see he feels bad about it? Obviously, it's an ear-cropping job..." She paused and looked hard at Angel's bobble ears. She had noticed they were different but had been too upset to see them clearly until now.

"...Gone terribly...terribly wrong!" she finished.

"Where are you from?" asked Bailiff.

I've been here all my life," Angel answered. "It was true when I first said it," he thought to himself, "and it's just as true now."

"We haven't seen you before," said Bailiff. "If I had seen you, I'd remember it."

"Did you drop from the sky?" Randy demanded.

"Sort of..." said Angel.

"I knew it!" Randy exclaimed.

"Stop it," said Bailiff. "Now, what happened to your head?"

"I don't know," said Angel, happy to think that for the most part, he was still telling the truth. "I might have been asleep when it happened."

"Haaaaaaaaaaah, uummmmmmmm," all the other dogs

nodded except Ben. He'd never been to the vet before.

"Listen," Angel said earnestly. "I know they look wrong and I do feel bad about it. But they're excellent ears! They hear very well, and look! I can point them!"

To demonstrate, Angel pointed his bobbles at a copse of trees some distance away on top of a small hill.

"I can hear another dog," he said. "And it sounds like he's annoyed."

"Boss!" said Bailiff.

"Let's go, pups," said Randy. "Time to join the pack."

"Maybe we don't want to join your pack!" Mimi sniffed.

"Well, you don't want to be out here all alone either, do you? " Randy asked and nipped her heel.

"Hey! You do not touch Mimi!" she snapped.

"No one touches Mimi unless Bob says so," Angel explained.

"Well, when Bob gets here, I'll ask him nicely," Randy said. "And when might that be?"

Mimi's big eyes filled with tears. It was true. She didn't know when Bob would come and she didn't want to be alone.

"I thought so," said Randy. "Now move it along, pups. Time for Night Court."

"Night Court?" they yelped.

"Don't be afraid, I'll be your lawyer," Randy used his sheep soothing voice. "Now let's move along."

"He's a really good lawyer," Bailiff said to Mimi. She blinked back her tears and joined the pack of pups padding down the slope then up the small hill to the trees. Randy brought up the rear, darting back and forth, keeping the group in tidy formation, nipping at stragglers, all the while thinking of his sheep.

Chapter Five

Night Court

The distant trees had been planted in a circle. When they reached the top of the hill, Randy herded them inside. Shrubs and bushes growing in between the trees formed a leafy wall. Inside the circle might have seemed cozy and protected if the four new dogs hadn't been so anxious.

From behind the trunk of a massive oak, a massive Rottweiler appeared. He strode back and forth, huge muscles clenching and unclenching, staring down each of the new four in turn. In his jaws, a giant bone was trapped between two rows of sharp teeth. He snapped his jaws and the bone rattled. The new four flinched.

"The Beast of Satan!" Angel whinnied softly. "Don't pee!" he commanded himself. "Don't!"

"Och, don't be such a quivering wee purse dog," Randy said quietly. "No offense, dearie," he said to Mimi. "You'll see. He looks mean but he's really just a big pussy cat."

"All sit up and beg!" Bailiff called out. "The Night Dog Court is now in session, the Honorable Big Boss presiding. Please turn off all electronic collars. If they go off in court, they will be confiscated."

Slowly and regally, Boss sat down. Still staring coldly at the new four, he placed the huge bone on the boulder next to him.

"Bailiff," he said, "Tell me, why are you here?"

"To call the cases, Boss," the little dog replied.

"And tell me, why are they here?" Boss pointed.

"To face the law," Bailiff nodded.

"And tell me, why am I here?" the big dog growled.

"'Cause you're the Boss!" Bailiff said.

"That's right!" the big dog growled again and showed his teeth.

"And what I say, goes," he said. "Let me explain it now. I'll make it very plain." He surveyed the new dogs' frightened faces.

"Don't pee on my leg and tell me it's rain. I've heard it all. I've heard it all before. So, toe the line. Or, there's the door," he pointed toward the entrance to the lair. All the dogs' heads turned.

"And if I say to jump," he said loudly, calling their attention back.

"We say, 'how high?'" said the Border Collie.

"And if you break the rules," the Boss dog continued.

"Time to die," Bailiff shook his head to convey that certainly no reasonable dog would do anything of the sort.

"And if you act like fools...........?"

Randy's expression assured him that no reasonable dog would think this a very good idea.

"My, oh my," he muttered.

"'Cause I'm the Boss," the big dog stated firmly. "And what I say goes. Now tell me, who's got the bone?" He picked up the huge fossil and rattled it in his teeth.

"You do, Boss!" said Bailiff.

"I said," the big dog spoke clearly through the bone in his teeth. "Who's got the bone?"

"We say, 'you do, Boss'" Randy said.

He put the bone down.

"I can't hear you," he said.

"Yes, Boss," said Randy and Bailiff. Bailiff gestured to the new dogs.

"Yes!" they all squeaked.

"That's better," the big dog said. "I'm happy now. A happy Boss!"

He looked them over, one by one.

"And now that we understand each other," he said, "Let's get to work. Bailiff, call the first case. No, wait!" He held up a paw. "You two!" he pointed. "Names!"

"Ben," shivered Ben.

"Jerry," squeaked Jerry.

"I don't need to hear your stories. Filthy coat," he pointed at Ben, "and ribs showing." And then to Jerry. "Easily traumatized, under-stimulated, hyper-stressed. Ran away!" His pointing paw moved from Jerry to Ben. "Ran away!" Ben and Jerry hung their heads.

"Ordinarily, this infraction would be cause for the ultimate judgment," he said. "You would be Bad Dogs." In a gentler voice, he said "But I can see why it might have been necessary. You're in, good dogs, go lie down."

Ben and Jerry couldn't move a step. They flopped down where they were, jostling Mimi.

"Hey!" Mimi said. Boss stared at her. "Sorry," she said softly.

"Call your next case!" he said to Bailiff.

"Dog number three, Angel!," Bailiff announced. "Angel appeared from nowhere, knows nothing about himself and has no idea how to be a dog. Angel is represented today by Counselor Randy Sheepherder."

"Mm, mm, mm," Boss dropped his head and shook it wearily.

"Thank you, Boss!" said Randy. He took a deep breath to continue but Boss held up his paw.

"Counselor Randy, is all that true?," he asked.

"Look at him, Boss!" Randy spluttered. "He's like a slobbery, wee pup! But he can't be a pup!" Randy nodded toward Angel's strange ears.

"Thick as two planks as well! Doesn't know the first thing about pack etiquette, doesn't know where he's from, and do we even know he's a dog?"

"I am a dog!" Angel said. "Look!" He panted and jumped around, wagging his beautiful tail. Randy pointed at him.

"What we may have here is living proof!" He waved his paw dramatically. "Earth-Dog-Space-Alien mutants do exist!"

"They do not," Bailiff sighed.

"It's an ear cropping job gone very wrong," said Boss. Angel was still romping around. He was having so much fun, he forgot where he was and that he had been frightened. The slimy tentacles swayed smoothly back and forth as Angel bounced, holding them all entranced.

"It's a wonder he knows his own name," Randy said softly. "Oh, your honor, we've got to keep him!" His voice was shaky now. "He won't last five minutes out there in the urban jungle!" Randy burst into tears. "Ah, look at him, the big stupid baby..."

"All right, counselor Randy, stop," Boss said. "Stop. Please. You're giving me a headache. Lost and alone, that's good enough. Weird new breed is an extra bit of interest." He pointed to Angel. "You're in, good dog, go lie down."

"Oh, thank you, thank you!" Angel cried. "But may I jump about some more? I'm so excited! I'm having so much fun!"

"Go lie down." The voice was kind but still meant business.

"Ok!" Angel flopped down near Ben and Jerry. They were already asleep. "They look so peaceful," Angel thought. "And happy. Aaaah, this is why...lying down on grass!" He felt himself drifting off. "This is fun too!"

"Next case!" said Boss

"Case number four," said Bailiff. "Aaaaaaaaa...this little dog."

"Mimi," she sniffed.

"Yeeeesssss, youuuuuu, youuuuu," said Bailiff. "Last night, this little dog ran away from her Friend and Home!"

Curious and skeptical, Randy and Bailiff cocked their heads at Mimi. After a second, they both looked at Boss.

"I don't see any reason why that would be necessary," Boss said quietly. "Do you have an explanation, little dog?"

Mimi drew herself up proudly and answered in a brave, assertive voice.

"I lived with my Friend Bob and he got a new girlfriend. She said she was allergic and their affair would end. Bob was thinking

42

about it! Before he could dump me, I ran away from home. Let's see how he likes that! And that's how I am here."

Randy and Bailiff glanced at each other and looked down.

"Spite," said Boss, "is not a good enough reason." Mimi sniffed but it came out more like a sniffle. Angel, awake again, was sorry to see her upset. "Who is this Bob?" he asked himself.

"Running away for spite," Boss spat, "is a very Bad Dog reason."

"Your honor," Bailiff broke the tension. "In stark contrast to the little dog's own report, reliable witnesses...." He paused and blushed. He was the reliable witness and would give a full report!

"Reliable witnesses report that this little dog was tossed from a topless red car last night! A lone female driver flung her from the moving vehicle!"

The other dogs gasped. Mimi's first full tear fell.

"She landed on her butt," Bailiff finished weakly. He didn't enjoy giving this full report. The little dog sobbed silently now. Bailiff felt very bad.

Ben and Jerry were awake now. "I'm sorry you have to hear this," Boss thought as he looked at them. "Your pain was physical," he thought. "This pain is almost worse."

"Ran away?" asked Boss gently. "Or what?"

"I didn't run away!" she said softly, head down, eyes streaming. "I was thrown away!"

She sat. She turned her damp eyes to the moon.

"I thought he loved me. I was his baby," she whispered. "Me! Mimi!"

She smiled at the picture in her head.

"Such a tall, handsome man, such a cute little dog," she murmured. She looked around at the rest of them.

"All eyes would turn to see us!" she said proudly. "We would go to the park and I would perform! I'd make him so proud! Chase the balls, do the tricks, I'd shake hands..." she paused. "And all

43

the ladies wanted to meet us."

The little dog's face, happy with the memory, now hardened.

"Away from the dog park, he met a new lady," she sneered. "She hated me!"

She looked at her audience. She knew it was almost impossible to believe. She shrugged. It had been true.

"She looked like a cat," she spat. "With her fangs, and her claws and her evil eyes! She was jealous!"

She laughed, but the sound was not pleasant.

"I said, oh, no, no, no, no! She's got to go now! Send her away!"

Imperiously, she waved her paw. She looked at them as if to warn of shocking events to follow.

"They just held hands," her voice soft now, "and looked at each other and not at Mimi! I barked and barked. Bob turned cold and indifferent. He said 'Bad pet!'". Sorrow and anger twisted her pretty features.

"Had I been wrong," she growled. "All these months…not his baby…but babe magnet? Chick magnet?"

Ben and Jerry had never had real Friends and didn't know what she was talking about. Randy waited for more details. Boss remained neutral. Angel had no idea what anyone was talking about and still appeared rather inappropriately excited about it all. Only Bailiff seemed to know her feelings. His sad eyes and sagging ears urged her to go on with the story.

"So, I went on a rage! I tore up her shoes! And I peed in her bag!" This last part made her smile. It was an unhappy, evil little smile.

"That was hard." Her smile faded.

"Bob shouted and scolded and left the room. I'm alone with the evil hag!"

She paused to review the details.

"Next thing I know, I'm stuffed in a bag," she continued. "And

44

she's driving the car! I think 'Well, ok, not too bad...' All of a sudden, I'm flying through air! And hitting the ground!"

All the dogs gasped. Mimi rubbed her rump.

"Little dog," Boss said. "Where's your collar?"

Mimi clutched her throat. For the first time, her face showed fear.

"She took my collar!" With everything else that had happened, she hadn't noticed the sound of her jingling tags was no longer there.

"Are you chipped?" the big dog asked.

Fear turned to shock as Mimi remembered.

"She was supposed to take me," she whispered. "That's why we were in the car!"

"Little dog," Boss's voice was gentle.

"I'm lost!" she cried. Tears flowed freely now. After a moment, she pulled herself together and wiped her eyes.

"But now we'll know," she said, hope fighting fear in her voice. "Now we'll know who he loves. Really loves! And it will be Mimi!"

The tears flowed again.

"He can't lose me," she whispered.

"He'll dump her!" she said firmly. "And then come find me and take me home...his Mimi...lost Mimi...me...." Her voice faded away.

A sad silence held them still for a heavy moment.

Ben spoke first. "Dude," he said. "Are you crying?"

"No," Jerry lied. "It's cold. I've got the sniffles."

"You're with us, Mimi," Bailiff said. "You're not alone!"

"He will come." Mimi shook off her tears and pulled herself up to her full tiny height. "You will see. Bob loves Mimi. You will see."

"Boss?" Bailiff asked.

"Lost and alone is good enough for me," said Boss. "You're

with us now, Mimi, if you wish."

"Yes, please," smiled Mimi.

"She can smile," Angel thought. "A real one. That's so pretty!"

"And next time," Boss said, "try to make Friends. With humans, the girlfriend usually wins."

"But she was evil!" Mimi burned.

"Especially when they're evil," Boss shrugged.

"That's everyone, I think," said Boss. "All you new dogs, sit up and beg."

Of the four newbies, only Mimi had been trained. She snapped to attention, sat back on her haunches and held her paws primly in the air. Angel tried to follow her lead but teetered unsteadily every time he lifted his front paws. Jerry could only manage one paw at a time. Ben fell over. Boss sighed. He looked at each hopeful face and smiled. Ben sat back up and lifted one paw like Jerry.

"By the power vested in me by the canine municipality of Dog Park, I now pronounce you good dogs and Night Dogs. " He waved his bone over their heads. "Court's adjourned, go play."

"I'm a Night! I'm a Night!" Angel exclaimed, thrilled to the core of his newly made heart. The heart skipped a beat when he saw Busy Angel floating over the shrubs between the trees. Busy was staring at him. His face was puzzled or disapproving, Angel couldn't tell which. He made a big Busy show of checking something on his clipboard. Then he stuck his nose in the air and followed its lead as he floated away. "Whew!" Angel thought.

"Night DOG!" Randy said loudly. "Night DOG! Not a night! This is night," Randy waved at the dark sky. "You're a Night Dog! Gosh, you're stupid!"

"But willing to learn!" Angel said. "Teach me, oh, sage!"

"Get off," Randy muttered and turned to Mimi.

"All right, little missy!" he said. "Dodged the hose hit there! Bad Dog! You were this close!" He held his paws together to show

how very close she had come.

"I'm not so bad," Mimi sniffed. "I'm not bad at all. I'm clever and mischievous."

Randy snorted. "Yes, that's what the ladies call it," he said. "Peeing in her bag, very clever."

"And difficult!" Mimi said. "She deserved it. If I see her again, I will rip her to shreds like one of Bob's silk ties. Besides, I'm sure I'm not the only Bad Dog here."

"No, you're not," Randy said. "Quite a few of us are clever and mischievous, nudge, nudge, wink, wink. Besides, bad dogs, that's all a myth."

"Like the good book says," he addressed them all. "There're no Bad Dogs! No bad dogs!" He lifted his snout and howled at the moon. "Whoooooooooo! Story time!" he said to Ben. "You first!"

"Once I ate a pot roast," Ben started. "It was bigger than my head. And then I rolphed it all around the floor." The other dogs nodded.

"I was a bit exhausted," he went on. "So I slept to rest my head. Then I ate it all back up and I rolphed some more!" He "rolphed" so convincingly all the other dogs giggled.

"And it made him mad!" Ben shivered remembering the Man's angry face. Ben had to dodge many, many kicks and belt swings that night. He looked at their giggling faces.

"But, was it bad?" he asked.

"No," Randy said firmly. "Not bad. 'Cause there're no bad dogs."

"No bad dogs," they all agreed.

"Whooooooooo," Randy howled. "Who's next?"

"First I chewed the sofa," Bailiff volunteered. "And then I chewed the rug. But my favorite thing was chewing underpants."

"I like socks," said Mimi. "And silk ties."

"I'd find them on the floor and say 'that's meant for me!'" Bailiff went on. "And they'd get so mad they'd do that little dance."

"The little dance," Mimi nodded. "The two-leg dance!"

"And it made them mad," Bailiff shook his head remembering the dire consequences. "So mad," he said, true sorrow in his voice. "But, was it bad?"

"No," Boss said firmly. "No, not bad. 'Cause there're no bad dogs!"

"No bad dogs!" Their agreement cheered Bailiff a little.

"Whooooooo!" the big dog howled. Unsure of their roles and his moods, the new dogs shrank back a little.

"My turn," he smiled and the new dogs relaxed.

"Now, if I spied a little kid with an ice-cream cone," he said, "I'd make sure that cone dropped on the ground!"

"Yum!" Randy said. "May I now, Boss? Thank you. And if I found a cat, peacefully sleeping...I'd BARK and make her jump and run around!"

Everyone laughed.

"I'd chase cats and ducks and chickens," Boss said. "And if I caught them, they were mine! It's nature, it's what we do, and it was fine."

"And I won't forget the day I found Manolo Blahnik shoes!" Mimi said, smiling now. "Sling-backs! And I licked and chewed and licked 'til I made them shine! What was left of them! Made them shine!"

Bailiff looked worried.

"And it made her mad," said Mimi with obvious satisfaction. "So mad."

She batted her eyes and offered her most appealing expression.

"But was it bad?" she asked.

A nervous moment passed.

"Manolo Blahnik," Bailiff said. "I remember that name. I think that's bad. Real bad."

48

"But there're no bad dogs!" Randy said emphatically.

"No bad dogs!" they all agreed and howled together.

"Whoooooooooooooooooooooo!"

As the final wooooooooooo floated up to the stars, all the dogs collapsed into fits of laughter. Even Boss rolled on his back and kicked his legs in the air. Ben and Jerry chased each other around the tree circle. Bailiff reminded himself that he had important work to do. No one noticed him slip away. "That's why I'm so good at my job!" he thought with pride. He'd do a quick tour of the park. "Reconnaissance!" he thought. "Very important! They should call me the Silent Stealth!" He would suggest his new nickname after he was done. While he was gone, the other dogs chatted and got to know each other

"Boss!" Bailiff cried when he returned, bursting through the shrubs and into the circle. "They're coming!"

"Who?" Angel asked.

"Animal Control!" Bailiff turned to Boss. "And they've got Spotty!"

"Spotty," Boss said sadly.

"Och, Spotty!" said Randy. "Why did it have to be Spotty? Of course it would be Spotty! Bit of natural selection there, if you ask me, the kibble-for-brains."

"You don't run from Animal Control!" Mimi was shocked. "They find you homes!"

"Been there," Ben said.

"Done that," said Jerry.

"Didn't work out," Bailiff said.

"Not for us, anyway," said Randy.

"And your friend, Bob?" Ben asked.

"What if he doesn't get there in time?" asked Jerry.

"What if they give you to someone else?" asked Bailiff.

"And besides, Boss couldn't go," said Randy. "His friend stays here, so he can't go to a new home. And we stay with him. What say you, Boss?"

"Ten shun!" Boss commanded. "Animal Control is almost here. Bailiff!"

"The Night Dog's Plan of Action!" Bailiff announced. The new dogs listened closely to the instructions.

"Run far away and go hide on your own," Bailiff said. "And pee everywhere along the way. Some time tomorrow, smell your way back here. Don't get caught! Come back and bring some food!" He looked at Boss and Randy.

"Night dogs rule!" the three dogs said together and stomped their paws on the ground. They looked at the new dogs.

"Night dogs rule!" they all said together and stomped their paws as one.

"Night dogs scatter!" Boss gave the quiet order.

They could see the long poles with neck loops over the tops of the shrubs. Hulking human shapes held the poles. They moved slowly and cautiously toward the tree circle.

"Go!" Bailiff shouted. "Go, go, go!"

For Randy, this was always the hardest part. Having spent his whole life keeping groups of sheep together, it felt wrong when he watched this new flock scatter in all directions. "We do what must be done," he thought. He noted with relief that Ben and Jerry ran together and Mimi led the way as Angel followed. "Good," he thought. "Two heads might make a whole brain there. They might actually find their way back!"

Boss and Bailiff were already gone. Relying on his breed's vastly superior speed and agility, Randy waited until he could see the faces of the humans.

"Those two!" he snorted, "Ha ha!"

He shot through the shrubs like a ball from a cannon. If lightning had struck, it would have missed him.

Chapter Six

One Dog's Win, Another's Loss

Lucy stood on her hind legs and stared out the window. She'd held that pose for a long time now and her hind legs were trembling with the effort. She clutched her favorite toy on the sill with one paw. It was a long squeak toy, shaped like a match and infused with beefy flavors. The squeak part was an embarrassment. She tried not to touch it. But at times like these, she would take the other end in her mouth and breathe deeply, the meaty fumes filling her snout with satisfaction. Then she would put it down. "Can't do that too much," she would scold herself. But now was not the time for restraint. She sucked on her toy and enjoyed the sensation. The scene unfolding below was just too delicious! She had to take in every detail!

"Buh-bye, Spotty," she whispered. "Buh-bye!"

On the street below, Animal Control Officers had the Springer Spaniel in a neck loop. They urged him forward toward their van. The dog seemed ambivalent. He wasn't fighting but would pause and stare back at the Dog Park, as if he would miss it and didn't want to leave. The Officers gave a little push forward. The dog took a few more steps, then stopped and stared again. When the van was only a few more steps away, one of the officers moved inside it. The dog turned his sorrowful eyes to the Officer, now crouching inside the van. Lucy saw the man smile. The dog cocked its head. The man reached into a jacket pocket and pulled out a bone. It was big enough that Lucy could see the hunks of meat on it. Spotty leapt straight up in the air and bucked around like a wild horse, then sat, panting and shaking with excitement, sad eyes now sparkling, and tongue lolling out.

"Let's try it," said the Man. "Stay!"

He held his hand out, palm flat, his face serious, bone in the other hand behind his back. The Spaniel's posture sagged a bit and he cocked his head.

"Now," the Officer said softly, palm still held out flat.

The other Officer twisted the pole and lifted the loop off

Spotty's neck.

Spotty looked at the one, then turned to the other, the one who held the bone. He waited, not wanting to hope too much.

Officer Bone smiled. "His face is nice," Spotty thought, "seems kind."

"Come here, boy!" said the Officer. Spotty wiggled backward a bit, assessing the jump. The Officers held their breath.

Gracefully and noiselessly, the Springer Spaniel sprung. He landed by the Officer's side, not a wobble, not a slide on the slippery floor, a perfect ten! He sat, waited and hoped.

"Good dog!" The Officer moved his hand from behind his back and offered the bone.

"Thank you," said Spotty.

When his eyes turned up and met the Man's gaze, they smiled together. Spotty moved slowly, cautiously, toward the bone and wrapped his teeth around it, nostrils flaring, sucking in the fumes.

"Good dog!" The Man let go of the bone.

Spotty fell on the floor in a state of absolute bliss. He stared at the Man and gnawed on the bone. "If this is heaven," he thought, "I'm there, dude!"

"Lord, almighty," said the Officer, smiling at Spotty. "I think I found me a dog!" Spotty found a meaty spot and gnawed all the joy in his body into that bone.

"Buh-bye, Spotty," said Lucy, "Buh-bye." She sucked on the squeakless end of her toy and enjoyed the taste. She started to move away from the window. Her hind legs were aching now but she couldn't resist one last look.

Spotty was still on his side, cuddling the bone, chewing and licking as if he'd never had one in his life. The man stroked his head and played with Spotty's long floppy ears. Lucy's heart softened just a little.

"Buh-bye, Spotty," she whispered. "And good luck!"

She surveyed the play room of the Doggie-Do-Right Day

Care Center where she and Lester were boarding for a few days. Ordinarily, they would be home now, cuddling with their Friends on the sofa and watching TV. Their Friends were on vacation, somewhere dogs couldn't go. "Sorry, kids," they had said, "but It's a Small World, not a dog world, after all."

"Think of it as a spa," Lucy tried to rally Lester. "They do bathing and grooming and trimming and fluffing and…"

"Yeah, yeah," Lester's voice was dull, uninterested.

"Sometimes," Lucy thought, "I just don't understand that boy."

Today, they had luxuriated in a total groom experience. They were bathed, dried, trimmed, fluffed, trimmed again, and sprayed with a finishing conditioner. The grooming lady worked feverishly. The Top Show Dog Champion meet was only a few days away! When they were done, Lucy had yearned for a photographer. "What a photo that would be!," she had sighed. "Look at us! Picture perfect! Our Friends could hang our portrait over their fireplace and gaze at us every night. Perfection!"

And they did look perfect, from the tiny bow in Lucy's fluffy top knot all the way down to Lester's ankle poofs and perfectly trimmed nails. And here was Lester, her beloved son, now rolling on his back and scooting around the floor. His perfectly shaped poodle poofs would be bent now. Some of the evil joy from earlier returned to Lucy's heart.

"Lester…" she said and then stopped.

"What, mother?" he asked, still rolling and pulling himself around the floor. She remembered the look of pure happiness on Spotty's face. She wished she could see that look more often on Lester's face. The news she had to bring was good, very good for her, but would make Lester sad. He was her baby and it killed her to see him sad but he had to be told for his own good. Still, she didn't have to gloat. She could deliver the news in an even voice, just the facts. He would have to be her little man and face it.

"Well, they got another one of your little hoodlum friends just now," she said lightly.

"Who was it this time, Mother?" Lester asked, still wriggling

53

around the floor.

"That Spotty one," she said, as casually as she could.

"Spotty!" Lester jumped up and ran to the window. He was tall enough to see out without standing on his hind legs. The Animal Control van was pulling away.

"Oh, no!" Lester moaned. "Not Spotty! Not Spotty!"

Lester dropped to the floor and pulled with his paws, dragging himself along the floor. "Not Spotty!" he said, rolling and dragging.

"He'll be fine!" Lucy said, a little too brightly. "The Animal Control Man seemed to like him! He gave the dog a bone!"

"I hope he'll be happy," Lester moaned and dragged. "And fed."

"He'll be fine," said Lucy, a bit too blithely, trying to keep the desperate nagging tone out of her voice. "And stop rolling around!" She gave up on bright and blithe. "We just had our hair done and we look perfect! You'll ruin it! Again!"

"Yes, mother!" Lester was rolling on his back. "And the sprays and the chemicals make me itch! All right, mother? Ahhhhhh," he moaned. "Spottyyyyyyyyyyyy..........."

That night, Lester's grief disturbed his sleep. Or was it anger that kept him awake? They had had all their usual arguments, leaving Lester angry and frustrated. Spotty was the spark point for every debate. Lester was reminded again and again of his loss. The sorrow would swamp over him and drain all his energy. Then his mother would say something else and the cycle would begin again.

"Don't 'oh, mother' me!" she barked. "That Spotty was a waste of your time!" She was spluttering now. "Filthy, undisciplined, wriggling all the time, and the fights you got into with other dogs! Your face is your fortune, darling," she whined with pleading eyes, "We can't have any scars!"

"The nose, mother," Lester sighed. "Follow the nose...." He tried the one trick that usually worked on her. Moving his head slowly and smoothly, he used his big nose to draw shapes in the air. Mesmerized, Lucy followed his movements. He drew bones and balls and chicken legs in the air. At one inspired point, he outlined the face of a cat and watched Lucy add whiskers to the cat face

"Can't take your eyes off it? Can you?" Lester chuckled and broke the spell. "It's huge, isn't it? Not the nose of a Number One Top Show Dog Champion or even a poodle, is it? I think you lied to me about dad, mother."

"Oh, stop, darling, stop!" she cried. "You know how I hyperventilate when you talk that way about your nose...about your father..." her voice trailed off, eyes cast down, lips nervously sucking the end of her match toy.

"Well, did you?" he demanded.

She ignored the question as always and went off again, traveling down the well worn path of all the usual subjects: she was a loving mother trying to protect her pup, if he would only listen and follow her lead he could be a prize winning show dog, the Show Dog life was the best choice for a dog like him...on and on. Finally, after exhausting all arguments and herself, she went to bed and slept.

Lester lay awake, listening to her noisy snoring. "A dog like me," Lester thought and got up from his bed. "What does she mean?" He stretched and padded round the room, carefully placing each paw so his nails wouldn't click on the floor. He sat in front of the wall mirror and stared at his moonlit reflection. Overall, he was quite a handsome dog, everyone said so. The second thing they said never varied.

"It's huge," Spotty had said. "Very impressive, but not really poodle."

"I know!" Lester exclaimed. "And so powerful! I think it's huge to fit all the extra nerve endings. Watch this!" He flared his nostrils dramatically. "Chili dog at ten o'clock, about a hundred yards down, check it out!" Spotty ran off to investigate.

He returned, eyes wide, his face amazed. "Exactly right!" His voice was awed and respectful.

"And there's cheese on it too, isn't there?" Lester asked, nostrils flaring and twitching. "Cheddar, I think, that smooth melty stuff?"

"Right again," said Spotty. "Your nose! It's awesome!"

"I know! But it's not a Show Dog nose."

"Not a chance," Spotty agreed.

Lester invented a game he called Smell and Seek. Lester would turn away and let a fixed amount of time pass. They always discussed what the time measure would be.

"In the time it takes for that kid to drop the cone," Spotty suggested. "Plus the time it takes for the Corgi to notice and lick it up. When the kid starts to cry, then you can look."

"Agreed," Lester nodded.

The child was small and wobbly. The Corgi was very quick. By the time the child realized what had happened, the ice cream was gone and so was the Corgi. The child puzzled over this for a second or two before picking up the empty cone. He stared at it, took a deep breath and wailed.

"OK," Lester said.

Spotty was an excellent hider. His choices were clever, unusual and altogether unexpected. "Good practice for Animal Control," he explained. Lester thrilled to the challenge and his big nose prevailed every time.

"Ha!" he enjoyed the triumph. "Covering your scent with that squirrel's nest! Genius!"

"And yet you found me," said Spotty, voice hushed with respect and admiration. "Uh, oh, here comes the squirrel mom!" And they ran away together to start the game again.

Lester won every time. Spotty didn't mind at all.

"You've got real talent!" Spotty said. "You should do something with that."

Some days they rolled and played until Day Care Guy said time to go. Other days, when Spotty's hunger made him weak and tired, they would sit together and talk.

"Sometimes, she makes me so mad," Lester would say, "I just want to rip things up!" He grabbed a fast food wrapper that was floating by on the breeze. "Rrrrrrrrr, rrrrrrrrr," he raged and ripped 'til the wrapper was reduced to confetti.

"Why do I have to be the Number One Top Show Dog Champion?" he said. "She wants to be Number One, not me! I wonder why she never won." He cocked his head to one side.

"I wonder why she lies about Dad." He cocked his head to the other side.

Spotty was a good listener. "Or maybe he's too tired to talk," Lester thought.

He wished he had remembered to bring Spotty a biscuit or a treat. Spotty breathed deeply and twitched his tail.

"Well, you're not a Show Dog," he said, "whatever she wants. What do you want?"

"I'm going to be a crime-sniffing police dog!" Lester sat proud and tall, the breezes ruffling his poodle poofs.

"You'd be great. You've got the nose."

"Danger! I'll hunt it down! I'll rip its pant leg!"

"Yes, you will!" Spotty roused himself and slowly stood up. "Let's go pee on all the bushes."

The poofs in the mirror were trembling. Lester realized he was crying. Not big girlie sobs, just a little bit. The sorrow of his loss brought him back to the present. Spotty was gone.

"Bye," Lester said to his reflection. "I hope you'll be happy. And fed."

He looked at himself and sighed. His poofs were torn up, bent and misshapen from rolling on the floor. He gazed at his nose, his favorite feature, his hope for the future, his ticket to greatness. He twitched it and focused until, on a soft breeze blowing in from the window, he found one last faint whiff of his friend.

"Bye, Spotty," he said. "Thanks for listening." He padded noiselessly back to his bed.

"I'm Jack Butts, poodle from Hell!" he thought as he circled and settled down. "Danger!" he sighed and then yawned. "I'll hunt it down," he started to snore. "I'll rip its pant leg...."

The Doggie-Do-Right Day Care Center

Chapter Seven

Witch from L

During the morning sunshine, the glare from the brightly painted sign blinded all who walked or drove by it. In whimsical script and charming colors it identified the building as the Doggie Do Right Day Care Center. The sign was the only bright or cheerful thing about the otherwise drab little building.

The building had once been a church. Its congregation had been small and poor and, as it turned out, feckless and unfaithful.

The Day Care Guy had used all his savings to buy the little church at a foreclosure auction. His last few dollars paid for the cheerful sign.

"It's a start," he thought. "As business improves, I'll make it all look as bright as that sign!"

Business would have to improve a lot before he could re-seed the weedy front lawn, or replace the flimsy picket fence that surrounded it. The pickets had warped to the point where the little front gate wouldn't stay closed. Day Care Guy often came home to find it flapping in the wind. The colorful sign called attention to the faded paint peeling off the front walls.

The front double doors to the church foyer had been stolen for their brass fixtures and never replaced. Day Care Guy didn't mind about that. He re-worked the inner door into a double dutch door. On warm and sunny days he could leave the top part open to let in air.

Inside the double dutch door, the large room that had been the congregation's seating area was now divided by screens or hanging curtains into several sections.

He had re-modeled the congregations' bathrooms into a large grooming station for the Day Care stylist. The center of the room was one big play area. He'd decorated the room's edges with doggie beds and stuffed toys. The low stage at the front which had been the church altar was now his spacious but sparsely furnished bedroom. The kitchenette was small but well-equipped and adequate for his needs. Near the kitchenette, he had arranged his old but comfortable sofa, a lamp, the TV and his favorite TV chair into a makeshift living area for himself.

Lucy and Lester often stayed overnight at the Day Care Center. Their friends were Frequent Flyers. "Bye, kids!" they would say. "We'd take you along but it's the world of Broadway, and not a dog world, after all." And off they'd go.

The L-Pups, as others called them, would often be waiting at the door bright and early when the daytime dogs arrived. Lucy enjoyed this part of the day.

"And here's Fifi! Hi Fifi!" she called, then turned her head away for a second. Her poodle poof shivered. When she turned back, she was smiling too brightly. She gulped.

"Another little "four-year-old-child-with-gum" incident?" she smiled, eyes blinking rapidly. "No, really. Nice haircut, it suits your face!"

As soon as Fifi passed by, Lucy put her head in her paws and shook with silent laughter. After a deep breath, she watched for the next arrival.

"Well! The L-Pups are in fine form today!" Fifi said to Lily when they reached the play area.

"Leave Lester out of it," Lili said." He's a great dog!"

"He is," Fifi nodded. "It's her."

"The Evil One," Lili said.

"Their Friends kept them together," Fifi shook her new haircut. "They probably thought it would be nice."

"Doesn't seem to be working out," Lili cocked her head.

"For anyone," Fifi cocked hers the other way.

"Melinda!" Lucy gushed. "And the puppies! Just look at them all! So many! How do you manage, dear?"

"Not today!" Melinda swept regally by. "Step aside!" she said loudly, shooing Lucy over to allow the pups to pass. All six Irish Setter puppies trotted by. Melinda turned her head and hung it down to Lucy's level. She bared her teeth.

"Just today," she snarled. "That's all I'm asking. Just today. Behave!" She flared her nostrils. "Can you do that, oh, Witch from L?" She looked up. "Hi, Lester!" Her tone changed completely. "How are you sweetheart? Your poofs are all crooked, honey, rolling again? The allergies? Love you, darling, you look great!"

She turned back to Lucy and her face lost the love.

"So," she said slowly, showing teeth. "Do we have a deal?"

"So!" Lucy snarled back, matching tone and teeth. "That's how it's going to be?"

"I'm…asking!" Melinda snarled.

"I'll …try!" Lucy growled.

"Hard," Melinda, trotted away. "Try hard!"

"High-maintenance witch!" Lucy muttered. "Watch out for those," she said to Lester.

"I heard that!" Melinda called from inside.

"Let's go in!" Lucy said.

"Witch from L! The L-pups!" laughed Fifi.

"Good one!" Lili sniggered. "But not the L-Pups. Not Lester. Just her."

"On wheels!" Melinda gasped and choked with laughter. "Oh, here she is! Hi Lucy!" She collapsed, writhing with giggles.

Lucy paid no attention. In the time it took to trot through the foyer, the argument started again, picking up right where they left it, as if it had never stopped.

"We have to talk about that Dog Park, Lester."

"Oh, Mother..."

"Don't 'oh mother' me!"

"I don't want to be a show dog, Mother!"

"Why not?" Lucy stomped her paws in exasperation.

The other dogs tried to be casual. They battered toys around, or quietly attended to personal grooming, trying to appear as if they weren't listening, while paying rapt attention to every word.

"I'm just a regular guy, Mom," Lester's world weary voice was close to a whine. "Kicking it back, hanging with my dogs. I'm not a show dog guy and it's not just the nose. I love my nose!"

Since they were trying to be casual, the others suppressed their gasps. Morning grumpiness gone, Melinda listened carefully. At the first opportunity, she would jump in and take Lester's part. "Heh heh," she laughed to herself. Her support for Lester's position was genuine. The chance to annoy Lucy was a delicious added benefit.

Lili and Fifi had dropped all pretension and were staring openly. Lester stared back.

"It's my favorite feature," he said loudly. "It's useful and powerful. You," he pointed to Lili, "had liver treats this morning."

"Any dog could smell that," said Fifi.

"You," Lester pointed to Fifi, "had liver treats three days ago. And we're going to see them again real soon, probably this morning." Fifi squirmed with embarrassment mixed with pleasure. It was nice to be the center of attention, whatever the reason! She flipped her hair around for everyone to see.

"There's nothing wrong with my great, big nose," Lester said loudly. He turned to Lucy and spoke more quietly. The other dogs leaned forward, straining to hear.

"And there's nothing wrong with being a show dog, Mother, nothing at all, except I don't want to!" he said. "And I hate this haircut."

"It's a classic look!" Lucy exclaimed.

"For a girl!" Lester retorted. "This is what gets me into fights, Mother. I'm a tough guy, a man-dog, and I look like a girl. They called me LuLu," Lester sighed and hung his head. "Spotty was my friend, he helped me. He never laughed at my haircut and he said my nose was the best in the whole world."

Seeing his sorrow return, Lucy softened a bit.

"My darling," she lied, "I am sorry about your friend."

She allowed her perfect posture a graceful slump. After a moment, she sat up straight again.

"You'll make new friends," she cooed encouragement. "How about that new girl there, that Papillion?" She pointed.

Papillion's recent introduction to the Day Care Center had been smooth and seamless. She didn't bark or nip. She didn't sniff. She responded politely to attention but didn't seek it. She wasn't aloof but, even while sitting right next to Lili and Fifi, she seemed absorbed in a world of her own. Her eyes would dart around the room, fixing on this dog or that, the Day Care Guy, or something out the window. Then she would fix her gaze and hold it. Lester couldn't figure out what she was looking at.

His eyebrows shot up.

"She's thinking!" he exclaimed.

"Don't be silly, darling," Lucy patted his paw. "She's a very nice girl."

Papillion twitched violently and fell over. As if nothing had happened, the little dog jumped to all fours, looked around, sat quietly down again and stared at something no one else could see.

"Just a little over bred," Lucy blinked rapidly. "That's all."

Papillion was interesting, Lester would agree with that. But as a partner for Smell and Seek?

"She's no Spotty," Lester sighed for his lost friend.

"You're not going to that Park!" Lucy said firmly.

"Mother, the Doggie-Do-Right Day Care Center's policy is

two walks per day," confidence returned to Lester's voice. "And there's nothing you can do about it!"

"I'll use my psychic powers," his mother answered.

All the dogs flinched, including Lester. They all had some psychic ability, all dogs do. Lucy's powers were extraordinary, as strong and well-developed as the nerve endings in Lester's nose.

"How else could she convince the world," Melinda thought, "that her son, clearly not a Toy Poodle, is also a purebred dog? A purebred Toy produced a purebred Standard, how is that possible? But everyone believes it! Their Friends, the AKC, everyone, even us until we're forced to think about it. Thinking!" She shut her eyes tight. "Ow! Stop it! Stop thinking!" She opened them again. "Look, she's using her powers now! What is she trying to do?"

Lucy's face was scrunched into a prune of concentration. Her tiny body trembled. "Bwah!" she released her breath and panted a bit. "There," she said. "Done. You'll see. Now, you're safe."

"From what?" Fear tinged Lester's voice.

"Bad influence," she said, her voice calm and certain. "Oh, I know it looks attractive from here, Lester," she went on, "but it's rough out there! You'll get sucked down with the rest of them, homeless, alone, wandering the streets, scavenging in garbage cans..."

"Yeah!" Lester exclaimed. "Danger!" he thought to himself, "I'll hunt it down!" "Running from Animal Control," his mother was still talking. "Running and

running and one day you just get tired of running and that's when they get you. And you end up in a row of cages, all pathetic and needy, oh, pick me! Choose me!"

"No, I wouldn't!" Lester said.

"And the days go by," she continued. "Pick me! Choose me!" her voice was desperate. "But your life on the streets is showing now. You're not as cute as you once were. No one wants you. And then one day...," she gurgled and squeaked, "...gone!"

"That's not..." Lester started.

"The point is," she interrupted, "you don't have to do that, Lester! Look at you! The Night Dogs would kill to have what you have. That's why you're getting into fights! You're not made for that world, Lester! You're made for this one! You could be Top Show Dog Champion if you would just apply yourself!"

"Here we go," Lester sighed.

Some commotion at the doorway distracted everyone. A huge shadow spread across the floor. All eyes turned.

"It is I!" the shadow's owner announced.

"Roo-FAAAAH-looooow!" Lucy exclaimed, rolling the R and over-pronouncing the rest. "Hi, Rufahlo!" she waved frantically.

The shiny red Doberman moved his magnificently sculpted musculature into the room. Every step was casually but perfectly placed, every movement fully followed through, each pause a pose designed to show off a different set of muscles. The ladies swooned and panted. Lucy turned to Lester.

"This is a show dog!" she hissed. "Watch and learn!"

Lester sighed.

As he did almost every day, Rufahlo greeted his day care companions with a series of rhetorical questions.

"Shall I...?" he started, his handsome face appealing to the girls.

"Strut across the room and give you all an opportunity to view my rippling muscles?" he asked. Without waiting for an answer, he demonstrated. All the girls sighed.

"Or shall I...?" he addressed Lester directly.

"Strike a pose which I have practiced, you could too, one of many that accentuates my rippling muscles?"

Lester made a face.

"One thing's for certain," Rufahlo ignored him. "With muscles like these...." He flexed for the girls. More sighs, a smattering of oooos and aaaahs.

"I'm a winner!" He smiled generously at his admirers.

"Shall I...." he addressed Lester again. "Tell you all the muscles you would have to have buffed up just to lift all of my trophies?"

Lester sighed and waited for the ritual to be over.

"Or shall I....?" Rufahlo continued. "Tell you how the elements of grace and style are highly prized commodities amongst the ladies?"

He paused for effect.

"And I love the ladies!" he swept his paw over the entire group, making sure each lady knew that he meant her in particular.

"Yes! I love the ladies!" he smiled at them all, then turned to Lester.

"And they love me!" he said just loud enough for all to hear. "And.....my.......rippling muscles!" He struck a heroic pose. More sighs.

"Yeah, yeah, fine," Lester muttered.

By the time he finished, there were no dogs left standing except the L-Pups. Satisfied with the effect of his performance, Rufahlo smiled around the room, pausing briefly at the Papillion.

"A new girl!" he thought. "Lovely!"

She was staring at something that was not him. She twitched.

"Hmmm," he thought. He turned his gaze to Lester and his show-biz self relaxed.

"Hello, my vastly inferior but still appealing and lovable friend!" He trotted over to give Lester some dog noogies.

"Hi, Ruffee," Lester sighed, his voice shaking from the noogie-ing.

"Roooo-FAAAAH-low, darling!" Lucy corrected him.

"Oh, he can call me what he likes, my little friend," Rufahlo said, still noogie-ing. "Hey!" He stopped and stared at Lester's head. "What's with the dread locks, poodle?"

"I'll leave you two alone," Lucy said and pranced away to pick a fight with Melinda.

67

Chapter Eight

Who's Helping Whom?

Melinda's sharp eyes focused on the boys. "Something's changed," she thought.

Lucy plopped down next to her.

"Look at them together," she cooed. "I'm so glad they're friends. Rufahlo is such a good influence for Lester. Such a proud, manly dog, a Top Show Dog Champion! Look at the way he talks to Lester, encouraging him, sharing all his tips and tricks, I'm sure."

Melinda was not so sure. When Rufahlo talked about himself, which was often, he sat up straight, head held high, chest thrust out. Even in conversation with just one other dog, if the topic was himself, which it usually was, he proclaimed his thoughts as if performing for a crowd of avid admirers.

As the boys talked quietly together, it was Lester now who sat up tall and proud, head held high, chest thrust out. Rufahlo's head hung down a bit and his face was turned towards Lester's ear.

"Look, that's so sweet," said Lucy. "He's talking quietly so Lester won't be embarrassed. It's tough being the #2 dog, always striving and straining to improve. You work so hard and still the prize goes to the dog with true star quality. No wonder Lester's discouraged."

"Something has changed," Melinda thought again. Lester did not look at all discouraged, quite the opposite. His quiet confidence seemed to be soothing Rufahlo, not the other way round. Rufahlo's face maintained its "Here I am!" expression but his eyes said something different. "Is he asking for something?" Melinda thought. "What could it be?"

"Look at him," Lucy gushed. "Begging Lester to be serious, to focus, live up to his potential! Aaaaah!" she sighed. "Such a good dog!"

"Begging," Melinda thought. "That's it!" Her pups' eyes looked that way when they wanted a treat or a toy. Whatever it was they wanted, their eyes said they wanted it more than anything in the world.

"He's begging!" Melinda thought. "For what?"

"Someday, he'll retire," Lucy said. "He can't go on winning the Top Show Dog Crown year after year after year."

"Retire?" Melinda said, "I don't think so. He loves the Show and he loves winning. They'll have to pry the Top Show Dog Crown from his cold, dead paws."

"And after he retires," Lucy ignored her, "Lester will finally have his chance. Oh Lester," she sighed. "Listen to him, learn what he knows! Your day will come and, if you work hard, you'll be ready!"

Rufahlo's "Here I am!" face worked almost as well as Lester's "Yes, Mother" face. All the girl dogs and puppies were drawn to his aura of confidence and contentment. Each, in turn, found some excuse, a toy thrown too far, a short walk to stretch the legs, a trip to the window to look outside, some reason to parade themselves in front of their hero and bask, however briefly, in the warmth of his acknowledgement and approval.

"Lili!" he said to the current passer-by. "Your Frise is fabulous today! So perfectly round!"

The little Bichon blushed and giggled and continued her trot to the window.

Rufahlo turned back to Lester. His face remained strong but the light in his eyes dimmed a bit.

"Lester," he murmured. "When we going to practice? I need to practice!"

Lester breathed in and puffed out his chest.

"First you assault me with noogies," he murmured back, "then you show off for my mother, and now you want my help?"

"Please, Lester!" Rufahlo mumbled then sat up straight.

"Fifi! New haircut? It suits your face!" The passing Shih Tzu tossed her golden locks and continued on her way.

"I got to know this stuff before you leave," Rufahlo's mumbling tone couldn't hide the catch of fear in his voice. "Please, Lester," he begged. "I've never done it alone!"

"I know. Don't worry," Lester murmured. "We'll practice. And I mean hard! I'm gonna work you like a dog!" He smiled at his friend. Rufahlo's "Here I am!" face relaxed. A ball hit his foot.

"Puppy! Which one are you? Buster? Good boy! But go easy on the ball, pace yourself, you last longer! Now, go play." The Setter puppy pushed his ball away and ran after it. Rufahlo turned back to Lester. Relief and gratitude softened the "Here I am!" face. He gazed at his friend with frank and sincere emotion.

"Don't cry on me," Lester mumbled, "I've had a rough night."

"I'm not! I won't!" Rufahlo said. His tone was shocked, as if such a thing would be inconceivable. They chuckled together for a second, each reminding himself that not only was such a thing conceivable, it could happen in a split second and was always quite messy afterwards. Since they were tiny puppies, they had used each other for sounding boards, tantrum targets, crying pillows and more. Each had done his share of crying and whining. Laughing together was always more fun.

"Look!" said Lucy. "Lester's listening! They're bonding!"

"Hmmmm," Melinda hummed.

"Papillion!" called Rufahlo. "Why are... are you ok?" He started to get up.

"I'm fine," she smiled, the shiver subsiding. She was still again. "Thank you," she added. She turned back and smiled again at something unseen.

"Why isn't she looking at me?" Rufahlo asked. "What is she doing?"

"Thinking," Lester answered.

Rufahlo's jaw dropped. "About what?" he exclaimed. "Ow!" he clutched his snout. "Ow! Stop thinking! Remember something! Oh, yeah..." The memory made him somber.

"What?" Lester asked.

"I'm sorry about Spotty," Rufahlo murmured.

"Thanks," Lester said. "He's in a better place. I hope."

"I hope so too," Rufahlo smiled, then laughed out loud. All the dogs turned to look. He dipped his face close to Lester's ear.

"I never forget that first show," Rufahlo said, his strange accent thickening. He gazed fondly at his friend. "Every command," he said, "you start early, so I could see what it was and follow. You showed me, and I did it but it cost you points!"

"I didn't need them," Lester smiled. "Mom wanted them, not me."

"You let me win," said Rufahlo, eyes misting with gratitude.

"I knew you wanted to," Lester answered. "And you like this stuff! You're better at it than I could ever be. Nothing my mother wants can change that."

"But, please, Lester," Rufahlo whined, very softly, but there it was. "We can't let your mother know! Oh, the shame! And also, she scares me. So we have to practice!" Rufahlo gave Lester a shove.

"Ok! Ok!" Lester laughed. "Chill! We'll practice!" He shoved back.

"Thank you, Lester," Rufahlo shoved harder, "Thank you! WHEN?"

"Later," Lucy trilled. She was sitting right in front of them.

The boys hid their panic. How long had she been listening? They might have been looking right over her head! What did she hear?!?!?!?

"Whatever it is you're doing," she said, "finish it later."

The other dogs were forming a group behind Lucy. Melinda trotted up next to her.

"Hello, boys," she said.

"Hello, Auntie Melinda," they answered together.

"Lester," Lucy trilled a little higher. "Almost time for walkies!" She smiled.

"The smile of Pure, Even-If-Well-Intentioned, Evil!" Lester shivered.

"Walkies!" Rufahlo announced. "Great! We're going to get some exercise, isn't that great? My muscles feel great now but they're going to feel fantastic after a workout! Are we ready to go, kids, are we ready to WORK OUT?"

"Yes! Yes!" the puppies and girl dogs jumped up and down.

"Lester!" Rufahlo shouted, throwing his whole fantastic body into a gracefully executed 180 degree turn. He aced the landing then paused.

"You're not ready?" he asked.

Lester was using the "Yes, Mother" face. Slowly and serenely and only just enough to keep his poodle poof from tilting, he cocked his head toward his mother.

"The Pure Evil, Even-If-Well-Intentioned face!" Rufahlo flinched. "Now, I have seen it! What could it mean?" Half his brain wanted to run away as fast as possible. The other half knew it should stay calm and maintain order.

"So, let's get ready to go, pups! Are you ready?" Rufahlo's 180 degree swoop back to the pups was still graceful but lacked spark. No one noticed.

"Yes! Yes!" the puppies jumped up and down. The girls decided to wait and see. They sat in a row, staring at him. Ordinarily, he would have enjoyed this but right now he just wanted to move his muscles and work them hard!

"So who wants to work out?" he said loudly.

"We do!" the pups jumped and squealed.

The girls remained seated. Papillion twitched and fell over.

"I'm fine," she said, getting up. She hadn't asked for help and Lili and Fifi hadn't offered any. She settled down and the three girls stared at him.

"So," said Lili.

"Are we going?" said Fifi, "or what?"

Papillion twitched.

Maintaining his confident smile and manner, Rufahlo turned back to the L-Pups.

The contented Evil Look still shaped Lucy's face. Lester was not happy but just sat, tall and proud, and waited.

"Come on, kids," Day Care Guy rattled the leashes. "Time for walkies!"

All the dogs rushed forward except the L-Pups.

"Hey! Hey! Easy! Sit! Everybody, sit!" Day Care Guy's hat fell on the floor and he lunged for it.

"Everybody sit!" Lester barked. The other dogs cocked their heads and obeyed.

"Good dogs!" said Day Care Guy, truly pleased. "Come on, puppies first, group leash, there you are, good babies!" He turned to the other dogs. "There isn't a better group of dogs in this world!"

"Thanks," Lester grumped.

"Fine!" Rufahlo said. "That's nice for you! Now, let's GO!"

"Good dogs!" Day Care Guy clipped a lead on Lucy's collar. "Let's all hook together. Not you, Lester. You stay home today, good boy."

Lester hadn't moved. His posture was proud, his face a mask.

"Good dog," said Day Care Guy, "You"ll go this afternoon. Come on, kids, let's go for a walk!"

"So that's what she's up to," Melinda thought. "She dog-motized the Day Care Guy into leaving Lester home." She planted her feet and resisted, ever-so-slightly, feeling the tension, measuring…

"Ok, pups," Day Care Guy was finally ready. "Let's go!"

The pups lunged forward. Day Care Guy stumbled.

Melinda resisted but only just enough to offset Lucy's straining forward. That was enough for now.

There was some new tension on the leash line, too slight for the others to notice. Papillion pulled backward, straining toward the half-gate door to the Day Care Center. "What this about?" Melinda cocked her head.

When the cross-bar dropped into the half-door catch, it was over. "That's it," Lester thought. "I'm home alone." His body shook. The tension rose until he reminded himself that there was no one there to obey or impress.

"Aaaaaaaaaaaaaaaaaaaaaaah!" he exhaled, "She makes me so mad," he hyperventilated, "I just want to....to....RIP THINGS UP!"

Day Care Guy was nice but very casual about things such as tidiness. Newspapers strewn on the floor were a feature of the Center, more than needed for the pups-in-house-training. Lester grabbed the style section of some give-away daily and let 'er rip.

"Rrrrrrrrrrrrrrrwwwwwwwwwwwwaaaaaaaaaah!" He finished with a flourish, surveying the confetti with satisfaction.

"Why do I have to be the Number One Top Show Dog Champion?" he panted. "She wants to be the Number One Top Show Dog Champion, not me! I wonder why she never won?" He cocked his head to the left. "I wonder why she lies to me about dad?" He cocked his head to the right. "I wonder how she does that psychic power thing?" He heard the groan and squeak of old wood moving and looked up at the gate. Two big eyes and a pair of big ears with drifting, feathery fronds of trailing hair could be seen over the half-gate. Above the two big eyes, the cross-bar weighed down on a very tiny cranium.

Day Care Guy had lost his grip on the puppies' leash. "Stay!" he pleaded to the other dogs. "Please! Just stay!"

"Melinda," Lucy shrieked. "Your babies!"

"They know where the food is," Melinda shrugged. "They won't go far."

"I don't understand you," Lucy said. "Or maybe I do! How many litters is this?"

"Not today!" Melinda snapped. "I think I'll scratch my butt on the half-gate."

"Disgusting!," Lucy muttered quite distinctly. She pushed her nose in the air and trotted to Rufahlo at the front.

Melinda backed her butt up to the gate and rubbed. "Aaaaaah," she said to herself. She looked at Papillion. "Now," she said quietly.

The little Papillion twitched with delight, fell over, got up and jumped onto Melinda's rump. She did not ace the landing but managed to hang on and to find herself two feet taller.

Papillion smiled down at Melinda.

"I can see for miles and miles," she marveled.

"Do it now, sweetie," said Melinda.

Remembering their telepathed purpose, Papillion smiled.

"When all else fails," she said, "use your head."

She wedged her tiny cranium under the wood block that locked the half-door. With a mighty heave, the tiny dog pushed the lever up, just enough.

"Lester!" Papillion whisper-yelled.

Lester saw the strangely oversized ears and big brown eyes just over the top of the gate.

"Good lord! That's the lock block on her head! How did she do that?"

Lester went zero to sixty in a second, then braked. He skidded skillfully to a stop just short of banging the door and sending little Papillion flying. Their eyes met.

"Thank you," he said.

"Thank you for stopping," she said.

Lester squiggled through the door with barely a ripple of motion. Melinda backed up again. With supreme effort and some help from Lester now using his own head, Papillion lifted the bar once again and lowered it slowly and soundlessly into the catch.

"Lester!" said Day Care Guy, panting, sweating, but back on the scene with all the puppies in tow. "How....?"

"Lester!" Lucy stomped her paws. "How...?"

"Sorry, Mother," Lester said, prancing past her. "Not!" he finished.

"Ok, Ok boy, you can come too," said Day Care Guy. "Can't remember why I was going to leave you home...strange...never mind, let's go!"

He braced himself and prepared for a walk between two leashes full of excited, happy dogs.

Chapter Nine

After Breakfast, A Walk

Randy looked around and counted heads.

"Let's see," he thought, "Doofus-with-the-strange-ears, New Girl, Doofus, Doofus, Bailiff, Boss and me. They all found their way back! Excellent!"

Every dog had successfully smelled his or her way back to the Park. This was a rare victory. Each of them had found some food. A triumph!

Boss had found a burrito gigante still in its bag. Neatly cut in half, with only a few bites taken out on one end, it made a luxurious breakfast for himself and Old Friend.

"Good dog!" Old Friend exclaimed.

He took the unbitten half and gave the rest to Boss. Boss chewed slowly, savoring the flavors. He knew he would get more. Old Friend wouldn't finish his portion.

"That's enough for me," he said. He put the rest down for Boss. "Good boy. You're bigger than I am and need it more, that's my baby boy." Boss always had seconds of whatever feast they had found. Old Friend was eating less and less as the days went by. Boss was concerned but when the food was put down for him, what else was a dog to do? Once it was on the ground, no human would touch that food again, as they had issues with dirt and doo. "It shouldn't go to waste," Boss thought as he sucked on a particularly tasty piece of carne asada.

Ben and Jerry had found half a bucket of fried chicken.

"Six whole pieces!" Ben said. "Big ones!"

"And we didn't eat one," said Jerry, quite proud of himself. "We brought them all back to share!"

"Except a wing," Ben said, "we split a wing to celebrate."

"If we break up the big ones," said Jerry, "everyone can have some!"

"The things humans throw away," Ben chewed on a juicy

piece.

"Lucky for us," said Jerry.

Mimi and Angel had stayed together through the night. Angel had discovered the food. He didn't know what it was and would have left it there. It didn't smell familiar. He showed it to Mimi.

"Sushirito!" she exclaimed. "They're good and good for you! Bob gets them all the time."

"What's in them?" asked Bailiff.

"Fish, rice and seaweed," Mimi answered. "Like a burrito but with fish."

"Seaweed?" Randy made a face.

"It's full of vitamins," said Mimi, "just try some."

It was surprisingly tasty and satisfying, Randy and Bailiff agreed, and one hardly knew the seaweed was there at all.

Through the whole night of searching and stealth, Bailiff hadn't found anything. Embarrassed and unhappy, not to mention very hungry, he returned to the Park.

"They're here!" He jumped for joy.

His favorite human visitors to the park had settled on their usual bench. They each had a paper bag from which they pulled out some food. It was only a matter of time, Bailiff knew, before they would forget about their food and start canoodling. Bailiff was very disciplined. He always resisted the steaming, half-eaten remains the man left right out in the open on the bench. It was safer all around to approach cautiously, silently, then grab the bag on the ground and be off. It was always fun to guess what would be in the bag. Half a sandwich? A bag of chips? The deep breathing required for running away brought the smells to his nose. "Corned beef!" he sighed, "And a bag of chips!" His pride restored, he went to find his friends.

"What did you get?" he asked Randy.

"The usual," Randy said.

Randy made a job of finding every bakery and bagel shop

within a five mile radius of the park. He knew what they had to offer and what they had to throw away. He knew the right times to be there. While the human scavengers were still asleep, Randy made his rounds.

"Muffin stumps," he said. "The carrot and raison ones are quite good. No!" he batted Angel's paw. "Not the chocolate ones! I should have taken those out."

"But they smell like…like…heaven!" Angel's vocabulary of earthly things was still limited.

"Yes, they do," Randy said, separating the chocolate ones from the rest. "But if you eat them, you'll feel like hell and no one wants that. They're poison for us, leave them for the humans."

"What a joyous start to the day," Old Friend licked up a last chocolate crumb and wiped his face. Shaking a bit and leaning on Boss for support, he stood. He hooked Boss's leash, took a deep breath and smiled.

"Come on, baby boy, let's take our walk."

Their goal was the public bathroom. Old Friend would wash a bit, brush his teeth, and give Boss a bowl of water.

"Later," Boss called over his shoulder.

"Onward!" Old Friend commanded and off they went.

Every morning after breakfast, or at more or less the same time, even if there was no breakfast, Boss and Old Friend set out to do their business.

"I envy you," Old Friend would say. "Pee anywhere you want, no worries. Me? I'm too shy for that. Need a little more privacy. You done? Onward!"

They struggled up the hill toward the dribbling water fountain and the street lamp.

"Challenge yourself!" Old Friend commanded. "Keeps you young and fit!" He stopped and stooped for a watery cough. He finished noisily and looked into his dog's eyes.

"And viable!"

Boss didn't know about any of that. He knew that hard work made his muscles strong. With strong muscles, he could do more without getting tired.

"Onward!" wheezed Old Friend and they began their climb anew.

"Here we go, "said Boss. "Hard work! And I'm ready!"

Gently, so as not to hurt the old man's feelings, Boss increased his pull on the leash.

"Good boy!" coughed Old Friend, "that's my good boy!"

At the top of the hill on the edge of the Park, they stood for a moment to calm their heartbeats. Boss was careful to position their feet away from the fountain's puddles.

Old Friend shaded his eyes and scanned the horizon.

"Now, which way did we go yesterday? Ooof!"

He exhaled as the leash snapped tight. Boss was already on the secret unseen path to where they were yesterday. It was a public bathroom on the edge of the park. If they didn't like the look of it, or felt in the mood for something a bit more posh, they would move on to the next destination. A dough-nut shop run by very kind people was just a little further on their daily path.

"Onward!" gasped Old Friend. Boss pulled and pulled. The old man struggled to keep up.

"Good dog! Hard work! It's good for you!"

Boss strained and pulled. Old Friend, trotted, stumbled and wheezed. Together, they took their daily exercise.

We Have to Keep Him! (Randy, Boss and Angel)

Chapter Ten

What's Going On Down There?

"Look!" said Bailiff. "Day Dogs!"

A gaping hole in the hedges formed the one natural entrance to the tree circle. The Night Dogs seldom used it. Randy advised that some anonymous spot in the hedge would be more secure. The thick brush would spring back together, erasing their comings and goings.

The natural entrance overlooked the one paved path into the Dog Park. Every morning as the Day Dogs arrived, the ovular space would fill with curious, panting dog faces. Even Randy could not resist the obvious breach of security. It was just too much fun. He felt confident that the Day Dogs were too dull from pampering and too self-centered to notice the wide eyed faces of the panting strays peering through the opening in the hedge.

The Day Dogs, whether traveling singly or in groups, always came in on the same paved path. Then, depending on individual preference, they remained on the path or not. A familiar group was stopped there, its dogs and Friend now making that decision.

They arrived every morning and most afternoons. They were a mixed group, with some who loved the grass and others who stuck to the pavement. This made for a lively show.

"Look at the human," said Bailiff. "He's like a rag doll."

"He lets them control him," said Mimi. "Stupid."

"Didn't you control Bob?" asked Bailiff.

"Shut up!" Mimi snapped. "We were different!"

"Wow," said Ben. "They've got some major babes!"

"Some big dudes too," said Jerry.

"Are they all angels?" Angel asked. "Do I see wings?"

"Look" said Bailiff, "there's the one who used to play with Spotty."

"Who are they?" Angel asked.

"Day Dogs," said Randy. "They have homes and human Friends."

"I read about that," Angel was excited. "On the Ethereal dot net!"

The other dogs looked at him with confusion or pity.

"That's what I thought I would be," he struggled to explain.

"You could be a Day Dog" Randy said. "You're goofy enough. "

"Excuse me?" Mimi's tone was dangerous. Her pretty eyes narrowed to slits and her teeth were showing.

"What's going on down there?" Bailiff asked.

Down on the path, Day Care Guy was pulled in all directions. Only Lucy pulled toward him while all the others strained as hard as they could to go their own way.

"You're not going near those strays!" Lucy's phenomenal maternal strength pulled toward Day Care Guy. "You'll ruin your hair!"

"Psychic powers!" Papillion cried. "Everyone focus!"

Everyone did, except Lucy.

"Leash off! Leash off! Leash off!" All the dogs chanted together.

"Ok, guys," Day Care Guy said. "Leash off. Go run around. And poop where I can see you!"

As if by magic, all the dogs and pups popped their collars. Only Lucy remained attached. "Fine," she said. "I'll stay with him!" They trotted off to a distant bench where Lucy would sulk while Day Care Guy sipped his hot drink and read the paper. She would avert her eyes when Lester went wild and ruined his hair again.

"You there! Croppy-Eared Boy!" Randy said. "Over here," he pointed.

All the dogs re-arranged themselves. Angel wriggled into the appointed place.

"As Earth-Dog-Space-Alien-Mutants go...," Randy started.

"Not this again!" Bailiff moaned, covering his ears. "Please, no!"

"You're quite okay! I was going to say! Before I was rudely interrupted!" Randy paused. "Wait for it."

"Ok, ok..." Bailiff waved a paw dismissively. "Sorry."

"Your ear-cropping job is just beyond comprehension. I'm sorry, laddie, but I just don't see the point. What were they trying to do?" He pointed at Angel's slug tentacles. "And the slime!" he finished and all the dogs stared. Angel slumped a little. He knew better than they did how it felt to be different.

"And yet, strange as they are," Randy's tone was respectful, "we've already had a show of what they can do. Most impressive." Randy said. Angel sat up straight.

"I used to hear very well," Randy went on. "Not as sharp anymore, I'm afraid. But I still love the gossip. Will you help me, Space-Alien-Mu..."

"Angel" Angel blurted. "Please, sir."

"His name is Angel," said Mimi.

"Angel," Randy said, nodding slowly. "Angel, will you point those slime sticks down at the Day Dogs and tell us what they're saying?"

"Yeee-ah! Please! Hurry up!" all the other dogs said.

Angel sat up very straight. The slimy ear-tentacles snapped forward.

"So, Ruffee," Lester said. "How about now? Want to practice?"

"Not here!" Rufahlo stage whispered through smiling lips and clenched teeth. "No one must see my imperfections!"

"No one's watching," Lester encouraged.

"No!" Panic edged Rufahlo's voice.

"Not here," he mumbled. "Let's play!"

The big dog bumped the smaller dog. They each reared back on hind legs and a paw fight commenced.

"Imperfections?" Randy exclaimed. "What do you care about that?" He addressed the whole group. "Do see what I'm saying? They've got everything! And all they want is everything else! What about those two there?" Randy pointed at a pair of fancy-girl, mini-dogs.

"I don't know," Lili sighed. "What's it all about?"

"What do you mean?" Fifi asked.

"We eat, we sleep, we take baths, we get dirty again..." Lili trailed off.

"I know," Fifi said. "I feel that way too. There's got to be something more!"

"Unbelievable," Randy snorted. "Why don't you get off your overfed behinds and chase a few sheep? There's something more for you!"

"But I feel that way too," Ben said.

"Shut up!" Randy couldn't believe his ears.

"I do too!" said Jerry. "Sometimes I get so frustrated, I just have to...to..." He grabbed the paper bag that had once held the corn beef sandwich.

Ben had the burrito wrapper.

"Rip things up!" they shouted.

Within seconds, the bag and the wrapper were confetti. Soft breezes caught the bits of paper and blew them out of the tree circle. Ben stretched. Jerry panted furiously. "That's better," said Jerry.

"I feel better too," said Ben.

"Ah, go way with you!" Randy said. "You have everything you

could possibly want!"

"Not everything," said Ben.

"And they've got more!" Randy continued. "And still they're complaining! Space-al..." he caught himself. "...Angel...what are they saying now?"

"Don't look now, Night Dogs checking you out," said Angel. "You too! If looks could burn, your hair would be on fire by now."

"Oh no!" Ben cried.

"They can see us!" Jerry panicked."

"Of course they can see us," Bailiff snorted. "They're fancy but they're not blind."

"Well, let them look," Angel said, still quoting the girls. "They have little enough in their lives. Maybe looking at us will make them happy."

Fifi tossed her hair around. Angel matched her movements and his tentacles flapped wildly.

"Hey!" Bailiff flinched. "Watch the slime!"

"Sorry!" Angel turned to Randy. "Can we go see them?"

"It's not the safest idea," Randy said.

"They're the only dogs here," Bailiff said, "and their Friend is oblivious."

"They know about homes and families!" Angel pleaded. "I want to learn from them!"

"What are they saying now?" asked Bailiff.

Angel aimed his tentacles and focused.

"I just wish I could feel..." Lili paused and Angel paused with her. "Imbued with purpose!" she finished.

Angel repeated her words and waited for more. Jerry started to giggle.

"I mean the eating, the sleeping, the baths, the hair-dos, it's all good...but..."

A noise interrupted Lili's thought. She looked up at the tree circle. The entrance was no longer filled with staring, panting dog faces. Several of the faces' owners were now rolling on the ground, heaving and yipping with joyous abandon.

"I wonder what's so funny," Fifi said.

"I don't know," Lili shrugged. "But look! Still checking you out!"

"You too," Fifi giggled. "Look! He is loving you with his eyes!"

"Too bad about the coat," Lili stared at Ben. "I hate to see a nice coat go all shabby like that. Why doesn't he get a bath and a comb-out?"

"I get so tired of hair issues," Fifi said. "That smooth one," she looked at Jerry. "Now there's a low maintenance 'do that always looks good."

"Papillion," called Lili, "come over here!"

"Papillion?" called Fifi. "What are you doing?"

"Thinking." Papillion twitched, stretched and trotted over the join them.

"I tried that once," said Fifi. "Never again!"

"I know!" said Lili. "I got so frustrated I just had to..."

She felt the urge. She glanced around, searching for something, anything! A sheet of newsprint floated on the breeze. She grabbed an edge.

"I just...have to..."

Fifi grabbed the other edge.

"Rip things up!" they screamed together and the rage-ripping commenced.

"Look at that!" said Jerry.

"They rip like we do!" Ben was astonished.

"Can we please go talk to them?" Angel pleaded.

"It would be better," Randy said, "if they talked to you. Safer that way. No one's Friend gets frightened by the strange dog bothering their dog."

"He's not paying attention," Bailiff was indignent. Day Care Guy's nose was deep in his newspaper. "It's like they're not even his dogs!"

"Still, better to be cautious," said Randy. "Let's move about, keep your distance, talk amongst yourselves. Maybe they'll hear something of interest and break the ice."

Chapter Eleven

May I Offer You Some Quality Ripping Material?

"Look!" Lili said. "They're all coming out!"

Slowly, casually, moving in pairs, the Night Dogs meandered away from the tree circle. Feigning interest in something on the ground, sparring in a fake paw fight, rolling on their backs, their progress toward the Day Dog play area was a study in purposeful nonchalance.

"Who do they think they're kidding?" Lili asked.

"Look at that one," Fifi pointed. "What kind of dog is that?"

The three girls stared at Angel. He tried to appear casual. He tried to focus on anything that was not the three beautiful girls. His tentacles waived wildly about.

"Watch the slime!" Mimi snapped.

"Sorry," said Angel.

Papillion's eyes bulged. She tilted into Lili.

"Get off!" Lili pushed her back up right.

"It's true!" Papillion whispered. "Earth-Dog-Space-Alien-Mutants do exist!"

"No, they don't," Lili said wearily.

"That's an ear-cropping job gone terribly wrong," said Fifi. "Tragic. What were they trying to do?"

"No one would do that on purpose," said Papillion. "That's a mutant!"

"No, it's your boyfriend!" Lili said. Fifi sniggered. Papillion growled.

"Fifi, look!" Lili changed the subject. "There's the old Border Collie."

"Snoopy old gossip," said Fifi, "and the Corgi's with him. Wanna have some fun?"

A wicked glint sparked in her eyes.

"They're such big braggarts," Lili explained to Papillion. "We get 'em all revved up and see how far they'll go. Ready?" The girlfriends nodded. Lili took a deep breath.

"My day has been a horror," she said loudly. "And I think my Friend's a dimwit! She dropped my china water bowl and put a big chip in it!"

"Oh, my god!" the other two girls whined.

"Chipped bowl? You were lucky!" Randy muttered quite distinctly to Bailiff.

"Here we go!" Lili elbowed Fifi who elbowed Papillion who fell over and got up again.

"My water bowl was a muddy hole my Friend made with his boot heel," Randy said to Bailiff. He spoke as if they were onstage in a very large theater.

"The rain would fall and fill the hole. I'd have it with my meals. Muddy swill."

"Muddy water? You were lucky!" said Bailiff.

"Eeeeeeeeew! Eeeeeeeeeew!" the girls snickered and giggled.

"My old Friend wouldn't bathe me, so I'd roll in mud 'til slimy," Bailiff proclaimed. "I'd dry it to a thick green crust, then shake it off, I'm shiny! And I'm clean!"

"Clean mud?" Randy questioned, "You were lucky!"

"Eeeeeeeeeeew! Eeeeeeeeeew!" the girls giggled softly. Trying not to laugh was harder than just laughing out loud.

"Make them stop!" Papillion gasped. "I'm going to pee myself!"

"Cause when you live out on a farm with cows and pigs and chickens," Randy gestured, "and goats and sheep any pile you'd leap right into probably…"

"No!" Lili gasped.

"Don't go there!" Fifi hiccupped.

"No!" Papillion twitched and fell over.

Randy noticed them and was very pleased. His little plan was working.

"Not clean mud!" he said, as Bailiff made a face. "That's all I'm saying!"

"Eeeeeeeeeeeeeeeeew! Eeeeeeeeeeeeeeeeew!" the girls gasped and sighed.

"Well, they might have all had homes once," said Lili, "but I guess they couldn't hack it."

"It takes a lot of guts and brains to make it in this racket," Fifi said.

Through the subterfuge of growling and fake paw fighting, Ben and Jerry had moved close enough to hear.

"Living outside is a challenge," Ben said indignantly to Jerry.

"Keeps the mind and body working," Jerry agreed. "And you don't end up all fat and dumb dumb like you would if your life was too easy," he added.

"Fat?" Lili challenged.

"Dumb dumb?" Fifi's hair twitched.

"Hmph!" Papillion pushed her little nose up in the air.

They'd had gone too far! Embarrassed, Ben and Jerry retreated. The girls put their heads together and conferred quietly.

"They whine and complain," said Lili, "but they like their life here."

"It's cute. Endearing," Fifi mused.

"But so dumb, dumb, dumb!" Papillion said.

"When you look as good as they do, you don't have to have a brain," a yearning note tinged Ben's voice.

"They're so cute," said Jerry. "Endearing."

"And so dumb," said Ben.

A quiet few minutes passed as each dog considered his or her own thoughts.

"I like my place. I like my life," thought Lili.

"I wouldn't trade for nothing," thought Randy.

"But I love to listen to all their lies," thought Fifi.

"They talk and I start laughing," thought Ben and Jerry.

"And I think to myself," thought Papillion, "I'm the lucky one!"

"I am!" thought Bailiff.

"I am!" thought Randy.

"I am!" Angel said out loud. No one understood him. He couldn't articulate very well through the sheets of newsprint and bags in his mouth.

"What are you doing?" asked Ben. Angel froze, the papers in his mouth flapping in the wind.

"Why is the hair on your neck all spiked up straight?" asked Jerry.

Angel cocked his head to one side and stared up at the stern visage of Busy Angel. No one else seemed to know he was there.

"What's he doing here now?" Angel thought. "Am I more slimy? No! Good!" He relaxed a little.

Busy Angel surveyed the scene and tapped the side of his halo with his pencil. Slowly, dramatically, he lowered the pencil to his clipboard and made a big check mark.

"Fine," Angel thought. "I'm still a dog and I'm going for it!"

Turning back to Ben and Jerry, he spit all the papers on the ground. He lolled his tongue out to rest it.

"These girls know about homes and families." He picked up the papers with his mouth.

"Dude!" said Jerry. "You can't just go right up to them...."

Out spilled all the papers again. "But I can approach," Angel explained, "bearing gifts." He pulled the papers together again.

"Ooooooooo!" breathed Ben and Jerry, slowly catching on. "Wow!"

Busy Angel tapped his halo.

"Pleah!" said Mimi, spitting out her collection of papers. "Here's some more. Not that one! It's got poop on it!"

"Thanks," said Angel and stuffed his mouth with the edges of papers and bags. Tentacles flipping and papers flapping, he trotted right up to the girls.

"Here we go!" Lili whispered.

"Oh, my god!" Fifi whispered.

"It's the mutant!" Papillion whispered.

"Pleah!" was Angel's opening line as he spit the papers at their feet. He tried to hold his tentacles very still and to smile in a warm and engaging manner.

"Good afternoon, ladies" he said. "My name is Angel. I'm a Night Dog. I couldn't help but notice that you seem to enjoy ripping things up."

"Yeah," said Lili. "We like to rip."

"We can rip," said Fifi.

Angel took a breath and stopped. Busy Angel hovered a short distance away. He was swishing the hem of his robe back and forth, brushing the noses of some red-colored puppies. They couldn't see it, of course, but the swishing made their noses tickle and they seemed to enjoy the sensation. They jumped and rolled over each other to get to the tickly feeling again and again. Before this, Angel had seen Busy only at night or in Heaven. He was surprised to see how sparkly he was in the daytime sun. If Angel didn't know better, he would have thought the Important One was enjoying himself. But he did know better and he knew that Busy had his spirit sights locked on Angel, passing judgment on his every move.

"So be it," Angel thought. "I'm still a dog, my purpose is to be useful and my goal is fun. Let's do it!" He looked back at the three girl dogs. They stared at him, waiting.

"May I offer you some samples of some quality ripping material?" he asked.

"Thank you," said Lili.

"Quite the collection," said Fifi.

The three girls started sniffing and pawing through the pile.

"This one's nice," said Papillion. It was the bag that had held the muffin stumps.

"May I have this one?" she asked.

"I brought them all for you," said Angel. "Take what you like. I thought we could rip together."

Sensing an opportunity to redeem themselves, Ben and Jerry crept closer.

"Yeah," said Ben. "A good start is to get a soft corner..."

"I like a hard crease," said Jerry.

"I like that it's there," said Lili.

Fifi grabbed a bag.

"Let her rip!" Ben shouted.

They ripped and panted and giggled and ripped some more until there was no piece larger than a senior dog's kibble bit. Angel watched with satisfaction. He had done this! He had made them happy! He wondered if this good deed would make his ears change back. He waggled them a little. Nope. Still slimy.

"Watch it!" said Lili.

"Sorry," said Angel. He heard a tap, tap, tapping. It was Busy Angel with his pencil. He pretended not to be watching but as soon as Angel looked up, he brought the pencil down to his clip board and made a show of making some notes.

"Something is different," Angel thought. Behind the stern expression and deliberate movements, Angel could sense something else. Could it be...approval? Happiness? "Why is he still here?" Angel thought. "Maybe he thinks Heaven is boring too. Maybe he likes being here, even if it's only to harass and worry me..."

Busy disappeared in an instant, as if some visibility switch had snapped off. The red colored puppies looked puzzled and poked at each other. Why had the tickling stopped?

Angel turned his attention back to the panting, happy dogs now lolling together in the sun. Tiny paper scraps, in the thousands it seemed, swirled in the breeze and fluttered on the grass. Lili was picking bits out of Ben's tangled coat.

"You need a bath," she said.

"A what?" Ben had never had a bath before.

"Now, ladies," Angel started. "I'm told you know all about homes with human families. May I ask a few…"

"What's all this?"

The angry roar could be heard in every corner of the park.

"Uh oh," Randy said.

Chapter Twelve

The Bone and the Bow

The sudden noise startled Lester and he dropped the bone.

"Don't lose it!" said Rufahlo.

While they were playing and chasing each other around, they had run inside the tree circle at the top of the grassy knoll. As many times as they had been to the park, they had never gone into the circle before. Spotty had always advised against it.

"It's our home," he had said. "Boss lives there with his Friend and he's quite territorial about it."

"Who?" Lester asked.

"Our Pack Leader," Spotty replied. "He's a really great dog and much kinder than he looks. If he likes you, you're in. But if he doesn't…"

"Never mind," Lester had said, "I don't need to see it."

But Spotty was gone now and here they were inside the secret circle. Lester didn't need to get close to the crumpled blanket to know that a human slept here often. He twitched his nose around while Rufahlo explored. "That one here and that one," Lester's nose identified where each of the Night Dogs slept. He didn't know their names but their smells were easy to separate and place in the overall picture.

"And that one and…wow! There's a girl here, too!" he said to Rufahlo.

"Never mind," Rufahlo said, "look at this!"

Hidden behind a big rock was the biggest bone either of them had ever seen.

"Wow," said Lester.

Carefully and respectfully, he picked it up with his teeth. It was very heavy and hard to balance in his mouth.

"Wha eye a ah i ah wa is?" he mumbled through the obstruction the bone made in his mouth.

"A buffalo?" said Rufahlo. "No, bigger! A dinosaur, maybe?"

Rufahlo's Friends watched the Discovery channel and Rufahlo knew a lot of things.

"Eye o o, " said Lester and dropped the bone. His jaws ached a bit already from stretching around its massive circumference.

"What kind of dog could keep such a thing?" he asked.

"Let me see," said Rufahlo. He picked it up in his teeth.

"Waaaaaooow," he said through the bone.

They paused for a moment, taking in the scene and what they were doing. The Wild Places! Rufahlo had heard of them but never imagined he would set foot there. Mischief glittered in his eyes.

"Ay!" Rufahlo shouted around the bone. "Ca ih!"

He took a deep breath and lowered his head. His beautiful musculature moved into a slow but steadily increasing spin.

"Oh no!" Lester said. "Not the discus throw! It's a great bone! It's probably his, the Pack Leader! Not the discus throw!"

A mini cyclone of dust rose around the spinning Rufahlo. With full body support, he whipped his neck outward and released the bone.

In the nano-second available, Lester gauged the distance. He leapt into the air with speed and precision a Border Collie would envy. The bone nestled softly into his teeth, as if it welcomed its own capture.

Then, the roar of rage filled the tree circle, bouncing and reverberating off the trees and rocks. Lester gasped, opening his jaws as his paws hit the ground.

"Don't lose it!" cried Rufahlo. He rushed over to watch its loss.

The bone had dropped from Lester's jaw and taken a mighty bounce off a rock in the dirt floor. It sailed over the shrubs and out of the circle. The boys rushed to the natural entrance and looked out. Slowly, beautifully, the bone sailed through the air. Gravity pulled it down, the energy of impact with every surface it found, rock, dirt, pavement, bounced it right back up again, always higher than before. Lester and Rufahlo watched in awe, their heads moving in sync with the bone's trajectory.

A final magnificent bounce concluded with a small splash as the bone dived into the decorative, man-made, Dog Park lake.

"Perfect ten," said Rufahlo.

"Bath time," Lester sighed.

"No! No, Lester! I don't want to get wet!" Rufahlo backed away from the edge of the lake.

"There's that whine again," Lester thought. "Rufahlo is just not happy these days."

"It's the right thing to do," Lester said. He looked at his friend. It was sad to see the show-biz eyes look so frightened.

"Never mind," Lester said. "I'll go."

"You'll ruin your hair!" Rufahlo protested weakly.

"It'll be fun!" Lester said. "Here, hold my bow."

He used his paws to unclip the top knot bow that Lucy made him wear in public.

"Image!" she would say. "Always be ready! Everyone is watching! Be the champion!"

It was a powder blue grosgrain ribbon styled like a man's bow tie, a small concession to the idea that a top knot bow was an unmanly and rather silly thing for a boy dog to wear.

He had worked out the removal technique on his own. It had taken long hours of practice, but now Lester could use his paws to unclip the bow and, at least, preserve that one thing for his mother. His hair would be ruined, that was a given. But, for her, he would protect the bow.

"Yeah!" he shouted and made a big belly flop into the water.

"Watch it!" cried Rufahlo, prancing backward to avoid the splashes. He made sure the bow was safe and dry.

"I'll have to carry it home," he thought. "He'll be so wet! Lucy will be very angry. She scares me! Protect the bow!" he commanded himself and moved a few feet further back.

Lester dove down and found the bone. It rested easily on the dirt floor and would be no problem to bring back up. Making the dive and assessing the job took all the breath he had and he pushed up to the surface. If he stood on his hind legs he could keep his head out of the water. He started to call to Rufahlo then paused.

Rufahlo's alert, excited face had sagged into profound sadness. His big head hung off to one side and his eyes stared unseeing at the ground.

"He really thinks he can't do the show without me," Lester thought. "And all I talk about is leaving."

Briefly, Lester considered how strange and different he must look with his poofy hair all wet and plastered flat to his body. "I really don't care," he thought. There was no emotion. It was a fact. That was it. He didn't care how he looked. The bone must be retrieved and brought back to the Pack Leader. The cool water felt wonderful. His hair would go flat and Lucy would have a fit. "There you are," he thought, "still worth it!" He looked at his friend. "He needs a boost," he thought.

Lester paddled his front paws as if he was struggling to stay afloat.

"Ruffee!" he called. "I found it! But it's stuck in the weeds and so is my leg!"

Lester paddled and splashed, sucked water and spit.

"I have to get it! I'm going down!" he shouted.

Rufahlo snapped up straight then stood at full attention.

"Wev-ah!" he shouted through the bow in his mouth.

"Get rid of the bow!" he thought. "Now!"

In his panic, Rufahlo made a spin-less discus throw, snapping his neck to the side. The bow soared through the air and was stopped by the chest of Papillion, who just that moment had pranced down to the lake on her own.

"Ow!" she squealed and fell down.

Out of breath again, Lester stood on his hind legs and saw the bow-shot hit the tiny target.

"Oh, no!" Rufahlo sprang to her side.

Lester paddled loudly in the dark water.

"I'm fine!" she said. "He needs help!" She pointed at Lester.

"I'm really stuck now!" Lester cried. "I can't get out!"

He sank his head dramatically into the water and blew bubbles.

"Lester!" Rufahlo shouted.

"Go!" Papillion screamed.

Rufahlo stared at her. This tiny dog was telling him what to do! That had never happened before.

"Go!" she squeaked.

"Lester!" Rufahlo backed up a step, prepared, and shot himself into the water. Much sooner than he expected, he hit lake bottom.

"Hmmm," he thought as he rolled, placed his feet and stood up. Standing on all fours, the dark water came up only to his chin. Lester was standing on his hind legs, he could see that now. The glee on Lester's face was mischief, not meanness.

"The water is wondershock! Don't you feel better?" Lester asked.

Rufahlo self-examined. It was his favorite hobby.

"And I do feel better," he thought. "He's right! The water is great! Bracing and cold! I feel great! But still..."

"You lured me here under false pretenses! You cried pup!" Rufahlo swacked a mighty splash at Lester.

"And you loved it," Lester swacked back and a water version of paw-fighting ensued.

"Ahem!" Papillion coughed.

"Huh?" The boys stopped swacking each other. They had forgotten she was there. She fell down.

"Whoa!" The boys started out of the water.

"I'm fine! I'm ok!" the little dog said as she righted herself. "Stay back! You're all wet! And smelly! Day Care Guy is trying to round us up to go home. There's some sort of ruckus in the bottom-of-the-hill play area. He'll leave one of us behind unless we help him. Let's go!"

"Get out, shake off," said Lester to Rufahlo. "I'll get the bone."

"And stand waaaaaaaaaaaay over there when you shake!" said Papillion.

Rufahlo stepped with care as he left the lake and went a good distance away. He placed himself so his path of spray would go side to side and not at her.

"Thanks," she said. "I'll take the bow and keep it dry."

When Lester emerged from the water, he struggled to balance the heavy bone. He paused to catch his breath and looked at his friends onshore. "Hmmm," he thought, watching them watching each other. He tried to be very quiet as he pulled himself out of the water.

Papillion's giggling made him stumble and drop the bone. He ducked into the shallow water and retrieved it.

"I'm sorry, Lester," she gasped.

Rufahlo joined him in the shallow water to look at the bone.

"With your hair all flat like that," she gasped, "your nose...," she coughed. "It's..."

"Hu!" shouted Lester. He gestered to Rufahlo to take the bone. "Huge!" he said after the transfer was made. "I love my great big nose! It's ok!"

"Thanks!" she said. "I'm sorry and thanks."

"Don't be sorry," he said. "I'm not."

"I've got the bow," she said. "Let's go."

They started up the hill to the play area.

"Wi oo a ah oh?" Rufahlo asked.

"Yes, give it to me," Lester said. They made the exchange.

"Papillion?" said Rufahlo and trotted a step ahead.

"Ay aah!" she said. Gently, she spit the bow onto a low bush.

"The bow must stay dry." Her gaze was frank and unwavering. She fell down.

"I'm fine!" she said. "I'm ok! I've got the bow. Let's go." She skittered unsteadily up the path.

"Let me walk near you," Rufahlo said. "I have a short coat and I'm almost dry. If you fall near a puddle, I could save the bow."

"Near is ok, next to is not," she said. "You're still wet. But thanks, and please do help me with the bow. The rest of the afternoon will be much more pleasant if we keep the bow dry." She paused and smiled. Rufahlo ducked his head and smiled back.

"Hmmmm," Lester thought, looking from one to the other.

"You know my mother, then, do you?" he said, laughing. "Let's move along then." He picked up the bone. "Uh aw, eh o!" he mumbled through its massiveness. They seemed to understand and continued up the hill toward the play area.

Chapter Thirteen

Why Don't I Come Over to Your House and Rip Things Up?

When they walked together through town, Boss took care to stay close to Old Friend's side. Sometimes, the old man would stumble. Boss would lean heavily against him to give support until he was steady again. Old Friend needed him for lots of things. Starting conversations was one example.

"Look at my dog," he would say to whomever they met. "Isn't he handsome?"

Whoever they met would often look doubtful. It seemed most of whomever they met found Boss more scary than handsome.

Old Friend would cup Boss's head in one of his big hands and rub his face. Always one to appreciate a good pet, Boss would close his eyes and relax against the old man's leg. They were the picture of familial bliss. Children would smile, mothers relax, teens would say, "He's awesome! Where'd you get him?"

"Oh, we've been friends a long, long time, haven't we, boy?" he gazed fondly down at Boss's big face. Boss would give his hand a lick.

"Can I pet him?" children asked.

"If it's ok with your mom, then it's ok with us," Old Friend replied. If the mother nodded, Boss would get treated to pets from a child. He loved to watch their faces change from shy to joyful as they realized the big, bad-looking dog really enjoyed their pets.

Proudly, he would think, "I'm an ambassador for my breed."

If the child seemed confident, he would give their face a gentle lick. Oh, how he loved the squeals and laughter and the tussling of children as they each tried to be the next to get a lick.

"Could you spare a little bit today?" Old Friend would say. "Yesterday, my baby boy had nothing to eat."

Sometimes they would get a dollar, or half a sandwich, or some homemade cookies out of someone's lunch. Sometimes they'd get nothing but "I'm sorry. Good luck." That was fine too.

Sometimes Boss needed to be strong and he could do that too. There were bullies and very cruel people in this world, he knew that. Sometimes they would target Old Friend.

"Your dog is ugly! And you stink!" they shouted. Old Friend would get flustered. He would stumble and lean on Boss for support.

"Whadya, drunk? Get lost, ya bum!" they would yell.

"I'm not drunk," Old Friend protested. "I've got a touch of the palsy, that's all. And I'd advise you to lower your voice. My dog may interpret your shouting as an attempt to hurt me."

"Attempt? No, I'm not attempting, here." Challenge would ring in their voices. "I AM going to…"

"WHAT?" Boss would bark. "You're going to do WHAT?

If the person was acting out of fear, Old Friend would pull Boss gently away and they would leave. If the person was a bully or just plain mean, the old man and his dog might decide to have a little fun.

"Careful now," Old Friend would warn. "I'm not as strong as I used to be. If he gets angry, I can't always hold him back."

Boss would fix his big yellow eyes in an angry, unwavering stare, boring into the eyes of the challenger.

"So what if you can't," the challenger might say. "What's he going to do?"

Depending on the sound of the voice, Boss would decide what to do next. If it quavered a bit or cracked, Boss would continue the growl but retreat closer to Old Friend. If the voice still said danger, Boss would raise the volume on his growl, strain forward and show his teeth. He had very big, sharply pointed teeth. Usually, this was enough.

"Watch yourself, old man," they would call over their shoulders. They tried to move away with dignity but Boss could tell they wanted to run away as fast as they could.

"You take care now," Boss would bark as they moved away. If they tried to say something else, Boss would show his teeth again.

"Good boy," Old Friend always said. "Maybe it's time to go home."

Home! Boss enjoyed their regular outings but, at the end of the day, he looked forward to being home. Home was the Dog Park and Old Friend would let him off leash as soon as they reached the edge. He could run and play and relax. Very few bullies or cruel people came to the Dog Park. Boss could stand down his vigilant watch and just have some fun.

To ease any fears about a big, mean-looking dog playing near other pets, Boss would spend the first ten minutes or so running into the park to stretch his legs. He would look around to see who was there, then back to Old Friend. When the other humans saw his human, they would relax. "Good. Someone is in charge of that dog." Some of them looked doubtful, perhaps wondering how much control this stumbling, palsied, raggedy old human could possibly have over the big, strong dog. When Old Friend cupped Boss's big head in his strong hand and the dog leaned in for a pet, the other humans would nod knowingly and go back to drinking coffee, reading newspapers and comfortably ignoring their dogs.

On his first run into the play area, Boss sensed something amiss. It was too soon to react. He had to run back to Old Friend at least twice before he could react to anything. That was his rule. Other humans would relax after two pets from Old Friend and then he could exert whatever authority was needed.

On his third run in, he realized what it was. The play area looked as if a piñata full of confetti had burst and spewed its contents all over the lawn.

"What's this?" he bellowed. "Who did this?"

All the dogs froze.

"Who did this?" he bellowed again.

He knew it was odd for such a big, mean-looking dog to be such a fuss-pot about tidiness but he couldn't help it. Look at this mess! All over the lawn!

"Who did this?" he bellowed again.

Ben hadn't moved since the first bellow. Lili looked at Ben and felt sad. She turned to Boss.

"We all did," she said. "We were having fun. That's what dogs do. Why are you so mean?"

Mean. There was that word again. Boss tried not to be mean. He had to maintain some sort of order but always tried to be fair and, if he could, to be kind. But here was this little, fluffy girl, getting all teary because she thought he was mean.

"He's our Pack Leader," Angel said, trying to be helpful.

"But he doesn't have to be so mean!" Lili was sobbing now.

"Yes, he does, sometimes," said Ben. "We're an unruly bunch."

"Day Dogs!" Boss sighed. Out loud, and very gently, he said, "Well, why don't I come over to your house and rip things up? Look at this mess! Who's going to clean this up?"

"Oh, Lili, don't be such a drama-pup!" called Fifi. "Come over here and help us!"

"Lili," thought Ben, "her name is Lili. That's pretty."

Fifi, Jerry and Bailiff were all helping Randy herd the Dog Park gardener. The four dogs urged the confused man closer and closer to the play area.

"Help is on the way," called Randy.

Lili and Ben ran down to join in.

"No! What are you dogs doing?" The poor man tried to fend them off with his leaf blower. "No! I'm not going near that big, mean dog!"

Boss saw Old Friend struggle up the hill toward the tree circle. "Ok, I'll go," he said and rushed away to help the old man.

106

"What is it, you dogs? Oh! Good Lord, what happened here?"

The gardener stopped in his tracks. Litter was everywhere. Someone had thrown confetti. As if on cue, all the dogs sat and looked at him.

"Ok, then," he flipped the switch on his machine from blow to vacuum.

Brrrrrrrzzzzzzzzzz! The machine sucked up all the papers and in just a few minutes the grass was clean again.

Settled down in the circle with Old Friend, Boss gazed out the entrance to watch the clean-up.

"Mean," he said. "I'm not mean. But when things are wrong, I say so. That's what I do. While I was yelling about things being wrong, the others worked together and got it right. What does that mean?"

A glittering flash made him blink. What was that? He squeezed his eyes shut and re-focused. He opened them again and fixed the cold, I-mean-business, yellow-eyed stare.

"My bone!" he exploded and jumped to his feet. "Give me back my bone!" he bellowed.

"What? What?" muttered Old Friend in his sleep. He shifted and snored again.

They were far away but Boss had seen the two dogs flinch. Like the bullies he met sometimes, the two dogs tried to be nonchalant but it wasn't working. Anyone else would think they were obediently going to their Day Dog Master. Boss knew they were trying to retreat with dignity, having been called on their conduct by a much bigger, stronger dog.

"I know those two."

The poodle had been good friends with Spotty. Boss knew they spent a lot of time together. The poodle would arrive at the park looking perfectly sculpted. When play time was over and the Day Dogs went home, Boss, watching for his Night Dogs' safety would see Spotty and the poodle take their leave. Invariably, the poodle would be a wreck of his former self. Boss found this interesting.

Spotty was a stand-up dog, a good judge of things as they were, not as one might want them to be. Spotty had thought enough of this Day Dog fluff ball to spend lots of time with him. At the end of each day, the fluff ball would be transformed, not always good in terms of his appearance. But a day spent with the Night Dog seemed to make the fluff ball bounce with new life and vigor.

"Hmmmm," Boss thought.

The other dog was also impressive but for reasons Boss didn't care for. Too Uber-Dog.

And yet, the overly-muscled, showy, shiny Doberman spent most of his park time with the deliberately-wreck-my-hairdo poodle, which was interesting.

Boss watched them struggle along, trying to balance his bone.

"Heh, heh, heh," he chuckled. He stopped, puzzled. He thought well of these boys. Why? They had stolen his bone!

"Heh, heh, heh," he shrugged. "I can get another bone."

He watched the two boys round up a half a dozen puppies and trot them back to their mother, the poodle waving the bone as if it were an arrow pointing to the place where the puppies should go.

"I know that face," Boss thought. "That's the 'I'll be nice unless you cross me' face. Where did he learn that?"

The Poodle must have had a swim. His carefully sculpted poofs had been pressed flat with the water. He looked and walked and seemed a different dog.

"Hmmmmm. How'd they get my bone? They must have been in here."

He sniffed and nodded to himself. Shampoo and liver treat smells mixed with the other smells in the circle. They had been here.

Old Friend coughed and stirred. Boss got ready. Old Friend relaxed again and snored. Boss relaxed and turned his gaze back to his bone leaving the park.

"I can get another bone," he said to himself. "Let's see what you got," he said to the Poodle.

"Lester! He sees us! Drop the bone!" Rufahlo cried.

"O", said Lester through the bone in his mouth.

The first rage roar, the one that made Lester drop the bone, sending it on its bouncy way down the hill and into the lake, had been caused, apparently, by some paper ripping incident in the play area. The girls were all talking about it, how big the dog was, how angry he had been, what he said.

"Then he said 'Why don't I come over to your house and rip things up?'" Lili squeaked.

"And the gardener wouldn't go near the mess 'til the Big Dog went away with his friend," Fifi shivered.

"I heard him too and I was all the way down at the lake!" Papillion marveled. "It was so loud and strong! I swear the shock waves hit me and made me fall down!"

"Maybe it wasn't the shock waves," said Lili.

"I mean, you fall down all the time," said Fifi.

"No, it was the waves," Rufahlo nodded. "I almost shed my coat!"

"Oooooooooooooo!" The girls were awed. Rufahlo never seemed afraid of anything.

The Big Dog was clearly a monster.

Lester put the bone down so he could speak clearly.

"Maybe he likes things tidy," he said. "I can get with that."

Except for his personal appearance, Lester was much the same way. He liked his few toys in order and never left kibble on the floor. Even his top knot bow, which he would prefer not to wear ever again, had to be in a certain place every night so he could find it first thing in the morning.

"He was right to be angry," he said. "We made a mess of his home. How would we like it if he came to the Day Care Center and did that to us?"

"If he came to the Center," Rufahlo said, "I really would shed my coat."

Everyone heard the next bellow. Everyone except Lester jumped and whimpered or ran around in excited circles. Papillion fell down.

"See?" she struggled up again.

"What did he say?" asked Lili.

No one knew. Lester picked up the bone and turned toward the source of the sound. Even this far away, he could see the gold eyes flashing, big muscles working. Lester heard the next roar quite clearly.

"Give...me...back...my...bone!"

Rufahlo jumped to catch Papillion before she fell again.

"Lester! He sees us! Drop the bone!" he said. He used his paw to push Papillion upright again.

"O." Lester said through the bone.

"Why not?" Rufahlo panicked. "What are you thinking? What if he comes down to get it?"

Lester put down the bone.

"Later," he said. "Let's get the puppies and go."

"Where's Day Care Guy?" Rufahlo asked.

Lester pointed with the bone.

Rufahlo snorted. "Typical. All the way down at the coffee kiosk, halfway home, and he hasn't noticed only two dogs with him!"

He could see Lucy and Melinda sitting at attention, waiting for whatever bit of biscotti they could dog-mo-tize him into sharing with them.

"Hmmmph!" Lester snorted and gestured to Rufahlo with the

bone. The two boys gathered the girls into a group and chased after the puppies 'til they were all together and ready to move as a pack. Up to a point, the puppies enjoyed this game,. When Lester's face turned serious, they knew it was time to stop fooling around and do what he said. Lester put down the bone and counted heads. "Ok!" he said. "Let's march!"

The little group started off and moved together toward the kiosk. Lester stayed behind them, encouraging the stragglers and discouraging the strays. He turned to look back at the gold-eyed Big Dog and swatted Rufahlo with the bone.

"Hey!" Rufahlo protested.

"Owee!" Lester said through the bone.

The gold eyes were gone.

The eyes were still there. The rage that made them burn had melted and their lights had dimmed.

Randy and Bailiff joined Boss at the entrance.

"He's quite good at that," Randy said. "Herds like a pro!"

"Responsible. Protective," Bailiff was impressed. "Those are good things."

Boss looked at his sleeping Old Friend. Yes, those were good things. Spotty was right. This Poodle was a good dog.

"Well," he said softly to the Poodle. "Let's see what else you got."

"Your bone!" Angel exclaimed.

"He's got your bone!" Mimi couldn't believe it.

"Kid's got your bone!" Ben was shocked.

Jerry opened his mouth but no sound came. He closed it again and gulped nervously.

Boss turned to the group.

"And which one of you thinks that because I have no bone I have no power?"

His voice was low but his sharp teeth flashed.

"Not me!" Ben said.

"I'm good with it," said Jerry.

"You're the Boss," said Mimi.

"Angel," Boss said. "I know it's a long way off, but see if you can focus those things on the poodle and his group, and tell me what they are saying."

Angel took a deep breath and puffed with pride.

He snapped his tentacles to attention, spraying everyone. Boss stared at the distant Day Dogs, his gaze unwavering.

"Sorry," said Angel and pointed his tentacles at the Poodle.

"...bring...it...back...," Angel said. "...get...to...meet...him."

"Hmmm," Boss smiled.

"You're crazy!" Rufahlo said. "He'll tear you limb from limb! You'll ruin your coat!"

"We'll talk about it later," Lester said. He picked up the bone. The two boys gathered the puppies and began the long march to the coffee kiosk.

Up in the tree circle, Randy nodded toward the poodle. "He's good!"

Boss nodded. His smile spread into a grin.

"Look at all my doggies!" Day Care Guy exclaimed. "All together and ready to go! And I didn't have to do a thing!"

"'Eah, 'eah," Lester said.

"Doofus," said Rufahlo.

"Lester! What is that?" Lucy choked on her biscotti. "Where did you get it?"

Lester put down the bone.

"It's a bone, mother. I found it in the lake. Why?"

"Nothing, nothing," Lucy spluttered. "It reminded me of

something else. Leave it here, it's dirty."

"No," Lester picked it up again.

"Hmmmm," Melinda thought, "What's this about?"

"The lake!" Suddenly aware of Lester's flat, stringy do, Lucy started in.

"How could you possibly…"

"Ok, kids," Day Care Guy fiddled with leashes and collars. "Let's leash up and go!"

"A Uh," Lester said.

"What?" Lucy demanded.

"I think he said later," Rufahlo offered.

"Hmmmm," Melinda took it all in.

Chapter Fourteen

Thinking Hurts

Up on the drying table, the two boys could finally talk in private.

All through the bathing process, Lester refused to let go of the bone. When she tried to take it away, Lester showed his teeth to the grooming lady.

"What's wrong with you today?" she asked. "Usually, you like this."

Lester certainly didn't like this but had accepted it as necessary. He was a competing show dog and his Friends expected to see him clean, perfectly groomed and expertly styled. Since he ruined his hairdo almost every day, grooming and styling had to be done often. The grooming lady didn't mind. She got paid extra for the service and Lester's behavior made him a canine ATM machine. His Friends, highly styled people themselves who didn't want for money, never questioned the cost. Lester didn't mind the process. Grooming was like a long petting session from friendly hands. It was the result he didn't like.

Finally, on the drying and grooming table, Lester put the bone down. The stylist reached for it and Lester showed his teeth.

"Growl at me one more time and I'll use the grooming leash," the stylist warned. Normally, Lester behaved so well during grooming, she never used it.

Lester shoved the bone toward his rear and sat on it.

"Or not," said the stylist, going back to her work. "Where's that top knot bow? Oh, thank you sweetheart," she said to Papillion who trotted over with the bow in her mouth.

"What do you want with this bone, Lester," Rufahlo asked. "Why didn't you just leave it there?"

Although Rufahlo's short coat didn't need styling, it was agreed that dog shampoo would smell better than muddy, moldy lakewater. He was bathed in the stall next to Lester. "Ka-ching!" said Day Care Guy. Now, they were both being dried, Lester with a wide-mouthed diffuser, Rufahlo with full-on blow.

"Why didn't you just leave it?" he asked again.

"Because," Lester said, "we didn't steal it. We played with it without permission and that was wrong. But when we lost it, we took responsibility and found it again. If there had been time, I would have dried it off and put it back. But there wasn't time. If I dropped it when he yelled, it would have looked like we stole it. We would have looked like cowards, running away 'cause we got caught."

"But we still have it!" Rufahlo protested. "So, how is it different from stealing?"

"'Cause I'm going to bring it back", Lester said. "Tonight. Surviving out there, you have to be tough and smart. Spotty thought the world of him, said he was kind, too. I want to meet him. I'll bring it back and explain what happened, I'll say we're sorry and sorry for the mess on the lawn. It's the right thing to do."

"Tonight!" Rufahlo gasped and almost pulled a Papillion tip-over. Only the grooming leash kept him upright.

"How you going to do that?"

"I don't know. I'll have to think of something."

"Thinking! Oww!" Rufahlo smacked his snout.

From across the room, little Papillion caught Lester's eye. For reasons apparent to no one, she was jumping up and down, straight into the air and down again, higher and higher each time.

"She's quite good at that," Lester thought. "Maybe it relieves the twitching."

"Oww!" Rufahlo smacked his snout again. "Why can't you do it tomorrow?"

"Because you never know what might happen overnight," Lester replied.

Lucy had joined Papillion and was now jumping up and down next to her. Clearly, she was trying to jump higher than the smaller, younger dog.

"Just can't give it up, can you?" Lester smiled. He really did love his mama and he knew she loved him too. She did everything she did because she loved him, he knew that. He moved his front paws back a little, closer to the bone. Although it was very heavy and would be difficult for her to move, he knew she would try to steal it and hide it from him. It reminded her of something she didn't like. She would try to protect him from whatever that was. When she wanted something, she usually got it.

"I wonder why she never won her trophy?" he thought. "Even now, she's got Top Show Dog style and enough determination to make up for the lack of mine. I wonder what happened?"

Rufahlo shivered. His eyes asked for answers.

"He keeps this bone for a reason," Lester said. "He might need it."

"Now that's what I like to see," Lucy cooed. "My Number One Top Show Dog Champion!" She snuggled briefly into Lester's side. When she pulled away, she used her paw to restore the fluffiness she had flattened with her snuggle.

"There…there…there! Perfectly round and smooth again," she sighed. "Now, please, please! Try to stay clean and keep that hairdo tight. The show is tomorrow and if…"

"It's tomorrow?" Lester asked absentmindedly, still checking his new look in the mirror.

"Yes, it's tomorrow!" Exasperation edged her voice. "Of course, it's tomorrow! What have we been talking about all week? Lester, you really need to…"

Lester's features molded themselves into the "Yes, Mother" face. He nodded slowly and tuned her out. Her jaw snapped and flapped but Lester was busy with his own thoughts.

He had focused his psychic powers on the stylist and, for once, it had worked. It was exhausting but the result was worth the effort. Of all the looks they teased and moussed into his hair, this was his favorite or, at least, the one that was least annoying.

"No, it's true," he thought. He stared at his reflection. "I like this one. It's a good look for me. Not girlie at all…well, not as girlie as the others…."

They called it the lion's mane. The stylist showed him a picture once as she flipped through the pages of a yellow covered magazine. Almost every page featured pictures of animals.

"There," she had said, holding up the page. "That's what you're going to be today! King of the Jungle!"

"King. Jungle. A jungle is a wild place," Lester thought. Rufahlo had seen one on the Discovery channel and told him all about it. "King of the Wild Places. That sounds good!" He sat very still and let the stylist work her magic.

Today, he focused as hard as he could. Over and over, he pictured it in his mind. At last, the stylist exclaimed "I know! Lion's Mane! Let's do that!" Lester relaxed and sat still for the treatment.

All the hair on his head, his shoulders and halfway down his back and tummy had been teased out to form a huge and perfect oval. She used some pleasant smelling waxy ointment on the roots to make the hair stick out from his body. After the oval was teased into shape, she sprayed on a fixing solution to hold it together.

"Not bad at all," he thought. The size and shape of the oval minimized his ear pom poms. His ankle poofs and tail pom had also been fluffed to the max but the mane was so imposing no one would notice them, another plus.

"You going to wear the bow?" Rufahlo asked.

Lester's thoughts came back to the present. Apparently, the nodding and the

'Yes, Mother' face convinced Lucy of his agreement with whatever it was she had been talking about. Without him noticing, she had stopped talking and wandered off to sit with Melinda. Next to his lion's mane in the mirror sat Rufahlo.

"Yes," he said. "I gave it a lot of thought."

"Thinking! Ow!" Rufahlo smacked his snout and shook his

head.

"In our world," Lester was serious, "this is our best foot forward. This is how we look when there's something important. Clean. Styled." He ducked his head a little. "And decorated. I want to look my best when I meet him. It's a sign of respect."

"But how you going to do it?" asked Rufahlo.

"I don't know yet," Lester said. "But I'm working on it." He picked the bone up in his mouth.

"Ow oo eye ook?" he asked.

Rufahlo's show-biz eyes sparkled. He started to giggle.

"Like an egg with a toothpick stuck in it!" He tried not to laugh. He failed.

Lester looked in the mirror then put the bone down so they could had a good rib-shaking, breath-heaving belly laugh together. They leaned against each other for support as their giggling subsided.

"Wait! Wait!" Rufahlo, pushed away. He used his paw to fluff out the mane that had been flattened by their contact.

"Whatever they spray on you, it really works," he said, fluffing and shaping. "Look, it spring right back into shape. Pick up the bone."

Lester put the bone in his mouth and they broke down again.

"Egg with a toothpick!" Rufahlo choked through his giggles. Lester put the bone down and shook with laughter, careful this time not to disturb his hairdo's shape.

"Oh! Ow!" Rufahlo was still laughing. "Ow, that hurts! Thinking hurts! But I think I have an idea!"

"Really?" Lester asked.

"I'm not sure," Rufahlo wiped his eyes. "I don't remember having one before. But something new come to my mind, that's an idea, isn't it?"

"Yes, it is," Lester was excited. "Let's hear it!"

"Yes," Rufahlo said, "but first, we practice."

"Really?" Lester was surprised. Usually, Rufahlo insisted on absolute secrecy during their practice sessions.

"I got to know this stuff," Rufahlo said. His head drooped toward the floor.

"You go out tonight, what if you don't come back? What if you get to be a crime-sniffing police dog and never come back? I have no more time. I have to risk everything now!" All the giggling was gone. His eyes showed fear.

Casually, Lester surveyed the room.

"Well, right now, everyone is busy, or napping," he said. "Let's do it. If anyone asks, we'll say you're coaching me."

"Rufahlo is so generous!" Lucy gushed. "Look at him coaching Lester!"

"Mmm hmm," Melinda nodded. Her tone conveyed agreement but she saw something different. "There's that look again," she thought. "Fear. Shame. Just a hint of it, but it's there. And if Lester's being coached, why is Rufahlo doing all the posing?"

"Look at that, he's trying to save his hairdo!" Lucy was happy. "I think he's really turned a corner. Lester!" She called across the room. "We learn by doing! Pose with him!"

"My hair, Mom," Lester called back.

"We can fluff it out again when you're done."

"Ok," Lester said to Rufahlo. "I wanted to do voice command only but they're watching. So, I'll do the voice command, then I'll do it and you follow me."

"But that's what we do at the show!" Anguish colored Rufahlo's face. "And you not going to be at the show! I'll be alone! I must do it alone!" A whimper crept into his voice.

"Ok, ok," said Lester. "Let's do it again. Sit!"

"No, wait, start again," Rufahlo was really flustered now. "I didn't know you were starting!"

119

"Siiiiiiiiiiiiiiiit!" Lester said.

Rufahlo's eyes went blank, then sparked again. He rolled over on his back and looked at Lester.

As gently as he could, Lester said, "I don't know, big guy."

"Aaaaaaaaaaa!" Rufahlo moaned. "What were you telling me to do?"

Lester sat.

"Why can't I do this?" Rufahlo whispered. "I know how to sit magnificently!"

He demonstrated. His posture was perfect, chest thrust out, head held high. He looked every inch a winner.

"But I hear the command," he was close to sobbing now, "and I roll over! Why? Why can't I do this?"

"It's ok, it's ok," Lester soothed. "Breathe….breathe…."

Rufahlo panted and calmed himself.

"Let's try another," Lester said. "Siiiiiiiiiiiiiit up!"

Rufahlo's eyes darted nervously. He shut them and tried to focus. The last thing he saw was Papillion staring at him. He opened his eyes and stared back. After a second, she glanced away. "That's the longest I've seen her sit without twitching," he thought. "Oh, wait! The command!" He thrust his beautiful musculature into an elaborate pointing pose.

He looked at Lester. He found the answer in Lester's sad eyes. "What am I going to do?" he whispered.

"We'll think of something," Lester tried to sound confident.

"Ow!" Rufahlo smacked his snout.

"I'll think of something," Lester's resolve filled the void where confidence should have been.

"If I wasn't so grateful," Lucy said, "I'd find this delicious! Look at poor Rufahlo, struggling with his emotions!"

"He's struggling, all right," Melinda said.

"Well, of course he's conflicted!" Lucy exclaimed. "He's helping Lester because they're friends! But he can see already that the more he helps him, the closer Lester gets to snatching the Top Show Dog Crown right out of his paws!"

"That would kill him." Melinda studied the two boys.

"Oh, he'd get over it," Lucy waved her paw.

"Really?" Melinda gave a hard, appraising look. "You never did," she said.

"No," Lucy said. The bitterness she held down in her heart swelled briefly to the surface. "No, I didn't," she said. Her eyes hardened. She clenched her jaws down tight.

"The I-don't-want-to-talk-about-it face," Melinda thought. "Fine. Later. But you will tell me, yes, you will."

"Looks like they're done now," she said.

The two boys seemed more at ease. Lester held the bone in his mouth, Rufahlo fluffed out Lester's unrumpled coat. She followed Rufahlo's gaze and found herself looking at little Papillion.

"Hmmm," she thought. "That's the longest I've ever seen her sit still without twitching."

Papillion fell over, got up, and trotted over to the boys. Rufahlo had called her over and now the three sat together. Rufahlo wore his show-biz face but the quiet voice was unusual for him; it seemed furtive and calculating. Papillion listened intently. Lester's eyes darted around the room.

"What are they plotting?" she asked, "and how can I help?"

"Look at that," she said to Lucy. "I think someone new has a little crush on Rufahlo."

Lucy said nothing. She stared straight ahead, eyes hard and unseeing. Whatever she was remembering consumed her completely.

"You will tell me," Melinda thought. "I will make you tell me why you never won that wretched Top Show Dog Trophy!"

Chapter Fifteen

Melinda Makes a List

All afternoon, Melinda went about her usual activities: grooming, napping, getting up for a snack or a drink of water, playing with the puppies, her every day routines. She kept her expression neutral and tried not to stare at any one thing for too long. The plotting threesome never sensed that every move they made was being observed.

She made a mental list of all she saw. This was tantamount to thinking and was therefore somewhat painful but she kept at it. Eventually, the items on the list would come together. A clear picture of the plan would be revealed.

Lester liked to play as much as any other dog but he was, at his most natural, a rather serious young dog. He wasn't all that interested in toys and didn't form attachments to objects as some of the others did. Lili, for example, would not lie down for a nap unless her little rag of a blanket was in her bed and she could smoosh it into a kind of pillow for her head. When it was given to her a long time ago, it had been a real blanket. Years of chewing and being dragged around floors had reduced it to the size of a washcloth. Still, she loved it and wouldn't settle down without it. Her Friend had to bring it with them every day and hand it to Day Care Guy. At the end of the day, the last thing he checked before they went home was whether or not they had her little blanket.

Fifi had a baby shoe she had stolen from her Friend's child. When her Friend discovered the chewed and mangled shoe, she threw her hands in the air. "Ok!" she said, "You can have that one but that's the only one you'll get!" Melinda wondered if the loss of the shoe was the reason the child kept putting gum in Fifi's hair, requiring ever more bizarre and un-Shih-Tzu like haircuts to remove.

Lester wasn't like that. He was calm and confident, comfortable in his own skin and didn't need any talisman or familiar objects to keep him balanced. So, it was interesting to see him, Rufahlo by his side, casually but clearly with purpose, take an interest in one of the stuffed toys Day Care Guy used for decoration. It was the figure of a dog in a curled-up napping position. Inch by inch, over a period of a couple of hours, the boys slowly moved the stuffed dog around the perimeter of the room, finally stopping close to Lester's own bed.

"Dark chocolate brown," she thought. "Same color as Lester. Mmmm. Chocolate! Yum! Wish we had some dog chocolate ... Wait! What's he doing now?"

The stylist was a bright and cheerful woman who fussed over the dogs and over absolutely nothing else. She'd gone home for the day, leaving all the dark brown hair she'd shaved off Lester's butt and hind legs on the styling area floor.

As casually as they had shifted the toy, the boys now moved all the smaller hair clumps closer together. Finally all the clumps were fused together into a mini-mountain of hair.

The nudging became a rolling motion and very slowly, taking turns as if it were a game, the boys were rolling the ball of hair in the direction of the stuffed toy of the same color. One of her puppies approached to join the game. Rufahlo, gently but firmly, said no and sent the little pup on its way.

"It's not a game," Melinda thought. "They're serious."

Since the Center was Day Care Guy's home, the very early arrivals would sometimes find him struggling to pull his robe on over his PJ's. If he was too rushed to find his glasses, he would nod and smile and greet dogs and Friends hardly knowing which pair he was talking to.

"Good morning! Small...round...white...raggedy blanket! Hello Lili! Good morning!" he'd say.

He truly loved each and every dog. He loved his job and considered himself very lucky. He was a happy man of simple tasks and comfortable routines.

Marching into the Center late in the afternoon with a smile that said, "I've got the best news ever!" was not routine.

"Kids! My baby dolls, listen up! I've got the best news ever!" He dropped to all fours, something he did when he had something joyful to report. He had read somewhere that approaching dogs at eye level would make them see him as a pack member. In times of great joy, Day Care Guy wanted to be their friend, not their leader and caretaker. He wanted to roll around the floor with them and feel their joy at the news he had to offer.

"This is such a coincidence! All afternoon, the phone is ringing," he said. He circled around on all fours to look at each and every dog.

"Mmmm," Rufahlo muttered to Lester. "I think he put on weight."

Lester spluttered and spewed and finally had to put the bone down so he could smother his laughter with his paws.

"Don't," he choked into his paws, "Please!"

Melinda noticed that the boys had carefully placed themselves in front of the toy and the hair ball, hiding them from Day Care Guy and most of the other dogs.

"Hmmm," she put it on the list.

"Every one of your Friends has called to ask if you could stay the night!" Day Care's eyes were shining. "Isn't that great?"

All the dogs stared. Day Care Guy took a breath.

"Everything's fine," he said in his soothing voice. "Parties going late, planes not arriving, sudden elopement, everyone's fine. And we're all going to be together tonight, isn't that great?"

"Wunderbar," said Rufahlo.

"Awesome," said Lester and they both cracked up again, snorting into their paws to keep it quiet.

Day Care Guy's back was starting to hurt. He got up on his knees and sat back on his heels.

"I get to have dogs in my bed! Who's with me?" He spread his arms.

"I guess someone should throw him a bone," said Lili.

"I volunteer you," said Fifi.

"I'm too big," said Melinda. They looked at Lucy.

"As if," Lucy said. They all looked at Papillion.

"I...I..." she said. She searched for words.

Melinda put that on her list.

"I...don't want to," she finished, ducking her head.

They looked at the boys.

"We're men," Lester said. "Men don't do that."

He ducked his head and shook with silent laughter.

"No! Ahem!" Rufahlo coughed. "Men stay on the floor."

"Oh, for dog's sake," Melinda got up and went to her puppies. Day Care Guy was happy to see any dog react but he was noticeably relieved to see the big dog walk past him and over to her pups. She would not be the dog in the bed tonight.

"Is he calling me fat?" she thought and chuckled as she sat to talk to her pups.

"Darling babies!" she said and they snapped to attention. She knew they hadn't understood a thing Day Care Guy had said.

"Big fun! " She smiled. "Your very first time! Who wants to sleep up high on the human bed?"

"Me! Me!" all the puppies jumped up and down, tumbling all over themselves.

"Whoever can make the jump gets to sleep up there! Who's with me?" Melinda called.

"Me! Me!" The puppies leap-frogged over each other as they followed her into Day Care Guy's spacious but sparsely furnished bedroom.

Day Care Guy got up and followed them. He stood and watched in awe as each of the six baby pups jumped, claw-climbed or were nudged up onto his bed by their mother. All the puppies stared at him, smiling expectantly.

"I meant tonight, sweeties, it's a bit early but, oh..." He gasped a few quick breaths.

"Don't cry," Melinda thought. "Really. Please don't."

"This is so great!" he finished. He flopped down on his bed and enjoyed a few minutes of being a puppy pommel horse.

One of Day Care Guy's comfortable routines was to have a hearty sandwich and a cup of tea for his dinner. Any dog boarding overnight learned to look forward to the making of the sandwich, an exuberant and sloppy exercise during which many unauthorized treats might end up on the floor.

"What'll we have tonight? What'll we have tonight?" Day Care Guy mumbled to himself as he peered inside the fridge. "Turkey? Salami? Here's some cheese!" he said. "That's it! Turkey, salami and cheese!" He pulled plates and platters and packages out of the fridge.

"Oh, darn," Lucy said. "Turkey! My favorite! But with all of you here, I probably won't get any."

When Friends were around, Day Care Guy presented himself as a rock of strict discipline.

"No unauthorized treats!" the Friends would instruct.

"Oh no, no!" Day Care Guy would reply, nodding his head in solemn agreement. But during sandwich making time, he reasoned to himself, if a bit of bread or meat flew out of his hands or off the edge of a knife and landed on the floor, purely by accident of course, what was he to do? And if he was too slow to bend down to get it, and some dog snatched it before he could pick it up, well, what was a fellow to do? The floor got cleaned, the dogs got treats, the Friends would never know and all was right in his world.

"Oh, look at that! I dropped a piece of cheese!" he would mutter as a morsel sailed out of his hand and down to the floor. He chuckled as he watched the dogs compete for it.

"Big crowd tonight," he said. "I'll make sure everyone gets a little bit."

"Turkey?" Melinda asked. "You like the turkey? I like salami better."

"I love turkey," Lucy sighed. "Love it, love it, love it! Probably won't get a lot tonight."

She looked at all the dogs crowding around the counter. Lester and Rufahlo sat politely at the crowd's edge, allowing all the smaller dogs to go first.

"Just as well, really," she said. "If I eat too much of it, it really knocks me out. I sleep like a dead dog, nothing wakes me up. Oh well, not tonight, I guess."

She settled down on the floor. Melinda looked at the crowd. All the other dogs were staring at Day Care Guy's busy hands. Lester and Rufahlo were staring at Lucy. Their eyes were saucers, their bodies taut with attention. Lester turned to Rufahlo and said something. Rufahlo's big head gave the slightest nod.

"Hmmm," Melinda put it on her list.

Earlier that week, Day Care Guy had roasted the small turkey himself. "Mmmm," he bent down to the dish and inhaled deeply. "That herb butter stuffed under the skin makes all the difference!"

"Ooooo!" Lucy whined. "The herb butter! I love that!"

Day Care Guy struggled and struggled with his dull carving knife. He hacked off some slices, set them aside, took a deep breath and plunged the knife in again. Something snapped and a whole turkey wing flew off the counter and onto the floor.

"No no!" he exclaimed. "Not the bones! No bones!"

He dropped his knife and bent to the floor where Lili and Fifi were tug-of–warring over the wing.

"No, sweethearts, no," he murmured and held onto the wing with one hand. With his other hand he tried very gently to pry one little dog's jaws and then the other's jaws off the wing. This took a while because each time he freed one little jaw and started on the other, the first would re-attach itself and the tug-of-war begin again.

"Come on, little ones," he said. "I'll give you something else but no bones. Let go of the wing, come on, let go…"

While Day Care Guy's back was turned, Lester swiftly and silently snatched a big fat turkey slice off the counter top. Rufahlo did the same. Softly, they backed away from the crowd and moved toward Lester's bed.

"Why aren't they eating it?" Melinda asked herself.

By the time Day Care Guy retrieved the wing and stood back up, Lester and Rufahlo were back at the edge of the crowd.

"What the…," Day Care Guy scratched his head.

"I could have sworn I cut three pieces…" He eyed the one piece left on the counter, then looked at the crowd of dogs.

Lester looked wide-eyed and hopeful. "Just waiting my turn," he said casually.

Rufahlo cocked his head to one side.

"Just hoping for a little bit," he said and lolled his tongue out for added effect.

"Oh, well, maybe I didn't," Day Care Guy said. "This dull knife makes it such hard work, it probably seemed like I cut more than I did. There's plenty more here. Oooop! Look at that! I dropped a piece of cheese!"

His hands fluttered over the counter and bits of food flew through the air.

"Here, mom," Lester said. "I got this for you."

Rich, buttery flavors filled Lucy's nose. The slice her son offered was as big as her head.

"Oh, Lester, you are the sweetest thing! Let's share it," she said. "What? You don't want any?"

"The butter," he said. "Gotta stay trim for the show!" Lester smacked his flat abs with his paw. "And I'm not hungry, anyway."

"Mmmm," Lucy chowed down, slowly sucking the buttery juice out of each little bite.

"Auntie Melinda, this is for you," said Rufahlo, offering his slice. "I had some cheese already and I'm full."

"Thank you, dear, that's so sweet!" She smiled and made cooing noises as the boys trotted back to Lester's bed. She took a small bite.

"Here, honey, you have it." She pushed the slice toward Lucy who was smacking her lips over the last of her first piece.

"Winning!" Lucy took a bite. "Really," she looked at Melinda and talked through her food. "How could you not want this?"

"Like I said," Melinda replied, "I prefer the salami."

She watched the boys talk quietly together. Whenever they glanced over, Melinda made chewing motions as if she too was enjoying her turkey slice.

"Hmmmm," she thought. "Ow!"

The list in her head was getting very long and hard to manage.

"This puzzle had better come together soon," she thought. "My head is killing me!"

Chapter Sixteen

A Puzzle, an Answer and Bob's Face in the Sky

As the last rays of sun left the Dog Park, Angel worked on a puzzle of his own.

"Ow," he thought. Having worked this puzzle for hours and not made much progress, he gave up. It was too hard. What if he didn't need to work the puzzle into an answer? Maybe if he just came out and asked the question, an answer would be given.

"Why are you still here?" he asked.

Busy Angel was startled by such bluntness. He flinched and as he did so, he dropped the baby bird he'd been cradling in his spirit hands. He gasped and lunged to catch it, then pulled back as the baby spread its tiny wings and fluttered.

"That's it," cooed Mr. Busy, gently flapping his two tiers to demonstrate. "Come on!"

The little bird flapped and flapped but was only strong enough to slow its downward progress.

"There's a good start," cooed Busy. "We'll try again tomorrow."

The little bird landed in his cupped hands and Busy floated up to put it back into its nest. He smiled and sighed with pleasure. Some things on this Earth were quite beautiful. Some things. He looked down at the little slug-dog. Some things still needed work.

"What were you saying?" he asked.

"Why are you still here?"

"You're very bold," Busy sniffed dismissively. "Such a question to ask."

"And you're stalling!" Angel surprised himself. "All right," he thought. "If I'm bold, let's be bold!"

"Why are you still here?"

"My assignment..." Busy searched for words. "...is to... monitor your progress."

"You don't have to be here for that." Angel stared at him. "You could watch me from Heaven."

"The eyes," Busy told himself. "Don't look at the puppy eyes!"

"There is…," he spoke carefully, "…particular interest in your… progress…"

"I've made lots of progress!" Angel exclaimed. "Lots! I've learned so much already! I'm learning all the time! Trying every minute!"

Progress could mean one of two things. Angel had to know which.

"Progress?" he whispered. "Or evolution?" He flipped his tentacles. "Still there, still slimy."

"Hey!" called Ben from the corner.

"Sorry," said Angel.

"You…have changed…" Busy said slowly.

"I have! I have?" Angel's heart filled with fear. With all his hope and hard work, was he changing? Which way? He strained to look at different bits of himself. His coat, was it slimier? His tentacles, were they bigger? Would evolution have its way and change him from the happy, four-legged, furry thing he wanted to be to a legless, hairless, slithering slime-ball?

"There, there," Busy soothed. "You're still mostly a dog. Relax!"

"I can't!" Angel cried. "You're still here! Watching! Judging me! Making little marks on your clipboard! Watching my heart break and taking notes!" He hung his head and sobbed a little. "Making your reports while everything I love is taken away," he cried. "I can't relax!"

"It's a good thing those eyes are cast down," Busy thought. "I'm having enough trouble as it is."

"Think of me," he said, "as a benign and neutral presence."

A weak smile disturbed his spirit face.

The sobbing ceased. The eyes looked up.

"Ow!"

"Uh oh!" Busy thought. "An idea! Look away! Don't look at the eyes!"

"You're my Guardian Angel!"

"Oh, Heavens, no!" Busy spluttered. "I'm assigned to monitor..."

"You don't have to be here to check my progress!" The little pup jumped up and down, bucking his hind legs like a wild horse. "You were kicked out to stay with me because it was your mistake I got here in the first place!" He spun around in circles, spraying slime everywhere. Suddenly he stopped and looked up at Busy.

"And you like it here! You like being with dogs! You think Heaven is boring too!"

"Shhh! Shhh!" Busy panicked.

"And you like me!" Angel triumphed. "You think I could get to be a real dog!"

Busy shrunk to the size of a fairy and floated near the little dog's ear.

"I never said this," he whispered into the tentacles. "You don't get to be a dog. You have to earn it!" He telescoped back to full size. "I never said that," he whispered.

"What? Said what? I heard nothing!" Angel was laughing now. He stopped and looked serious again.

"And I'm earning it," he said. "I'm trying very hard."

"And I'm watching," Busy said.

"You like it here!" Angel giggled softly. "You like being with dogs! Admit it!"

"Watch...yourself!" said Busy. Poof! He disappeared.

"I'll get my wish! " Angel danced. "I'll get to be a dog! Or, at least, I have a chance!" He bucked and pranced. "He's my Guardian! He likes me!"

"Here comes your Boss," Busy's voice entered Angel's head.

"I can hear him," Angel said. "They're still a few minutes away." He danced with wild abandon.

"He's an odd one," said Ben. The little dog had cried, then laughed and was now hopping around the circle like a rabbit crazed on cilantro, all for no reason Ben could figure out.

"But he's fun," said Jerry. "Let's dance too!"

Bucking their legs and shaking their ears, they followed Angel's dance. Slime flew everywhere. The other dogs were used to it now and hardly noticed.

A small slime ball hit Mimi in the ear and she flicked it away without comment. She sat in the natural entrance, sheltered by the shrubs, watching the day go by. She'd watched the sun go down, the stars come out and now she watched Boss and Old Friend make their slow and steady progress up the hill to the circle. Alternately pushing, offering support to steady him, then pulling, Boss helped the old man move slowly toward their destination, their home, their bed.

"Hard work," the old man wheezed. "Keeps you young and strong. Pause a bit, baby boy, let me catch my breath."

They stopped. The old man coughed, then dragged in a few deep breaths.

"OK," he said and the struggle began again.

"I couldn't do that for Bob," Mimi thought. "He's too tall. I'm too small. He'd better not get old." Sorrow shrouded her heart. It seemed such a long time since she had seen Bob at all. Was he old now? Was he too old to find her?

"Hello, little pretty thing," Old Friend wheezed. "Still here? I'm surprised," he said. He bent down to pat her head and started to tilt over.

"Whoa," said Boss and leaned hard to keep him up straight.

"Whoa! Whoa, there," Old Friend said. He put his hand on Boss's head for support and leaned down again.

"Don't worry, little baby," he stroked her forehead. "I know someone will come for you soon."

"Thank you," Mimi whispered and leaned against his leg.

133

"Yes, they will," he cupped her head and rubbed her cheek. "There you are, yes, they will."

He pulled himself up.

"Look at this!" he said. "It's beautiful!"

Mimi had pulled and pulled on each corner of the tartan blanket until it was perfectly flat and free of wrinkles. She had carefully pulled off every leaf and blade of grass. She had licked every stain and some of them had come out. She had placed his bag of extra clothes where he could use it as a pillow. She had swept over the area around the blanket, removing rocks and trash, leaving it smooth and looking very tidy.

"It's a palace!" Old Friend exclaimed. "I must be a king! Look at this, Boss, isn't it beautiful?"

"Yes, it is," Boss smiled. "Lovely, Mimi, thank you."

"Angel helped," said Mimi. After his joyful dance, Angel had rushed about licking up all the slime bits that had landed in the blanket area.

"Good dogs," said Boss. "It means a lot. Look at him! He's so happy!"

Humming a jaunty tune, Old Friend pulled his tattered coat tightly around himself. Carefully, he sank onto one side of the blanket and placed his head on the pillow.

"I'm a lucky man," he reached for the far edge of the blanket.

"We'll do it," said Boss and nodded to Mimi. He picked up one far corner of the blanket and Mimi picked up the other. Moving together, they pulled the two corners until the other half of the blanket covered up Old Friend.

"Not a king, perhaps," murmured Old Friend, "but a lucky, lucky man." And off he went, sound asleep, snoring gently and rhythmically.

Mimi smiled at Boss and trotted away. She sat down under the shrubs of the entrance and looked out into the night. After a few minutes, when he was certain Old Friend was softly dreaming and would be all right, Boss lay down next to her and sniffed the passing breezes.

Mimi looked at his face. She was relaxed now and looking down rather than frozen with fear and looking up. His face seemed different now.

"That really made his day," he said. "He used to have a wife. She kept things tidy. Whenever he thinks of her, he hums that little tune. He'll sleep gently all through the night." Boss stretched. "Makes a nice change for me," he yawned. "So, thanks again."

Yesterday, his face frightened her. Today, it seemed a nice face, big nose and all.

"Don't stare at the nose," she bossed herself. "Look away. Gosh, that's huge! Look away!" She turned toward the stars.

"Are you Friends a long time?" she asked.

"Best years of my life," Boss yawned again. "I had other Friends but..." he shrugged, leaned toward her and pointed to his shoulder.

Mimi gasped at the size of the scar.

"Do I look like a rough dog to you?"

"I'll take a chance here and be truthful. Yes." She tensed and waited. Would he be angry?

"Well, that's how they used me," he said. "Rough." He looked at the stars and yawned. "Then he came along," he exhaled. "He saw good in me and that's been my life ever since, all good."

He rested his head on his paws.

"So good," he said closing his eyes. "I got lucky," he snoozed, "and I'm so grateful."

Mimi looked at the sky. It had never occurred to her to be grateful. Bob was all she'd ever known. She had taken his love for granted. "Maybe we both did," she thought and the tears welled up again. She focused on a group of stars and tried to see through the watery blur. She squinted, gasped and looked away. She shook her head, wiped her eyes and looked back up. In her group of stars...the face of Bob!

She blinked and blinked. Bob's kind face was still there.

"Have I lost you already?" She kept the tears down and cried deep inside, the better to see him clearly. "Are you in heaven?" she asked. She looked away and then looked back.

"Did you lose me or did I lose you?" she asked the star face. It smiled back but gave no answer. After a few minutes, she sighed, settled down next to Boss and closed her eyes.

Chapter Seventeen

Antiques Roadshow Interrupted

In less than an hour, the turkey had worked its magic. Lucy's head lolled to one side.

"Oh!" she said, waking herself up. "Oh, I'm going to be sooooooo asleep, very soon." She grinned a goofy smile at Melinda. "It's just intoxicating, that turkey," she mumbled and slurred. "I love the way he makes it. " Her front paws slid forward and her belly hit the floor. "Oooops," she giggled. She lay like the sphinx, head up, eyes open, but Melinda could tell she didn't see any of the excitement building up across the room.

"Come on!" Lester said. "Let's do it now!"

"Your mother's not asleep yet," said Rufahlo.

"She looks pretty out of it to me," said Papillion.

"And Auntie Melinda's still wide awake," said Rufahlo. "Maybe the piece I gave her wasn't big enough. And I have to be convincing. I can't just fake having to pee. I have to really mean it. Couple more minutes."

"You know he won't get up during his favorite TV show," Lester said.

Day Care Guy had finished his sandwich and tea and changed into his jammies, robe and slippers. He puttered around the room, setting things up for a night of TV viewing.

"An actor must prepare," Rufahlo said with a haughty sniff.

"Oh, come on!" Lester snorted.

"I can fake it now! Watch!" Papillion shut her eyes, held her breath and squeezed 'til her little bottom shivered.

"Little one, do you have to pee?" Day Care Guy paused his preparations.

"No!" said Rufahlo sternly.

"No," said Papillion.

"Cause if you have to, let's do it now before my favorite show begins...No? Well, OK." Day Care Guy resumed his preparations.

"Why not?" Lester was exasperated and anxious to get going.

"Think about it, Lester!" Rufahlo used his "I Know More Than You Do" voice.

"Papillion is new, he doesn't know her. And she's very small. He would be careful to get her leash and then the plan falls to pieces. Me, he knows well and trusts. And I'm big and strong. When his show comes on and I have to go, he'll just open the door. He knows I'll come right back."

"All right," Lester admitted. "You're right."

"Thank you," said Rufahlo. "If it's one thing I know, it's show-biz," he said to Papillion.

The sound of a soft thud made them turn.

Lucy's head had hit the floor. She lay flat out and was snoring rather loudly for such a little dog. Melinda lay flat too, curled around the sleeping Lucy.

"Auntie Melinda. She's not snoring," Rufahlo thought.

"Ok, they're gone," said Lester. "How does the big boy look?"

Slowly, carefully, the boys had shifted Lester's bed so it was now almost hidden behind a cardboard box the puppies like to play in. With one swift movement, Rufahlo placed the stuffed dog in the bed and pushed down. Only a bit of the stuffed toy was visible over the bed's rim. Papillion had helped them arrange the ball of hair clippings into a lion's mane mound over the toy.

"Well, if I was where they are," Papillion said, nodding slightly toward Melinda and Lucy, "and all goofed up on too much turkey, I might think that was you. Should it wear your bow?"

"No," Lester said. "I have to wear the bow."

"Ok!" Rufahlo said. "Now, I have to pee! It's show time!"

Melinda opened one eye.

"Lester," said Rufahlo," go get the bone and take a moment to prepare."

"I'm ready now," Lester said.

"Take a moment," Rufahlo insisted. "Visualize what you're going to do. It's an acting technique, you rehearse now, you're more convincing later."

"Fine!" Lester shook his mane and trotted off.

Rufahlo turned to Papillion.

"You sure you want to do this?" he asked. Even through his strange, garbled accent, she could hear the concern in his voice. "It's not safe and Day Care Guy might get really mad," he finished.

"No one stays mad at me for long," she smiled prettily. "I'm just that cute."

"Yes, you are," Rufahlo thought.

"I'll run right near you," he said, "in case you fall down."

"You don't have to," she said. "I can do it."

"You fall down, he catches you before Lester is gone, it's over," Rufahlo said. "Lester needs time to disappear. Besides, if I'm with you, then he can be mad at us both."

"Eye reh ee," Lester said through the bone in his mouth.

"Let's roll," said Rufahlo.

Day Care Guy was still getting ready when his favorite show's theme music started to play.

"Antiques Roadshow!" he sighed. "I wonder where they are this week?"

He liked to have everything just so before he sat down. With everything he needed nearby, he wouldn't miss a second of the show. What else should he get? Maybe a nice glass of wine...

"Ahem!" Rufahlo coughed. Standing by the door, he skittered his feet and looked anxious.

"Now you have to go?" Day Care Guy was annoyed. "You couldn't do this ten minutes ago when I asked?" He opened the door wide enough for Rufahlo's big chest to squeeze through.

"OK, boy, but hurry up and come right back!"

He went back to watch the show.

"Art Deco night!" He clapped his hands. "Tiffany! Erte!"

"Ahem!" Papillion coughed. She was standing next to the open door.

"Papillion! No!" Day Care Guy panicked. "Stay!"

She bolted.

Without pausing to find glasses or turn on the Tivo, Day Care Guy rushed through the door after her. The picket gate was open and flapping against the fence. He could see two vague shapes moving down the sidewalk away from the house.

Two shapes? One big, one small?

"Bad dogs!" Day Care Guy exclaimed. "Rufahlo, I'm surprised at you!" He hurried after them.

Angling the bone so the door wouldn't open any wider, Lester slipped through and ran into the night.

The puzzle pieces came together. Melinda gasped. Lester was running away! Why?

"Lucy!" she hissed, trying not to wake the other dogs. "Wake up! Lester's gone!"

"'Course he is," Lucy mumbled. "Bound to happen, sooner or later…"

"That's the turkey talking!" Melinda hissed and shook her hard. "Snap out of it!"

"He's fine," Lucy grumbled. She jerked her head up and stared fuzzily at Melinda.

"He's MY son!" she slurred. "Whatever he does, he'll be fine…." She sighed and relaxed back down to the floor.

"What are you talking about?" Melinda was frantic. "Wake up!"

"Can't," Lucy muttered and snored again. Melinda looked around the room. All of the other dogs had succumbed to turkey fever and were sleeping soundly. Even Lester…

"Wait a minute!" she thought. She could see curly brown hair peeking up over the edge of Lester's bed.

"What the...?" She got up to go look.

She stared at the stuffed toy covered with Lester's hair.

"Hmmm. Just stay put," she thought. "That's the best thing to do. This story's not over yet!"

Rufahlo pranced backwards, keeping pace with Papillion and watching.

"What are you doing?" She gasped from the running and the talking and started to tilt. He pushed her back up with his paw.

"Going...going...gone! Lester's gone into the park. We stop now." He threw himself down and blocked her path. She tumbled into him, slapping against his belly.

"What! Are you doing?" she hyperventilated.

"This way I look like a hero," he smiled. "I stop the little dog and keep her safe."

"Hmmmm." Papillion stared at him.

"Her stare is unnerving," Rufahlo thought. "Day Care Guy is very slow," he said. "He needs more exercise!"

"Papillion!" Day Care Guy was almost in tears. "What were you thinking? No, no, bad dog," he said as he cuddled and kissed her.

"Very poor training technique," sniffed Rufahlo. "Reward the dog for bad behavior just because you have emotions!"

"Don't be jealous," Papillion sniffed back.

"Rufahlo!" Day Care Guy's half-sobs turned to wheezing. He stroked Rufahlo's head and took several long, deep breaths. "You stopped her! Thank you, big boy!"

Rufahlo couldn't help himself. He smiled the "Aren't I fabulous?" smile.

"Mmm-hmmph!" Papillion sniffed over Day Care Guy's shoulder. She gave Rufahlo a look. He couldn't read its meaning. She licked Day Care Guy's face.

"Uh oh," Rufahlo thought. "She's very smart..."

"Come on, kids," Day Care Guy's panic had passed and he breathed easily now.

"It's Art Deco Night! Tiffany! Erte! Aaaaaaaaaah! And I left the door open! Let's go!"

The man and the big dog ran back to the house. The little dog, bouncing in the man's arms, looked down at the big dog and had a thought.

"Strange. Thinking doesn't hurt me at all."

She looked back down at the big dog and thought some more.

"Uh, uh,...uh, uh, uh!" Day Care Guy, still not wearing his glasses, counted heads around the room. Still holding Papillion tight, he ran to his bedroom. "Six puppies! Good!" He sagged with relief. "All present and accounted for. Shall we watch TV?" he asked Papillion. "Look!" he pointed to the screen. "I have a vase just like that one!" He sat down in his chair.

"Nice," Papillion said and cuddled down in his lap.

Rufahlo settled down in his bed but couldn't sleep. What if Lester didn't come back? What about the show tomorrow? His head pounded. It felt like a tractor beam from some alien star ship had attached itself to his ears. He had seen such things when his Friends watched the Discovery Channel.

"No good," he muttered and opened his eyes.

The source of the tractor beam flared her nostrils.

"Where is he?" Melinda hissed, her eyes glowing yellow with rage. "What's going on?"

"Auntie Melinda!" Rufahlo jumped to his feet. Auntie Melinda was almost as big as he was and he couldn't avoid her eyes.

"Who?" he squeaked. "Everyone's here!" His voice dropped to a whisper. "It must be the turkey talking, maybe you should go lie…"

"I had one bite of turkey," Melinda hissed. "I gave the rest to her!" She jerked her head towards the loudly snoring Lucy. "And a blind dog could see that's not Lester!"

Her rage-filled eyes narrowed. Their tractor beams intensified.

"Where is he?" she growled. "What's going on?"

"What's going on there, pups?" Day Care Guy glanced over his shoulder. "Go to bed now."

Papillion's head rested on the arm of his chair. She opened one eye and looked at Rufahlo.

"I'll be back," Melinda hissed. She moved slowly and deliberately back to her place with the snoring Lucy.

Chapter Eighteen

A Big Nose Knows Another

After the initial bolt from the door, Lester slowed down.

"Running attracts attention," he thought. "Looks suspicious. Especially with this thing in my mouth. Trotting along, not a care in the world, anyone watching will think my Friend is just lagging behind, reading his newspaper, or tweeting." He trotted up the entrance path and into the Dog Park.

Vague shapes moved through the dusk. No shape paused or seemed to take an interest.

"Keep trotting," he told himself.

When he could see the tree circle at the top of the little hill, he stopped and sat for a minute. He put the bone down and breathed in deeply through his nose.

"Uh, uh..." he counted off the Night Dogs by their scents. "Uh, uh,...the Human Friend...uh, uh, uh. OK." The girl seemed right up front in the smell combination. "She must be outside."

He started, then stopped. The grass was very wet.

He paused and thought.

"Thinking doesn't hurt me at all. That's strange."

The dew would destroy his ankle poofs. OK, OK, he had ankle poofs and he wasn't always happy about that but...

"When you go somewhere important, you look your best," he thought. "Soggy ankle poofs..." He slapped himself and laughed.

"Oh, mom," he gasped, "I sound just like you!"

An uncontrollable fit of giggles seized him. "Rufahlo would enjoy this," he thought. For a moment, he missed his friend and wished he could be here.

"I'll have to seek forgiveness for him too, he was involved." Lester looked at the grassy little hill.

"No set path," he thought. "I'll have to prance and hope for the best."

He paused and thought some more. He took a deep breath.

Earlier that day, all the dogs had lounged, or sat, or rolled around on this little hill. He could put a name on the Day Dog smells and a face on the Night dog smells. He smelled a small, distant but still distinct hint of Spotty.

"Hello, my friend," he thought. "I'm glad you're here."

If he followed those smells, he would find the spots where their lounging had flattened the grass. He could prance from spot to spot and keep his ankle poofs much drier than if he just plowed through the grass up the hill.

He sniffed and found spot number one.

"Start prancing!"

"Strange," he thought, jumping from spot to spot. "Thinking doesn't hurt me at all."

Boss got up and went back to his Old Friend's side. His place next to the fitfully snoozing Mimi was soon taken up by Bailiff.

"Is that Bob?" Bailiff pointed. Mimi shook herself awake.

A Corgi is not a pointing dog by any means and it was difficult to follow his lead. The areas he described were vast and formless. After a few seconds he would fixate on a completely different area. He would jump up, point his snout, and waggle his eyes at her to see if she was looking. It was dark and the few humans left were only vague, silhouetted shapes. This was the hundredth time they'd had this dialogue and Mimi was exhausted. .

"No!" she said wearily.

"Is that Bob?" Bailiff launched his body in a different direction. Another vague silhouette moved through the dusk.

"No!" she cried.

"Is that Bob?" Bailiff sprung again, landed and pointed.

Mimi couldn't tell if he was joking, or trying to get her attention, or if he really thought Bob might be out there. Whichever was true, Mimi was done for the day.

"No!" she barked. "Stop! Just stop!"

"Bailiff," said Boss, gently but firmly. "Time to go to bed. Now."

Bailiff's face sagged a little.

"Okeeeeeeeeeeeeeeey...." He turned to go.

"He was trying to help," Mimi thought. "Or trying to get a laugh. Or both. But it wasn't mean."

She blocked his path with her paw.

"Thank you for trying," she said. "It's night now and if Bob was here, I could smell him. Tomorrow, I'll tell you what he looks like and you can refine your search."

"OK!" Bailiff brightened up again. "OK!" He wandered off to the other Night Dogs and flopped down at their feet.

"What a serious little dog, such a jobber," Mimi thought. "He's not trying to be funny, he's really sincere. But it is funny, or it would be, if it wasn't about Bob." She paused. "No, it's funny. Until it gets really annoying. And then you tell him it's annoying. That's it! No more!" She practiced how it would go tomorrow.

Tomorrow. This would be her second night without Bob.

"Where is he?" she gazed into the darkness. "What's he doing? Is he all right? Why hasn't he come for me?"

In all fairness to Bob, she didn't know where she was. They had never come here before, she was sure of it. No smell was familiar and she would have remembered these dogs.

"What is he doing?" she wondered.

He was probably putting up posters around their home, the last place Mimi had been seen.

On the awful night, Mimi remembered a long drive. After all the familiar smells were gone, the collar was ripped from her neck and the bag she was in left the car seat. It floated briefly through the air before crash-landing in this strange place.

"I'm too far away," she thought. "No one who sees those posters would come here. I wonder if he's posted on Craig's List?"

"I wonder if he's looking at all," was the thought she did not dare think. Still, it was there, a vague silhouette lurking in the dark corners of her mind.

Two nights now, she'd been away. Did he miss her at all? Was he looking? If so, how hard? With vigor and due diligence or half-heartedly for appearance sake? The evil hag girlfriend, what about her? Were they still holding hands and fixed on each other? Was he glad Mimi was gone so he could be with his girlfriend in peace? What could or should Mimi do?

"Wait. Stay here and wait."

Her head sunk onto her paws. How long would she have to wait? Wait for what? Would he come? Could he come, ever? What if life with Bob was over? Was he done with her? Even if he wanted her back, could he find her? Tears welled in her eyes.

Through the blur of tears, she saw another vague shape moving through the darkness. Unlike other shapes, there-in-a-blink and then gone, this shape moved steadily toward her, the silhouette sharpening as it approached. It was a sort of egg, with a toothpick sticking out each side. Blinking away her tears, she could see the egg had legs and smartly prancing legs at that. But why would a giant egg with a toothpick be prancing toward them at this hour of the night?

"Will you look at that?" said Randy, suddenly at her side.

"What is that?" said Bailiff, suddenly at her other side. He hadn't mentioned Bob and for that she was grateful.

"Boss!" Randy called softly. "Look at this!"

"No," said Boss quietly. "I'll stay here. Let him come to me."

When Rufahlo forced him to rehearse, Lester had been impatient and annoyed. Now, he was profoundly grateful. This was the moment they had planned for.

He hadn't planned on all the prancing to avoid soggy ankle poofs. After his final jump to the lounge spot nearest the entrance, he thought about his facial expression. He knew it was probably goofy and happy-looking. Being out alone at night was new excitement for him, a step toward the wild places of freedom. This, on top of the sheer fun of prancing around, would put that happy goof look on his face.

"Wait!" he said to himself. "I like prancing? It makes me happy? Isn't that part of what I'm always complaining about when Mom talks about the show? The prancing? Hmmmm," he thought. "Ow!" He flinched in surprise. That thought had hurt!

"Hmmmm." He thought about that and the pain went away. It was time to focus. He composed his handsome features into a serious and, he hoped, dignified expression. Surprising himself, he touched his bow and re-assured himself that it was still on straight.

He picked up the bone, made a final leap and landed in the center of the tree circle's entrance.

He was very, very grateful that he had rehearsed the next part.

His face wore the serious expression and his landing was graceful and clean. He made brief contact with the yellow eyes that had burned him from a hundred yards away. He ducked his head then slowly put the bone down to rest at the front of the entrance. He dropped to the Sphinx position, carefully placing himself so his paws and his head were a respectful distance behind the bone he was offering.

Without looking up, he said, "We're sorry we played with it without asking. We never meant to steal it."

Mimi glanced back and forth between man and boy. She felt no tension. She chanced a longer look at Boss. He was smiling!

"Bring it to me," Boss was grinning from ear to ear. "I need to examine it, see if you've caused any damage." He growled and chuckled at the same time. Lester was enthralled, and frozen.

"Sit down here," the big dog pawed the place next to him. "Stay with us a while."

Lester still couldn't move. Boss gestured to him.

"I'm kidding about the damage! Just sit here!" He slammed his paw down and laughed, then stopped and stared. The yellow laser eyes flashed, then faded. "Just sit here," he said, "stay a while."

Lester grinned, picked up the bone and obeyed.

"Aynk ooo," he said through the bone.

He trotted over and put the bone down in front of the big dog. Then, following the paw's directive, he lay down by the big dog's side. He couldn't stop grinning. He glanced over. The Big Dog was grinning too. He was also staring, which was a little unnerving. Lester, a seasoned Show Dog, was used to being stared at. It didn't bother him. He didn't care what they thought. But this Big Dog's opinion was important to him. Why?

"Nice bow," said the Big Dog, grinning.

"Thanks," Lester said. "You want it?"

"I think I would," said the Big Dog. "But don't you need it?"

"My mom will get me another," Lester sighed, then caught himself. No sighing in front of the Big Dog! There it was, though, he had sighed in front of a dog he didn't know. They weren't friends. Yet. To cover his embarrassment, Lester launched into the bow removal procedure. In a matter of seconds, he had the bow in his paws in the offering position. It was still starched and shiny after all the necessary manipulations.

"I took your bone, after all," Lester said. "So, you should have my bow."

"You brought my bone back," he said. "So, I won't keep the bow. I'll wear it for now. For fun. I've never been fancy. I always wondered what it might feel like. Can you hook it on my collar?"

Lester had practiced this so often, it took no time at all.

"Lovely," said Mimi.

"Very posh," said Randy.

"Very..........jaunty!" Bailiff squeaked and collapsed with giggles. All the other dogs, slowly, quietly, carefully joined in, even Lester.

"I know, I know," said Boss. "But let me pretend for a while." Then he collapsed too and they all giggled quietly so as not to wake Old Friend.

After the giggling, the dogs relaxed and went back to minding their own business. Some of them considered it their business to eavesdrop on Boss's conversation with the exotic new creature.

"How is it you're out alone at this time of night?" Boss asked. "Where's your Friend?"

"Our Friends are Frequent Fliers," Lester replied. "We board at the Day Care Center when they're gone."

"We?" Boss asked.

"My mother," Lester held back a sigh. He glanced at Boss. The Big Dog stared at him, grinning from ear to ear.

The staring was warm but intense. Lester made a decision. He stared back. Slowly his smile stretched from ear poof to ear poof.

"What?" he asked.

"You've got a big nose," the Big Dog said. His smile stretched even further.

Lester took a breath. "I'll take a chance here," he said carefully. He leaned in a bit and spoke more softly. "You would know," he said.

"Exactly right!" Boss choked back a big guffaw. His body shook with quiet laughter. The other dogs wished they'd heard the joke.

"Exactly right," he pounded his big paw against the dirt floor.

The laughter stopped.

"Yes," he stared unblinking. "I have a big nose. And I know how to use it. How about you?"

"I do OK," Lester said. "I think I'm pretty good."

"We'll see," smiled the Big Dog. "We'll see."

No wind stirred that evening and the tree circle was cozy. The other dogs dozed peacefully while Boss and Lester chatted away.

"What about your mother?" Boss asked. "Does she know you're out alone at night?"

"I fed her some turkey," Lester said. "She's a very small dog.".

"That doesn't sound right," Boss said. "But..."

"I'll be back by morning pee time," Lester said. "No one will know. We have it all worked out. Rufahlo will help me." Lester ducked his head. "He's sorry too. About the bone."

"Fine," said Boss. "No worries."

He stared again. Lester stared back.

"Your mother," Boss said. "And a Friend. You're so lucky. And yet you're here at night. What is it? Your mother is..."

"She wants me to be a show dog," Lester spilled all the sighs he'd been holding back.

Boss was puzzled. He looked Lester up and down.

"But you have all that and a bag of chips!" he exclaimed. "How is this a problem? Show dog. That's a good life!"

"Yes," Lester struggled. "Yes, it is a good life. I know dogs who want it more than...cheeseburgers." Several dogs lifted their heads when he said cheese. He thought of Rufahlo who would trade all future cheeseburgers in his life if it meant he could compete with confidence.

"But I don't want to be a show dog!" He held Boss's gaze and took a deep breath. "I want to be a crime-sniffing police dog!" Emotion rippled the edge of his voice.

Boss's smile faded. He looked away from Lester and stared into the night. His yellow eyes flickered and twitched. Memories filled his head.

Trying to cover his nervousness, Lester soldiered on.

"I'm gonna be Jack Butts, Poodle from Hell! I'll hunt them down, I'll rip their pant legs!"

Startled from his reverie, Boss looked at Lester and grinned.

"Jack Butts?" he chuckled. "Boy, what's your real name?"

"Lester," he said, hoping there would be no "Lulu" jokes.

"You sure you want to be a crime-sniffing police dog? That's what we did," Boss nodded toward Old Friend. "And we were good. Until he got hurt. It's dangerous out there…"

"Danger!" Lester stared into the middle distance. "I'll hunt it down, I'll rip…"

"Are you sure you wouldn't want to just play one on TV?" Boss tried to joke. A few dogs chuckled and he silenced them with a murderous glare.

"Acting?" Lester was confused. "I should take up acting?"

"All of the fun and none of the danger," Boss said, concern in his voice. "It's kind of a show dog life. Maybe your mother would like that. I knew a show dog once…."

"Service," Lester's voice was quiet and focused. "I want to be of service. Look at this thing!" He pawed his nose. "And I do know how to use it!" He kept his voice quiet but his passion bristled.

"I don't want to just preen and pose and prance around for applause!"

He paused for a moment, remembering how much he had enjoyed prancing through the grass to get to the tree circle. "Yes, prancing is always fun," he thought, "but I want more!" He took a deep breath.

"I want to do things. Important things. Things that need to get done. I want to be the dog that makes it happen. My nose was made for service, not for show!" He was out of breath now. Saying it out loud and all at once had made his dreams seem very real.

"And I think it's more than just 'pretty good'," he said cautiously. He glanced at Boss. The power of the big, warm smile made him suddenly shy. He looked down.

"I think it's…" He glanced at Boss again and this time held his gaze. Joy filled his heart. The Big Dog seemed to understand him. Lester pulled himself up to his full height. "I think it's…awesome!"

The two dogs grinned together. The very idea made Lester happy. He looked right at Boss.

"My nose is awesome! I want to learn how to use it, so that I can be of service! That's it! That's my plan! That's what I want!"

Old Friend stirred, shivered and slowly sat up. He shook his head and looked around the circle. Brushing back the tartan blanket, he huffed to his knees and puffed to his feet.

"Moonlight!" he said. "Beauty and utility all on the same nickel. Stay here, boy, I'll just be a minute."

He bent and half-crawled through the entrance and was gone.

"No time like the present," Boss said. He tapped his paw at Lester's feet.

"Stay there," he grinned. He moved to the entrance and gazed into the darkness.

"Wait 'til I tell you, then come sit next to me." He turned and peered into the night.

Chapter Nineteen

One Small Smell Among Many

Boss settled down in the sphinx position.

"Now," his voice was soft. "Come."

Lester tiptoed to his side and sat upright. If this was going to be a test, he wanted his nose in the air where all smells were available and away from the ground where only a few scents were strong.

"He does this sometimes," Boss murmured. "He'll say he has to pee and tell me to stay. Sometimes he comes right back. Other times, he wanders off. I should go with him but he told me to stay. So I try to keep a nose on him in case he gets into trouble."

He turned and grinned at Lester.

"Find him for me and tell me the route he took. Show me what you got."

Lester flared his nostrils and sucked in air. "Thousands of smells out there all inter-mingling," he thought. Feet, hair, breath, clothes, humans were walking clouds of competing scents. In the fog of Old Friend's human fug, Lester had noticed a tiny molecule of something different. He knew that smell. He could find that tiny bit and follow it. He wouldn't say anything and maybe Boss wouldn't ask. He didn't want to tell him about this particular smell.

He flared his nostrils wider.

"There it is," he thought.

"He went straight down the slope to the 'all dogs on leash' sign," Lester said.

"Stumbled down, you mean," Boss smiled, "and stopped himself by hitting the sign. Then what?"

"He went left." Lester breathed. "He stopped at the children's sand lot. He had a pee there."

"Really?" Boss lifted an eyebrow, wrinkling his forehead.

"Ok, he peed himself but only a little bit. He managed the

clothes and most of it went on the weeds around the sand circle."

"Hmmm," Boss nodded approval.

"Then he went forward, crossing the sand," Lester paused. "And on to the overgrown rosemary bushes near the coffee kiosk. He pushed inside the bushes and...whoa!" Lester gasped.

"I know," said Boss. "I think that's why he goes for the rosemary. Covers the smell."

"Not really," Lester pulled his nostrils tighter.

"Interesting," said Boss. "They're very careful about ours. Pick it right up with their little plastic bags and into the trash it goes. Their own?" He shrugged. "Leave it right where it drops."

Lester didn't know what he was talking about. His own friend had never dropped anything so vile and certainly never dropped anything outside of the tiny room of mystery inside their house. Lester had examined the tiny room of mystery with great care. Never a sign of anything dropped. The shining bowl of water was very nice and he lapped from it often.

"Focus!" He snapped back to the present. He searched the vile cloud until he found the one tiny molecule of smell. It was unique and could easily be followed.

"Then he moved right, following a sort of zig-zag pattern but steadily forward...."

"Sounds right," Boss nodded.

"He stopped at the lone willow tree," Lester paused.

"Their initials are there," Boss said. "Himself and the wife. I helped him do it," he smiled. "Chased around and menaced, kept people away until he was finished," he sighed. The memory was sweet but still made him sad. "That was before he got hurt."

"He moved swiftly down the slope to the lake," Lester was excited now. "There he is! I can see him!"

"The lake!" Boss sat up. He squinted and made out the figure of his human. He was pacing the lake's edge, flapping his coat. He looked at the moon and spread his coat like a pair of wings.

"Angel?" Boss called gently. "Are you awake?"

"Yeeeesss," Angel mumbled.

"Come here and point those things. Tell me what he's saying. Please."

Angel shook off sleep and stumbled over. It took a second or two to control the tentacles and to point them in the right direction.

"He's howling," he said. "No, wait, he's singing."

"The words," Boss said. "What is he singing?"

"Sometimes I live in the country," Angel sang, "sometimes I live in town. Sometimes I get a great notion..." he paused and looked at Boss nervously. "To jump into the river and drown."

The tentacles lost their focus and flapped about. "Hey!" Lester flicked slime from his lion's mane.

Boss hung his head. "He told me to stay," he murmured. "Time to disobey."

He looked up and took a deep breath.

"Will you come with me, boy?" he asked. "Help me bring him in?"

"I will," Lester said. "The lake's not deep. I can drag him out if we have to."

"I'll come," said Angel. "I can listen and tell you if the song changes."

"I'll be there too," Randy yawned and stretched. "I'm the herding expert."

"I can...well, I can watch and make reports," said Bailiff.

"We'll keep people away," Ben said. "If there's anyone there."

"That's what we do," Jerry said and hung his head.

"I'm not staying here alone!" Mimi squeaked.

"Myself and the boy in the lead," Boss barked. "The rest of you stay back and do your jobs. Angel! Tell me if the song changes. Let's go!"

Lester kept pace with the Big Dog. His ankle poofs dissolved completely in the wet grass and dragged down like dirty mops. He was thrilled. Adventure! The wild places! There he was, living the life!

Angel stayed a respectful pace behind them. It was hard to focus the tentacles while walking. The man was not singing now. Angel looked ahead. He saw the man, his coat spread like wings, standing at the edge of the water. Above him, huge and floating but very, very still was the Big Busy. He smiled that calm, beatific smile they all did in Heaven and held his arm out straight, palm up, in the "stay" position.

The man dropped his arms and the coat collapsed to his sides. He stepped back a pace from the water's edge, flapped the coat wings and sang.

"He's singing," called Angel. "It's different!"

"What?" called Boss, "What is it?"

"Baaaaaawn in the you ess aa-aa," Angel tried to match the inflection and convey the emotion. "Baaaaawn in the you ess aa-aa! I'm a long gone daddy from the you ess aa-aa-aa."

"OK," Boss said. "Slow down, everyone. Approach softly. He's better now."

"Thank you," Angel whispered.

"It's what we do," the Big Busy replied.

When they finally reached him, Boss nuzzled the old man's hand.

"Baby boy!" he exclaimed. "I thought I told you to…" He looked at his big dog's pleading eyes.

"Well, never mind. You're here now. Let's look at the moon."

He sat on the ground, not noticing the damp, and put his big arm around his big dog's shoulders. Lester sat on his other side.

"And the fancy boy's here too!" Lester winced at "fancy" but no one laughed.

The old man rumpled his fingers through the lion's mane and scratched Lester's ears. No one ever did that. No one ever wanted to muss his carefully sculpted hair. It felt very, very nice. Had Lester been a cat, he might have purred.

Mimi put her paws on the old man's thigh and settled her head between them.

"And the little one too!" He scratched her ears. The other dogs whimpered with longing. Old Friend looked over his shoulder.

"Everyone's here!" he said happily. "It's a party! Let's howl at the moon!" He threw his head back and took a deep breath.

"Let's not," Randy growled. "Animal Control! I don't feel like running."

"Me neither," said Boss. He stretched his big body across the old man's legs.

"No? You're right," murmured Old Friend. He stroked Boss's flanks with deep, strong pets. "Best to enjoy the quiet. I'm tired too."

Ben and Jerry closed their mouths and quietly let out the air taken in for the howl.

"Isn't it beautiful?" Old Friend said. The other dogs crept forward and leaned against his back and against each other, making contact for comfort and warmth. Together the furry little group gazed at the face of the full, shining moon.

Lester was disappointed. "Real dogs like howling at the moon," he thought.

"I was looking forward to that." He didn't know why they would resist such fun but if Randy said so and Boss agreed, there must be a very good reason. He leaned closer to Old Friend. After a few minutes, Mimi shivered.

"The ground is wet," she said. "I'm cold."

"You're right, my poor little one," said Old Friend. "It is cold. Let's go home, my babies."

He struggled to his feet. The dogs yawned and stretched.

"Why did you all come out?" he asked. "Did everyone have to pee?"

Jerry lifted his leg and let fly at a clump of weeds.

"Is everyone done now?"

Ben lifted his leg and showered some wild poppies.

"Well, let's go home. You can finish along the way."

Alternately leaning on Boss, who was strong, and Lester, who was tall enough to counter-balance, the old man struggled across the field and the playground. Busy Angel floated behind the group, brushing stragglers forward with the hem of his robe. With Boss pulling and Lester and Randy's support from behind, they finally made it up the hill and into the tree circle. Mimi had scampered ahead and smoothed the tartan blanket into an inviting bed.

"Ah, little one," the old man sighed. "You're a gem."

As he settled down, a ripple of worry disturbed his mind. "These two new ones," he thought. "The little one, so pretty. The other one, a poodle! A carefully groomed one. Someone will miss these dogs."

"What will they do when they find them with me?" he thought. "What if they think I stole them?" His first care had to be Boss. But if they took one, they could take them all, even Boss! This was as much worry as his old, tired mind could handle. "We'll rest and enjoy ourselves now," he thought. "We can do something tomorrow." He drifted off to sleep.

The other dogs cuddled like puppies and were soon warm enough to sleep. Boss and Lester sphinxed themselves at the entrance and gazed out together at the soft, quiet night.

"You'll have to go back soon," said Boss.

"It's all worked out," Lester said. "Rufahlo will help me."

"Good," said Boss. "In the day light, people will look at us and wonder why you're here."

"I know. I'll go back at first light. I'll slip into the crowd when they're out for the morning pee."

"Good," said Boss.

"I'll be back, though," Lester said. "May I come visit?"

"Always welcome. No one will question two big dogs having a play together."

"Thanks." Lester tried not to grin too wide but couldn't help it. He had made friends with the biggest dog in the park, the dog everyone else was afraid of!

"Now, let me ask you something," said Boss

Lester cocked his head.

"A nose that knows what it's doing," Boss said, "looks for the one small thing that's unique to that person. When you find that one thing, you focus!" Boss lifted a paw and made graceful waves toward his very big nose.

"The nose follows that one smell where it leads." He stared at Lester. "Is that what you do?"

Lester nodded slowly.

"What did you find in my Old Friend?" Boss rumbled. "What did you follow?" His yellow eyes glowed softly.

This was the question Lester hoped would not be asked. He glanced away, considering many possibilities for his answer.

"Tell me," said Boss. "Go on."

Lester looked at the ground.

"It's OK," Boss sighed. "I already know what I think. I could use a second opinion."

Lester dared a sideways glance at Boss. The glowing yellow had dimmed and the eyes were asking.

"I've smelled it before," Lester said. "A long time ago." He smiled at the memory.

"When I was a baby, my Friend's mother lived with us. She loved me. She sat in her big arm chair all day long. When I came to her, she would laugh and pick me up and give me a cuddle. When I was big enough to jump, she'd pat her lap and I jumped up to be next to her. We watched TV."

He looked at Boss.

"That's when I first smelled it. Mixed in with the perfume and clean clothes and the food and her breath, there was a tiny note of something very different. None of the other humans had this smell. I didn't know what it was. No one else had it. Why did she? What was it?"

Boss nodded encouragement. "Go on," he said.

"As I grew bigger, she seemed to shrink smaller. Bit by bit, day by day, the smell grew larger and larger, gradually taking over all the other smells in the mix," Lester frowned, concentrating hard. He tried to remember the sequence of events and to find the right words.

"One day, my Friend told me not to jump up on the chair anymore. He said I was too big and might hurt her," Lester blinked as the memory filled his heart.

"I would never want to hurt her, so I sat by her feet. She would rumple my hair and scratch my ears, just like Old Friend did tonight. It was nice."

Boss smiled. "Go on."

"Then my Friend asked her not to rumple my stupid hair!" Lester started to shake. "My stupid hairdo must always be ready for show!" Lester took a deep breath to calm himself. "So, we managed. She would pat my butt or my stomach where the hair shape wasn't so important. She would smile at me and rub my belly and we were happy together. Time passed, I grew more and she grew less. The smell got stronger," he paused for breath.

"One day, she didn't come to her chair. I followed the smell to her room. She was still in bed. My Friends were there and other people too. The others wore white coats and spoke very softly. She saw me and smiled. I was very young and without thinking I jumped on her bed. Everyone gasped with horror but she laughed. 'Oh, let him stay here!' she said. She mussed my hairdo and my Friend didn't say anything. The room was a great confusion of smells. Perfumes, soaps, clothing, cleaning agents, feet, all mixed together in one big cloud of fug. But the one smell that stood out was hers. It was very strong now."

"Every day, I would jump up to be next to her. She would smile

161

and pet me. Every day, the one smell would be bigger and her pets would get smaller, her smile a little weaker." Lester stopped. This part really hurt and he didn't want to speak of it.

He looked at his new friend and knew he had to tell the truth.

"Then one day, she went to sleep. She didn't wake up. That smell was the only one left in the room. It had taken over. And then, she was gone."

The two dogs stared at each other. Lester had to look away.

"That's the smell I found on your Old Friend," he said softly. "Very small, just the beginning, but that's the one I followed."

"Thank you," Boss murmured. "I thought so myself but it's good to have another 'big nose' opinion."

The two dogs stared at the moon.

Mimi squiggled herself between them.

"So nice and warm!" she sighed. "Achoo! Achoo!" she batted Lester's mane away from her nose. "Too much hair!"

"I know," said Lester. "Sorry."

"I'll just sit on this part here," she said. "That's better, out of my face, anyway."

The three of them gazed at the stars.

"Where's Bob?" Mimi thought. "No, no. Mustn't cry. He'll come for me. He will…soon…I hope…."

She blinked and sighed, then snuggled into Lester's mane and closed her eyes.

Chapter Twenty

Asleep, Awake, and the Chicken Dog

Lucy's eyes glared. Melinda knew they saw nothing. Lucy was having a dream.

"He's my son!" she said. "He'll be the best! I taught him that!"

Melinda tried an experiment.

"Lucy," she said softly, "maybe Lester doesn't want to be a show dog."

Lucy's eyes closed. "I know," she said. Her head sank between her paws and she snored a bit.

"What do you think of that?" Melinda murmured.

"I taught him to work hard, to be the best," Lucy muttered. "Discipline matters more than the goal."

"Wow," said Melinda. "That doesn't sound like you."

"I can't live his life for him," Lucy muttered. "I taught him to work hard. Hard work will get him what he wants."

"What you want," said Melinda.

"I want my boy to be happy," Lucy mumbled. She rolled over and snored loudly.

"In the morning, I'll remind you that you said that," Melinda whispered to the sleeping poodle. She gave the small dog's body a gentle shake.

"Now stop snoring!" she hissed.

Lucy sputtered a bit, settled down and breathed quietly.

"Thank you!" Melinda whispered. She put her head down between her paws and tried to sleep.

Worry disturbed Rufahlo's sleep. He shifted and stretched but could not relax. He opened his eyes to see Papillion staring at him. She twitched.

"What's the plan?" she whispered and twitched again.

"Make sure Day Care Guy's glasses are missing," he

murmured. "Make sure he doesn't have them when he opens the door. We'll get the girls all excited to go out to pee, so he'll be too distracted to wake Lester. You go out. If Lester's there, bark three times, your loudest 'this is important!' bark. When I hear it, I get rid of the toy and the hair. Lester comes back and gets into bed. That's it. I hope."

"What if Lester's not there?" she whispered.

"I don't want to think about that." Rufahlo put his head down, closed his eyes and desperately hoped for sleep. If he was too tired come morning, he wouldn't be able to think fast or react to whatever the situation might be.

"Thinking fast is so hard, even when I'm fresh and strong. How hard will it be if I'm tired?" He twitched. That made him smile.

"Twitching! Just like little Papillion!"

He felt something warm against his belly. Papillion had curled up next to him and was now asleep.

"So warm," he thought. "So nice...." He curled his big body around her to get more of her warmth. The warmth was comforting, her breathing calmed him and very soon he too was sound asleep.

When the very first color glowed in the sky, Boss sat up and stretched. Old Friend snored peacefully.

"Oh, please," Boss prayed. "Let him be ready. I just want to go back to sleep...well, look at that." Boss cocked his head.

Lester was awake, alert and ready.

"Good boy," Boss nodded.

"We come here every afternoon," Lester said.

"We take our walks," Boss nodded toward his friend. "But if we're here," he smiled. "You and I," he squinted. "We're going to play!" He growled and smiled again. He pawed Lester's shoulder. Lester's mane seemed off-kilter. The lower left quadrant had collapsed under Mimi's weight. Boss found himself fluffing it. "It should be symmetrical," he thought, then caught himself and stopped.

"And don't forget," he said, yellow eyes flashing. "Follow your nose!"

"Could we talk more about that part? I want to train this thing." Lester pawed his nose. He sat up very straight and spoke with conviction.

"I want to be Nostrildamus! When can we talk?"

"We'll figure something out," Boss's voice cracked. "Nostrildamus?" His face collapsed and he struggled to smother his laughter. Lester struggled to do the same. They failed. The other dogs slept, undisturbed.

"Time to go," Lester stage-whispered.

Boss watched as the young dog pounced and pranced down the hill. The ankle poofs were already ruined. Why bother to be careful now?

"Someone's taught him well," he thought.

They would see each other again. He knew it. The idea was comforting. He didn't know why but it was. He lay back down with Old Friend and slept.

It had all started out so well.

No one needed encouragement to go out for the morning pee. When Papillion woke, the girls were huddled and shivering by the front door.

"Come on!" Lili whined. "I've got to go!"

"Me too," Fifi squeaked.

"Oh, that turkey!" Lucy moaned. "I'm going to lose it!" She hunched herself in the dump position. "Lester!" she yelled. "Get up!"

"Oh, that turkey!" Melinda faked it. She hadn't eaten any but placed herself between Lucy and the Lester toy and hunched in the dump position.

"Oh, no!" she moaned and shot Rufahlo a look that would have killed, had he been awake to see it. His body was stretched across the toy Lester. He snored peacefully. Papillion was jumping up and down, nipping at his nose.

"Oh, no!" she moaned again and squeezed her eyes shut.

"No! Girls, no!" Day Care Guy exclaimed. "My robe! My glasses! No!"

He grabbed his robe and struggled into it.

"Forget the glasses!"

He fumbled at the door locks. Finally, they sprang free.

"Go! Go!" he shouted as the girl dogs rushed into the small front yard. Within seconds, the air filled with strong smells and sighs of relief.

"That was close!" Day Care Guy rubbed his eyes.

"How come the boys are still asleep? Oh, well," he thought. He gathered his bundle of plastic bags. He found his glasses near the bags and put them in his pocket.

"Still early," he thought. "No need to see straight yet."

He went outside. After a few seconds, six little setter puppies waddled and staggered into the yard where they greeted their mama and had their morning pee.

"Bark, bark, bark!"

In his dreams, Rufahlo pranced joyfully through a field of wild flowers. Up on a small hill, little Papillion, surrounded by daisies and daffodils, waited for him. She spoke.

"This is my important bark! Bark, bark, bark!"

She was smiling sweetly but her voice had a harsh, desperate sound. Rufahlo stopped and cocked his head. He was confused.

Papillion took a deep breath. He watched in horror as her face swelled up like a balloon and her sharp little teeth became fangs of death. Her face twitched with rage.

"Wake up!" she screamed. The terrifying fangs clamped onto his nose.

"Ow! What?" He brushed at his nose.

"WAKE UP!" she screamed again.

"Huh?" Rufahlo's shook his head and opened his eyes. He was back in the Day Care Center. Shaking in front of him was Papillion. He heard the clumsy stomping of Day Care Guy's feet on the front stairs.

"Lester is here! Day Care Guy's seen him! He's coming back!" she squeaked.

"Ditch the toy!" she gasped and fell over.

The plan! It all came flooding back into his head. He sprang to his feet, knocking the little Papillion sideways.

"I'll see if I can stall him!" She scrabbled out the front door.

"Little one, be careful!" the man said. "Ooof! Ooops! Almost tripped me! Now, let's go see what's what."

Rufahlo grabbed the toy dog in his mouth and started spinning. At the last second, he slowed a bit and loosened his grip. His soft snap release sent the toy sailing through the air. It landed among the other toys where they first found it. Only a few stubborn tufts of Lester's hair still clinging to its velveteen skin suggested the toy had been anywhere but right where it sat. The rest of Lester's clippings now covered the styling area floor.

With Papillion worrying his feet, Day Care Guy came stumbling through the door.

"Now!" He fumbled with his glasses.

"Now!" he said, the glasses in place. Lester peaked in behind him. Rufahlo sagged with relief.

"I could have sworn..." he paused. He looked carefully at the bed where the toy Lester had been. He looked hard at Rufahlo.

Rufahlo stretched first his front, then his back legs.

"Such a nice dream I was having," he said. "Except some monster dog bit my nose!" He looked pointedly at Papillion.

"Had to," she shrugged. "Sorry."

"I'll go pee now," he trotted past Day Care Guy.

"I'll go with you," Lester turned and followed.

Papillion skittered her feet on the shiny floor, found a grip and launched herself after them.

Glasses firmly in place, Day Care Guy surveyed the scene.

"I could have sworn I saw Lester asleep in bed. I go outside and he's there! I come back in, there's nothing in the bed after all!" He shook his head. "Too much turkey," he muttered, "and perhaps a bit too much wine." He scratched his head and looked around. He didn't remember the styling room floor being this messy. Clumps of chocolate colored curly poodle hair were everywhere!

"I must speak to Francine about this," he said. "Francine...," he smiled at the thought. He wandered toward the kitchen to get some coffee. "Less turkey," he resolved. "And less wine."

The three co-conspirators huddled together in a corner of the yard.

"Well?" Papillion demanded.

"Well...yes," said Rufahlo. "I think it went very well."

"I think you should have been awake!" she snapped.

"I think it all went very well," Lester soothed. "And thank you both!"

"I couldn't help it," Rufahlo tried schmoozing the tiny, angry dog. "I didn't want to wake up. I was dreaming of you."

"Oh, please!" Papillion snarled. She twitched and fell over. Rufahlo caught her fall and righted her with his paw.

"So?" he asked. "What happened?"

Lester launched into a very excited monologue. His two friends paid rapt attention.

"Look at him," Lucy said. "How does he do it?"

Melinda, tackled to the ground by six hungry puppies, turned a glazed eye toward Lucy.

"What?" she challenged.

Relieved of morning concerns, Lucy was relaxed now and could focus on her favorite subject.

"His lower left quadrant is smooshed flat. Whoever tried to fluff it up must have used a garden claw. His whole mane is off-kilter! And the ankle poofs! How does that happen overnight? I'll…"

"You'll do nothing!" Melinda flopped a weak paw and landed one overgrown toe-nail on Lucy's collar.

"What the…?" Lucy struggled. "Let go!"

"Last night, you said," Melinda waved her other big paw, "that you wanted him to be happy."

"Well, I do," Lucy said.

"Then don't pounce on him because he slept wrong and his hair is crooked. They're going to fix that! Ka-ching! You know they love fixing that!"

"Well, they'd better fix it," Lucy growled. "The show is today!"

"A show, one show is today," Melinda sighed. "There's another on Thursday." She was tired now. The puppies had finished and wandered off. She was sleepy.

"And I've got to win that trophy!" Lucy hissed.

"Don't you mean Lester's got to win that trophy?" Melinda yawned. "You said 'I'. Melinda let go of her collar. "Lucy, I've known you a long time." Her head went flat on the grass and she looked up at the little dog. "What happened?" she asked. "You were the number one show dog, everyone knew it. Why didn't you win your trophy?"

Lucy raised her face to the bright morning sun and enjoyed the warmth, then looked down at the ground.

"I have a past," she muttered.

"Do tell!" Melinda was wide awake now, head up, ears twitching.

"It wasn't pretty," Lucy sighed, "but I was." She winked at Melinda.

"I loved the wrong man," she shrugged. "We had no future but he is my past." She closed her eyes and turned her face to the sun.

"Well…?" Melinda urged.

"He was deliciously wrong for me," Lucy shivered. "A junk-yard dog with a big nose."

Melinda gasped.

"But he was sweeter than cheese." Lucy looked at her friend, eyes soft with the memory.

"And…?" Melinda demanded.

"And when he said please, that's how I got my past," Lucy said in a rush and looked away.

"Well, this is fun," Melinda said, "but what's it got to do with the show?"

"Oh, why can't a dog just be judged on her merits?" Lucy cried out, her voice a little too loud. Dogs turned to look. She coughed and spoke more softly.

"I was top show dog champion!" she hissed. "At least in my mind."

Her face grew hard.

"Our pups, perfect Toys," she said. "All except Lester. They laughed, they snubbed us and robbed me of my precious prize! My prize!"

"Oh, you are so not alone," Melinda comforted. "My youth was wild and crazy too. So happy and free…" she smiled.

"Hey!" Lucy snapped. "Back to me! This is not about you!"

"Well, sceeeeeyouuuuse me!" Melinda snapped back. "Go

on."

"My boy." Lucy's voice was hard now. "Yes. My Lester. My son will avenge me." Her eyes squinted. "He'll pull back together my pieces of pride," she sagged just a little.

"He's smart. Strong and handsome, a fine Standard Poodle!" Her voice was shaky now.

As gently as she could, Melinda asked, "Pure-bred?"

"OK," Lucy hung her head. "Junkyard-dog-doodle!" She sat up sharply. Her eyes were fierce now, her voice steady and strong. "And I think that's fine!"

"Me, too," Melinda said. "He's a wonderful dog." Melinda searched Lucy's sad face and decided to take the chance.

"And all that's well and good," she said, "but how do you imagine he could ever beat Rufahlo?"

"Oh, Rufahlo," Lucy waved her paw dismissively. "Today's supernova, tomorrow's black hole. Someday, he'll retire. And when he does, Lester will have his chance."

"Would it be so bad if he wanted something different?" Melinda asked. "The show is not for everyone."

"I want him to want this," Lucy stomped her paw. "This is safe." She looked at the ground. "His father's life wasn't safe."

"Lucy, Lester doesn't want to be a show dog," Melinda said softly.

"Don't talk nonsense," Lucy replied but her heart wasn't in it.

"That's why he won't focus," Melinda said. "His heart wants something else and his head's growing into it."

Lucy cocked her head.

"I don't know what it is," Melinda said. "And maybe he doesn't either. But he will."

They sat quietly for a moment. Melinda had an idea.

"Ow!" she rubbed her forehead.

"Lucy, why do you insist on living through Lester? Why don't you take another chance? Look at you! You could still compete!"

"Oh, stop," Lucy waved her paw but Melinda knew she was pleased. "I'd feel silly prancing around at my age...."

"No you wouldn't!" Melinda knew she was right. "You'd love it! You know you would! You always did!"

"Oh...,"Lucy sighed. "I just can't."

"You mean you're chicken!" Melinda exclaimed.

"Am not!" Lucy said. "I'm too proud."

"Bwack, bwack, bwack," Melinda chicken-barked.

"Stop it!" Lucy snapped.

"Imagine you, too chicken to go up against the likes of Lili and Fifi," Melinda was laughing now.

"I am not!" Lucy snapped. "I just don't want to come in second or third to the likes of Lili and Fifi."

"Chick-chick-chick-en," Melinda got up and trotted toward the house.

"Stop it or I'll yank your tail right off!" Lucy followed.

"Winning or losing won't matter," Melinda wapped her tail and brushed Lucy's angry face. "You love strutting up and down, everyone looking. You'd have fun!"

"I would not," Lucy sniffed.

"Chicken!" Melinda hissed and bounded into the house.

"That's it! The tail's mine!," Lucy screeched and bounded after her.

Chapter Twenty-one

Two Shows That Week

Melinda was right. There were two shows that week, the first one that very day. Francine, the stylist, gasped in horror when she saw what had become of Lester's coat.

"How did you do that, just overnight?" she mused. "I'm going to have to use stronger spray."

Lester sighed. He went through all his usual paces of protest against the indignities of it all. As usual, Francine ignored his moods and worked on his hair. Lucy would sit at the head of the styling table, eyes blinking back emotion. She loved to watch the transformation. Francine made it look so easy. A few clips, a few fluffs, some strong spray and some expert work with a diffuser and Lester was, once again, the polished, high-style poodle Lucy knew he could be.

"I don't want to be a show dog, Mother!" Lester would say.

"I know, dear," Lucy used her hypnotic voice. "Just do it for mama."

All during the grooming and protesting phase, Rufahlo seemed quite anxious.

"Curious," thought Papillion. For some reason, thinking didn't hurt her the way it did the other dogs. She enjoyed thinking and did quite a lot of it.

"He always wins. Why would he worry about whether Lester goes or not?" she wondered. Twitching quietly at the edge of the crowd, Papillion watched them all in turn, Lester, Lucy, Rufahlo, back to Lester, and so on. Lester kept talking, Francine ignored him and continued her work. Lucy was almost chanting now.

"Do it for mama," she hummed, her voice buzzy and captivating. "Just do it for mama."

"Ma ma ma ma ma ma." The puppies seemed in a trance, chanting together in soft puppy voices.

Rufahlo seemed more and more anxious.

"Hmmm," Papillion thought.

"Oh, all right, Mother," Lester said, at last. "One last time."

Lucy turned away. Her smile was sly and triumphant. Papillion could swear she heard Lucy say "Score!" under her breath.

As soon as Lester said "Oh, all right," Rufahlo visibly relaxed. As the show preparations continued, he was his old self, bragging happily, flirting outrageously and posing for all to admire.

"Hmmm," thought Papillion. "He wants Lester to come. Why?"

From the other side of the room, Melinda, too, had watched the scene develop.

"Hmmm," she thought. "Ow!" she said and rubbed her forehead.

Watching the show was always fun. Francine sat in the stand, holding all their leashes, laughing and cheering as Day Care Guy trotted round the ring, first with Lester, whose mane bounced prettily as he pranced, and then with Rufahlo. Hums of admiration and approval filled the air when Lester pranced. Gasps of awe would greet Rufahlo.

"Oh, I wish our Friends were here," Lucy moaned. "Day Care Guy doesn't show well at all."

"He's doing fine with Rufahlo," Melinda said.

"And he gave Lester short shrift, I saw that too!" Lucy spluttered. Melinda rolled her eyes.

"Politics," Lucy hissed. "It's all politics and popularity! I wish Lester would play more to the crowd!"

Rufahlo was doing just that, zigging and zagging ever so slightly as he pranced around the ring, rippling all of his sculpted muscle groups in turn.

"Obedience," Francine clapped. "Here we go!"

A dozen dogs and their handlers stood around the ring. The judges, a man and two women, strode to the center of the circle.

The first woman spoke softly into her microphone.

"And now…the first command!"

With a dramatic sweep of one arm, the man gave the command.

"Siiiiiiiii….." he called, voice rising in pitch.

Lester sat. Rufahlo nodded slightly.

Papillion cocked her head, staring intently at the performance.

"…iiiiiiiiiiitttt…" the man intoned, hitting the 't' very hard. Rufahlo sat. His posture was proud, his aura calm.

"Uuuuuuu…" the man continued.

Lester flinched. The man wasn't finished! It wasn't sit, it was sit-up!

Lester sat up and coughed. Rufahlo glanced at him, panic in his eyes. Lester jiggled his paws up and up again.

"…uuuuuuuuuuup!" the man finished, spitting the 'p' and giving another flourish with his hand.

Rufahlo sat up and forced his frightened features into a show dog mask. He smiled at the crowd. They oooohed and aaaaahed and applauded.

"Hmmm," Papillion thought.

"Ow!" Melinda smacked her forehead.

"My Lester sat up first!" Lucy called to the judges.

"I think that's the problem," said Melinda, crossing and uncrossing her eyes to relieve the pain of thinking.

"Ah-haaaah," Papillion nodded to herself.

The judges held the microphones away from their faces. Papillion read their lips.

"A bobble!" said the first one. "That will cost him."

"Bobble-schnobble," said the man. "Look at him! He's magnificent!"

"Let's just give it to him anyway," said the other lady.

All three judges nodded, stroked their chins, and gave the

appearance of thinking things over very carefully.

At the end of the show, the result was what one expected. Rufahlo, once again, was Best in Show. Lester was rewarded with Best Bouffant and Bow. Everyone got treats and most went home happy.

"You must learn to wait for the command," the man judge told Lester. "You are too eager, my poodle. But so beautiful!" He fluffed Lester's mane.

"You really are, you know," Rufahlo said.

"Shut up," said Lester. "And sorry about the sit-up thing."

"I almost shed my coat," Rufahlo muttered. "But it didn't seem to make much of a difference."

"That's how much they love you," Lester said. "You could play dead and they'd still give it to you. You don't need me at all."

"I do, Lester, I do, don't say that," Rufahlo kept his show face on but his eyes were pleading.

"I know," Lester said. "Don't worry. And don't laugh when they call me beautiful."

"OK," said Rufahlo," and you're not, you know, not beautiful at all! You're handsome!" Rufahlo flashed his most engaging smile.

"And manly," said Lester.

"Very manly," said Rufahlo, " and you wear a nice bow!" The two boys cracked up and tussled each other.

"The hair!" Francine squealed. "Rufahlo! Don't muss his hair!"

Lester's 'do was the talk of that day's show. Francine received many complements on her work and several new grooming appointments were made.

"Ka-ching!" Francine was excited. "Oh, Lester! You're going to be my walking advertisement!"

"Uh oh," Lester said.

"Mm mm mm," Rufahlo shook his head.

A few days later, for the Thursday show, she created a new look.

"What shall we call this?" she mused as she admired their reflections in the mirror.

"How about 'my last shred of dignity gone'?" Lester replied to her smiling mirror image.

"That's too long," Rufahlo tried to be helpful. "Too hard to remember. A name should be short and snappy."

Lester growled at him and showed his teeth.

"No, no," Francine cooed. "Such a pretty dog should not be growling!"

Lester knew better than to growl at her. He stared at his reflection. Sorrow weighed down his heart. All of his efforts to be taken seriously as a strong, smart man-dog, gone, lost in the frou-frou and ribbons of Francine's handiwork. Today's show would be very hard to get through. And then, at the park…

"I hope none of the mean dogs come today," he sighed. "I don't think I could run fast enough.

Francine had divided his mane into hundreds of small sections. She had rolled and twisted and wrapped each section of hair into a charming little nubbin. Lester's head and body, even his ear and ankle poofs were covered with rows and rows of charming little nubbins. They stood up like seeds on a strawberry. The nubbin rows on his head varied in size and were arranged to resemble the crowns he had seen in pictures of human kings and queen. To make matters worse, she had tied a length of very thin ribbon around each of the nubbins on his head, making dozens of sweet little bows with long fluttery tails.

"They're blue, at least," Rufahlo said hopefully, "the ribbons…"

Lester didn't move, didn't speak. The sorrow paralyzed him.

"Princess Diana!" Francine clapped her hands. "That's what we'll call it! No, wait," she stroked the ribbon tails. After a moment, her skilled hands moved quickly.

"There we are," she said. "I'm glad I left the tails so long. Woven together, they look just like the veil she wore under her crown. That's what we'll call it! The Queen Victoria!"

Lester turned his mournful eyes to her.

"What's the matter, baby?" she said. She thought for a moment and then caressed the nubbins that formed his "crown."

"I know, I know, you're a boy," she said.

"Thanks for noticing," Lester's voice wobbled a little.

"You're not a princess or a queen, so what will we call this new style?" she asked.

"You look like Uncle Fester," Rufahlo said sadly. Uncle Fester was the puppies' favorite toy, a round, rubber squeak toy with a goofy face. Uncle Fester's body was covered with soft, floppy, rubber nubbins that the puppies loved to chew.

"Uncle Fester!" Francine exclaimed. She jiggled his head nubbins with an affectionate hand. "That's what we'll call it!"

Lester hung his head. Hoping to give comfort, Rufahlo nudged him with his paw.

Lester was a pro and took his responsibilities seriously. Although his heart still hurt, he put sorrow aside and moved through the paces of the show. His legs pranced high as ever, his posture was regal and he dutifully jumped the cues so Rufahlo could see them and follow.

"Why does he do that?" Lucy was exasperated.

"Hmmm," hummed Melinda. She shook her head to relieve the pain of thinking.

"A blind dog could see why," Papillion thought but didn't say anything.

Rufahlo took Best in Show, as expected, but all of the after-show attention came to Lester.

"What a gorgeous 'do!" the ladies ooohed and aaaaahed.

"Look, it's a tiara," one lady said. "Just like Princess Diana!"

"Well, no," Francine said, "I wove the ribbons together to make a veil. It's the Queen Victoria!"

"Oh, I see it now," another lady said. "She's just beautiful."

"He," said Francine. "He's a boy."

"He's just darling! And you're a genius! You must work on my baby and give her a new look. When can I have an appointment?"

"Ka-ching!" murmured Day Care Guy, smiling with pride and joy.

Francine made six new appointments that day.

"Oh Lester," she hugged him. "You're my hero!"

"I'm glad you're happy," Lester sighed. He meant it. Francine was nice and he was glad he could help. The Day Care Center needed all the help it could get.

"I think we'll leave this in for a few days," she cooed. "Let's see if we get more appointments."

That did not make Lester happy. He scratched at his head nubbins.

"No, sweetie, no," she said. "Let's keep it nice for the Dog Park."

Lester sagged. His sorrow returned. All week long, he had looked for Boss at the Dog Park but Boss was always out on walks with his Old Friend.

"If he's not there today, well, so much the better," Lester thought. "I can't let him see me like this."

Rufahlo came to his side and nudged him gently. Lester leaned on his friend and tried not to cry.

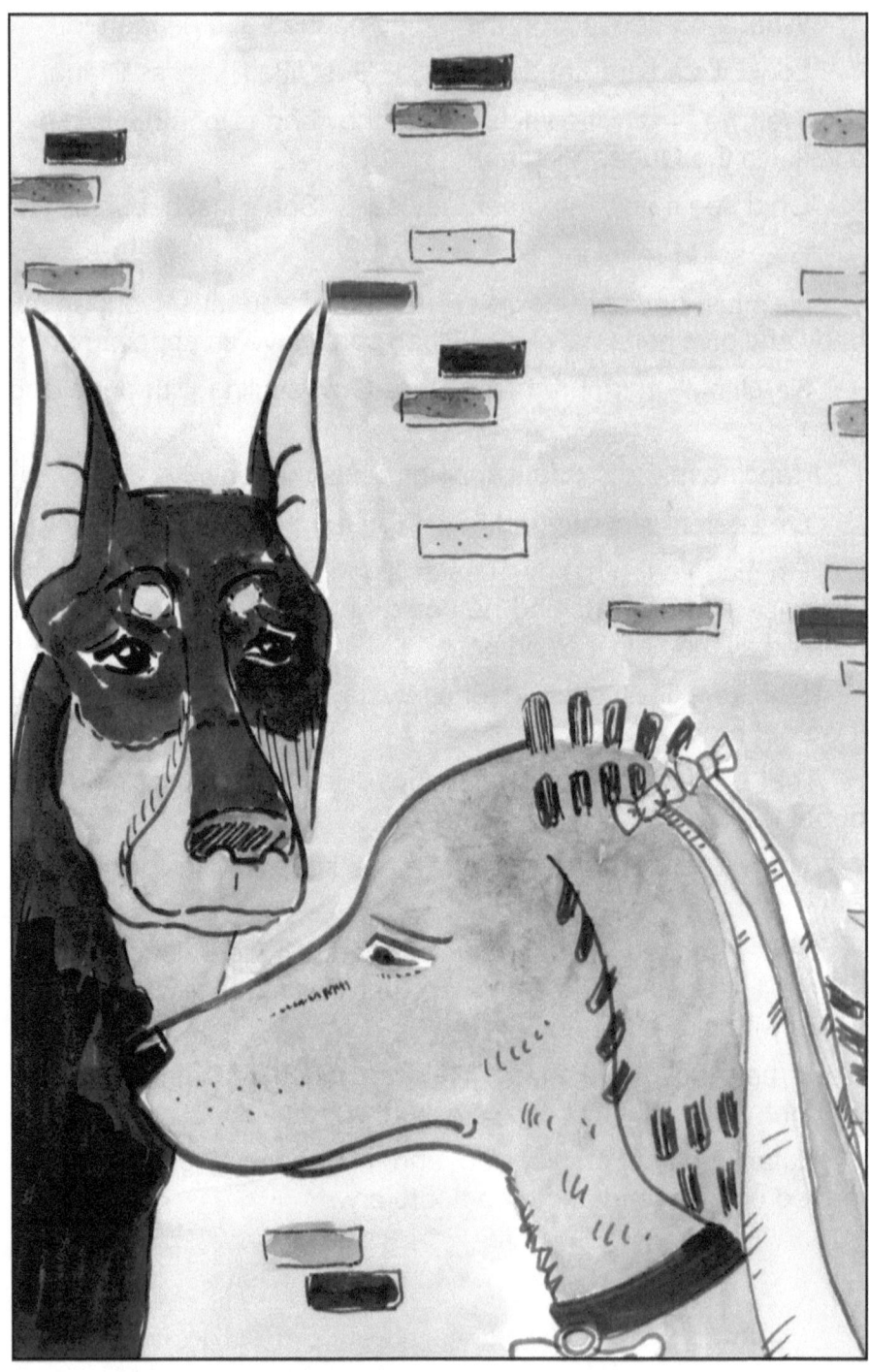

Lester's Worst Hair Day Ever

Chapter Twenty-two

Never Mind What You Look Like, Show Them What You Can Do

Randy and Bailiff saw Lester come into the Park.

"What the…?" Randy said.

"He looks like Uncle Fester," said Bailiff. "If Uncle Fester wore a blue babushka."

Lester bolted away from Francine and hid under a bush. Francine put her hands on her hips and called after him. When he didn't come, she turned back to the crowd of admirers already assembled and continued with the chatting about hair-do's and appointments.

"Well, let's go tell him," said Randy.

"Don't say anything about the hair," said Bailiff.

"I wouldn't know what to say," Randy started toward Lester's hiding place. "It's a good thing none of the mean dogs are here today."

"Hello there," Randy called.

"Hi guys," Lester mumbled. "Boss isn't here, is he?"

"No," said Bailiff, "but he said to say hello."

"Tell him I said hi back and I'll see him," Lester paused, "later."

Randy and Bailiff looked at each other. Randy cleared his throat.

"Interesting 'do. Did it take long to put together?"

"Leave me alone," Lester's voice was flat and lifeless.

"I know what Boss would say," Randy tried.

"Me, too," said Bailiff.

"What?" Lester asked, his voice small and sad.

"Never mind what you look like," Randy said.

181

"Just show them what you can do," Bailiff finished.

Lester didn't answer. An awkward silence filled a few seconds.

"Boss said we should help you," Randy said.

"Really? How?"

"Follow your nose," Randy said. "Train it and make it work for you."

Lester's spirits lifted a little. The big dog had thought of him and wanted to help. That made him feel good. He smiled weakly but said nothing.

"Remember that game you used to play with Spotty?" Bailiff asked.

"Spotty," the thought of his friend made him smile again. "We used to play Smell and Seek."

"Boss said we should put Smell and Seek together with one of our games," said Bailiff, "and use it for training exercises.

Lester peeked out from under the bush.

"What's your game?" he asked.

"Steal Things and Hide 'Em," said Bailiff.

"As opposed to Steal Things and Eat 'Em," said Randy.

"That's not really a game," said Bailiff. "I mean, we have to eat."

Lester crawled out from under the bush. He made sure the bush still hid him from Francine's sharp eye.

"How does it work?" he asked.

"You steal something and hide it," said Randy.

"I like small and shiny items," said Bailiff.

"They get all upset," Randy explained. "Then you make out like you found it."

"You get treats," said Bailiff. "Score!"

"Now, us," said Randy, "we can't do this too often. Someone might notice our 'no Friend' situation."

"But you could do it all day!" said Bailiff.

"But how does it work with Smell and Seek?" Lester was puzzled.

"That's the training part," said Randy. "This was Boss's idea. We steal the stuff and let you smell it."

"Then we go hide it," said Bailiff.

"When they get all upset, you go up to them and smell them. We take things like wallets, phones, keys, whatever we can get out of their pockets or purses," said Randy.

"Keys are tricky," said Bailiff. "They jingle."

"So when they get upset, you go smell their pockets or purses. We already let you smell whatever we stole, so you know what you're looking for," said Randy.

"You reinforce the smell by sniffing their pockets," said Bailiff. "Then follow the smell to where we hid it."

"Try to engage them, make sure they follow you," said Randy. "When you find it...."

"And you will," said Bailiff. "Follow your nose."

"You'll get treats," Randy finished.

"Which you might share with us," Bailiff was hopeful. "If there's enough."

"Sounds good," Lester was smiling now. "Let's go."

Francine was showing pictures she had taken at the show. Lester had refused to sit still and pose but, during the Obedience Test, she was able to get some good, focused shots of his head and back.

"He's adorable!" the ladies cooed. One put her big bag on the ground so she could take Francine's cell phone in both hands and hold it close to her near-sighted eyes.

"The Silent Stealth strikes!" Bailiff thought as he crept toward the bag. He put his head deep inside, pulled it quickly out again and trotted nonchalantly to the bushes where Lester waited with Randy.

"Pink," he said, offering the leather wallet. "Easy to see. And it was right next to a pack of spearmint gum. I almost took the gum."

"She wouldn't miss the gum," Randy snorted.

"Which is why I took the wallet," Bailiff retorted testily. "I'm off! Don't look where I go, that's cheating," and he was gone.

Lester kept his eyes closed while Randy watched the group.

"Right...about...now!" he said. Lester opened his eyes.

"Let me give you my card," the lady was saying while she picked up her purse. "You'll call me when you have an opening." Francine nodded and smiled while the lady dug through her bag.

"My wallet," she was puzzled. "Where...? My wallet! My wallet is gone!"

Francine and all the ladies chattered with excitement and concern. Lester ran full tilt up to the group and with a final, dramatic leap, landed before them with a thump loud enough to get their attention.

"There you are!" Francine said.

"What am I going to do?" the lady wailed.

Lester jumped up on his hind legs. He waved his front paws in the air. He had seen horses do this in cowboy movies Day Care Guy liked to watch.

"Oh, now you want to show off!" Francine smiled.

"All my bank cards, my driver's license," the lady wailed.

Lester jumped again on hind legs. This time he held his right paw back while he pointed his left paw right at the weeping lady. She stopped crying.

"Is he pointing at me?" she asked.

Lester dropped to all fours and went right for her purse. He was tall enough to get his chin over the lip and pull it down to get his head inside.

"What is he doing?" the lady cried.

"Looking for your wallet?" Francine asked, trying to cover the fact that she had no idea what he was doing.

Lester did the wild horse pose again and took off, nose to the ground.

"He's…" Francine was at a loss.

"Sniffing!" Day Care Guy finished for her. "He's got the scent of something and he's tracking it down!"

"Should we follow?" Francine asked.

"He's too fast," the lady dug some more through her purse.

Lester zigged and zagged around the park. His blue veil made him easy to see, even for the near-sighted lady.

He stopped at a group of low shrubs.

"Come on, man!" he said to Bailiff, who was crouched down behind the shrubs. "Give me a challenge!"

He picked up the pink wallet and balanced it gently between his teeth. As he ran back toward the ladies, he felt his legs stretch to their fullest. His leaps were long and dramatic. He felt good.

"Look!" cried the lady. Although near-sighted, she could still see colors at a distance.

"It's pink," said Francine. "He's got something pink!"

With a final leap a ballet star would envy, Lester landed neatly at their feet. He smiled and placed his prize gently on the ground.

"My wallet!" the lady screamed. "Oh, you wonderful girl!" She hugged him and cried.

"Boy," said Francine. "He's a boy."

"Whatever," said the lady. "He's a hero! And he's going to get a great big treat!"

She dug some more in her great big bag and pulled out what Lester knew had to be half a bacon sandwich left over from her lunch.

"Bacon!" he beamed. "Must share," he reminded himself.

He held the half sandwich in his mouth for a minute while all the people finished ooohing and aaaaahing and marveling at his genius.

"Please! Take my card!" the lady said to Francine. "I want the first appointment you have!"

His work here done, Lester turned and ran off to find Randy and Bailiff. Francine and Day Care Guy were too busy collecting calling cards to notice he was gone again.

"Bacon!" squealed Bailiff.

"Lucky dog!" Randy marveled.

"You two have it," Lester said. "I'm too excited to eat."

The Night Dogs eyes met briefly. They seemed to say to each other "What kind of crazy talk is this? Well, his loss!" Their heads bumped together over the sandwich. Their jaws locked on either end and they pulled it apart almost perfectly in half.

"I'm bigger," said Randy through the meat and cheese and tomato. "I should get more."

"Shut up," said Bailiff through the bread, avocado and sprouts.

"Who's next? " Lester eyed the playing field.

They kept it up all afternoon. They stole wallets and cell phones, billfolds and i-pods, money clips and pocket watches and, in one spectacular lapse in judgment, a bag of brand new ladies underwear with the store tags still attached.

"Stick to wallets," Lester came back treatless. "Ladies underwear. It looks a bit weird."

"Was she mad?" Randy asked.

"Oh, yeah," Lester said. "She thought I was going to eat them."

There was one very close call.

Angel wanted in on the game. He pled so hard that Randy and

Bailiff decided to give him a chance.

Very slowly, silently, the strange little dog crept close to a couple on a park bench.

"Nice approach," said Bailiff. "Good instincts."

"I don't know," said Randy. "What if they see him? He's…so…"

"Very odd," Bailiff finished.

"It's not what you look like," said Lester, "it's what you can do."

"Please don't turn around," Randy said to the couple on the bench.

Next to the man lay something shiny.

"Keys!" Angel thought.

"Keys!" Randy panicked.

"No!" Bailiff panicked.

The little pup's jaws closed around the prize and he stepped back. The keys jingled. The man turned.

"Hey!" he shouted. Angel froze with fear. The man grabbed the strange dog's odd looking ear. Angel twisted and the slimy tentacle slid out of the man's hand.

"What the…eeeeeeeew!" the Man rubbed his hand on the bench. Angel turned and ran for cover.

"Drop the keys!" Randy shouted.

"Drop them!" Bailiff screamed.

Angel, too frightened to think, forgot to drop the keys.

"Get him!" the Man ran after the slimy little dog.

"Go!" Randy said.

Lester burst from their bush hiding place. He traced a wide arc of fast and graceful leaps, drawing attention from the crowd and cutting off the Man's forward progress.

"That dog!" cried a lady. "He found my phone!"

"And my money clip," called a man. "He'll find what's missing!"

"I want the little, thieving…dog, if it is a dog," the Man growled.

"And when I find him...."

The Man set off again in the direction of Angel's flight. Lester cut across his path and sped toward Angel's smell. He found the little dog not very well hidden in a group of young trees.

"I'm sorry," Angel whispered.

"Don't worry," said Lester. "Give me the keys and go!"

"I lost them!" Angel's voice trembled.

"What?" Lester cried. In the not so far distance, he could hear the Man stomping and shouting.

"Quick!" Lester commanded. "Let me smell your jaws!" He made a quick once over of the little dog's face. "Got it!" he said. "Now go! Run!" Lester took off.

Angel couldn't move. His tentacles were focused on the sound of the Man's approach. Fear froze him to the spot.

"You!" the Man said, pointing at him and snarling. He moved forward. Angel cringed.

The Big Busy floated down from the tree tops. He aimed his robe to cover the shivering pup.

"What the...!" The Man himself was now shaken and fearful. The dog-maybe-not-a-dog had disappeared before his eyes. He blinked and felt his forehead. A jingle jangled behind him. It was the hero poodle with the keys in his mouth. The poodle set the keys down.

"Good dog," the Man's voice was shaky. "Good dog."

He picked up his keys and ruffled Lester's nubbins.

"Silly hair," he said, "for such a smart dog.

"I know," Lester said. "Let's go."

The Big Busy used his force field to pick the trembling puppy up and cuddle him in his spirit arms. He folded his wings around the shivering pup.

"I'm sorry," Angel cried. "I made a mistake."

"That's how you learn," said Busy. "Tomorrow, you'll do better."

He floated them to the tree circle and set Angel down on Old Friend's blanket.

"Rest now," he said. "Ask your friends to teach you more tomorrow."

"Thank you," Angel collapsed into sleep.

"It's what we do," Busy said softly.

By the end of the afternoon, Lester's veil had unraveled and the ribbon tails waved dramatically in the wind. The bows had come untied making the tails even longer. He posed proudly as Day Care Guy gathered the other dogs. Francine and many of his new admirers snapped his picture.

"There's one for the web site," Francine said proudly.

"It's not what you look like," Lester thought to himself. "It's what you can do. Look what I did! No one's talking about my hair now!"

He was wrong about that but it didn't matter anymore. He was proud of himself.

"I wish Boss could have seen me," he thought. "Where could they be? That's one very long walk!"

Chapter Twenty-three

Hundreds of Mimis, but No Bob

"A wondrous day! Let's wander!"

Old Friend stroked Boss's big head. "He's trembling..." Boss looked at the pale and wheezing old man.

"Come on," his Friend smiled. "Let's have a new adventure!"

They sat in the sun at a table in front of the doughnut shop run by very kind people. Old Friend had had a good wash in the bathroom. He smiled and waved to the kind people and went outside to Boss.

"There's no one else here," he said to the dog. "Maybe they won't mind if we sit for a minute and soak in some health-giving sun."

Apparently, they didn't mind at all.

"Slow day, yesterday," the kind man said when he came outside. He was holding a tray.

"Lots of left-overs," he put the tray down in front of Old Friend. "Would you like coffee?"

They feasted on day-old treats.

"Mmmm," hummed Old Friend as he chewed on a tea cake and sipped hot coffee.

"Yeah," Boss mumbled through a bite of ham and cheese croissant.

"We'll save a few for the boys and girl," Old Friend filled his pockets with dough-nut holes and muffins.

Fortified by food, they walked past the edge of their territory.

The sad and tatty neighborhood of the doughnut shop gave way to wider streets, neater lawns and more brightly colored houses.

"Isn't this nice?" asked Old Friend. "I wonder if there's a park?"

Eventually, they turned a corner and saw a wall of trees and shrubs and flowers.

"Excellent!" Old Friend said. "The entrance must be at the other end. Let's just take this short cut."

They pushed and picked their way through the shrubs and flowers. When they moved past the last big tree and saw the open, grassy field, they stopped dead in their tracks. Boss's jaw dropped. Old Friend's eyes opened wide. A broad smile filled his face.

"I've never seen anything like this," he said. "Look how cute they are!"

Boss was speechless.

The field was filled with Mimis, dozens of little round dogs with pointy ears, big wide-set eyes, and silly curlicue tails. Boss began to chuckle.

Dozens of well-dressed young people were there with their dogs. Some had seen them and were pointing, saying things to their friends.

"Best we stay back here," Old Friend decided. He went to the nearest bench and told Boss to lie down. "We're not members of this club," he said.

Together, they sat quietly and enjoyed the show. Soon, they were both giggling. Old Friend laughed out loud, wheezed and coughed, then wiped his eyes and laughed some more.

The little Mimis were just too funny. Dozens of little, round dogs, running and jumping, rolling each other, play-fighting, real fighting, and barking all at once!

Two well-dressed people pulled their fighting dogs apart.

"We're just playing!" said the one dog.

"Put me down!" said the other.

The people exchanged words and moved away from each other. They put their little dogs down. Within seconds, the two dogs were rolling and snarling again.

"Uh oh," said the one dog. "Here come's my Friend again!"

"And mine. Let's do something else," said the other.

"Look at that big dog!"

"Let's go!"

The two boy Mimis belted over to Boss. Their two owners froze with fear.

Boss sat up.

"Hi!" said the one.

"Hi!" said the other.

"Hello, there," said Boss and smiled.

"Can we smell you?" said the one.

"Wanna play?" said the other.

"Lucius! Come here right now!" the well-dressed lady called.

"Nothing doing," said the one. "She didn't bring treats today," he explained.

"Ah," said Boss.

"Kermit! Come!" a young man called.

"Later," said the other. "Come on! Let's play!"

Kermit threw himself at Boss. He bounced off Boss's solid body and rolled a bit.

"Whee!" he squeaked and threw himself again.

Boss chuckled and lay down. Lucius and Kermit jumped on him again and again, rolling and pawing and gnawing with glee. Half a dozen other Mimis soon joined in. Old Friend laughed so hard that tears came and he had to use his scarf to wipe his eyes.

Boss lay on his back and laughed as little dogs jumped on his belly, sniffed at his tail and licked his ears.

"Oh!" wheezed Old Friend. "I haven't laughed this much in a long, long, time!"

"I know," Boss gasped. "We should come here again."

When they saw how gently the big dog played with their babies, some but not all of the well-dressed people relaxed and turned back to their lattes and cell phones.

"Lucius!" The well-dressed lady stomped her high heeled shoe.

The heel sank into the lawn, causing her to stumble sideways.

"Lucius!" she shrilled.

"Maybe you better go," Boss said.

"Naaa," said Lucius. "She didn't bring treats. She can come and get me!"

All of the Mimis had worn themselves out laughing and playing. They were all lying down now, snuggled next to Boss, panting hard, tongues hanging out.

"Which one of you is Lucius?" Old Friend murmured as he gently pet the little dogs and looked at their collar tags.

"Here you are," he scooped up the squirming pup.

"Hey!" Lucius barked. "Put me..."

"Pipe down!" Boss used the quiet voice that still meant business. "You'll get us in trouble."

"Oh," Lucius stopped and looked sadly over Old Friend's shoulder.

"Time to go to Mama," Old Friend murmured, stroking the little dog's back.

"I wasn't done yet," Lucius whimpered as Old Friend carried him away.

"We'll see you again," said Boss. "Be good."

Cautiously, Old Friend approached the lady. As he came closer, she shrank smaller. Her face went pale and her rouge looked raw against her skin.

"Is this little prince your dog?" he asked, holding the puppy at arm's length toward her. "Is this Lucius?"

Without a word, she snatched the pup and cuddled him hard.

"Ow!" Lucius squirmed.

"I have a dog like this," Old Friend said.

"Oh, really?" she snapped. She looked around, eyes desperate.

"Terry!" she called and waved a frantic arm. "Terry! Wait!"

She turned and stomped away. Her heels sank into the grass with every step. As she strode forward, the shoes sprang back and slapped her feet, making a thwack, thwack, thwacking sound.

"Oh, well," Old Friend sighed. "I tried."

He sat back on the bench and pet the other puppies. His conscience bothered him now.

"Our little one," he said to Boss. Boss nodded. "She should be here."

"She belongs here," Old Friend mused, "or someplace like this. With people like these, young, well-dressed."

"With homes," Boss added.

"She had a home, she must have," Old Friend stroked Kermit's belly. "What happened? Why is no one looking for her?"

He sat up straight, put his hands on his knees and sighed.

"What will happen if they find her with us?" he said to Boss. "What if they think we stole her?"

Old Friend looked around and studied people in the park. The owners of the pups still at his feet seemed content to have someone else minding their dogs. No one was looking at them now, no one pointing.

"Her owner might come to a place like this to look for her," he thought.

He studied the faces, looking for someone alone and sad, someone searching for something that couldn't be found.

"No one here like that," he thought.

Bob had already gone.

He had come to the park to ask other members of the Frenchie Connection, as they called themselves, for advice. No one had much to offer. As he watched the little dogs play, his heart had ached for Mimi. When he could no longer bear it, he left. He posted his sad "Lost Dog" signs on the bulletin board at the park's entrance. Anyone coming into the Park by a shortcut would not have seen them. Old Friend led Boss out the way they came in so they never saw the sign. Two men and one big dog went home that night, hearts heavy, wondering what to do about little lost Mimi.

"We'll bring her here," Old Friend decided. "Maybe someone will know her."

Chapter Twenty-four

Trouble, Memories and Make-Overs

"Well, what have we here?"

Old Friend's voice was tired. Their walk today was the longest they'd had in quite a while. Finding their way back had been hard going. They had to stop for rest several times. The last stop was a bus stop bench. Breathing hard, Old Friend took note of their surroundings. They had come far enough to reach the edge of the tatty neighborhood. Further on was the doughnut shop where they had feasted this morning. They were on the right path but still had a long way to go. Twilight was gathering and the streets ahead were rough and unfriendly. For a while now, two young men had been following their same path. Although they stayed about 100 feet behind them, Old Friend could tell they had matched their pace to his own, coming no closer but falling no further behind. His policeman's instincts sparked. Unhappily, he noted that when he stopped, they stopped too. He stopped at a bench, a place to sit down, a place for the dog to lie down at his feet. Where they stopped, there was nothing, no reason to linger. Silently shifting their feet, they feigned interest in the tired, shabby street around them. One of them lit a cigarette.

"Loitering," Old Friend muttered, "with intent."

Under his cover of tired and muttering old man, he continued his fact-finding survey. He saw without looking, listened for clues and listed the facts in his head. At his feet, Boss was not so subtle. He stared fixedly at the two men and briefly flashed his teeth. The smoking man flinched and looked at the ground.

"Not so young," Old Friend thought. "Experienced. Lean and hungry. Willing to do harm to get what they want."

What could they possibly want? His floppy hat? His dirty coat? His dog? Without changing his face or moving his eyes, he smiled at the thought.

"Good luck with that," he muttered and stroked Boss's head.

Still staring at the men, Boss gave a long, low growl. The non-smoker coughed and tried to look casual.

Big motors rumbling and belching exhaust, a bus pulled round the corner and stopped. The doors opened. Old Friend waited. When the doors started to close, he said, "Now!" In an instant, man and dog were on the bus with the doors closed tightly behind them. The bus rattled away from the stop. Boss heard shouting. Old Friend didn't react. The bus driver glanced in his rearview mirror.

"Those two," he muttered and stepped on the gas. "Not a chance," he said. "I'm on a schedule!" he shouted. "Wait for the next one!" He gave it more gas and glanced in the rearview mirror again. "Ha!" Look at 'em run!"

"Trouble?" Old Friend asked.

"Always," said the Driver. "Don't need it. Nice dog." He smiled at Boss.

"He is," said Old Friend. "Better than he looks. To me, at least." He took a deep breath. "I must apologize," he said humbly. "I confess I have no fare."

"I figured that," said the Driver. "There's no one else here. I'll take you a few stops."

They rode together to the doughnut shop.

"I turn here," the Driver said, "and I think you go straight on."

"How did you know?" Old Friend was puzzled.

"My cousin owns this place," the Driver pointed at the shop. "He's talked about you. And your dog."

"Good talk, I hope," Old Friend was pleased but still cautious.

"You don't remember, do you?" the Driver asked. "Years ago, you were a cop. Big boy here was your partner. A very young dog then." He looked fondly at Boss. "A teenage boy dog. You saved my cousin from a beating. Those very guys."

Old Friend looked blank. Boss was relieved. They had worked hard to forget such things.

"Yeah, you saved him," the Driver went on. "But you got pretty beat up yourself. Real bad. But you got one guy and the dog got the other. My cousin made it to the phone and called for help. Those two went down and were put away for a long time. We didn't see you after that. I heard you went to the hospital. They said you'd been stabbed."

Old Friend's mind stirred. He couldn't remember specifics – just pain, long illness, losing...losing.... He couldn't finish the thought. He didn't want to remember such things.

"Years later, here you are," the Driver said. "And you still have your dog."

"I do," Old Friend smiled. The pain and loss melted away. "I still have my dog."

"It's nice to see you," the Driver said. "If I see you again and there's no one here, you can always ride with me."

The two life companions stood in front of the doughnut shop and watched the bus pull away. Old Friend waved. Boss wagged his stub of a tail.

"I still have you," Old Friend stroked the dog's big head.

"We have each other," said Boss, leaning hard against the old man's leg.

Old Friend felt completely refreshed. "Happiness will do that," he thought.

"Let's go, shall we?" he said. "Our pups will be waiting."

As if all that wasn't enough to make the day memorable, on the rough street leading to the dog park, a fluttering movement caught their eye.

"Ten dollars!" Old Friend exclaimed. "A fortune!" he picked it up. "How did it get here?"

Busy Angel's big shoulders sagged. He'd flapped his wings very, very hard to bring that bill to their attention. If he had a body, it would be very tired by now.

"Mission accomplished," he floated away.

They took their treasure into a Subway shop, holding the bill up to show they were paying customers. The kids smiled and made him two huge foot-longs stuffed with meat and cheese.

"More than enough to share," Old Friend said. "Everyone eats tonight!"

Even with the energy, happiness and anticipation of delicious food, the way back to the tree circle was still long and slow. Boss pulled very hard to get them up the last small slope to the entrance. Old Friend wheezed and stumbled and finally struggled through the low opening. He flopped down on his blanket and caught his breath.

"Strange," he thought. "They don't seem to notice the food. What's going on?"

"What's this?" said Boss. "What happened?"

"Well, what have we here?" Old Friend asked, his voice tired but happy. "A brand new dog?"

Ben smiled shyly and ducked his head.

"Ben?" Boss said, his face a question. "Is that you?"

Ben nodded and rubbed his nose with his paw. He wasn't used to attention, especially good attention, and he had had plenty that day.

"It's not a new dog!" Old Friend said and set the sandwich bags down on his blanket. Bailiff sniffed loudly and crept closer.

"Wait for it!" said Randy. "Let Ben have his due."
"It's you!" Old Friend couldn't believe his eyes. "It's really you!" He stroked

Ben's head and ears. Ben rolled over and offered his belly.

"Oh, how I wish someone could talk!" Old Friend rubbed the belly and scratched Ben's ears. "This must be quite a story!"

"Tell me," Boss coaxed.

"I...well, I..." Ben started.

"I'll tell it," said Jerry. "Enjoy the pets."

Now that the ice had been broken, Ben and Jerry settled into a comfortable routine. Every day, when the Day Dogs arrived, they would romp and play with the three fancy girl dogs. Everyone enjoyed their games of "chase me 'til you roll me" and "jump over my head." After checking to see that the play was for fun, the humans stopped watching and they could play with wild abandon. The girls were small and not used to exercise so it didn't take long to tire them out. Eventually, the little twitchy one would wander off to find the Doberman. Ben would sit with Lili and Fifi with Jerry. They would pant and chat together, go drink some water, then lie down to chat some more. Some days, they would rest until ready, then the play and pant cycle would start again. Other days, when the sun was warm and the winds were quiet, they would spend most of their time resting, rolling on the grass, and telling each other stories.

Today had been a roll in the sun day. It was more than warm, it was hot. They were quite content to lie on the grass and watch Lester's antics.

"Look! He's got something pink!" said Lili.

"What is that?" said Fifi. "What's he doing?"

"It's called 'steal things and hide 'em'" said Ben.

"We play it sometimes," said Jerry. "You get treats. Watch."

"Look!" said Lili. "He dropped the pink thing in front of that lady!"

"She's hugging him!" said Fifi. "And..." she paused and squinted.

"Now, he gets a treat," Jerry finished for her. The lady pulled something big from her bag. Lester trotted away, holding the something in his mouth.

"Probably going to share that with Randy and Bailiff," Ben said.

"Lucky dogs," Jerry sighed.

"Boss said to teach him," Ben explained. "It's for training."

"He wants to be a service dog," said Jerry.

"We know," said Lili. "His mother doesn't want that."

"She wants him to be a Show Dog, like Rufahlo," said Fifi.

"He doesn't want that," said Lili. "He hates the hairdos."

"Well, I hate that one," said Jerry. "It's just stupid."

"Where's his mother?" asked Ben. "Doesn't she come to the park?"

"She does," said Lili, "but she stays with the humans and sulks."

"She doesn't like to see him wreck his hair," said Fifi. "She's a witch."

"Sounds like it," said Jerry.

They watched in silence for a while. After a cycle or two, the girls saw the pattern. The Corgi or the Border Collie would sneak up to a human. Quick as cats, they'd snatch something from a purse or bag or even a pocket and be off with it. Lester would smell the thing and wait. The other dog would disappear. After a few moments, Lester would sniff the air, the ground, then the air again and be off. It never took long for him to re-appear, carrying the something in his mouth. He would approach the human slowly and drop the thing gently at their feet. Squeals of joy, hugs and pets and treats would follow. After a short time, presumably spent consuming the treat, they would re-appear and the whole thing started again.

"Sweet!" said Lili.

"It is," said Ben.

"We play it sometimes," said Jerry, "when we're really hungry."

"Not today, I hope," said Fifi. "I had a big breakfast and just want to lie in the sun."

"We're not that good at it, anyway," said Jerry.

"Not half as good as Lester," said Ben. "Boss said so himself. He should be a service dog, he'd be great at it. If that's what he wants to be…"

"Oh," said Lili. "He wants it."

In warm and happy silence, they watched the show. Ben thought about what he wanted. Wistfully, he said, "Tell us about your homes." It was his favorite subject and he never tired of hearing about it.

"And your families," said Jerry. "We never had one."

"What's it like?" Ben asked.

Lili took a deep breath.

"Well, there's a mommy and a daddy," she started.

"Or two mommies," said Fifi, talking about herself.

"Or two daddies," said Lili, talking about Rufahlo.

"Or more, or less, sometimes it's just one person. That's the best," said Fifi. "You have them all to yourself."

"Sweet," sighed Ben.

"And sometimes there are children," said Lili, "or cats."

"Nasty," Ben muttered.

"Not always," said Jerry. Ben cocked his head and looked at him.

"Oh, they're ok," said Fifi. "Leave their food alone and they'll just ignore you."

"If there's no children," Lili went on, "then you're the child. That's the best!"

"Hugs! Pets! Treats!," Fifi squeaked.

"And you eat and play and sleep," said Lili.

"What's your job?" Ben asked. "Randy says a dog needs to do a job."

"I don't know," said Jerry. "We had jobs. Wasn't great."

Lili raised her brows at Ben.

"My face," she said, hissing the "c" in face. "My face is my job, honey."

"And my hair," said Fifi.

"So people look at you? That's your job?" Ben asked. As many times as he'd heard it before, Ben could not get his mind around the concept.

"Sweet," said Lili. She paused. "Isn't it?"

Ben wasn't sure. Lili herself sounded doubtful.

A few moments passed.

"Isn't it..."Jerry searched for words. "Kind of...passive?"

"You mean boring?" Fifi asked.

"Well...yes," Lili said. Both girls sagged a bit.

"But we get lots of pets," said Fifi.

"And treats," said Lili.

Sounds like heaven to me," Ben sighed. "How I wish," he went on," but no one wants to look at me." He put his head down on his paws.

"Or me," said Jerry sadly.

"Maybe when we go to heaven, we could get reincarnated," Ben said, a smile coming back to his voice. "We could be fluffy little poodles or Bee-Zone Free-zays or something." He gave Lili a playful swat.

"No," Jerry said. "My mind is made up. I want to be...." He paused and took a deep breath. "A cat."

"Dude!" Ben's head snapped up.

"I can't believe you said that," said Fifi. "Lili? It's time!"

"Ok! Ok!" Lili was excited. "Listen up. We've been thinking..."

"Ow!" said the boys and slapped their heads.

"I know! I know!" said Fifi. "It really hurts but Papillion helped us and we've decided!"

"We want to be service dogs too!" said Lili.

"We want to do something!" said Fifi.

"So we looked around," Lili went on, "and asked ourselves 'what are our best talents? How could those talents be of service?'"

"You two are OK, you could get a good home," said Fifi. The

boys cocked their heads. No one had ever said that before.

"You're just going about the whole 'find a good home' thing the wrong way," Lili explained.

"So we're going to help you," said Fifi.

"We're going to give you..." Lili paused for dramatic effect. The two girls' eyes met. They took a deep breath.

"Day Eye for the Night Guy Make-Over!"

They squealed and shrieked and rolled on their backs, kicking their legs in the air. Ben and Jerry's eyes made contact.

"Please!" said Ben's eyes. "Let's do this!"

"What?" said Jerry's. "What are they talking about?"

"Grooming. Accessories. Deportment," said Fifi.

"Huh?" the boys said.

"Behavior," said Lili. "But first, grooming! You need a bath, mister!"

"A what?" Ben asked.

"Papillion can spell it out," said Fifi. "We need two big dogs to help."

"I'm a big dog," said Jerry, "and I don't mind getting wet."

"Good," said Lili. "Let's get Papillion. If she comes, Rufahlo will help and he can be the other big dog."

Chapter Twenty-five

A Brand New Dog!

Once again, Rufahlo found himself fascinated. Speechless! The little dog's brains and leadership! So impressive!

"And," he thought to himself, "I'll just say it. She's so bossy!"

Papillion had quick-marched the little group to the far side of the decorative man-made lake.

"No people over here," she said. "If we upset the ducks, no one will notice."

"Ducks!" said Jerry.

"Yeah!" Ben chimed in.

"Forget the ducks!" Papillion snapped. "Leave them alone. We have work to do and we don't need humans flapping around about some ducks!"

"Look at them!" Rufahlo mused, dutifully trotting along behind the group. "Five times her size and still she dominates them!" He chuckled. "Look at me!" he thought. "One hundred times her size and I'm following orders too! A natural leader! So impressive!" He smiled at the sight. Two big, rough, street dogs and another strange little stray, meekly taking their cues from a tiny, twitchy girl and her fancy girlfriends. "This will be fun," he thought.

When they reached the far side of the lake, Papillion took them to a quiet spot hidden behind some large stands of lake grasses.

"Here," she said. "We have everything we need."

She turned to face them and barked instructions.

"You," she said to Ben. "In the water. Now! A quick dip, them come out and shake yourself off. We need hair that's damp, not saturated."

Ben hesitated.

"Don't be afraid, dude," said Jerry. "It's not deep."

Rufahlo stepped up.

"We all go," he said. "We jump together! Ready? Go!"

The three boys belly-flopped into the murky water. After such a long time in the sun, the cold water was a pleasant shock. Ben dunked his head. Jerry paddled after some ducks.

"Me, too!" Angel threw himself into the water.

"Oooo, oh! Deeper than I thought," he gasped and flailed to stay afloat.

"What an odd looking dog," Rufahlo thought. "Or…is it a dog at all?" He had heard stories. He would make discrete inquiries. "Later."

"Leave the ducks alone!" Papillion barked. "Come out now!"

Angel gasped and gulped and struggled to shore with the three other boys.

Following her instructions, the boys gave themselves very vigorous shakes.

"Oooo," Lili giggled when the spray hit her face.

"Ow," Fifi spluttered as the spray got up her nose.

"Again!" Papillion barked. "Shake!" She twitched and fell over. Rufahlo caught her with a paw and set her right again.

When she was satisfied that Ben's fur was the desired state of merely-damp-not-wet, she gave the next instruction.

"Here," she led them to a stand of weeds. The weeds were topped with balls of tiny white pods and flowers.

"Roll in this," she told Ben. "Rub the flowers and pods all over your body. The pods have a milky juice that's like soap. Roll! Rub!" she barked.

Ben rolled and rubbed and dragged himself on his belly through the stand of weeds. Angel followed his every move.

"I want a bath too," he said. "I've never had one."

"Me, neither," said Ben. "Not a proper one, with soap."

"If it cuts the slime a bit," said Jerry, "that would be good."

"Am I slimier now?" Angel asked. "More than before?"

"Little bit," said Jerry.

"Less talking!" Papillion barked. "More rolling!"

After the two dogs had completely flattened the stand of weeds, Papillion made them lie down on their stomachs. "Rub!" She pointed Jerry and Rufahlo towards Ben while she worked on Angel with Lili and Fifi.

"Rub the milky juice deep into their fur," she demonstrated, rubbing her tiny paws on Angel's butt.

"Lucky dog," Rufahlo sighed.

"Rub 'til you see bubbles," she said. "We might need more water."

"I've an idea!" Jerry slapped his forehead. He ran to the lake, took a mouthful and sprayed it all over Ben. Rufahlo did the same and then the same again for Angel.

"Allow me, ladies," he said and sprayed.

"Thanks," said Lili.

"Yes," said Fifi. It's bad enough my paws are all gooey but I really can't get my hair wet."

They rubbed and rubbed 'til Angel and Ben were all gooed over with the juice.

"A bubble!" Papillion squeaked and fell over. She got up and examined Ben closely. "There!" she said. "A bubble! On to the next step."

She told Ben and Angel to get back into the water and walk or swim across the lake.

"We need a thorough rinse," Papillion explained, "so make sure to dunk your heads and more than once!"

"Okeeey," Ben was still nervous about the water.

"Come on, dude," said Jerry.

"Us boys go together," said Rufahlo.

They waded in. The girls began their trot around the lake to the other side.

Soon, Angel's legs could no longer touch bottom and he

started to swim.

"Dude, are you shrinking?" asked Jerry. "You were almost up to my chest before and now you're not."

"I'm not?" Angel asked.

"I'm not sure," said Ben, "but I think your back legs are shorter than your fronts."

"They weren't like that before," said Jerry.

"Hmmmm," Rufahlo thought. "Ow!"

Angel had been paddling like a seasoned water dog. Hearing their assessments, he began to worry. His strokes struggled.

"I'm going to dunk," he said.

"Me, too," said Ben and they both went under water.

Shaking his head in the cold, sweet water, Angel made a list.

"I'm shrinking, my back legs are shorter, my coat's more slimy…" He struggled to the surface and gasped for air.

"Are my…" he spluttered. "Are my ears bigger?"

Jerry cocked his head. "Yeah," he said. "Little bit."

"They are," said Ben, "I can see it now."

Angel's heart sank and dragged him below the surface.

"Evolution," he thought as the bubbles of air left his mouth. "It's really happening…" He sobbed in some water and started choke.

"Maybe it's better this way." Bubbles of air left his lungs. "I'll go back to heaven and start over…hey!"

Something lifted him up and up and all the way out of the water. He choked and coughed and spluttered and wiped his eyes with his paws.

"You're a good swimmer," said Rufahlo, "but you must train your muscles, build your endurance. Rest now and ride on my back."

"Put him on mine," said Ben. "We'll dunk and rinse together."

Gently, they made the transfer and Angel clung to Ben's neck.

"Thank you," he whispered.

"May I ask a question?" said Rufahlo. His curiosity had overwhelmed him and the inquiries would not be discrete.

"You're a very ...unusual dog," he said, carefully. "Are you, by any chance...um...well, I've heard of earth-dog-space-alien mutants...." The little dog flinched. Rufahlo was sorry he asked.

"I don't know," Angel fibbed. "I don't remember." He laid his head weakly on Ben's neck. "Randy says I am..." he whispered.

"And Bailiff says that's all a load of poop," Ben snorted. "He says Randy's crazy."

"Which he is," said Jerry. "You're a dog. You went to the vet, something happened, that's all. You're some weird new breed that I've never seen but you're a dog!"

Angel hugged tightly on Ben's neck.

"Thank you," he said softly. He knew they weren't correct but their kindness soothed his heart.

"We're almost there," Rufahlo said. "One last dunk and rinse!"

The four boys went under together and wriggled through the water. Angel let go of Ben and swam the rest of the way to shore.

When Angel was out of earshot, Rufahlo turned to the others.

"They make breed like that on purpose?" he asked softly. "What were they

thinking?"

"No idea," Ben said.

"Beats me," said Jerry.

"I heard that!" Angel called from the shore.

"See that, dude?" Jerry called back. "You are a dog!"

"His hearing is phenomenal," Ben said to Rufahlo. "Maybe that's what they were going for."

"And he's a good swimmer," said Rufahlo. "We should make a name for the breed," he said. "That will boost his self-esteem."

"I don't know," said Jerry.

"Where to start?" asked Ben.

"Never mind," said Rufahlo. "We ask the Papillion." He couldn't help but sigh when he said her name. The boys looked at him.

"She'll think of something," he said quickly. "It doesn't hurt her head to think."

Jaws dropped.

"I know!" Rufahlo stage-whispered. The boys shut their jaws.

"Wow," said Ben.

"Powerful," said Jerry.

"Tell me about it," said Rufahlo and they muscled up the last few yards to dry land.

Back on shore, Papillion took the lead once again.

"You," she said to Angel. "Just run around and air dry. You'll fluff back up in no time."

Angel saw Randy and Bailiff engaged in some sort of game with Lester. "I'll play too," and off he went.

Papillion pointed to a bed of purple flowers.

"Roll in that," she instructed. "It will make you smell nice."

Ben rolled and rubbed and the air filled with the scent of lavender.

"Lovely," said Lili.

"Very nice," said Fifi.

Next she had him lie down on his belly.

"Now," she said, "we girls will give him a comb out. Not you," she said to the boys. "You just watch. Our paws are small and it won't hurt so much."

The three girls pulled their paws through Ben's matted, tangled fur.

"Ow! Ow" Ben squawked.

"Hang in there, dude," said Jerry.

"You're doing great," Rufahlo encouraged.

"What are you girls doing?" a lady's voice asked, her tone disbelieving.

"Uh oh," said Lily.

"Francine!" said Fifi. "Why aren't you all café latte with Day Care Guy?"

"I've…almost…got…this one!" With a final, mighty pull, Papillion ripped out a big knotted mass of Ben's fur. He flinched and squawked with pain. The force of the pull knocked Papillion backwards and she rolled into Rufahlo's leg.

"And why is this poor dog letting you do it?" Francine cooed as she sank to her knees. Gently, she stroked Ben's damp head. He leaned against her thigh and begged for more.

"What a sweet dog," she murmured, "to let you play on him like that. Another dog would have eaten you for lunch!" she told the girls in her no nonsense voice.

"And he smells like lavender soap," she said with approval. She rubbed Ben's back.

"Hmmmm," she said, feeling the knots and tangles. Recovered from her roll, Papillion trotted over and dropped her clump of knots on Francine's knee.

"Oooooh," said Francine. "I see…I think. Oh, girls, you'll never get them out like that. It would take forever and hurt his skin. Isn't that right, boy?"

"Yes," Ben moaned. "It really hurt."

"Let's see what I can do," she reached into her pocket, "with these!"

She whipped her favorite pair of trimming scissors out of the pocket and twirled them like a baton. She tossed them into the air and they landed in perfect position in her hand.

"Stand back," Lili said.

"She's in the zone," Fifi said.

"Watch the magic," Papillion twitched and fell over.

The three girls, Rufahlo and Jerry watched in awed silence. Ben closed his eyes and hoped for the best.

Her artist's hands and nimble fingers moved too fast for the dogs to follow the action.

"It's all a blur," said Lili.

"Of fur," said Fifi. "Everywhere!"

Clouds of hair clumps filled the air and billowed in the breezes. Francine's hand flew over Ben's body, snipping, clipping, shaping.

"There," she said at last. "That's better."

"It is!" said Fifi.

"Dude," said Jerry. "You look awesome!"

"Wait!" said Lili. She nosed her snout into Francine's purse and pulled out something blue.

"Perfect!" Francine said. She rolled the blue bandanna into a tube and tied it around Ben's neck.

"There you are," she said. "You're so handsome!"

"You are!" said Lili.

"Yes! Really!" said Rufahlo.

"Man!" said Jerry. "Dude! You look…"

"You look," said Francine, "like a …."

Her face changed. Fear filled her plump, pretty features.

"Like a completely different dog!" She gasped. "Oh! What have I done? Where's your owner? Oh!" she flapped her hands. "Oh, girls! What have we done?"

"Owner talk!" said Jerry. "Let's go!"

"Thank you," Ben licked her face.

"I'm sorry! I'm so sorry!" she cried, "I couldn't stop myself!"

"If you were my Friend," said Ben, "I'd love you forever." He licked her again. Jerry was already moving away. Ben trotted off to follow.

"Come on, girls!" Francine was in full panic mode. She scooped up Lili and Fifi and stuffed Papillion into her bag.

"Let's get out of here before his owner finds us and kills us! Rufahlo! Come!"

She hustled away as quickly as one could while holding three little squirming girl dogs.

"Tomorrow!" called Lili.

"Accessories," called Fifi.

"You look great," called Rufahlo. "Like a top show dog champion!"

Papillion felt quite satisfied with her day's work. She smiled and snuggled deep into Francine's bag and fell asleep.

"Wow!" Boss chuckled. "That's quite a story! Sounds like someone likes you!

Ben blushed and rubbed the ground with a paw.

"Someone nice likes you," said Jerry. "That's better."

After all the pets and excitement, Old Friend turned his attention back to the overstuffed foot-longs.

"This is going to be quite the job," he said. "Good thing the bread is soft."

With practiced hands, he tore each sandwich into four equal parts.

"Now I know this isn't exactly fair to the bigger dogs," he said, handing out the pieces. "Maybe the little dogs will have some leftover to share."

"Don't count on it," said Mimi, "I'm starving!"

"Just go ahead," said Boss. "We had doughnuts today."

"And we had so many treats," said Bailiff. "I think I can share some of this."

"Never mind," said Ben. "I'm too excited to eat."

Randy and Bailiff exchanged glances. It might make sense, coming from a day dog like Lester. But a night dog, always hungry, always on the lookout for food, too excited to eat?

"That's crazy talk," said Randy.

"Save it for later," said Bailiff.

"I'll have it," said Jerry.

Ben had changed his mind and the sandwich bit was already gone.

Angel ate more slowly than the rest. First he licked each individual element, the meat, the cheese, the bread, even the lettuce and the sprouts.

"Sometimes, I wish I had a body," Busy Angel said. "Eating looks like fun."

"That's desire," Angel spoke through a mouthful of cheese. Busy Angel snorted and waved a dismissive spirit hand.

"If you're not careful, that could turn into envy," Angel teased. He took the end of a slice of roast beef in his teeth and very slowly, bit by bit, pulled the rest of it into his mouth.

Busy Angel harumphed and looked away. Angel giggled and made smacking sounds with his lips.

From somewhere deep in one of his several bags, Old Friend pulled out a sheet.

"My new, clean boy shouldn't sleep on the dirt," he said. "At least for one night."

He spread the sheet out next to the tartan blanket.

"Here, boy," he said to Ben. "And the rest of you cuddle in where you can."

Soon they were all asleep, Boss and Old Friend on their blanket, Ben on the edge of the sheet closest to the blanket, and all the others crowded round him.

"Nice and warm," thought Ben.

Angel placed himself on the edge of the sheet. When the only sound left was breathing, snoring and the occasional fart, he got up and crept softly over to Busy Angel's spirit feet.

"What's happening to me?"

He wanted to be strong and demanding but his little whisper was more like a prayer.

"Evolution," said Busy Angel. "I told you. It will take a few days."

"Why?" Angel cried. "Why? I'm a dog!"

"You weren't meant to be," said Busy, a note of regret in his spirit voice. "Don't look at the eyes," Busy reminded himself. "Avoid the eyes at all cost!" Recovering his composure, he continued in his voice of authority.

"We can't change what is written," he said but slipped again. The note of regret was loud and clear.

"You can't look at me, can you?" Angel whimpered.

Busy's spirit eyes examined the trees.

"I'm a dog! Why change me now?" Angel whined. "It's so inefficient!"

Busy sighed. His head dropped, his eyes closed and his halo tilted off axis.

"We can't change what is written."

"I did," Angel said.

"And look what happened," said Busy. He chanced a look at the puppy eyes. "Big mistake," he thought, as regret turned to sorrow in his spirit heart. His two-tiered wings sagged. The puppy trembled a bit.

"There won't be much to guard when I have no legs and no hair and can't do much except slither through the dirt," he murmured.

"And eat," said Busy. "You still get to eat. All God's earthly creatures get to eat."

He meant well but it sounded hollow. The puppy looked down and scraped the earth with a paw.

"Look at the bright side," Busy tried. "This could be a good thing! You'll be a very tiny creature with a short life span. One big shoe and boom! You're back in heaven and ready to try again!"

Angel was not comforted. "So inefficient," he murmured. He turned his heart-melting eyes away from Busy and gazed at the man and the pile of sleeping dogs.

"I want that!" His voice was soft but fierce with ambition and desire.

"I'm a dog," he said. "I want to be useful and bring joy to someone's heart." He stood up and stretched. His short back legs held his butt just barely off the ground.

"I want to be one with my person," he said. "I'd help them, like Boss does. I'd be their reason to go on living."

"Doglike thoughts," said Busy. "Very noble."

A deep rumble filled the sky.

"Thunder?" Busy thought. "There aren't any clouds..."

Angel's back legs shivered and itched. He turned and gave them a chew.

"Dude!" whispered Jerry. His sleepy eyes open, he lifted his head up off his pillow, which was Ben's hind leg. "You're legs!" he whispered. "They grew!"

Angel stretched again. It was true! His back legs were longer now and held his butt higher off the ground. He stared at Busy.

"Dog-like thoughts," said Busy. "Thoughts become action."

Angel grinned from ear to ear and stretched his still short back legs. They weren't fully restored but they were definitely longer.

"Swimming!" said Jerry. "We'll do it again tomorrow! Like Rufahlo said, build up your muscles, train for endurance!" He put his head back down.

"And food," he murmured, "more food. Growing dog needs food. Fun..." and Jerry was snoring again.

"Dog-like thoughts," said Busy.

Still grinning, Angel moved back to the dog pile. Confident of his dryer, cleaner coat, he snuggled between Ben and Boss.

"You're learning," said Busy. "Education is good. Opens doors..." He paused. He was going a bit far. He was there to guide and protect after all, not to interfere. He chose his words carefully.

"If I were a new dog," he said, "I'd go have a chat with that poodle. Get a different perspective. Broaden the horizons."

"I could thank him," mumbled Angel. "He saved me from the Angry Key Man."

"Good thought," said Busy. "Good dog thoughts."

Someone farted and Angel drifted off to sleep.

Chapter Twenty-six

More Brand New Dogs and a Newly Discovered Talent

The next day, Francine was still so upset she didn't want to go to the park at all.

"What if he hates it?" she cried. "What if his owner hates the new look? Oh, why did I do it?"

"Don't worry," soothed Day Care Guy. "Come to the park. Have some lattes. I'll tell you what I know about that dog.

Jerry asked Rufahlo to help and together they marched Angel to the far side of the lake.

"Practice," said Rufahlo. "You must practice every move. Practice builds strength and endurance. We swim together now and see how far you get before you sink."

Angel jumped in and started swimming. He kicked his back legs out as far as they could stretch.

"I'm a dog!" His concentration was complete. "I'm a water dog! I love swimming!"

Jerry and Rufahlo waded in and walked behind him.

Two thirds of the way across, Angel gasped and sank.

"Good!" said Rufahlo, lifting him out of the water on his back. "Farther than yesterday. Good! Ow! Watch the nails! Your back leg almost got my jugular!"

"Are they longer?" Angel asked Jerry.

"Little bit," Jerry said. "I think."

Angel caught his breath, jumped back in and swam the rest of the way.

"Good! Good effort!" called Rufahlo.

When they reached the shore, the little dog was stretched out flat and panting.

"They are longer, dude," Jerry said. "I can see it!"

Angel kicked his growing legs in the air and danced for joy.

After a thorough shake, they went to join Ben and the girls. Lili was fussing with Ben's blue bandanna collar.

"Grooming," said Lili. "We covered that yesterday. Very important."

"Now, accessories," said Fifi. "Try these on. I stole them from Francine's bag. Spiky for you...."

"No!" Jerry cried. "No! I don't want to be spiky!"

"What?" Fifi was startled. "Why?"

"It's stylistically consistent with your overall look," said Lili.

Jerry looked at the collar, the shiny black leather, the studs, metal stars, the sharp and angry spikes.

"No!" he cried. "No, I don't want that. I don't want to be that guy!"

"You look like that guy," said Lili.

"That's the problem," Jerry was crying now. Shocked, the girls looked at each other in silence.

"I'm a big, mean-looking, scary dog. People don't like me," he sniffled. "I don't need a scary collar to make it worse. I'm not mean! I don't want to be scary...."

His voice trailed off. The sorrow weighed him down. He lay on the ground and closed his eyes. "Bad people want a mean, scary dog. I can't go there again. Can't do it."

The girls looked at each other.

"Well," Fifi said, "the only other choice I have is sparkly...."

"Yes!" Ben jumped to his feet. "I want sparkly! Please, let me be sparkly!"

"All right," Fifi sighed. "Stylistically, it's completely inconsistent but...."

Jerry lay back down and Lili helped Fifi connect the Velcro bits on the ends.

"Wellllllll…" Lili said.

"It works," Fifi's tone was firm. "You're Mr. Sparkly!"

Jerry smiled. His breathing calmed. "I wish there was a mirror," he said shyly.

"Oh, look at that!" a human girl voice said.

A young couple had stopped a few feet from their group.

"Look at the pit bull!" she laughed. "Such a mean-looking dog but he's got a rhinestone collar, how pretty!"

She bent down and stretched her hands toward the group.

"Come here, boy," she said.

"Who, me?" Jerry was stunned. This had never happened before.

"What's the matter, big, boy," she cooed. "Are you shy?"

"She means you," Ben encouraged.

"Get over there," Fifi snapped. "Make friends!"

Cautiously, Jerry approached.

"Careful," said the young man, stepping back.

Jerry stopped. The girl made a fist and stretched her arm a little closer to Jerry.

"Come on, big boy, have a sniff," she said. "Let me see your pretty collar."

Jerry crept closer and carefully sniffed her hand. It smelled like peanut butter. In a heady rush of joy, Jerry forgot himself and gave the hand a thorough, gentle licking.

"See?" the girl turned to the young man. "He's just a little love muffin! Come here, big boy!" She gave Jerry's back some long, smooth strokes. Jerry leaned against her legs and began to cry again.

"A mean dog would never look so pretty," she scratched his ears.

"Bye bye, big baby, have a nice day," she said, planting a kiss on Jerry's forehead. She strolled away, holding hands with her young man.

"That guy," Jerry sniffled. "The guy she saw. Mr. Big Baby Sparkly Love Muffin. I wanna be that guy."

"Well, that's it then," said Fifi.

"Mr. Sparkly you are," said Lili. "That means you," she turned to Angel. "You have to be Mr. Spiky."

"OK!" Angel was happy to be included.

Lili and Fifi hooked the Velcro bits together. Angel sat up and looked for their reaction.

Lili giggled.

"Stylistically," she gasped, "totally inconsistent!"

"But somehow it works!" Fifi collapsed on the ground, giggling uncontrollably.

"Dude!" Ben laughed. "You look hilarious!"

"In a good way," said Jerry. "You'll make people laugh!"

"They love that! Really!" laughed Rufaho.

"Really?" Angel asked, wishing for a mirror.

"Absolutely," said Rufahlo, his strange accent surging. "Here's how it works. You are very goofy looking, very unusual, but still very cute in a goofy, puppy way. The spiky collar seems to say 'Look at me! I'm a bad dog!'"

"Which is why I don't want it," said Jerry, not laughing anymore.

"But you're so little and cute and you have such limpid pools for eyes," said Rufahlo. "The collar makes a big joke and people laugh because it brings them joy to look at you."

"Just like us!" said Lili. This was a new thought. "Ow!" she squeaked and slapped her forehead.

"Look!" said Fifi, "the collar has a tag!"

"Where'd Francine get that," asked Lili, rubbing her temples. "What's it say?"

"Killer!" said Rufahlo and the whole group laughed some more.

"Killer!" Fifi squeaked. "That's perfect!"

"Killer and Mr. Sparkly," Lili squealed. "Score!"

She high-fived with Fifi.

"The accessories lesson is now complete," she said. "Tomorrow? Deportment."

"Wha...?" the boys said.

"Behavior," the girls said and then rolled on their backs in the grass.

Angel saw Lester rolling on his back and remembered Busy's advice. He scampered over and looked down at the writhing poodle.

"Hi," he said, "I wanted to thank..."

Lester opened his eyes and flinched. He stared up at Angel, a smile spreading on his face.

"What in the world are you wearing?" he laughed. "Where did you get that collar? That's hilarious!" He rolled on his belly and laughed into his paws. "In a good way!" he choked, wiping at his eyes. "Let me see," he said, peering at the tag.

"Killer! That's perfect!" His whole body shook with giggles. "Is that your name now?"

"I don't know," Angel said. "What do you think?"

"I think people will love it," Lester chuckled.

People would love it. That made Angel feel good. He hadn't had much contact with people so far.

He remembered his purpose.

"Thank you for saving me," he said.

Lester looked puzzled.

"The Angry Key Man," prompted Angel.

"Oh!" Lester remembered. "No problem. If they're not your

Friend," he went on, "they don't have the right to be mad at you or mean to you. Your Friend matters, keep your eye on him. Or her. And all their Friends." He rolled some more, then stood up and shook his whole body.

"And it doesn't take much to keep them happy, you'll see," he said.

"I'd like to," said Angel.

Lester dropped to the ground and rolled again.

"What are you doing?" Angel asked. "Do you have fleas?"

"No," said Lester, "it's the nubbins."

Angel looked him over. Half the nubbins had come undone and their hair was floating in the breeze. The other half were still together. Lester's hair went from cloud to nubbins and back to cloud again. Angel started to giggle.

"You look pretty funny yourself," he said.

"I know!" Lester said. "Francine was all upset about something this morning and didn't comb me out. I don't mind looking stupid but the nubbins itch!"

He writhed on the grass and grunted.

"Maybe I could help," Angel offered.

"Work away," Lester said.

Angel scraped at the nubbins with his front paws. Several came apart and the hair fluffed into a cloud.

"I think it's working," said Angel.

"Do them all! Please!"

Angel scraped and rubbed. After a while, the stimulation to his paw pads caused slime to secrete.

"Uh oh," he said, "maybe I should stop."

"No, please," Lester begged. "Do them all!"

The slime seemed to nourish Lester's hair. As each nubbin burst apart, the hair seemed to stretch its follicles toward the sun. The slime made it look glossy and shiny. The hair smoothed itself into orderly curlicues. The curlicues molded together into an organized shape.

"The lion's mane!" Lester said. "That's my favorite."

Angel did them all, even the ankle poofs.

"Thank you," said Lester, "I feel normal now."

"Normal," Angel thought. He wagged his tentacle ears. "I wonder what that feels like?"

"You're a very unusual dog," Lester said. "They tell me your ears are quite powerful. The collar looks great, by the way, very cute."

"Oh yeah," Angel said. "When I point them, I can hear all kinds of things. Want to see what else they can do?"

Lester grinned.

"I just learned this today," Angel was excited and wanted to show off. He snapped the tentacles straight up into a V.

"Watch that leaf." He pointed to a large maple leaf, swooping and swaying gently on the breeze.

"Now!" Angel snapped the tentacles forward.

A thin stream of slime spewed out and hit the leaf. It dropped like a stone and bounced when it hit the ground.

"Cool!" Lester said. "Do it again!"

Soon the ground around them was littered with gooey leaves, slimy bits of paper, and a few unfortunate bugs.

"That is so cool," Lester said. "Show me the hearing thing now. See those two over there?" He pointed his snout at Day Care Guy and Francine. They were sitting together on a bench. Their faces were serious and their lattes sat forgotten as they talked.

"Can you tell me what they're saying?" Lester asked.

Angel shook his tentacles. "Sorry," he said, as the spray of excess slime hit Lester's mane.

"It's OK." Lester rubbed it into his hair. "It's kind of like conditioner."

Angel pointed his tentacles and listened.

"And his dogs really love him," Day Care Guy was saying. "I saw them the other night when I came out for air after 'Antiques Roadshow'. I'd left my glasses so I couldn't see clearly but I could tell it was him. He was down by the edge of the lake. For a second, I thought he'd fall in. Then his main dog, the big, ugly one, came to his side and licked his hand." Day Care Guy paused. He looked sad.

"He stepped back from the edge and sat down with the big dog. Then all the other dogs came. They leaned on each other and stared at the moon." Day Care Guy looked at the ground.

"I envy him," he said. "His dogs really love him." He rubbed a hand on his face and reached for his latte.

"My dogs don't love me," he said sadly.

"Aw, come on," Lester said. "We like you well enough."

"They're not your dogs," Francine said gently. "They have their own homes."

"They only like me when there's food," he said.

"That's not...entirely true," Lester protested weakly.

"Sometimes I think they're laughing at me," Day Care Guy sighed.

"Well...that is true," Lester said. "I feel kind of bad about it now..."

"So the dog who got a haircut?" Day Care Guy said. "That's one of his dogs. The old man. They live in the tree circle." He pointed at the circle and smiled at Francine. "He probably likes the haircut," he said.

"He does!" Angel said. "He really does!"

"They're homeless?" Francine was shocked. "But how...?"

"Not homeless," said Day Care Guy. "They make their home with him. They love him. They seem well fed and happy and they don't bother anyone. I wouldn't worry about the haircut." Day Care Guy sighed again. "His dogs really love him."

"You need a dog of your own," Francine said.

"I love them all," he smiled at her. "How could I possibly pick just one?"

"The right dog will pick you," Francine patted his hand. "The right dog will make you pick him…or her."

Angel snapped his head towards Lester. Slime sprayed everywhere.

"Dude, I think I'm conditioned enough," Lester rubbed it into his hair.

"He needs a dog of his own?" Angel squeaked. His big eyes bulged with excitement.

Lester grinned. "Go for it!"

Angel streaked toward the bench and skidded to a halt at their feet. He sat waiting, ears up, tongue panting.

Day Care Guy looked up. He cocked his head to one side, as dogs do when they see something they can't understand.

"Hello, little…puppy?" he said.

Angel put his front paws on the man's knee and stretched himself toward the puzzled face.

"Pick me! Choose me!" Angel said.

"What a very strange dog," Francine said. "Nice hair, though. Looks conditioned."

"That's not a dog," Day Care Guy said. "That's a science experiment."

Angel sagged a bit.

"Come here, little one," Day Care Guy lifted Angel into his lap. "Let's have a look."

He looked him over and scratched his back. Angel licked his cheek. "Ha ha," Day Care Guy laughed. "Look at him!" He held him up and continued the examination. "This is a science experiment." This time, his voice was gentle.

"Go on," Angel heard Busy's voice in his head. "Tell him about yourself."

"I can do tricks," Angel said. "I can sit up, lie down and then stay and wait for you."

Angel hesitated. This next part wasn't entirely true.

"They're not lies," said Busy's voice. "They're puppy dog tales. Go on!"

"I don't eat much," Angel said. There wasn't much to eat, so that was true. This next bit was a little more suspect. Angel took a breath.

"I don't shed," he said and waited for fire and brimstone. None came. His confidence grew. He was sure about this next part.

"I'll always be there for you", he said. "I'll adore you."

Day Care Guy was smiling now.

"I will guard you," Angel said, "and protect you from all harm. I..." he paused.

"Soldier on," Busy's voice prompted. "In for a penny, in for a pound."

"I won't bark. Won't bite. Won't howl at night," Angel said. Still no brimstone. Angel finished in a rush.

"I'll be just perfect! And you'll be so proud of me!"

Day Care Guy started to laugh.

"Pick me! Choose me!" Angel said.

"Very strange but very cute," Day Care Guy said. "Nice collar too. Whose little dog are you?" Day Care Guy cuddled him on his lap and looked for the tag.

"You'll be mine, I'll be yours," Angel said.

"Killer!" Day Care Guy laughed. "Your owner has a sense of humor!"

"That collar," Francine said. "It looks very familiar. I think I've seen it before."

Day Care Guy still laughing, wrapped Angel in a big hug.

"I wish you were my little dog," he said.

"I am!" Angel said. "I will be!"

"I wonder who your owner is," Day Care Guy looked around.

"Owner talk," said Jerry, trotting past the bench. "Time to bale."

"No..." Angel whined and licked Day Care Guy's face.

"Yes," said Busy's voice. "Always leave 'em wanting more! You'll try again tomorrow."

Angel wriggled.

"OK, OK," Day Care Guy put him down.

"Look at that," he said. "At the base of these...ears...who the heck did that to his ears? But look!" He showed Francine.

"Tufts of hair, right here at the base! I swear they weren't here a second ago!" He held the puppy up again. Angel grinned and wriggled.

"OK, little one," he put the puppy down.

"New tufts!" Angel licked the man's knee.

"Dog like thoughts," he heard Busy's voice. "Thoughts can become actions."

Brimming with happiness, Angel scampered after Jerry.

"So long, Killer," said Day Care Guy. "Hope to see you tomorrow."

"That collar," Francine mused. "It looks so familiar." She shrugged and sipped her latte.

Much later, Francine said, "It's like silk! Feel it! I can run my fingers all the way through it!"

Day Care Guy stroked Lester's mane.

"Mmmm," he said. "And look, it molds right back into shape!"

"Who did this?" Francine marveled, still running her fingers through Lester's hair. "Who would comb out a dog they didn't know? Much less apply conditioner!"

"The same sort of person who'd give a stray dog a haircut?" Day Care Guy grinned.

Francine's eyes narrowed.

"OK, OK," Day Care Guy, hands in the air, backed away.

Francine stroked and pulled and fluffed and molded.

"This conditioner," she mused. "It must be very expensive."

She twizzled a lock around her finger.

"There's no show tomorrow," she said. "And I have a great idea for a new look. Come here, boy."

Lester closed his eyes and hoped for the best.

Chapter Twenty-seven

Train Your Nose and Make It Work For You

"I call it the 'Our Life with Dogs'." Francine waved a graceful hand toward Lester.

Cameras and phones snapped and beeped and whirred.

The Dog Park ladies and some of the men ooohed and aaaahed. Francine handed out business cards. Lester yawned and stretched and struck another heroic pose. The cameras snapped and whirred.

Lester liked this look a lot.

"This is not for the show," Francine had said firmly. "This would never do. This is for us. For fun."

She had divided his hair into sections, then sub-sections and even smaller sub-sections. Starting with the larger sections, she braided his hair so it lay close to his body. The braids formed patterns, whorls and waves, straight lines and zig zags. The patterns became a series of pictures. His head and neck were crescent moons and stars. The left side of his body showed a lake and a forest of trees. His right featured stick figures, two-legged and four. The four-legged figures had tails. Some of the two-leggeds were large. Smaller ones had bows on the circles that made their heads. The two-legged figures were playing with the four-leggeds under the beams of a smiling sun. The little clouds of his ear poofs became pictures of clouds in the sky, his ankle poofs the waves of a very tiny ocean.

"How long did that take?" a lady asked.

"Hours and hours and hours," Francine mimed total collapse from exhaustion.

"And hours," Day Care Guy said. "I had to give her dinner and a very late night snack." He looked rather pleased.

"But I had to finish," Francine said. "I just had to finish before I went home."

Day Care Guy looked wistful.

"It was quite late," he said softly. "A lot of overtime."

"What's that on your butt?" asked Melinda.

"What?" Lucy looked closely.

"You tell me," Lester said.

"It's a four-legged…" said Melinda. "It's a dog! And it's pooping!" She giggled.

"Subtle," Lucy sneered. "Really nice."

"Oh, lighten up," said Melinda. "You look stunning," she told Lester.

"Well, that's the right word," said Lucy. "Stunning."

"And your body looks so different without all the hair," Melinda went on. "Very muscle-y."

"I like it," said Lester.

"There's nowhere to clip on your bow!" Lucy protested.

"I really like it," Lester stood proud.

"Look, it's me!" Boss pointed to Lester's hind leg. "And my Old Friend! There's his hat, there's his coat and I'm bigger than all the other stick dogs. Ha ha," he laughed. "She got me! She's very talented."

"I can't quite see," Lester bent himself in half to look at his leg.

"It's me all right," said Boss. "Where's your bow?"

"No place to clip it," Lester grinned. "I like this look. How come you're here? No walk today?"

"We're taking a day off," Boss replied. "Long one yesterday. Too long. Ran into some trouble."

Lester's brows shot up, wrinkling the stars on his forehead.

"It was nothing," Boss shrugged. "Two guys. But he needs to rest today. We're doing it again tomorrow."

Boss told Lester about the new park, the Frenchie Connection, and their plan to find Mimi's friend. Lester talked about his hopes and dreams, his aspirations.

"Follow your nose," Boss said. "Believe in yourself. It might not happen just the way you planned but if service is what you want, then work on that, dream toward that and keep training that thing on your face."

"Tomorrow's another show," Lester sighed. "Hours of hairdo, hours of posing, Rufahlo wins again, when do I have time for training?"

"My boy." Boss patted the tiny waves on Lester's ankle. "You will need everything to make it in this world. Brains, muscles, strength, hustle and your heart."

He looked at Lester's starry forehead, his yearning eyes.

"You'll need everything you've got."

"Heart is important," said Bailiff.

Randy sniffed. "Brains are important."

"But more," said Boss, "yes, even more important..." He patted his own huge nose. "The compass that guides you, that sniffs out the path to friend or foe..." He twitched his nostrils. "And you're the only one who knows. There's awesome power in that nose!"

"That nose," Randy and Bailiff said softly.

"Thousands of nerve-endings twitching and tingling," said Boss

"So many smells, all inter-mingling," said Lester.

"Sorting them out," Boss gave his nose another pat. "That's the big boy's job. He's got to know a lot and work very hard." He gave Lester the fierce stare with flashing yellow eyes.

"You have to train your nose. Give it a work out. Look for subtleties, nuances, whiffs and hints that make a scent." He banged his big paw on the ground. "You tell the big boy what you want to know," he said. "And where he leads, you go."

Randy and Bailiff sniffed the air.

"Follow your nose," Boss said. "Steal-things-and-hide-'em.

When the boys gave you an object, what did you do?"

"Gave it a thorough smelling over," Lester said.

"Looking for what?" Boss said. "Remember, no smell exists on its own. It's the combination you want. The combination is the roadmap. Me, for example? What's my combination?"

"It helps to close the eyes," said Bailiff.

"Observe the world through your nose hairs," Randy said.

"Twitch it to the left," said Bailiff.

"Then right," said Randy.

"Then all around and pull it together," said Boss.

Lester closed his eyes and followed their instructions.

"Richly composted soil..." Lester breathed in, measuring, calculating. "Doughnuts...," he exhaled.

"We had them yesterday," Boss encouraged.

"Garlic fries?" Lester opened one eye.

"My favorite," Boss grinned. Lester closed the eye.

"Lemon thyme...and mint!"

"Good!" said Boss. "Very good."

"Lemon thyme and mint?" Lester asked. "What is that?"

"There's a patch of it near our tree circle," Boss smiled. "I roll in it every day. So if you ever have to find me, that's the first thing to pull out of the air."

"Unless there's an Italian restaurant nearby," said Randy.

"And if there is," Boss gave Randy the fierce stare, "what next?"

"Garlic fries," said Lester.

"Italian restaurant again," said Bailiff.

Boss flashed the eyes at Bailiff.

"What then?" he said.

"The soil?" Lester asked.

"We're sitting on soil now," said Randy.

"Dirt is everywhere," said Bailiff.

"But mine," Boss used his shut-up-now voice, "is richly composted. I'm often sitting on or near flowerbeds. And who," his tone said this-is-important. "Who is it I sit next to?"

"Old Friend!" Lester exclaimed. "I smell him now! He's in there!"

"That's what you look for," Boss nodded. "The soil, my Old Friend, and you know what I mean, the thing we talked about the other night…"

Lester nodded.

"The lemon thyme and mint. Those are the constants. Food items come and go. Let's try another. This isn't exactly fair, since she's not here right now but what if you had to find Mimi?"

"Lavender bouquets," Lester smiled.

"Ben rolled in lavender yesterday," Randy cautioned.

"Plus…!" Lester held up a paw. "Ladies leather shoes."

"Girls are everywhere," said Bailiff. "And they all wear shoes."

Lester closed his eyes and worked hard to remember.

"A tiny hint of men's cologne," he said.

"Bob," said Bailiff.

"That's fading fast," said Randy.

"And…and…Old Friend, again!" Lester said.

"She sneaks in next to his belly every night," Boss chuckled.

"She makes me move over," Bailiff complained. "Not fair! I was there first!"

"That combination," said Boss. "That's Mimi. Well done! And you haven't smelled her that often, very impressive."

"She's a girl," Lester grinned. "A guy pays attention."

They spent the rest of the sunny morning testing Lester's skills. Boss found himself quite pleased with the boy's focus and drive. Once again he wondered at his fondness for this fancy boy from the privileged world.

"He works hard," he thought. "He's got a big nose. Hard work, a little help, he'll know how to use it."

At the day's end, he thought of Lester again. "Good boy. He'll have a good life. I hope. He deserves it."

He looked over his shoulder at Old Friend. He was lying on his blanket chatting away to Mimi, playing some kind of game with her. The little dog bounced up and down and wriggled with glee.

"Look at you, my old soldier," Boss thought to himself.

"Sometimes you get so low, I think 'This is it! What should I do?' Then you bounce right back." Boss turned his face to the stars so no one would see his watering eyes.

"And I think to myself 'there's still some time!'". He shook his head and wiped a paw across his face.

"My good friend," he thought. "Let's have a little more time together. Please"

"…and we'll see if anyone knows you," Old Friend told Mimi.

"Really?" she squealed. "Really? The Frenchie Connection?"

"Lots and lots of little dogs just like you."

"I know them!" she squealed. "They know me!"

"Maybe someone will know who you are."

"Bob!" she cried. "Bob!"

"We'll see," Old Friend gave her head a tender stroke.

"We must try," he settled his head on the bag that was his pillow.

"And sooner rather than later," he murmured, then drifted off to sleep.

"Bob?" asked Bailiff. "Where's Bob?" He jumped to the entrance and pointed at a passing shadow.

Mimi was so happy she decided not to bite him. She moved to the entrance and sat between him and Boss.

"As a matter of fact," she couldn't keep the excitement out of her voice. "We're going to find him tomorrow!"

"Really?" asked Bailiff.

"Really?" said Boss.

"We're going to try," she said. "We're going to take a very long walk and look for the Frenchie Connection!"

"Wow," said Bailiff.

"Mmm," said Boss.

"What?" she asked.

"Nothing," said Boss. "It's good he's asleep. He'll need everything he's got to get us there." He looked away.

Mimi looked at Old Friend's tired, ragged, body. She knew why Boss was concerned. But the chance to find Bob, to see him again…!

"But that's him" said Bailiff. "If he said he'll do it, he will."

"Yes, he will," said Boss. He put his head down on his paws. "We'll do it together. It'll be fine."

Mimi licked his ear. "Thank you," she whispered.

"No worries," Boss smiled. He got up and stretched, then lumbered over to his spot next to Old Friend.

Chapter Twenty-Eight
Nothing to be Done

"What?" Angel asked.

"Nothing…" Busy's voice trailed off.

His spirit eyes were narrow, worried and sad. They were fixed on Boss and his Old Friend.

"It's not nothing," Angel said. "It's always something. What is it?"

"I didn't finish my sentence," Busy turned his spirit face away from the sleeping pair. "I meant to say, 'Nothing to be done.'"

"Meaning what?" Angel challenged.

Busy puffed back to his old self.

"Meaning," he said sternly, "that it's night and time to go to sleep so I can be off the clock for a few hours! So will you stop fooling around with that muffin and just finish it already?"

"OK…," Angel grinned. "The muffin…" He cuddled the pecan and walnut confection close to his body and gave it a tender lick. "So, I should eat the muffin…"

"Yes!" Busy snapped. "Now!"

"Why?" Angel asked, eyes twinkling. "Everyone's busy."

He tilted his head toward the other dogs and smiled. "No one seems interested."

The other dogs were absorbed in some new game they had learned.

"No one here wants it," he grinned. "That is, no one who could actually eat it…"

"Fine!" Busy snapped. "Fine! Yes! I can't eat a muffin!"

"Or anything else," Angel said.

"I can do this!" Busy flashed himself up and out to the size of the tallest tree in the circle.

"And this!" He shrunk himself down to the size of a small,

glowing bug.

"A firefly!" said Jerry. "I call dibs!"

"Look out," said Angel. "You can't eat but you might get eaten."

"And this!" Busy's head swelled to the size of Boss's big stone of power. His little body dangled below.

"Wha...?" said Jerry, backing away.

"And this! And this! And this!" Various parts of Busy's spirit body swelled and shrank and shimmered and, at one point, actually sparked.

"Fire!" Jerry cried.

"No, there's not," said Ben. The spark had disappeared.

"Oh," said Jerry. "Sorry."

"But, no, I can't eat a muffin!" Busy finished, his spirit body panting from the effort.

"Thoughts become actions," Angel said. "They can. You said so yourself." He thought about licking the muffin but decided against it.

"I know!" Busy roared. "So, would you please just eat the da.....arn muffin so I can think of something else?" His two-tiered wings twitched and shivered.

"Who wants a muffin?" Angel called.

Ben and Jerry pounced. The muffin was gone in a heartbeat along with the paper it was baked in.

"Thank you!" Busy settled his wings and relaxed.

"What are you guys doing?" Angel asked.

"Deportment," said Ben.

"What?" Angel's brow furrowed.

"Behavior," said Jerry. "How to behave when you want to get a good Friend."

"The girls taught us," said Ben. "We're practicing."

"Yeah," said Jerry. "See, we never had a good Friend."

"So, when we were at the pound," Ben continued, "we'd be all 'don't see me, don't pick me.'"

"Look away," said Jerry. "I'm not here."

"Turns out," Ben got excited, "that gave us exactly what we didn't want!"

"Bad people want a frightened dog," Jerry said.

"So, to get what we want, a good Friend," Ben started bouncing, "we have to look like good dogs!

"Happy dogs," said Jerry. "Fake it 'til you make it! That's what Fifi said."

"So, when we see a good Friend prospect," Ben was eager to demonstrate, "instead of looking at the ground or cowering in the corner, we do this!"

Ben and Jerry both got up on their hind legs and pranced around in circles, eyes bright, tongues lolling out. Moonlight sparkled off the jewels of Jerry's new collar.

"You look happy!" Angel laughed.

"A Corgi would have a hard time with that," said Bailiff. Jerry recognized the sorrow in his voice and dropped to all fours.

"Then just wriggle," he said. "You could do that!" He wriggled and wiggled and made a happy face.

"Let's try," said Angel and the two smaller dogs followed Jerry's movements.

"You look great!" Mimi joined in. "Here's something else," she was eager to help. "Move your ears in different directions. They love that!"

She looked at Bailiff's huge pointed ears. "You could do that really well," she said.

Bailiff grinned. "You think so?" he asked shyly.

"Let's try!" she said. "Move them all around!"

All the dogs practiced pointing their ears north, south, up, down, east, and west. Angel was especially enthusiastic.

"Yow!" Ben yelped. "Watch the slime!"

"Sorry," Angel's tentacles sagged toward the ground.

"Look at that stuff," said Jerry. "Let me rub it around. Dude, you look all glossy!"

"It's like conditioner," Mimi said. "You look beautiful!"

"Do me!" said Jerry. "Give me a spray!"

"Me too!" said Bailiff.

"And me," said Mimi.

"Me as well," Randy said. "Can't be left behind on the glossy circuit."
    They spent a few happy moments with Angel spraying, the others rubbing it into their fur.

"Watch my shiny ears," Jerry pointed them first left, then right.

"And mine!" said Bailiff, pointing one up and one down.

"Watch this!" Mimi pointed hers straight out to the side and then flat back.

All the boys cracked up and rolled on the ground.

"You look like a cat!" Ben gasped.

"Not that there's anything wrong with that," said Jerry. "I kind of like them…"

"Ahem," Boss coughed. All the dogs froze.

"Quiet time," he said softly. "Settle down."

"Sorry," said Bailiff. The dogs all looked at each other. Bailiff waggled his ears and everyone had to choke back giggles. Happy, for once, the strays settled down for a sound sleep. Randy wasn't down long before he was up again. Softly, quietly, he paced about.

"What's he doing?" Angel asked.

"Ask him," said Busy.

"Randy?" Angel whispered.

"I miss my sheep," he paced some more. "All this fol de rol for humans. Bah. I was lucky, I had a good one. I worked hard and he respected me. I liked him but I miss my sheep." His voice cracked.

"He needs to tell someone," said Busy. "Let him."

"Hopelessly stupid," Randy's eyes watered. "And helpless. And smelly. They needed me," he sighed deeply and tried to steady his voice.

"They trusted me. Followed me. They stared at me..."

A breeze fluttered leaves on the edge of the tree circle.

"You're not the only one with a guardian," said Busy.

Half a dozen little balls of light moved through the air. When they reached Randy, they sprouted wings. The winged balls flew around his head. The balls slowly formed into heads and bodies. The bodies sprouted legs. Half a dozen winged sheep surrounded Randy and drew in close.

"What'll we do now, Randy? What'll we do now? What'll we do now, Randy? What'll we do now?" they chanted.

Their adoring eyes looked up at him. He sat at attention and softly barked his orders.

"First we'll assemble into a tight, group formation, for the sake of warmth and personal security. This formation is otherwise known as a circle!"

The little spirits scrambled to follow his directions. He chuckled.

"And then," he said, "we'll eat some grass!"

"Grass! Grass! We get to eat some grass!" the spirits chanted, bouncing up and down, jostling each other.

"Och!" he sighed. "They made me laugh."

He lay down and the little spirits made a circle around him.

"Oh, how I miss them," he sighed. The spirits trotted around his body.

"Oh, my wee angels," he whispered. "Thanks for coming to see me. You know I can't sleep without counting you like I used to. Same time again tomorrow, eh?"

One by one, the little sheep angels jumped over his head.

"One…," he said softly. "Two…thr….." And he was gone from this world, safe in the peaceful land of sleep. The little spirits hovered for a while, then floated away.

"Wow," Angel whispered.

"Off you go," said Busy.

Angel snuggled between Ben and Randy and tried to be a quiet little sheep-dog. Very quickly, he was gone to the land of peace in sleep.

"Wish I could go to sleep," Busy thought. "Well, I'm sort of off the clock, at least."

He set himself up comfortably on a tree stump, struck a meditative pose and resigned himself to the usual long night of waiting for the clock to start ticking again. His steady gaze was drawn to gently snoring Boss and his Old Friend. His spirit eyes narrowed. Worry and sorrow drew them down as he looked at the sleeping life partners.

"You're right, sir," he sighed. "Better sooner than later. Nothing to be done."

His spirit chin sank to his chest. All he could do was twiddle his spirit fingers and wait.

Chapter Twenty-nine

She Sees Into the Black Pit of My Wretched Soul

"What's he doing?" Francine asked.

More roughly than he meant to, Rufahlo pulled another piece of stuffing from the ruined toy bear's head.

"His daddies tell me he does this before every show," Day Care Guy shrugged. "Imagine that. A dog with stage fright."

"Lester's calm," Francine said.

"He never wins," Day Care Guy replied. "There's not so much at stake. I'm not sure Lester cares. He does it for fun!"

"And the hairdos," Francine said. Day Care Guy looked at her and smiled.

"She's here late," said Lucy.

"Again," said Melinda.

They made eye contact.

"Someday soon, I think we'll have a new Day Care Mommy," Lucy said.

"Good," said Melinda. "He needs someone to talk to. Someone who talks back."

"Rufahlo's not talking," Lucy shrugged. "For once."

"He seems worried," said Melinda. "Lester will cheer him up."

"There's still more stuffing in his leg," Lester said.

"I get to it," Rufahlo mumbled through a piece of arm stuffing. He spit it out and tore at the arm fabric.

"Why are you here tonight?" Lester asked.

"She want to use new product for the show," Rufahlo said.

"Spray it on, let it dry, buff me up and make me shiny like a new penny. Take a long time, have to start early. My daddies have opera tickets so it work out good for everyone."

He spit the arm fabric aside and started on the one remaining leg.

"I don't know what she'll do with me," Lester said. "When these braids come out, I'm going to look like the wild dog of Borneo."

Rufahlo tugged at a stubborn knot of stuffing. It wouldn't come out. With a moan of frustration, he shoved the toy aside and put his head in his paws.

"What's wrong?" Lester asked.

"She knows," Rufahlo whimpered.

"No, she doesn't," Lester said. "Wait. Who are you talking about?"

"Papillion," he whispered. "She knows!"

"No, she doesn't."

"Look at her. I can't. She's staring at me. She sees into the black pit of my wretched soul!" Rufahlo reached for the toy and began to worry it again.

Lester cocked his head. Papillion didn't seem different. She was sitting quietly, as she usually did, staring into space, twitching a bit, talking to herself from time to time. She was staring in their general direction.

"She's just admiring your rippling muscles," Lester said.

"Lester, I tell you, she knows!" Rufahlo's whisper couldn't hide his pain. "She knows I'm not what I seem. When I am revealed, what will she think of me?"

Lester didn't know what to say.

"When those braids come out," Melinda said, "Lester's going to look like a Brillo pad! What is she going to do with his hair?"

Lucy shrugged.

"You don't care?" Melinda was shocked. "Lucy, what's wrong with you?" Her warm eyes glowed with concern.

"Everything changes," Lucy said softly. "Even my baby. When he was young, I'd look at him and see only myself. Now, I see something more."

"A junkyard dog with a big nose?" Melinda asked gently.

"A good dog, a wonderful dog, with a kind and generous heart," Lucy whispered. "And a big nose," she finished.

Melinda smiled.

"And you're right," Lucy said.

"Dear lord, let me remember this day!" Melinda cried softly.

"He doesn't care about the show," Lucy said. "I care about the show. He does it for me," she said. "I need to let him know that."

Melinda looked at Rufahlo's sad face and the pile of ruined stuffing. Lester was talking quietly and urgently.

"Maybe not just for you," she said. "I think."

"What?" Lucy cocked her head.

"Ow!" Melinda squeaked and slapped her temples.

"Is she an angel? Do I see wings?" Rufahlo's head lay on his paws. His jaws barely moved as he mumbled. Tufts of chewed stuffing ringed his head. He turned sad eyes up to meet Lester's gaze.

"She is the sum of my favorite things," he said softly.

Lester looked at Papillion. She twitched and tilted sideways. She caught herself, sat straight and panted.

"Really?" he said.

"Her tragic flaws are endearing to me!" Rufahlo roused himself, lifting his head a few inches from the floor.

"I wish you...I wish the whole world could see what I see...." His head plopped down on his paws.

Lester thought he should say something.

"Hmmmm," he hummed.

"I have trophies," Rufahlo mumbled. "Many, many trophies. What does that mean if the one dog I admire...besides yourself, of course....What good is it if she cannot admire too? I'm a fraud," he moaned. "And she knows it!" His eyes bulged with fear.

"She doesn't know..." Lester started. "Uh oh, here she comes!"

"Hide me!" Rufahlo cried. He grabbed Lester's middle and dragged the smaller dog across his face.

"Dude, come on...Hi Papillion!" he said brightly, paws scrabbling on the floor. "What's up?"

She stared at them with alarming focus. The boys cringed.

"Unless you walk through the pet door, you can't play in the garden," she said.

Rufahlo's eyes bulged. Lester made a squint and cocked his head.

"What?"

"I know what you're doing," she said.

The boys hung their heads.

"And I have an idea," she said.

The boy heads snapped to attention. Rufahlo slapped his temple.

"Look at that," Lucy said.

"I know," said Melinda.

Day Care Guy had walked Francine to the door. They lingered there and talked some more.

"It's so late now," Lucy said. "And they want to start so early, she may as well just stay here."

Francine opened the door and stepped outside. She stood on the landing, still talking, the porch light glowing on her face.

"I wonder why they didn't think of that," Lucy asked.

With a final wave, Day Care Guy closed the door. After the door clicked shut, his face fell, his posture sagged, he sighed deeply and leaned against the door.

"I think somebody did," Melinda said.

"Boys are so odd," Lucy said. "They act so tough and strong but a girl can change all that in an instant."

"Case in point," Melinda nodded toward the boys and Papillion. Rufahlo lay flat on the floor, surrounded by the ruined stuffing. Papillion spoke with passion, waving her paw at his nose. After one big paw movement, she tipped over. Without moving the rest of his body, Rufahlo stretched out his paw, caught her fall and set her right again. His face, still on the floor was cowed and fearful. Lester was talking too. Papillion looked fierce and commanding. .

"What in the world are they talking about?" Lucy wondered.

"I have an idea," Melinda said, "but I'm holding it back. My head is killing me."

"What?" Lucy demanded. "Tell me!"

"Ow," Melinda moaned.

Papillion turned and focused on Lestor. Her face was fierce. Her talk was quiet but intense and she gestured with her paws. Lester's head dropped to his chest. He looked just as cowed as Rufahlo. He glanced toward his mother, flinched, and quickly looked away.

"What is that hyperactive mouse saying to my boy?" Lucy was on high alert. "Look at him! She's crushing his spirit! On the day before a show! What is she saying?"

Melinda got up and stretched. "Maybe it's time we found out." She shook her head.

Lucy was halfway across the floor.

"I'll put a stop to this," she muttered.

"You're in this just as deep as he is!" Papillion waved a paw at Lester. "And don't pretend you're not!"

Lester looked at the ground. He batted a bit of stuffing with his paw.

"You deceived your own mother and helped him lie to us all!" She stomped her paw. "You have to come clean too!"

Lester cringed.

"You can't go forward until you face this!" Papillion stomped again. "You have to tell her!"

A noise distracted her. She turned to look.

"And right now would be a good time," she said. "Here they come."

The boys saw the ladies approach. Lucy's fierce face mimicked Papillion's.

"Hide me," he whispered to Rufahlo.

"Lester," Rufahlo whispered back. "Walk through the pet door. With me!" Rufahlo lifted his head and leaned on his elbows. He smiled and gave Lester a friendly swat. Lester grinned through his fears. He closed his eyes and listened to the angry click of Lucy's polished toe-nails on the linoleum floor.

"What's going on here?" Lucy snapped.

"Hello, ladies," Papillion said. "The boys here...BOTH of them," she glared at Rufahlo first, then Lester. "Each of them has something to say."

"Well?" Lucy demanded.

"Boys?" Auntie Melinda raised her brows.

The boys hung their heads.

"Go on," Papillion said. She turned to Rufahlo. "You first."

"I'm a fraud," Rufahlo moaned.

Lucy waved her shiny toe-nails.

"Oh, that's just pre-show jitters...."

"No!" Rufahlo's voice was strong now. He looked at Papillion. She smiled and nodded. He took a deep breath.

"I really am a fraud!" He was determined now and it all came spilling out.

"I only won because Lester helped me!" he said. "I...I have a problem!"

Eyes wide, ears focused, the ladies sat at full attention.

"I hear one command, I do another. I don't know why," Rufahlo sagged a bit then recovered. He took another deep breath and squared his shoulders. His head dropped again to his chest.

"I could never win on my own." His eyes stayed focused on the floor. "Lester jumped the cues so I could see what the command was and I could follow. He let me win. I owe it all to him." He looked at Lester. His eyes said, "Your turn."

Lucy's eyes were unreadable. Lester cringed again. What did he see there? Sorrow? Disappointment? Rage? He couldn't tell. All his energy drained away. His head fell on his chest and he stared at the ground.

A long, uncomfortable silence made the boys squirm. With a quick glance to each other, they stiffened their wills and mustered their courage. Together, they would endure whatever punishment was given.

"Lester," Lucy said softly. "Is all that true?"

He couldn't look at her. Eyes fixed on the ground, he nodded into his chest.

Another silence followed. Melinda couldn't take the tension and flopped on the ground.

"So all this time," Lucy murmured, "You were the real Top Show Dog Champion?"

"Yes," Rufahlo said. "He should have been."

"Well, maybe not," Lester stammered. "There are lots of other dogs...."

"No," Lucy said. Lester, startled by her tone, dared to look up. She was smiling!

"You two were the only real competition there," she said. "And always, you let him win? Every time?"

"He needed to," Lester murmured. "He wanted to."

"I did!" said Rufahlo.

"And I didn't," Lester said quietly.

"My boy," she said softly. "My wonderful, generous, boy. You are MY champion!" she rubbed her face on his shoulder. Lester was so relieved he almost pulled a Papillion tip-over. Rufahlo pushed him back up.

"And you!" Lucy sat up sharply and turned to Rufahlo. He cringed.

"You cheated to win the Top Show Dog Champion Crown?"

"Had to!" Rufahlo stammered. "I had to win! I was obsessed with winning! It's another one of my problems...." He cocked his head and turned to Papillion.

"I love talking about my problems!" he marveled.

"See?" she said. "It helps...."

"Oh, Rufahlo," Lucy was laughing now. "You know how I love my Lester," she gazed fondly at her son, then back to Rufahlo. "But maybe you're the son I should have had!"

"Really?" he squeaked.

"I would have driven you less crazy," she chuckled.

"That's for sure," Lester said.

Melinda laughed. All tension melted away as the five friends dissolved into giggles.

"But what about now?" Melinda asked when the giggles faded away. "What about the show? What about your friends?"

"Oh, they be OK with it," Rufahlo said. "Just the other day, they were complaining about all the time it takes to dust my trophies."

He cocked his head and marveled. Only an hour ago, the show meant everything to him. Now, he knew he could be happy just as he was.

"I'm a loser!" he said joyfully. "A big, happy, loser! Oh, it's so good to have it all in the open! What a weight off my chest!"

"You don't have to win all the time," Melinda said.

"Look at Lester," Lucy said. "You learn a lot just by showing up and taking part."

"That's true," Lester said.

"I will always want to win," Rufahlo mused. "But I can't. I have a problem. I must learn to seek joy in other things." Without meaning to, he had addressed this last remark to Papillion.

"You can conquer your problems," she said. "Everyone has problems. Want to know what mine is?"

"Well," Rufahlo said gently, "I think we can all see what your...."

"I like to steal things and hide them," she interrupted.

"Me too!" said Lucy. "I like small and shiny items!"

"If my teeth marks show when I bite 'em, it's gold!" Papillion's eyes sparked with excitement. She tipped over. "Score!" she said, sitting back up.

"I like to take their keys and stash 'em," Melinda joined in.

"Oh! Their lives are trashed without 'em," Lucy laughed. Lester couldn't believe what he was hearing.

"And when I make out like I found 'em," Melinda went on, "I get treats!"

"Score!" Lucy squealed.

"Oh! It's so hard being good," Papillion moaned, "all of the time."

"I chill with the thrill that I'm feeling when I'm being bad," Melinda said.

"Once in a while," Lucy added primly.

"I had to win all of the trophies," Rufahlo sighed. "I did wrong for applause and the glory. But now that you know my story, I'm done! Aaaaaa!" he sighed and shivered with new happiness.

"I'm so perfect, all of the time," he said.

"Me, too," said Lucy.

"Me, too," said Papillion. They all stared at her.

"The pressure gets to me," she said. "I just have to do something bad!"

The staring continued.

"Once in a while," she said.

"Tomorrow," said Lester, "let's find a school kid's lunch and steal it!"

"Let's find a flower bed and pee on it," Rufahlo was excited.

"After the show," Lucy said, "we'll spend a jolly afternoon just being bad!" They laughed and laughed, jostling each other and rolling around on the floor.

"Kids!" Day Care Guy had his hands on his hips.

"Quiet down! Big day tomorrow and a very early start! Go to bed!"

He tightened the belt of his ratty bathrobe and slapped back to his bedroom on floppy slippers. One of the puppies had settled down on his pillow. He smiled and forgot his annoyance. He turned off his light.

"What about tomorrow?" Melinda whispered.

"I guess I lose," Rufahlo shrugged.

Lucy said nothing but an image of Lester and a big, shining trophy filled her head. She smiled.

"Papillion," Lester said. "You had an idea?"

"Ow!" they all said.

"What is it?" asked Melinda, holding her temples.

Papillion outlined her plan. They all agreed it was risky but it just might work.

"I could do this!" Rufahlo was very excited. "I think I could! I can't wait to try!"

"And you're going to compete," Lucy said to Lester. "For real?"

Lester promised he would.

"Oh, yes, Lester!" said Rufahlo, his old self again. "Maybe tomorrow will be your day!" He chuckled.

"Not!" he finished and laughed some more.

"Shhhh!" Lucy shushed. They settled down together on the floor. Different thoughts and dreams sparkled through each head. Sleep was a long time coming.

Chapter Thirty

Don't Let the Sparkle Fool You

The next day, Francine was there bright and early as agreed but looking a little ragged.

"Couldn't sleep," she said.

"Me, neither," he said. "The puppies kept sitting on my head. Coffee?"

"Oh, yes," she said. "A latte. Please."

They shook the can of new product and started to spray.

"Oh," she said. "This doesn't look right. It's splotchy!"

"Spray slowly and evenly," he said, "not too much in one place. Besides, it has to dry. I'll do his ears."

Day Care Guy sprayed the stuff onto his hands and rubbed Rufahlo's head and ears.

"Hmmm," he said. "Sticky."

"Look at him!" she cried. "It's streaking! It's splotchy! It's... it's...changing color!"

"Let's just wait," he soothed. "It has to dry and then we have to buff him. It'll be fine."

Francine's fearful eyes blinked.

They started on Lester's braids.

"Oh, why did I make them so tight?" she cried, tugging and pulling.

"Ow!" Lester said. "Ow!"

"Calm down," said Day Care Guy softly. "Take a deep breath."

He showed her a pair of chopsticks.

"I whittled these down last night," he said, "when I couldn't sleep. Look! It works pretty well on the big ones."

He showed her how to work the stick into the braid and pull out one length. With the one length out, the other two fluffed free.

"Very clever," Francine said with a nervous smile. "I never

would have thought of that."

They picked and pulled 'til all the braids fluffed free.

"Wow," Day Care Guy wiped his forehead. "That was hard work."

"But look at him!" Francine cried. "It's awful! What am I going to do?"

Lester looked at himself. His hair stuck straight out from his body. It bent and kinked and pointed in all directions. Clumps formed, some sticking way out, others sagging sadly toward his feet. His ankle poofs were ragged mops. His ear poofs zig-zagged out in little lightning bolts.

"Brillo pad," Melinda smirked. "I told you."

Lester grinned. "Cool!"

"Oh no, oh no," Francine's hands were clumsy. "His top knot! It won't stay up! It won't stay together! It's a disaster!" She put her face in her hands and sobbed. Day Care Guy looked panicked.

"I told all these people we'd be there today and have smart new looks!" she gasped and gulped. "Oh, this is so not what I meant!"

"Look!" said Day Care Guy. He snatched a mini-dog jeweled collar from a shelf.

"We'll pull the top knot together like this..." He wrapped the collar around the hair and clipped it on its tightest setting.

"There!" he said. "And we'll take these little jeweled bobby pins, the ones we use on Fifi sometimes and..."

He curled and pinned and placed the jewels so they formed a diamond pattern.

"We'll call it the Jeweled Pincushion," he said.

"That would work, I guess," Francine sniffled and dried her eyes. They worked together until all of Lester's hair was curled and pinned. The jewels made diamond triangles all over his body.

"That's it," said Day Care Guy. "Perfect!"

He looked at Francine's face.

"Well, good enough for today," he added hopefully.

"You did a great job," she said softly. "He looks…OK. We'll pretend we meant it that way."

"Fake it 'til you make it," Day Care Guy chuckled.

Lester looked at himself and made a wry face.

"The first one who laughs," he said, "I'll bite them."

The ladies and Rufahlo struggled hard to hold it in. Papillion fell over.

"I'm not laughing!" she said. "I'm hyperventilating!"

"Now, Rufahlo," Francine said and picked up her buffing brush. She rubbed and buffed and wiped.

"That stuff smells!" Lucy scrunched her face. "I'm leaving!" She trotted away.

"It's not working!" Francine cried and buffed harder.

"That's not the spray that smells," said Lester. "What is that?"

"Lester!" a girl's voice cried.

"What have we here?" said Day Care Guy.

Mimi stood outside the half door gate.

She held a dirty rag of denim in her mouth. Behind her stood Randy, Ben, Jerry and Angel. They all looked very worried.

"It's the haircut dog!" Day Care Guy said. "And Killer! Hi, Killer" He bent over the gate and picked up the little dog.

"No time for cuddles!" Angel squirmed.

"And these two and this girl…these are his dogs. The old man. What are you doing here?" he asked.

"Look at Lester," Francine said. "It looks like they're talking.

Melinda appeared at the gate with all six pups.

"Pee-time!" she said.

"OK," said Day Care Guy.

Melinda and the pups ran out and the Night Dogs all pushed in.

"He was taking me to find Bob," Mimi sobbed. "He carried me and Boss walked on ahead. Two men jumped out and grabbed Boss! They put a bag over his head and tied two ropes to his collar! He couldn't get to either of them. Old Friend ran up and they hit him and knocked him down. I went flying! One of them was smoking and he stuck it into Old Friend's arm and burnt him!"

Lester gasped.

"The other one kicked him. Kicked him! An old friend lying on the ground and he kicked him! I leapt at him and bit and he kicked me away. But this piece came off of his pants and I kept it. Smell it!"

"I can smell it from here," Lester said. "Then what happened?"

"They tied the ropes to their truck and drove away. Boss had to run to keep from being dragged! Pee, Boss, pee! Pee everywhere along the way, I yelled. A bus driver stopped and picked up Old Friend. He drove us here to the dog park. Old Friend lay down on his blanket and cried. Bailiff stayed with him and we came here."

Tears rolled down her face.

"You're the best nose ever!" she cried. "Boss said so himself. You've got to find him, Lester! Old Friend looks…very bad…"

She laid the rag at Lester's feet.

"This is their smell and you know Boss's. That's the combination! Please find him!"

Lester breathed in.

"There's more smell here than just that rag," he breathed again. "That smell is here!"

"Help! Help!" Melinda's voice, small and frightened, floated in from the garden.

Lucy came running, charging like a wild bull, knocking over Mimi and Papillion on her way to the still open half door.

"Melinda!" she screamed.

All the dogs followed her into the garden. Puzzled, the humans went after them.

"Melinda! Melinda!" Lucy licked the red dog's face. "Wake up! Get up!"

Lucy was crying now. She turned to Lester. "They hurt her!"

Lester could see that. He was busy counting frightened puppies.

"One, two..." he said.

"Three, four..." said Day Care Guy. "Only four? Where's Larry and Moe?"

"They took my babies!" Melinda gasped. "They leaned over the fence and grabbed my babies!"

"What's this?" Francine picked up a long cigarette butt. It was still lit and burning.

"I jumped to bite them and they stomped me," Melinda sobbed. "I think something broke in my chest!"

"It's them! It's them!" Mimi cried.

"I got this piece of his sleeve," Melinda pointed to the rag.

"What's this?" Day Care Guy picked it up. "No, boy, you don't want this," he said.

Lester ignored him, grabbed the rag out of his hand and breathed deeply.

"It's the same smell!" he said.

"No!" Mimi cried.

"Yes!" Lester spoke softly so Melinda wouldn't hear.

"They think they can make him fight," he said.

"Who?" Lucy cried.

"And they'll use the puppies as bait!" Lester choked back tears.

"Who?" Lucy demanded. "Who are you talking about?"

"Auntie Melinda," rage and purpose filled Lester's heart. "Don't worry, I'll find them!"

On this day, of all days, for once the picket gate was closed.

Lester ran to the fence, choosing the farthest corner so he could build up speed. He leapt and cleared the fence, his back legs extending and pointing as gracefully as a ballet dancer.

With more agility than grace, Randy followed, holding the sleeve rag in his mouth.

"Lester!" Day Care Guy yelled.

"Dude," said Ben, "I can't make that jump!"

"Me, neither," Mimi cried.

"Allow me," said Jerry. He backed up a few paces, set himself and charged. He threw the full force of his massive, dense body into the gate. The flimsy pickets exploded on impact.

Francine screamed. Ben, Jerry and Mimi ran full tilt through the hole. Mimi carried the pant rag in her mouth.

"No, boy," Day Care Guy grabbed Rufahlo's collar. "Someone's got to stay here with us!"

Groaning from the impact and aftershock, half the remaining fence fell down. Lucy and Melinda sobbed and tried to comfort each other.

"No!" Francine was crying now. "The little one! She's running in the street! The car!" she screamed.

"She's OK," said Day Care Guy. "I see her. She made it!"

Without thinking, he wrapped his arms around Francine. She sobbed into his chest.

"She's one of his dogs," he soothed. "The Old Man. She's going home. She'll be OK...." He felt something tug at his leg.

"Killer!" he said. In spite of everything, he couldn't help but smile at the strange little dog tugging his pants.

"I can help!" Angel cried. "I can help!"

"But Lester...the others, where did they go?" Francine wiped her eyes.

"To look for Larry and Moe?" Day Care Guy thought out loud. The little pup paced back and forth, jumped up and down, his strange ears waggling every which way.

"I can help!" Angel cried. He snapped the tentacles straight up then pointed them in the direction of the fleeing dogs. He looked at Day Care Guy and pointed the tentacles again.

"I'll get the car," said Day Care Guy. "We'll all go look. We'll find them!"

"You've got the nose," said Randy. His voice was calm and steady even though they were running faster and farther than Lester had ever run in his life.

"But I've got the speed," he continued. "Endurance. And the eye," He winked. "Add my smell to the mix and follow. I'll keep up with them. You lead the others there."

He was off in a black and white blur of flying feet.

Lester slowed to a stop and breathed.

"Can't give out," he thought. "Must pace myself."

He slowed his breathing 'til it was steady and regular. His nostrils twitched.

"Yep," he thought, "we're going the right way."

"Hurry up!" he yelled to Ben and Jerry.

"Is that dog following us?" the smoker asked.

His legs ached from peddling the rusty bike. The puppies squirmed and scrabbled in the bag on his back, throwing him off balance. His lungs hurt.

"Let's stop," said the non-smoker. "Let him catch up. I'll cut him."

He snapped his knife open.

"Look at him", the smoker said. "Now, he stopped."

"Hmm, hmm, la la la la la." Randy smelled some flowers.

"Minding my own business here, just having a pee on the flowers…"

He lifted his leg and sprayed.

"It's a Border Collie," the non-smoker shrugged. "They're crazy."

"Hey! Shut up!" The smoker smacked at the bag. "Damn puppies!"

The non-smoker laughed.

"They peed, man! Peed all down your back! It's dripping on the ground!"

He laughed some more. The smoker swore and smacked the bag again.

"He's gone now," said the non-smoker. "Let's go."

"Learned a thing or two from Bailiff, haven't I?" Randy said, watching the men from behind a rosemary bush. "I must tell him."

He waited until the men propelled their creaking bikes a little further then followed, his sharp eye never leaving their backs.

Angel sat in Francine's lap, his tentacles focused out the window. Papillion leaned on his back, sniffing as hard as she could. Rufahlo propped Lucy on his shoulder, their two noses twitching out the back window. Melinda, her four puppies clinging, dragged herself up to Rufahlo's side.

"What is their smell combination?" he asked.

"Mother's milk, puppy poop, lemon thyme and mint," she moaned.

"Lemon thyme and mint?" Lucy asked. Her eyes were wide.

"There's a big patch at the park," Melinda said. "They saw some big dog roll in it and now I can't keep them out of it."

Lucy turned her head back out the window. She stared, unseeing, and sniffed.

Angel moved the tentacles back and forth, scanning the streets for sound. He heard the thundering of padded feet, and snorts of labored breathing. He held the tentacles still and focused.

"Dudes!" Ben's voice said. "Wait up!"

His tentacles snapped toward the sound.

"That way!" he barked.

"That way!" Silent and invisible, Busy flapped his robes, blowing the resting scents toward the car.

"Lemon thyme!" squeaked Papillion.

"Mint!" Rufahlo barked.

"Pee!" Melinda whimpered. "They peed here!"

"That way!" Lucy screamed.

Watching Angel's ears, Day Care Guy turned the car.

"Killer pointed this way," he explained. "We'll try here."

"There!" Francine pointed. "Down at the very end, in those bushes! The hair-cut dog!"

Day Care Guy squinted and focused, just in time to see Ben's butt disappear through the brush.

"Let's go!" he said and hit the gas.

"I should take you to a doctor," said the Bus Driver.

"No," Old Friend whispered. "Please. I must be here."

The Bus Driver covered him with the tartan blanket.

"He'll come back," Old Friend whispered. "I must be here."

He chuckled then moaned with pain.

"Those two," he smiled but winced with the effort. "No match for my dog."

He grimaced and collapsed onto his pillow.

"There's shelter here, at least," the Bus Driver thought. A gentle breeze fluttered the edge of the tree circle. The Corgi licked the old man's forehead.

"My cousin sent sandwiches and coffee," the Bus Driver said.

"And here's a doughnut for your buddy here."

"I'll have it later," Bailiff said. "After I finish this." He licked the old man's forehead with long smooth strokes.

"He's not well," Bailiff said. "Nothing cures like a thorough coating of dog spit."

"Good boy," the Bus Driver gave the dog a pat.

"And if he can't come back," Old Friend whispered, "or if he can't get here in time…"

He paused for rest and breathed.

"If you see him," the old man's eyes pleaded. "Just tell him I loved him and thought about him every minute of the day."

"Shhh," said the Bus Driver. "Rest now. We'll get him back. I know those two and a couple places they hang out. I'll drive the bus and have a look."

"Thank you," Old Friend whispered. He closed his eyes.

The Bus Driver stumbled from the circle and wondered which way to go.

"That way," Busy fluttered his robes, blowing the breezes in the right direction.

"And hurry up!"

Hiding behind the last stand of trees before the open space, Randy and Lester assessed the situation.

"A box car," said Randy. "Wide open. Abandoned. Good place to hide. Room for the bikes."

Lester sniffed at the sleeve rag then put his nose high in the air.

"This is it, all right," Lester's nostrils flared. "There's Boss and the puppies. Look! Behind the box car!"

At the far edge of the box car, the wheels of a truck could be seen.

"And the bikes," Randy pointed to the corner of the truck's bed. A rusty handle bar hung over the side.

"What's the plan?" Jerry tip-toed the last few feet to join them.

"What should we do?" Ben was right behind.

"When there's danger," Randy said, "an old dog should face it. That would be me. You lads have a good few dog years left." He scanned their worried faces and settled on Lester.

"However, having said that, you look...and I'll say this as delicately as I can...you look the least threatening of us all. You could get farther without raising fears."

Day Care Guy's hair pinning job had survived the journey. Lester remembered the little jeweled collar on his top knot. The diamond pattern on his body was still in place.

"Don't let the sparkle fool you," he growled.

"Good lad!" Randy said. "Approach with caution and check it out. Call us and we'll come running."

Lester nodded and tiptoed into the open.

He crept softly toward the box car's wide open doors. No one was visible but he could hear growling and men's voices

"Yeah! Yeah!" said the smoker.

"Eat the damn puppies!" said the non-smoker.

Boss's head, his face a rage of glowing eyes and snapping teeth, appeared in profile from behind one side of the doorway.

"Careful, man," said the smoker.

"Just throw 'em," said the non-smoker.

Moe and Larry sailed through the air toward Boss's snarling face.

"Babies!" Boss commanded. "Get behind me! And stay there!"

Lester could hear Moe and Larry whimper.

"Damn dog!" said the smoker. "Eat the damn puppies!"

Boss's face showed again past the door frame as he strained forward and roared.

"That's it," said the non-smoker. "I'm going to cut him!"

Lester charged and leapt into the box car.

"What's going on here!" he roared.

"Lester!" Boss cried. A short chain stretched from his neck to a bolt in the floor.

"What the hell…" the smoker shielded his eyes. Lester turned and saw two men on the other side of the open box car door.

"I said, what's going on here!" Lester roared.

The sun reflected off the sparkly jewel pins and blinded the two men. They held their hands in front of their faces.

"A…a fancy dog!" The non-smoker couldn't believe his squinting eyes.

"Lester!" Boss roared, his face a mask of rage once again. "Act like you hate me!" He snapped his huge teeth.

"OK!" Lester roared back. "What's the plan?"

"If they think I want to fight you," Boss roared, "they'll let me off the chain!"

"OK," Lester roared and snapped his own teeth. "I hate you! I really hate you!"

"I hate you back!" Boss screamed. "Your hair looks crazy today!"

"You…you've got a big nose!" Lester yelled.

"Big nose!" Boss strained at the chain. "Look who's talking!"

"Well, at least I know how to use it!" Lester screamed. "How do you think I got here?"

"Good boy!" Boss shrieked and growled and strained against the chain. "The training worked!"

"Look!" The non-smoker smirked. "He wants to fight the fancy boy!"

"You bet I do!" Boss showed more teeth than Lester had ever seen.

"You got nothing, old man," Lester yelled. "Come over here

and try me!"

"This should be good," the smoker crept forward.

"Careful," said the non-smoker.

"Don't worry," Boss screamed. "It's him I want!"

"Oh, yeah?" Lester shouted. "Bring it! Come and get me!"

"Yeah!" the smoker said. The chain fell to the floor.

"Oh, yeah!" the boys yelled. They jumped together, stood side by side and roared at the two confused men.

"What?" The smoker moved as far back as he could.

"What now, genius?" said the non-smoker, trying to get behind him.

"Guys!" Lester yelled. "Now!"

The boys hadn't waited for their cue. In an instant, Jerry was next to Boss, growling and snapping his own terrifying jaws.

Ben and Randy stood behind them, flanking the frightened puppies.

"Don't let the sparkly fool you," Jerry snarled, flashing his collar.

"What now?" Lester yelled.

"I don't know," Boss roared back. "Make noise while I try to think!"

The five boys opened their jaws.

"You too, little pups," said Randy.

"Make some big, bad noise," said Ben.

Chapter Thirty-one

Mother, Father and Earth-Dog-Space-Alien-Mutants

The roars and puppy screams were so loud Angel moved his tentacles to shield them from the noise. The humans looked confused.

"In there!" Angel pointed again.

"Oh, my God!" Francine whispered. "What will we do?"

"I don't know," said Day Care Guy. "Let me think!"

"No time to think!" Angel cried. "I'm going!"

He scampered toward the box car.

"Little one, wait for me!" Rufahlo cried. "I help you make the jump!"

He stopped and turned.

"Girls stay here!" he commanded.

"You're not the boss of me!" Papillion snapped.

"Or me!" Lucy moved forward. "My Lester's in there! I can hear him!"

"My babies are there," said Melinda. "I'm going too!"

Rufahlo made a face. "Well, stay behind me, at least!"

He galloped forward and lowered his head. Angel leaped onto his neck mid-gallop and the two of them sailed through the box car door. Angel tumbled off Rufahlo's neck and rolled a bit, coming to a stop at Jerry's feet.

"What's going on here?" Rufahlo joined the roar.

"Oh, crap," said the smoker. "Another big one!"

"With teeth," said the non-smoker.

Lucy pushed Melinda's butt and helped her into the opening. Moving with pain, Melinda bent, grabbing first Lucy's collar, then Papillion's and dragged them in.

"Mommy! Mommy!" Moe and Larry cried.

"My babies!" Melinda sobbed. "Are you hurt?"

267

"You beasts!" Lucy screamed. She threw herself across the open space and got the smoker by the shin.

"Ahhh!," he screamed. "Get off me!"

He kicked at her until her jaws released, then picked her up by the top knot and started to throw.

"Stop!" Francine screamed.

Everyone stopped. The men stood there stunned, their jaws open, their eyes frightened.

"Ow! Top knot! Ow!" Lucy squirmed.

"Lucy!" Boss said, his voice filled with wonder.

She turned toward the voice and went limp.

"Boss!" she whispered. "Ow! Top knot! Ow!" She squirmed again.

"Mother?" Lester's face questioned.

Lucy smiled.

"Father," she pointed to Boss. She shrugged and started to squirm again.

The boys' turned to each other. Their eyes met. Each pair of eyes traveled down to the other one's nose. They flashed a quick grin.

"Later," they said and turned back to the men.

"Take your hands off my mother!" Lester roared and started forward.

The knife snapped open in the non-smoker's hand.

"Wait," Boss held Lester back.

Francine gasped.

"These your dogs?" the non-smoker said.

"Some of them...," said Day Care Guy.

"Call them off or the poodle gets it," said the non-smoker, waving the knife.

"She bit me," said the smoker. "I think she gets it anyway!"

The dogs roared and screamed, the sounds bouncing off the box car walls. Angel stuffed his tentacles into Ben's fur to dull the noise.

The non-smoker, unsure if this was really a good idea, slowly raised the hand that held the knife.

"Quiet!" yelled a voice no one had ever heard before. Everyone stopped. Francine looked at Day Care Guy and trembled.

"You took our puppies," he said. "Don't make it worse for yourselves."

"You can't prove nothing," the smoker said.

"You stink like pee," Melinda yelled. "And I have your sleeve! A blind dog could see you did it!"

"You stink like pee," Day Care Guy said. "Each dog's pee is singular to itself. One lab test would prove it."

"And your dog bit me!" the smoker yelled. "I'll sue!"

"You'll have to get past these dogs first," Day Care Guy said. "And they don't seem to like you."

The non-smoker sneered. "Let's not forget who's holding this." He waved the knife.

The group growl started again.

"Anyone makes a move," he yelled, "and the poodle gets it!"

"Ow!" Lucy cried.

"Let go of my mother!" Lester screamed.

"Wait!" Boss commanded, holding him back.

"Lester!" a small voice said. Lester saw the strange little dog at his side.

"Let me!" Angel said, waggling his tentacles. "Let me try!"

He waggled them again and winked.

Lester's eyes grew wide. He remembered that day in the park, the slimy maple leaves, the soggy bugs.

"Go!" he said softly. "Go!"

The little dog marched into the no man's land in between the angry men and the angrier dogs. He sat and waggled his ears.

"What the..." the non-smoker said. He stopped waving the knife.

"Killer!" said Day Care Guy. "No!"

"Pick me," Angel said. "Choose me. Make me your puppy dog."

"That's not a dog," the smoker was confused. He lowered the hand that held Lucy.

"That's a science experiment," the non-smoker said.

"An earth-dog-space-alien mutant!" said the smoker. "I've heard of that!"

Lucy wriggled. The smoker looked at her and shrugged. He tossed her to the ground and grabbed Angel. Day Care Guy moved. Francine held him back. Lucy scampered behind Boss and Lester and peeked out between their legs.

The smoker held the little dog at arm's length, looking him over.

"I'm very unusual," said Angel. "Maybe I really am an earth-dog-space-alien mutant."

"I knew it!" Randy whispered.

"What a freak!" the non-smoker sneered.

"Yes!" Angel said. "A freak! You could sell me on E-bay for a lot of money!"

"That's it!" Lucy cried. "Focus! Everyone!"

"Sell me on E-bay!" she chanted and they all followed.

"Sell me on E-bay! Sell me on E-bay! Sell me on E-bay!"

"A lot of money! A lot of money! A lot of money! A lot of money!"

"Damn!" said the smoker. "I bet we could sell him on E-bay!"

"For a lot of money," said the non-smoker.

"OK," said the smoker. "Here's the deal. We'll take this one and the rest of you can go."

"No!" said the voice no one had ever heard before.

"None of these dogs go with you," Day Care Guy snarled.

The group growl started out low.

"We're back to that, eh?" said the non-smoker, moving the knife again. "Don't forget..."

"Look at him!" said the smoker. "What a freak! What's he doing now?"

Angel's tentacles had snapped up straight into the V.

"Get ready," Lester whispered.

"He's kind of cute..." the smoker cracked a smile.

"Now!" Angel yelled.

The tentacles snapped forward. A thick stream of slime hit the smoker right in the eyes.

"Gleah!" he yelled and tossed Angel into the air while he swiped at his eyes.

Moving through the air and twisting to re-focus, Angel's aim on the next spew wasn't quite true. He missed the non-smoker's eyes. The slime hit the ugly man's nose, and went into his open mouth.

"Blwaaaah!" he yelled and grabbed at his face. He forgot to drop the knife and cut himself on the nose. Blood spewed everywhere.

"Aaaaah!" his scream gurgled through the slime.

He threw the knife aside. It's sideway's path crossed Angel's descending path and sliced through a piece of the flying dog's tentacle.

"Killer!" screamed Day Care Guy.

"Now!" Boss and Lester roared as one.

Together, the two dogs leapt forward. Boss's huge paws caught the non-smoker square in the chest. His massive weight knocked the man flat on the floor.

Lester's aim was true but he was lighter and could only make the smoker stumble.

"Get down!" Rufahlo roared. He leapt over Lester's head. The smoker fell flat on his back.

"And stay down!" Rufahlo growled into the frightened man's face.

Jerry had his huge jaws wrapped around the non-smoker's throat.

"Just stay still and no one gets hurt," he mumbled into the man's neck.

Ben was having trouble.

"Ow!" he said. "I can't open that wide!"

"Trade places," said Rufahlo. "See? Mine are so big I can cover half his face and also his neck!" He made a happy face. "The slime," he said. It's quite tasty!"

Ben and Melinda draped themselves across the two men's bodies. Randy covered all four feet.

Lucy and Papillion stood poised over the men's pant zippers.

"I don't want to…" Papillion warned.

"Ugh, no!" Lucy made a face. "But I will if I have to!"

"Little…needle…teeth!" Papillion twitched.

"We have little needle teeth," Moe and Larry said. "Can we help?"

"Sure, sweeties," Lucy said. "We'll take turns"

"What do we do now?" Day Care Guy asked, his face anguished. He cradled the bleeding Angel in his arms. "Killer has to go to the hospital and so does Melinda!"

Francine was already dialing her phone.

While they waited for the police to arrive, Day Care Guy fretted over Angel. Francine cleaned up the slime and the Night Dogs made their plans.

"I gotta go," Boss said to Lester and Lucy. "I've got to get back to my Old Friend. They hurt him…"

"Go," said Lucy. "We'll be all right."

"I'll go with you," Lester said.

"Yes!" Lucy nodded. "If Lester's with you, no one will be scared. You'll be two friends, one big and one sparkly, out for a walk together. The people will leave you alone."

"I'll see you soon," said Boss. He bent and licked her face.

"Isn't that cute?" Francine said. "Lucy's got a boyfriend."

Day Care Guy looked up from the bleeding Angel and gave a weak smile.

"Stay here, boys, and help these people," Boss said. "As soon as the cops arrive, scatter and get back to the Dog Park."

The Night Dogs understood.

"Where are they going?" Francine cried as the two dogs took off running. "Lester!"

"They'll go back to the Dog Park," Day Care Guy said. "We'll find them there. What are you doing?"

Francine had dug deep into her bag and pulled out an empty face cream jar.

"I'm cleaning these boys up a bit," she said. "Who knows what's in this stuff?"

She scraped the jar's edge over the men's faces and necks. The men seemed grateful and, even if they weren't, they were still held down by Jerry and Rufahlo's big jaws on their necks.

"Please don't struggle," Rufahlo said politely. "You'll force your jugular into my very sharp incisors and that would not be good. For you."

"What he said," Jerry growled.

"Why don't you use a facial wipe?" Day Care Guy was puzzled. Francine continued scraping. When she'd collected as much as she could, she brought the jar over to Angel and Day Care Guy.

"My sweet, strange, little creature," she murmured, stroking Angel's head. "What a very brave thing you did for us!"

Angel cuddled into Day Care Guy's chest.

"Do you think you could spit out a little more slime into this jar?", she asked. "For me?"

"Francine..." Day Care Guy held Angel tighter.

"It's for science!" she said. "Could you honey? From your one good ear?"

Angel looked up at Day Care Guy.

"She's your friend," he said, "and you're my Friend. Therefore, she's my friend too."

Weakly, he snapped his one good tentacle up straight. She held the jar close. With the little strength he could muster, he shot the tentacle forward. A thin stream of slime spewed lazily into the jar.

"Thank you, darling," she said. "This might be enough."

"I'll sleep now," said Angel. He closed his eyes.

"Killer!" cried Day Care Guy. "Don't leave me!"

"I won't," Angel said. He snored a bit so the man would know he was alive.

"Where are the cops?" Day Care Guy moaned.

"They're here!" said Randy. "Night Dogs scatter!"

Angel Risks It All

Chapter Thirty-two
How to Explain This?

The first cop scratched his head.

"Let me get this straight," he sighed. "A Rottweiler, who is not here now, knocked you down."

"Yes!" the non-smoker said.

"And a pit bull, also no longer present, had you by the neck?"

"Yes!" the non-smoker said.

"And you," the cop turned to the smoker. "A poodle..." He tried not to snigger.

"It was a big poodle!" the smoker was indignant.

"...covered in little sparkly jewels...." The cop had to stop and collect himself. He took a deep breath.

"The sparkly poodle, who is also no longer present, knocked you down," he continued, "and that doofus there..." He pointed to Rufahlo.

Every bit the show dog, Rufahlo was prancing around on his hind legs, rolling in the dirt, making stupid faces and waggling his ears. Papillion laughed so hard she fell down and couldn't get up. He nosed her up and began the display all over again.

"That...clearly vicious dog there," the cop said. "He held you down by the neck."

"Yes!" the smoker said.

"And this dog," he pointed to Melinda who was cuddling Larry and Moe. "Who seems to have a broken rib and is clearly in a lot of pain, helped hold you down?"

"Yes!" said the smoker.

"And the Border Collie held down our feet!" said the non-smoker.

"Also not here now," said the cop. "The Border Collie."

"Yes!" the two men nodded.

"And of all these vicious dogs," the cop said, "it was the Toy Poodle that bit you?"

"Yes!" said the smoker. "And I'm going to sue!"

"Let me see your leg." The cop looked at the smoker's shin.

"Well, there is a bruise," he said. "But your pants aren't torn, there's no clear teeth marks and the skin's not broken...what about this?" The cop pointed to the smoker's other pant leg. A large piece of shin cloth was missing.

"Another dog did that," the smoker said.

"Who is also not here now?" the cop asked.

"Yes!" the smoker said.

"What about your sleeve?" the cop said to the non-smoker.

"She did that!" He pointed to Melinda.

"When you were stealing her two puppies!" Day Care Guy exclaimed.

"Sir..." said the cop.

"Sorry," said Day Care Guy.

"Oh," said the cop. "Lest I forget. This little...dog? Who is cut on the...ear? And clearly weak from the loss of blood, this little dog is actually an earth-dog-space-alien mutant..."

"Yes!" said the smoker.

"Who sprayed you in the eyes..."

"And my nose!" said the non-smoker.

"With a thick stream of venomous slime..."

"Yes!" said the smoker.

"Which has now evaporated completely..."

"She's got some in a jar!" the smoker pointed to Francine. Francine shrugged as if to say, "What? What are they talking about?"

The cop sighed and turned back to the smoker.

"...leaving no trace?" he finished wearily

"Yes!" said the smoker.

"Except that punk's hair is now lustrous and shiny," Francine thought to herself. "And curled into fantastic style! I knew it!" she thought. "It's the slime!" She pushed the face cream jar further down into her bag.

"Whose knife is this?" the second cop held the knife up by its belt clip.

"Mine," said the non-smoker.

"And whose blood is on it?" the cop asked.

"Mine," said the non-smoker.

"And his!" Day Care Guy pointed to the cut on Angel's ear.

"That was an accident!" said the non-smoker.

"You cut yourself in the face?" the cop asked.

"After the space-alien-dog-mutant slimed me! Yes!" the non-smoker said.

The two cops looked at each other. The first one looked at the ground and sighed deeply.

"I think what we have here, ladies and gentlemen," he said, "is a draw. No harm, no foul, everybody go home now."

"But they stole our puppies!" Francine exclaimed.

"To feed to the Rottweiler who is not here now," the cop said. Francine nodded.

"And you didn't actually see them do it."

"But they smell like pee, and there's pee all over that bag!" Day Care Guy protested. "A dog's pee is individual to the dog! One lab test would prove it!"

Day Care Guy desperately hoped this was actually true.

"It's true," the cop said. "These boys do smell. But there's lots of smells in there and I don't think the fact that some dog peed on that bag would really prove anything."

"So, we can go now?" Day Care Guy asked. "We have to get him, and her, to the hospital."

"This your dog?" the cop smiled. "The earth-dog-space-alien mutant?"

Angel opened his eyes.

"Am I?" he asked. "Am I your puppy dog?"

"Yes!" Day Care Guy said firmly. "He's my dog."

Had he felt better, Angel would have danced for joy. As it was, he sighed with perfect happiness and closed his eyes.

"Or he will be," Day Care Guy said. "I have to ask him."

"Who?" said the cop, "Ask who?"

"The old man," said Day Care Guy.

"What old man?" the cop said.

The smoker looked nervous. The non-smoker inched toward the box car door.

"The old man in the park!" a loud voice called.

Outside the box car, standing in the sun, the Bus Driver pointed an angry finger at the two men.

"The old man these two kicked to the ground and left for dead when they stole his dog!"

The non-smoker tried to bolt but the second cop grabbed his collar.

"What kind of dog was it?" asked the first cop.

"A Rottweiler!" said the Bus Driver.

"Ah," said the cop. "The Rottweiler!"

"You can't prove nothing," yelled the smoker.

"My bus is equipped with a camera," sneered the Bus Driver. "I've got it all on tape!"

"Cuff 'em," said the first cop. "For now..."

"If you want to ask him," said the Bus Driver, "you'd better hurry. He was old and sick before they knocked him down. He's... not doing too well...." The Bus Driver swallowed. "I don't think he'll last much longer...." His voice trailed off. "You'll find him in the tree circle."

"The what?" said the cop.

"I'll show you!" said Francine. "You take the car and get these two to the hospital," she told Day Care Guy.

"I'll take the lady and the other dogs on my bus," said the Driver. "Follow us!"

The cops stuffed the two men into their car. They drove off after the bus, each one wondering how in the world they would explain all this in their daily arrest report.

Working systematically, Bailiff moved from one hand to the other, then Old Friend's neck, his cheek, then back to the hands, giving each part a careful and complete going over with his tongue.

"Nothing cures like a thorough coating of dog spit," he said. "I wish he'd turn over so I could get the other cheek."

"It can't hurt," said Mimi, "but I think he needs more than that."

Old Friend hadn't moved since the Bus Driver left. The coffee was cold and the sandwiches still in their bag, unwrapped. The old man dozed fitfully. Several times he'd shot up with a start. He'd lift his head, look around, sniff the air and call for Boss. When no Boss came, he'd closed his eyes and dropped his head back on his bag.

Mimi hadn't moved from the entrance. For hours, she scanned and searched every section of the park. Twilight was gathering and she was very tired. A distant twinkle caught her eye.

"It's not a star," she thought. "It's on the ground. It's moving."

She followed the twinkle as it flashed on the entrance path to the park. The twinkle paused. Lumbering and limping behind the twinkle, a large, dark shape moved toward their little hill. She breathed in.

"Lemon thyme and mint!" She turned to Bailiff.

"You can stop now!" she said. "He's here!"

The fear that gripped Boss's heart made the last few yards very hard to climb. Lester nudged him forward. Boss looked to the tartan blanket. Old Friend's face was very pale and still.

"Too late!" he choked.

Mimi nudged him.

"Not too late," she whispered. "Just in time."

Boss crept forward. He sat in front of Old Friend, looked him over, then bent and licked his face.

The old man's eyes opened slowly and focused.

"My baby!" he cried. "My baby boy! I knew you'd come back to me!"

He reached out and cradled the big dog's face.

"My baby boy," he murmured. He pulled himself up slowly and gathered the huge dog in his arms.

"My boy," he hugged and swayed and stroked the big dog's fur.

"My baby boy! You're safe!" he cried. "Thank you for coming back to me!"

Boss licked his cheeks. The old man hugged him for a long time and then released.

"I can rest easy now," he lay back down on his pillow. Boss bent to lick his face. Old Friend smiled and stroked the dog's cheeks. A sparkle caught his eye.

"And look, the young one's here." He looked at the two dogs sitting side by side.

"Did he help you?" he asked. "Is that why he's here?"

"Yes, he did," said Boss. "I'm so proud of him. And grateful."

The warm light from his yellow eyes filled the circle.

"My Old Friend is here," he smiled and spoke softly. "And I have a son."

Overwhelmed, Lester looked at the ground, scrabbling the dirt with his paw.

"My brave, smart...sparkly boy," Boss said. Lester looked up and they grinned at each other.

"I'm so very proud," Boss said. "So proud of my sparkly boy... and his great big nose!"

The dogs chuckled quietly. Bailiff rolled on his back.

Side by side, the two boys looked at Old Friend. His face filled with wonder.

"Such different dogs," he said softly. "But your faces...your eyes...your noses! You could be father and son."

"We are!" said Boss, grinning widely.

"Really?" asked Bailiff.

"Yes," Lester nodded. "We learned that today."

The two dogs grinned.

"I can see it," said Bailiff.

"Incoming!" said Mimi, staring out the entrance. "More dogs!"

Randy, Ben and Jerry approached with caution. Mimi's smiling face was reassuring but they couldn't let their guard down until they were safe inside the circle. When they saw that Boss was there and Old Friend was awake and smiling, they all relaxed, collapsing on the ground.

"Everyone helped," said Boss. "Thank you all!"

Rousing himself to play host, Old Friend unwrapped the sandwiches.

"Mmmm, sourdough," he struggled. "Good, but not so easy to tear apart."

But he managed it and soon handed round the bits of sandwich to all the grateful dogs.

"Have mine," Lester said to Boss. "I get enough to eat."

"I will," said Boss. "I've been through a lot today. Thank you."

"Have mine," Bailiff said to Randy.

"Ah, go on, have it yourself," Randy said. "A Border Collie never eats much. But thanks."

The proffered bit was gone before he'd finished the word "thanks."

"People!" Mimi spoke through a mouthful of bread. "People are coming!"

"Bob?" said Bailiff through a mouthful of meat. "Is it Bob?"

"No," Mimi snapped. She peered into the gathering darkness.

"It's the lady who cut my hair!" said Ben.

"And the bus driver who brought us home," said Mimi. "And... some others..."

Chapter Thirty-three

Memories Don't Always Hurt

The Bus Driver crawled in first.

"Hello, come in!" Old Friend smiled. To ease any fears the dogs might have had, he spread his arms wide and spoke in warm welcoming tones

"Look who's home!" He stroked Boss's head.

"You said they were no match for your dog," the Bus Driver said. "And you were right!"

He had brought more food from his cousin's doughnut shop: hot soup for the old man, more sandwiches for the dogs and doughnuts for anyone who wanted them. While Old Friend sipped the soup, the Bus Driver explained what the other people wanted.

"The Police are here," he said. "They have the two men who attacked you. They want to show you pictures. And there's a lady here. I think this is her dog," he pointed to Lester. "I think this one helped your dog escape. She wants to see if you're all right."

A fluffy white head peaked through the entrance.

"Can we come in now?"

"Lucy," Boss smiled. Lucy couldn't wait any more. She rushed to Boss's side and leaned against him.

Old Friend set down the soup.

"This dog," he said. "I don't remember much these days, but she looks very familiar."

Lester moved to sit next to his mother.

Old Friend looked at the three faces in a row.

"I do," he said. "I do remember you, little scamp." He gave her head a pat.

"The hair," Lucy said. "Don't crush the hair."

"Still the same little snoot you always were," Old Friend murmured. He scanned the three faces again.

"Good lord," he said. "It must be true." He chuckled.

"That would make you my grandson," he said, ruffling Lester's topknot.

The Bus Driver had no idea what he was talking about.

"Are you ready?" he asked. "Can I tell the policemen to come in?"

"Yes," Old Friend chuckled. "I'm remembering things. Let's take advantage while we can."

Into the circle crawled the two cops, followed by Francine and Rufahlo.

Francine was charmed by the tableaux of Old Friend and his big, rough dog sitting next to her two fancy charges. She asked to take a picture and the little family posed together for her phone. Rufahlo's eyes grew very wide. He looked at Lester, questioning. Lester's own wide eyes looked first to his mother, then to Boss, then back to Rufahlo. He raised his brows and nodded.

Rufahlo's jaw dropped. He settled in the sphinx position and looked at Lester again. Lester shrugged and grinned. Rufahlo grinned and covered his face with his paws.

"Can I show you some pictures?" the policeman reached for his phone.

Old Friend remembered very well. He told the whole story of how they had set out to find Mimi's owner. The two men had followed. They'd jumped out from behind bushes and put a bag on Boss's head. They had knocked him to the ground and kicked him. He showed the cigarette burn on his arm. The cops took pictures. Proudly, he told how the little girl dog had attacked one man's leg and been kicked away. She tore a big rag off the man's pants. She had disappeared with it which had him worried. She came back to the tree circle some time later, still holding the rag in her mouth.

"Would you happen to have that rag now?" asked the policeman.

"Little one!" said Old Friend. "Dirty thing?"

"I hid it," said Mimi. "It was smelly."

She ran to the edge of the circle and came back with the rag in her mouth.

"Can we take this?" asked the policeman. "If it's a match for the hole in his pants, that would be a help."

"Please do," said Old Friend.

"It's smelly," Mimi wrinkled her nose.

"And I have the sleeve rag from the other man at home," said Francine.

The cop had pictures of the suspects on his phone.

"Oh, yes," Old Friend said. "That's them."

"You're sure?" asked the cop.

"Oh, yes," said Old Friend.

"And you don't remember them other than today?" the cop asked.

"Should I?" Old Friend asked.

There was a sniffling noise. The Bus Driver wiped his eyes.

"I think I know you, sir," said the policeman. "You're Joe Whelan. Sergeant Joe."

It had been a long time since Old Friend had heard his real name.

"Am I?" he asked.

"And this big man here," the cop offered his fist for Boss to smell. Boss gave it a generous lick. The man stroked his head.

"He was much younger then," said the cop, "but he was The Boss! Sergeant Joe and the Boss! I was just a rookie then."

"I'm glad we're remembered well," Old Friend wanted to be polite.

"You were legends," said the cop. "A great team. There was... an incident.

I heard you were hurt. We didn't see you again. A great loss for the department."

Old Friend smiled.

"There's a lot I don't remember. Don't want to. I'm glad you're only asking about today. Today is still with me. My boy is home and safe. Life is good."

"I'm glad to see…" the cop took in the surroundings. "I'm glad to see you're safe…with your family." He sighed and looked down for a moment.

"Did you get all that?" he looked up at the other cop.

"Yes," said the man.

Francine had been using her phone too. She shut it off and put it in her purse.

"Thank you for talking to us," said the cop. "I'll come check on you tomorrow, see how you're doing."

The people got up and left. Boss could hear them murmuring outside.

"Did you hear that, my baby boy? We were legends!" Old Friend smiled. "I wish I could remember that part."

"We tried to forget," Boss said fondly.

Lucy cuddled to Boss's side. Lester sniffed the air. Boss looked at him. Lester looked away.

"Oh, I'm so tired now," said Old Friend, "and so happy. I'll sleep for a long, long, time."

He settled down and very quickly started to snore. Lester looked up and met Boss's eyes. They sniffed together.

Boss settled into his nighttime position, curled next to Old Friend's body, front leg draped over the old man's side.

"Good night," whispered Lucy, giving him a lick.

"Tomorrow," Lester whispered. Their eyes met. Lester held his gaze until Francine called.

"I'll leave them be tonight," said the cop. "But tomorrow…"

"He's been here a long time," Francine said. "He hurts no one."

"I know," said the cop. "But I can't. I'll bring Social Services. They'll find him a place, they're good at that. But the dogs…"

"His dog!" Francine cried.

"They can't take dogs," the cop said. "They'll go to the pound. They'll find new homes."

"But…what's the use? Where's the good in that?" Francine was crying now.

"I…" said the cop. "I…I got nothing. I have to do my job. I'm sorry," he said.

Francine swallowed. She worked to put a smile into her voice.

"Day Care dogs! Time to go home," she called.

Rufahlo bounded out of the circle. Slowly and reluctantly, Lester and Lucy followed.

Old Friend

Busy Angel

Chapter Thirty-Four

Please Don't Leave Me

"She'll recover very well," said the vet. "And the puppies are just fine. You can take them home now." She put Moe and Larry into Day Care Guy's arms.

"The other one has to stay here," she said. "I'll be honest. I can't...I can't tell you he'll be fine. I'm not sure what's wrong with him. We've stitched up the...ear? And given him as much blood as he should need but...he's not responding well..." her voice trailed off.

Day Care Guy did not want to leave. He thought of the four more puppies still in the car and of Papillion. Francine had texted him about going to the park and leaving the little dog at home. She had included instructions for dinner. Papillion had a special needs diet.

"Can I come back?" he asked. "Can I stay with him?"

"Sure you can," said the vet. "We find it helps the pet to have their loved one near. We'll set up a cot," she said. "It's an extra fifty dollars."

"Ka-ching," Day Care Guy thought.

He drove the Irish setter family home.

Papillion was very glad to see them and scarfed down her special needs dinner. She then placed herself in front of Melinda and barked bossy instructions to any pup that came near.

"Your mother needs her rest!" she barked. "Go rip up a toy!"

The other four meekly obeyed.

"Can we lick her face?" asked Moe.

"We were scared too," Larry whined.

"Let them," Melinda said weakly.

"Ok," said Papillion," but just licking!"

The boys kissed their mother then scampered off to play. They ripped apart several plush toys before wending their way into Day Care Guy's room with the other four. When they realized he wasn't there, they crept out of the room and over to the bed where their mother slept. Papillion growled. Moe and Larry settled down, resting their heads gently on Melinda's rump. Papillion nodded and the other four settled down with their heads on Moe and Larry's rumps. Everyone snored in unison. Papillion smiled. She pulled her little pillow over to Melinda's side, settled in and went to sleep.

Day Care Guy held Angel's paw in his hand.

"Don't leave me," he said.

"I won't," Angel thought.

"I've never had a dog of my own," the man said. "I take care of other people's dogs and…and, I love it!" he said. He looked at the sleeping creature.

"But you're mine," he said. "Or, I hope you will be. I have to ask the old man."

He paused and thought.

"Francine said the right dog would pick me! You picked me! I know you did!"

Day Care Guy looked at his feet. He was glad everyone was gone and no one could hear his sad confessions to a sleeping dog.

"You're…unusual…like me," he said.

He joined his one hand to the other and stroked the sleeping dog's paw.

"And you're happy! Just as you are! Like me…I like to think," Day Care Guy's voice faded.

"Come be my puppy dog," he said. "We'd make such a great team!" His eyes stung and he pressed them hard. With a sigh, he settled on the cot, reached out to hold the dog's paw and went to sleep.

Angel felt his loving touch and smiled.

"Yes!" he thought. "I am your dog! I wonder why I can't move?"

This thought was too complicated. He set it aside for later and drifted off to sleep.

In his mind, Old Friend felt himself moving faster than the speed of light. In Boss's eyes, he wasn't moving at all.

"Still breathing," Boss thought, "but only just."

He was lying down at Old Friend's back, front leg draped around the man's chest. For years and years, this was how each day ended. They would lie down together, think about the day and dream about tomorrow. Boss sighed. Very gently, he laid his head against Old Friend's cheek. The man's face twitched a very tiny smile. A shaky hand found Boss's cheek and rested there.

The other dogs had gathered close and formed a circle round them. Their breath warmed the air.

He knew the answer but he had to ask one last time.

"Please don't go," Boss thought.

The shaky hand gave his cheek a gentle squeeze.

"I'll be there," Old Friend said without speaking. "My love will never leave you. You'll feel me."

"I'd rather hear your voice," Boss thought.

The shaky hand lay still.

"And take our walks," Boss cried in his head.

"My love will never leave you." The frail hand slid slowly from the dog's cheek. Softly, it came to rest on the tartan blanket. Very gently, Mimi licked the lifeless fingers. Boss rubbed the still warm cheek.

A tiny poof of light glowed dimly in the tree tops.

"Do you feel me?" said Old Friend's voice. "Do you hear me?"

"I do," Boss cried inside. He hugged the mortal vessel that

had been his friend and cried out loud. The other dogs cried with him and they mourned through the night.

Chapter Thirty-five

Waiting for the Future to Arrive

Randy woke up just before dawn. Reverently, he picked up Old Friend's big, floppy hat and laid it gently over the old man's face. Mimi pawed the extra sheet out of one of his bags. Bailiff helped her open the sheet and pull it over his body.

"Thank you," Boss whispered.

Soldiering on through sorrow, Boss called the troops to order. Shaken and exhausted, the dogs tried to understand what he was saying.

"People will be here soon," he said. "Those cops will come back, or that lady will come to see how he is, or the Bus Driver..."

He hung his head and took a deep breath.

"When they realize he's gone," Boss continued, "Animal Control..." He stopped.

No one moved.

"I'm done," he said. "I'm not running anymore."

Ben and Jerry glanced at each other and looked down. Mimi put her head in her paws. Bailiff shifted around, then followed Mimi's lead. Randy cocked his head to one side.

"So," Boss sighed. "Go on. Scatter. Run far away. Don't get caught, come back and bring some food." He smiled at the memory. "Night Dogs rule."

"When you get back, I'll be gone," he said. Mimi sniffled softly. "Thank you for helping me with my friend." Boss's voice faltered. He swallowed hard.

"I know we made him very happy," he said. "He lived well and he died in peace, surrounded by love. We should all be so lucky." Boss looked around, studying each face.

"I'll never forget you," he looked away.

"I'll stay here with you, Boss," Mimi said.

Ben and Jerry nodded.

"We're your pack," said Bailiff.

"You shared him with us," said Randy, "so…we thank you. "

Flailing his left hind leg within an inch of his ear, Randy spent a second trying to make contact with an itch. After a few seconds, he snorted and stopped.

"Without him, there's no family. Without you, there's no pack. We were dead lucky to find each other," Randy grinned and gave Bailiff a swat. The smaller dog showed his teeth and swatted back with a smile.

"I doubt I'd be so lucky again," Randy said. All the others nodded.

"We'll wait with you," Randy flailed his back leg again and gave his ear an approximate scratch. "And we'll all go together as a pack." He yawned and stretched.

"To be honest," he said, "I'm a wee bit fed up with all the running and hiding myself." He flopped on the ground. "One square a day would be fine for a while, even if served in a cage."

That decision made, all the dogs relaxed. They lay down, or got up and stretched. They stared at the trees and at the lovely lawn that was their Dog Park. They trotted around in search of one last good sniff of a favorite haunt. They reminisced about treats, pranks and tricks. Some wondered where Angel was and hoped he was all right. Boss had one last good roll in the lemon thyme and mint, then lay back down next to his Old Friend. Lost in their own thoughts and together as a pack, they passed the time pleasantly while waiting for the future to arrive.

"And he was a hero," the cop said. "Himself and the dog. The Boss! A great team!" He looked up.

His nephew looked down. His nephew blogged for the local newspaper's online division. He was not paid for this work. If his blog earned advertising money, he would get paid. Earnings to date were zero.

"So far," the nephew sighed, "I've got homeless man living in Dog Park with dog."

His Uncle, the cop, stared unblinking. The Nephew shrugged. His posture said, "This is not news. This is life. This is how it goes sometimes."

He held his uncle's gaze and lifted his hands.

His Uncle grinned. The grin spread slowly across his face. The nephew was reminded of butter melting on waffles. His Uncle dropped his face into his hands and appeared to hyperventilate. He made strange noises. His Nephew became concerned.

His Uncle looked up, waved his hands and slowly calmed his breathing. When he could speak again, he said, "It's a story of human interest."

A faint twitch of a smile crossed his features. "And what else do you have to blog about?" His Uncle's eyes sparkled. "Just come along. This man is worth a story. Later on, we could have some lunch...maybe a hot dog?"

The Nephew hadn't moved.

"Come on," the Uncle said. "Get some experience," he smiled. "Help me tell this his story and I'll get lunch."

"I don't do meat anymore, or anything unhealthy," the Nephew said. "I'll need an hour and a ..."

"Twenty minutes," the Uncle interrupted, eyebrows raised. "Other people are coming. Meet us there. Twenty minutes."

His Nephew stood. His Chrome bag was on the table. He packed small, plastic coated items into every pocket.

The Uncle's eyebrows relaxed.

"I'll see you there," he said. "About twenty minutes," he smiled over his shoulder.

"Give or take a doughnut or two..."

The Nephew grinned and worked on the packing.

"Homeless Man Living in Dog Park with Dog" was worth a few paragraphs anyway and worth doing just to please his uncle. The real story he found at the park would fill his blog for days and provide inspiration for his award-winning, based-on-a-true-story novel. "This is huge," the Nephew thought.

The novel would then be optioned and made into a major motion picture starring George Clooney or Bruce Willis or maybe even Vin Diesel. He knew it!

He tried to keep his facial expressions somber, or at least neutral. Someone had died here. It would be insensitive to get too happy about an exclusive first look at such a big story. He wore a skinny tie, stood up straight and maintained a professional presence. His Uncle watched with pride.

The homeless man had been a policeman, just as his uncle had said. Apparently, he was quite well-known in his day, famous for solving big crimes and helping those in need. Several other cops had come along with his uncle. The young cops had hoped to help a fallen comrade, find him a place to stay, get someone to look after him. Instead, the four stood silent, hats in hand, and said some silent prayers. The old man had died during the night.

The lady from social services made a few calls. Young men came and took the old man's body down to an ambulance parked at the bottom of the hill. His dogs followed the gurney down the slope.

The dogs all lay down in the sphinx position. They stayed focused 'til the ambulance doors closed. When the door clicked shut, their heads dropped to the ground. After the ambulance drove away, they all got up. The big dog led and the other dogs followed him back to their lair.

A pretty lady sat on the slope and wept, a take-out container of soup steaming at her side. Dogs were everywhere, fancy dogs, rough dogs, big ones, small ones.

At the entrance to the tree circle where the old man had lived and died, six dogs sat very still. These were his dogs. Now orphaned, they would end up at the pound.

"Let's get to work," the Nephew told himself.

He interviewed, videoed, posted, and blogged.

His Uncle admired his focus and marveled at all the little bits of equipment he had at his disposal.

The cops told stories of the old man's heroics from back in the day. They were rookies then and the old man had taught them the ropes.

The pretty lady told him about the events of the day before.

"He was trying to find the owner of this one," she said, lifting the little French Bulldog to her cheek. He framed the picture so their two sad faces filled the screen.

"He was on his way to the other park when he was attacked!"

She told the story of his huge dog and her big poodle, how they had worked together to overpower the two crooks and save the rest from harm.

Animal Control officers led the orphaned dogs into their van.

"This will be the last image," he thought as he filmed the sad parade.

"I've been trying to catch this one for years," one of the Animal Control officers said. He rattled the leash of the old Border Collie.

"I wonder why he gave up?" he asked.

"You never caught me," Randy said. "You have that right! But, here we are, all the same..."

The Nephew zoomed in on the faces of dogs being herded into the Animal Control van.

"Oh, I do hope they'll find new homes," sobbed the pretty lady.

His phone rang. He gave thanks that he had just finished filming and the call hadn't spoiled the images.

The newspaper had seen the clips he had posted and read the few paragraphs he'd written while on the scene. They wanted a full story, with pictures, for the Sunday edition. The pretty lady offered some video she had on her phone.

Her video was the old man being questioned by his Uncle, the Cop, just the night before. The whole story of the old man's last day was there! He thanked her and promised to mention the now-orphaned dogs in need of new homes in his piece.

His phone rang again.

The local TV station had seen the clip of the pretty lady and the French Bulldog.

They wanted a full three minutes for their evening newscast! His Uncle said to be sure to mention the funeral services being organized for tomorrow. He promised he would.

The phone rang again. It was a local literary agency, asking if he had representation. When he finished that call, he stood quietly for a moment. He wasn't a religious young man.

"Still," he thought, "I'd like to say something..." He paused for a moment. He clasped his hands together and looked at the ground.

"Thank you, sir," he said to the old man's now-departed spirit. "Thank you."

"Don't forget to mention that my dogs need new homes," the old man's spirit replied. "Especially my Boss!"

"What?" the Nephew shook his head. "What? Who said that?"

Two tiny lights flashed in front of his face.

Fireflies? In the daytime? He swatted at them but they were already gone.

"What's the matter?" his Uncle asked. "Never seen a dead body before?"

"Not one that talked!" His Nephew's face was pale. The cop's big brows shot up.

"Maybe it's time for that hot dog."

"With chili," the Nephew nodded, his voice flat and frightened. "And cheese"

The cop put an arm around his nephew's shoulder and they left.

"You're really getting the hang of this spirit thing," Busy's little firefly self said to Old Friend.

"Yes," Old Friend smiled. "It's kind of fun. What now?"

"One more place to go," Busy said. "One more thing to do, then we ascend."

The two tiny points of light streaked across the sky.

Chapter Thirty-six

Everyone Watches TV

Just before 6pm, televisions turned on, computers powered up, phone apps activated and people across the town waited for the news of the day.

Bob sat alone at his computer. His new girlfriend was still at work. The green smoothie he'd blended lacked something and was not appealing. His screen saver was a close-up of Mimi's face. His whole life lacked something. He put down the smoothie, hung his head and sighed. Looking at her picture made him sad. Clicking away from her screen-saver face also made him sad.

"Enough moping," he told himself.

He took a big glug of smoothie, made a face and moped some more. He positioned his mouse and clicked.

"Hmm," he said. "I clicked, I know I did. Why is Mimi's picture still there? Wait a minute! Who's that lady?"

The lady on the screen was crying. The story title at the bottom of the screen read "Hero Cop, now homeless, found dead in Dog Park".

The crying lady said, "He was trying to find the owner of this one."

She brought the little dog's face next to her own. Their two sad faces filled the screen. Bob's jaw dropped. His hands were shaking.

"He was on his way to the other park," the lady sobbed," when he was attacked! And this little dog…"

"Mimi! Bob shouted. He jumped out of his seat, knocking over the glass of green smoothie, which sloshed all across his keyboard, causing his computer to spark then ignite. Small flames spit from the CPU.

"No! No! Mimi!" Bob screamed. He grabbed a fancy throw his new girlfriend had purchased and tried to smother the flames. Unfortunately, the throw was made of highly flammable material.

He stomped until the flames went out then doused the mess with the rest of his smoothie.

"TV news! TV news!" he shouted. "Where's the remote? Where's the remote?"

He ran around the room, peering under chairs, throwing cushions to the floor and moving piles of paper. When he finally found it, he pointed it at his big screen and hoped for news.

A couple of time zones away, having concluded a day of very important business, Lucy and Lester's Friends were now getting ready for an evening out.

"A nice dinner," the Lady said. "And perhaps some salsa dancing."

"Mmmm," said the Gentleman. He wasn't all that keen on the dancing part but he liked to keep her happy.

The Lady sat at the hotel's fancy dressing table and looked into the mirror. She had set up the table the way she liked it: jewelry boxes to the left, make-up case in the center, her lap top on the right. She liked to watch the news while applying cosmetics.

Halfway to its target eye, the hand holding the eyelash curler suddenly froze mid-air.

"It's Lester!" the Lady exclaimed. "He's on TV!"

"Good lord, look at his hair!" the Gentleman said. "And who is that huge dog sitting next to him? What's going on?"

The screen caption read "Hero Cop, now homeless, found dead in Dog Park".

While the camera held on the two dogs' faces, a lady's voice described how they had acted together to overpower two crooks who had stolen her puppies.

"It was as if they planned it!" the lady's voice said. "Like they had talked about it and decided what to do. They gave each other signals!"

The two dogs looked at the camera, then at each other and back to the camera.

"I think they smiled at each other!" the Lady said.

"I know it seems odd," said the Gentleman, "but do you see a resemblance? I do."

The Lady looked from one big nose to the other.

"I do too," she said. They cocked their two heads to one side and stared at the screen.

"I'm so grateful we met again," Boss said to Lucy.

The Animal Control officer attached a lead to his collar.

"The memory will fill what days I have left with great happiness."

The Officer tugged on the lead and Boss got up.

"And my son," he said to Lester. "I'm so proud to know you."

The Officer pulled again but Boss had more to say before he moved. He gazed softly at Lucy then bent to lick her face.

"I'll never forget you."

"You won't have to," she said.

Boss cocked his head. The Officer pulled harder. Boss moved a little bit, then held firm.

"I'm already working on it," she smiled.

Boss didn't understand. The Officer pulled harder and Boss moved as slowly as he could.

"Goodbye, my love. Goodbye, my son."

"Not goodbye," she said. "Au revoir."

Boss looked over his shoulder as he moved toward the van. His face was puzzled.

"She means it," said Lester. "And she's good! Au revoir."

Boss's face scrunched with confusion.

"It means we'll see you soon," Lester called out.

Their sweet naivete made him smile. With heavy steps, Boss moved the last few paces into the van.

Lucy's eyes glazed over. She stared unseeing into the middle distance. Her body trembled.

"Pace yourself, Mom," Lester said. "Our Friends aren't even back from their trip."

Her head snapped in his direction and she showed her teeth. Lester had never seen her look so angry.

"You don't want to explode," he cautioned.

"Oh, will you be quiet!" she hissed. "Now, I have to start all over again!"

Her eyes glazed over, she stared and her body trembled. Lester decided to be quiet.

The Gentleman sat down hard on the hotel bed and rubbed a familiar spot on his forehead. Right there, at the top of the bridge of his nose and between his eyes, he sometimes felt a sharp little ping of deep pain. It always subsided quickly. He had no idea what caused it. He had noticed that soon after these little pings, new and interesting ideas came to mind. He liked this one very much. It was something he had thought about for a long time.

"You know," he started cautiously. "We could use a guard dog. I mean, yes, Lester's big for a poodle but look at him."

Francine had been too exhausted to do anything with Lester's hair. It was half in and half out of the diamond pincushion look and the little jewel pins sparkled randomly.

"He's hardly intimidating," the Gentleman said.

"Oh, nonsense," the Lady said, finally finding her lashes with the curler.

"Besides, Lucy would have a fit."

"Yes," the Gentleman said, turning her by the shoulders

toward the computer screen. The Lady leaned forward and took the curler off her eye.

While the TV lady's voice described how the crooks had held the Toy Poodle by her top knot and threatened to kill her with their knife, the camera held steady on the three dogs. Boss was lying down with his head on his paws. Lester sat behind him. Lucy leaned on Boss's shoulder. Their faces were very close.

"Yes," the Gentleman said again. "I can see that Lucy is very upset."

A hand with a lead came into the frame. The hand attached the lead to the big dog's collar. Lucy leaned harder against his body. The hand tugged the lead and the two dogs got up. The lead tightened but the big dog didn't move. The two dogs gazed at each other. The big dog bent and licked Lucy's face.

"Good lord," said the Lady.

"Ow," said the Gentleman, rubbing his forehead. "I think it's time we packed our bags and got home."

His wife gave the mirror a sharp look. Her reflected gaze caught his eye.

"After a very nice dinner, of course," he soothed. "And some salsa dancing."

All across the town and in several other time zones, people watched the sad story unfold on their TV screens. Some read the blog on their computer and watched the videos embedded in the story. Others noted the day as Saturday and wondered if the Sunday paper would have a feature. They all made note that the Animal Control Shelter would be closed until Monday.

Fifi danced in front of the big TV screen, her movements mimicking a prancing Pit Bull who was part of the story.

"Look at his sparkly collar," said one of Fifi's mommies, pointing at Jerry. "And his color! They match!"

"We could use a guard dog," said the other mommy, stroking her child's hair.

"I mean, she barks and that's OK, but let's get real."

"And she seems to like him," said the first mommy. Fifi jumped on the couch and squiggled herself between them.

"Look at Lili," said Lili's Dad, pointing at the TV. "She's hanging all over that sheep dog!" He stroked Lili's head. She looked at him with pleading eyes.

"What a little hussy," he smiled.

His wife adjusted the baby in her arms and shook the bottle.

"We could use a guard dog," she said. "I mean, she barks and that's good but let's get real..."

"You mean it?" the husband squeaked. He cleared his throat and rubbed his face. Walking a big, bad, boy dog alongside the small, fancy girl would be a great improvement over the current situation. The current situation was him, big, buff, toned and sweating in his jogging clothes, prancing along behind the tiny, fancy thing his wife loved so much. He saw the faces of people staring. It wasn't entirely comfortable. He wasn't comfortable.

"Really?" he asked.

"Well, they seem to like each other," the wife said.

Onscreen, Ben was straining against the leash that pulled toward the Animal Control van, while Lili strained at her leash to stay near him.

"We'll go on Monday," the wife said. "We'll have a look."

Lili rubbed her head on the wife's leg.

An older man sat down in front of the telly. His younger wife wheeled in the stroller that held their silent toddler. The man leaned forward.

"Look at that," he said. "A Border Collie. An old fella," he smiled. "Used to have a few of those when the farm was working."

He allowed a brief memory of different times and smiled.

"And look at that," he said. "Mr. B.C. has himself a little friend."

On the TV screen, Randy was looking down at the much smaller Bailiff. Bailiff was showing off his newfound ear wiggling talent.

"What's the little one doing?" asked his wife.

"It looks like the hokie pokie," said the farmer. "With his ears."

Bailiff pointed them straight up, then down, then straight out flat to the sides. Randy collapsed to the ground and covered his face with his paws.

"Ha, ha, ha!", the toddler laughed. He pointed to the screen and looked at his parents.

"Ha, ha HA!" the toddler chuckled and banged his stroller.

The parents looked at each other.

"That's the first time…" his father said. He choked and stopped speaking.

"We'll go Monday," the mother's jaw was set, her voice determined. "We'll have a look." Their eyes met. Hope sparkled between them. They looked at their son. He was looking at the screen, still pointing, still smiling. The screen image changed. The child's hand returned to the stroller tray. His head lolled to the side, his usual position.

"We'll go Monday," his mother said.

"You look very nice on TV," Day Care Guy said. "You're very photogenic."

"Thank you," Francine said. "I wish my eyes weren't so puffy but I couldn't stop crying."

"You looked wonderful," Day Care Guy said. He fiddled with the collar in his hands.

On the TV, Francine was telling the camera how all the dogs had worked together to save them from the crooks.

"And then," she said, "as if they'd planned it, the old man's big dog and our poodle jumped the two men and hit them right in their chests. The big dog knocked his man down but our poodle, well, he's smaller and the man stumbled but didn't fall." She cuddled Rufahlo's sleek head against her hip.

"Now this one and the poodle are the best of friends, always together. So when the poodle hit the man but didn't knock him down, this one..." she stroked Rufahlo's ears. Her teary eyes widened in awe.

"He launched himself over the poodle's head and hit the man square in the chest and down he went. Then he wrapped his jaws around the man's throat and held him down until the police arrived!"

Away from home on a weekend mini-break, Rufahlo's two daddies had just finished their post golf game showers and yoga stretching. One powered up the lap top to check on the news from home.

"Look!" he said, pointing to the screen. "It's our baby!"

The other listened to the story.

"Oh, my lord," he said. "He's a hero!"

"Hero, schmero," said the one. "Why are they putting him in danger? Wasn't there a show yesterday? Why weren't they at the show? We have to go home right now!"

"Show, schmow," said the other. "We have enough trophies. All that dusting! And he's a hero! Look at him!"

"That poodle," said the one. "He's the one who's in all the same shows, the one who always jumps the commands."

"Yes," said the other, "I recognize him now. Sad hair."

"Very sad," his partner agreed.

They watched for another minute.

"Look at our baby, he knows he did well," said the one.

"And it's real life," said the other. "He's been different lately. I think he's tired of the show. Look at him!"

On the screen, their huge, beautifully sculpted Show Dog was rolling on his back on some grass. A tiny Papillion jumped over his stomach and back again.

"Oh, that's crazy talk," said the one. "He'll never give up show biz." He looked at his partner.

"You're right," the partner said. "It's probably time to go home."

Papillion crawled across Francine's lap. She leaned over and licked Rufahlo's ears. He looked up and smiled.

"Yes," Francine said, "your boyfriend is a hero, too."

"Down in front!" Lucy snapped. She was cuddled on Francine's other side.

"I can't see the TV!"

Papillion moved back to her place on Francine's hip.

"Are you sure you don't mind staying?" Day Care Guy asked.

"Not at all," she replied. "There's some tasty turkey in the fridge. I'll make a sandwich."

"I roasted it myself," Day Care Guy smiled. "The herb butter makes all the difference."

"And that bread," Francine said. "I toasted some today. It's delicious! Where'd you get it?"

"I made that too," Day Care Guy blushed and looked away.

"Really?" Francine asked. She gazed at him until he looked up. He smiled and looked away again.

"How's Killer?" she asked.

"The same," he said. His shoulders slumped. The collar in his hand dropped to the floor.

"The vet said one more night," he said softly. "Then, we have to make a decision."

When he bent to pick up the collar, the hand Francine had extended to touch his shoulder missed its mark. She pulled it back and put it on Lucy's rump.

"No, no!" said Melinda. "Try again! Lucy, make her!"

"I'm busy," Lucy said, thinking of Boss and her Friends.

Powered by the pain in her still aching ribs, Melinda shot Lucy a vicious and demanding stink-eye. "Do it!" she hissed.

"Fine!" Lucy hissed back and scrunched her face in concentration.

Francine's hand touched his shoulder. He looked up, startled and more than a little flustered.

"I'm sorry," she said. "Killer was a hero too. And those crazy ears! We'll hope for the best…what's that you're making?"

"Oh!" he was grateful to have something else to talk about. "This?" he asked, waving the collar. "Just another little invention of mine," he said. He held it up for her to see. She leaned in closer, her hand still on his shoulder.

"I've made a little leather pocket to attach to the collar," he said. "There's room in the pocket for two or three poop bags, depending on their size. The dog carries the bags until you need them. You'll never be caught without a bag again. I call it the Doggie-Doo-Right Pocket Collar." He blushed again and looked away.

"Kind of silly, I know. The dogs inspire all kinds of things in me."

"Not silly at all," said Francine, adding it to her list of future projects. First item on that list was the conditioning slime she'd preserved in the face cream jar. The collar would be the second.

"Quite a good idea," she said.

"Thanks," he fiddled with the collar in his hands.

"Go stay with Killer," she said softly. "We'll be fine. I hope you can bring him home."

Chapter Thirty-seven

It is Written

Perched up high on what used to be a picture rail in the Victorian house that was now the animal hospital, two tiny points of light, the firefly-sized spirits of Busy and Old Friend, looked down on the sleeping Angel. They dimmed their lights when Day Care Guy came in.

"So, how did he do it?" Old Friend asked.

"He changed the writing," said Busy.

"What? How?"

"He was supposed to be a slug," Busy explained. "But he wanted to be a dog. So he took the spirit pencil and connected the s to the L so it looked like a d. Then he closed the u to make it an o. I pronounced him dog and here we are."

Old Friend looked down at the odd little creature.

"Desire becomes thought," he said. "And thought becomes action."

"Yes," Busy said. "Much to my misfortune. He…"

Busy pointed his tiny, two-tiered wings heavenward and raised his brows.

"He…was not pleased. I had to impose the original order. But since he was already here on Earth, evolution was the only way. Very slow."

"He's still a dog," said Old Friend. He cocked his spirit head to one side.

"Come to think of it," he stroked his spirit chin, "I did see some changes. The ear tubes were growing, his legs were shrinking and the other dogs had slime all over them from his coat and ears. Made their fur look smooth and glossy."

"Evolution," said Busy. "Slow but sure."

"No," said Old Friend. "Then it stopped. His legs stretched back out and the ear tubes sprouted tufts of hair."

"I saw that myself," said Busy. "I thought it best not to comment."

He looked down at Angel.

"I'm not supposed to interfere," he said sadly.

"He thinks he's a dog," said Old Friend. "No. He knows he's a dog. Thought became action."

He looked down at the sleeping creature. The man at the little dog's bedside looked very sad. He stroked Angel's fur and murmured.

"You didn't have to interfere," said Old Friend. "He did it himself. Look at him and everything he did. Loyalty, bravery, self-sacrifice...."

Down below, the man reached out and wrapped a hand around the dog's front paw. He rubbed his eyes with his other hand.

"And connection." Old Friend finished. He looked at Busy.

"He made the connection. He thinks he's a dog. That man thinks he's a dog too. That man," Old Friend flapped his fledgling wings for emphasis. "That man wants him to be his dog! That's it. He's a dog. He's made it happen."

Busy frowned and rubbed his spirit forehead.

"Was the order ever changed," Old Friend's little wings fluttered. "The written order. Was it ever changed back?"

"Let me see," Busy muttered and fumbled around in his robe.

"Here it is," he unfolded the spirit paper and looked up at Old Friend. His spirit eyes were wide and shining.

"No," he said. "No, it wasn't. It still says 'dog'!"

"There you are," said Old Friend. "So be it."

"Indeed," Busy grinned. "It is written."

"And he's earned it, I think," said Old Friend.

The sad man was now asleep, his head cradled on the arm that draped across the little dog's paw.

"So be it," said Busy. He focused the laser beams of his spirit eyes on the little dog's head. Angel sneezed and shifted.

His whole head glowed with warm light. He lifted his head and opened his eyes. The glow faded and he sank back down on the bed, yawned and went back to sleep.

"Our work here is done," said Busy. "Ascend!"

The two points of light streaked through the solid walls, shot into the sky and were gone, lost among the billion stars sparkling in the night.

Angel woke with a start and looked around him. He yawned again and stretched.

"I can move again," he thought. "I'm getting better!"

His head felt warm and itchy. Moving slowly so as not to disturb his sleeping Friend, he sat up and scratched his ears. He was still tired, so he put his head on Day Care Guy's hand and went back to sleep.

Day Care Guy dreamed that a strange creature with a dog's face and tubes for ears was licking his face.

"Stop, stop," he murmured and chuckled at the tickling sensation. He stroked the dog's face. The fur felt very real. The tube-eared dog licked his hand. He opened his eyes.

It was real! His little dog was sitting up on the hospital bed, awake and wagging his tail.

"Killer!" he cried. Careful of all the tubes still attached, he gathered the pup in his arms and gave him a hug.

The little dog wriggled and licked his face.

Something was different.

He released the dog and sat back to look him over.

The ear tubes with tufts of hair were gone. In their place were two silky, downward draping, normal dog ears.

Day Care Guy stared, open-mouthed. He blinked and rubbed his eyes.

The puppy smiled back at him and cocked his head. The lower ear hung down gracefully. The red-gold hair was long and shiny.

"What the...?" Day Care Guy couldn't believe his eyes. He reached for the ears and massaged them with his fingers. They were real, all right, no doubt about it.

"How is this possible?" Day Care Guy murmured. "Am I going crazy?" he asked himself. "Or was I crazy yesterday when I saw something different?"

"Good morning," trilled the vet as she came through the door.

"Someone looks much better!" She smiled and turned her attention to the dog. She set her stethoscope and listened to one spot, then another.

"All better! I think he's ready to go home! Isn't that wonderful?"

"Wonderful," Day Care Guy said softly. "He looks all right to you? He doesn't look...different?"

"He was sick and now he's well," she said. "That's different."

She ran her fingers over the silky ears.

"The wound is all closed up and scabbed over. Be careful of that when you bathe him. Otherwise, he seems just fine. Aren't you fine, my little darling?"

She cuddled his head and let the dog lick her face, then turned off the bedside machines and started to remove the tubes.

"We were worried about you," she said. "You're a walking miracle. One for the books."

"A miracle," whispered Day Care Guy.

"How is he?" Francine's head poked in from behind the door. Day Care Guy sat back so she could see the dog. Her eyes stretched wide and her mouth dropped open.

"All better," said the vet. "Isn't that great?"

Francine came in and slumped down next to Day Care Guy. Their eyes met. He made a small shushing gesture.

"Really great," he said to the vet.

"I'll get his release papers ready." The vet left the room.

"What…" Francine spluttered. "How…?"

"I don't know," Day Care Guy said. "But I'm glad you see the difference. That tells me I'm not crazy."

Angel stretched his front legs, then his back legs. He shook his head. The silky ears flapped freely back and forth.

"A miracle," said Day Care Guy. "One for the books."

He put his arm around Francine's shoulder. She leaned against him. The little dog stretched and shook, wagged his tail and jumped around on the bed.

Chapter Thirty-eight

What Do I Have To Look Forward To?

Sunday was a long and lonely day at the Animal Control Center. It was closed to the public. The only human the Night Dogs saw was the weekend worker who, either from job dissatisfaction or a head-burning hangover, was not particularly inclined to engage with his charges.

Ben and Jerry practiced what Lili and Fifi had taught them. Jerry radiated Mr. Sparkly Love Muffin. Ben pranced around on his hind legs. The indifferent worker schlumpfed by their cages.

"He didn't even look!" Ben said.

"I don't feel good about this," said Jerry.

"Me neither," Ben flopped on his stomach.

"That guy's a tool," Mimi said. The Night Dogs looked at her, shocked by such language from the fancy girl.

"The real people will come tomorrow," she said. Bob's face flashed through her mind. "Goodbye," she said sadly to herself. Out loud, she said, "We'll all find new homes. What do you think, Boss?"

Boss lay flat on his cage floor. He hadn't moved since the morning light had roused them all from sleep.

"I think I'm done," he said. "Someday soon, I'll just go to sleep. If they let me in, I'll be with my Old Friend again."

This shocked them more than Mimi's bad language.

"Don't say that, Boss," Mimi protested weakly. "We'll all find new homes...."

"I don't want one," Boss said to the floor. "I'm tired."

The Night Dogs exchanged nervous glances.

"Boss..." Mimi started. She couldn't find words to say.

"I think to myself," Boss said, "what do I have to look forward to? Sitting outside a trailer, like Ben?"

The image frightened Ben and he hid his eyes.

"Or alone, in a warehouse, like Jerry?"

Jerry rubbed his sparkly collar. "I won't go there again," he told himself. "I won't!"

"No," said Boss. "It's enough. I had one Friend. He was good to me and he loved me but he's gone now. I won't find his like again. I could go on trying but why? I couldn't love again."

"You could, Boss!" Mimi cried.

"Sure you could," said Randy. "And you don't have to love them. I never did," Randy thought of his true loves, his sheep.

"Just do your job and be a good dog," he said. "That's all they want."

"I've busted through walls," said Boss. "I've put out fires. But start all over again? I'm too tired."

"Oh, please don't despair, Boss, keep your hopes up!" Mimi cried. "Someday soon, we can all begin again!"

She looked over the motley crew of Night Dog faces. Bob's face blurred her vision. Her sudden anger warped his image.

"And give our whole heart away to someone new," she spat. The bitterness in her voice curdled the air.

"No!" she said. "I'm with you, Boss. I had one Friend. He was false in his love and he betrayed me. I won't do that again. I could go on trying, but why? I couldn't love again!"

"Mimi!" Bailiff squeaked. "Don't give up!"

"Girl," Randy said, "you could love again. You know you will."

"No," she settled on the floor, her face in her paws.

Ben's heart shook. Jerry hyperventilated then forced himself to stop. He flopped down next to Ben. Bailiff went down soon after.

The message was clear. If a great dog like Boss and an A-lister like Mimi had no hope, what hope was there for them, the C and D list dogs? Only Randy stayed up right.

"Humans," he thought to himself. "What a lot of palaver over humans. Why worry? It's all a crap shoot, anyway." In his head, he rolled the dice and it came up sheep. He smiled at the thought. The door opened and the Sunday worker schlumpfed in.

"Lunch!" Randy said. No one else moved.

Chapter Thirty-nine

Unexpected Developments

Monday brought an unexpected and very welcome surprise.

"Spotty!" Randy shouted. "Kibble-for-brains! How you keeping?"

"Great!" said the Spaniel. He ran up and down in front of the cages, greeting all his old Night Dog friends.

He told them all about his new life with the Animal Control Officer. They had a nice home, with a big yard where he could play.

"And the food!" he smacked his lips.

"Yeah," said Bailiff. "You look a little fat."

"It feels great!" Spotty said. "I've got so much energy!"

He had a job, he told them. The Officer brought him to work every day. His job was to greet all the new dogs and to cheer them up while they waited for new people and homes.

"Hello!" he said to Mimi. "You're a Night Dog?" He couldn't believe his eyes.

"Yes," she said firmly. "I am. I'm a homeless stray," she looked at the others with pride.

"Not for long, I think," said Spotty. "The lobby's full of people!"

The first one through the door was Lucy's Gentleman Friend. He and the Lady had been away in the desert, looking for business opportunities. He had risen later than expected. In the rush to get out of the house, he had put on all the desert clothes he'd worn the day before. The broad brim of his Australian outback hat flopped up and down as he walked. The folds of his duster coat billowed with movement.

Boss sat up.

"My Old Friend!" He couldn't believe his eyes.

"He's well! He's young again! Oldie! It's me! It's me! Boss! Your baby boy!"

Lucy and Lester stood by the man's side.

"Hello, Boss," she said.

"Hey," said Lester.

"Oh," said Boss. "Not my Old Friend. I thought…"

"I know," said Lucy. "He's not. But he will be."

She scrunched her face. Her body shook.

"Watch the magic," Lester whispered.

"You," said the Gentleman. He rubbed his forehead. "Big boy!" he said. "I like you."

He put his fist near the cage. Boss gave the hand a cautious lick.

"My wife," he said. "She likes the poodles. But you're going to be my great big baby boy! They can go to the shows…"

Lester's face fell just a little.

"And guess what we're going to do?" he asked.

"No! I can't guess! Just tell me!" Boss shivered.

"We're going to go fishing!"

"I love fishing!" Boss jumped to all fours.

"And swimming…"

"I love swimming!" Boss shivered so hard all four paws left the ground.

"I could love it too!" Lester murmured. His sad eyes stared at the man who had never paid him much attention. The Gentleman considered poodles to be show toys for his wife. Lester tried not to sigh. This would all be good news for Boss and he didn't want to spoil it. Still, the sorrow for himself was too much to ignore. He dropped his head and looked at the ground.

Lucy looked at her sad boy's face. She made up her mind and scrunched her face again.

"Ow!" said the Gentleman, rubbing his forehead.

"And we'll bring Lester with us," he said. "Enough of this show dog lark. Yes, you're a poodle but you're also a boy and a big one!"

He patted Lester's head and ruffled his top knot.

"This man-dog here is going to help me dog you up!"

"Yes!" Lester yelled. "Thanks, Mom!

After they left with Boss, two ladies came in. One of them held Fifi in her arms. The other one towed a little girl by the hand. When she put the dog down, Fifi ran right over to Jerry's cage.

"Their colors!" said the lady. "They match!"

"Work it!" Fifi snapped. "Show them who you want to be!"

Fifi got up on her hind legs and jumped around. Jerry followed her movements. He pranced and smiled and angled his new collar so the sun shot sparkles at the ladies' eyes.

"They really match," said the other lady. "And she seems to like him."

"We'll take him!" said the first lady. "Won't we, sweet-pea?" she said to the little girl who giggled at the dancing dogs. She nodded her head and took a wad of gum out of her mouth.

"No, no," said the lady.

"Well, at least he's got short hair," said the other lady.

After they left, a young couple came in pushing two strollers. The lady's stroller held a smiling baby. Sitting up like a queen in the man's stroller was Lili. She jumped out and ran over to Ben's cage. He bent to lick her face, then sat up straight and still. He made confident eye contact with the man and smiled.

"Good!" said Lili.

After a moment, Ben couldn't sit still any longer. He jumped to his feet and wriggled. He danced around, never breaking eye contact with the man. The tension was killing him. He bowed to the lady and the baby. He looked back to the man and gave a soft, tiny woof.

The baby laughed.

The man smiled. He looked at the lady.

"I like him!" he said.

"So does Lili," said the lady. "Let's take him!"

Another couple came in. They also had a stroller. The child in the stroller was a toddler, not a baby. He stayed very still. His head lolled off to one side.

"They seem worried," Bailiff said.

"So, cheer them up," said Randy.

"Is that the baby?" said Bailiff, pointing one ear.

The child stirred.

Bailiff gave a little woof and pointed the other ear.

"Is that the baby?" he said.

The child looked at him

"Are you the baby?" Bailiff asked and pointed both ears toward the child. Then he shot them straight out to the sides. Randy cracked up.

"Ha ha ha," said the child. He pointed a stubby finger. Bailiff waggled his ears every which way he could.

"Are you the baby?" he woofed. "Are you the baby?"

"Ha ha HA!" The child laughed and pointed and looked at his startled parents.

"Ha ha HA!" The child banged his stroller and pointed at Bailiff. The man wiped his eyes.

"We'll take him!" said the lady.

The lady took Bailiff and the stroller and left. The child held onto Bailiff's ear while they walked out together.

"Ha ha HA!" His little voice faded down the hallway.

The man stayed behind and spoke to Randy.

"I had a farm. A long time ago…" he said.

"So did I," said Randy, his interest piqued.

The man shook his head.

"Got too old for that," he sighed. Randy knew how he felt. He rubbed his head against the cage. The man scratched the dog's ears.

"Had to make a change," he said. "Now I have an Agricultural Education Center. Children come to learn about farming," he said.

"Sounds good," Randy said.

"There's a petting zoo," the man said. "I have goats and chickens, some young cattle."

"Lovely," Randy said.

"And half a dozen sheep."

"Sheep!" Randy snapped to attention.

"We could herd them around the yard," the man said. "Show off for the kids."

For the first time in his life, Randy was speechless.

"Come on, old fella," the farmer said. "You still have it in you. I can see that."

And they left.

Mimi was alone.

"I'm a Night Dog," she told herself. "A homeless stray. I can take care of...."

The door opened and Bailiff's head poked in. He was straining at his new leash.

"Ha ha HA!" The child was still laughing.

"Come on, boy," a lady's voice said.

"Mimi!" Bailiff said.

All her brave resolve left her.

"Don't..." she whispered.

"Is this Bob?" he asked.

"Come on, boy," the lady's voice said. Bailiff's head disappeared. Mimi sagged to the floor.

The door opened with a bang.

"Mimi!" a voice screamed. "Mimi! Don't you know me?"

"Bob!" Mimi screamed and jumped high enough to hit her head on the cage top.

Bob opened the cage and took her in his arms.

"Mimi!" he cried. "I saw you on TV! Where've you been?"

They sat together and hugged and cried for a minute.

Mimi jumped away and accused him with her eyes.

"That girlfriend of mine? She said you ran away! Then I found your collar in her car!"

"Jealous, lying witch!" Mimi growled.

"Jealous, lying witch!" Bob muttered. "So I dumped her!"

Mimi jumped back into his arms.

"I've got a new girlfriend now," he murmured into her fur.

She jumped away again, burned him with her eyes and growled.

"No! You'll like this one, Mimi! You'll see!"

He fumbled in his pockets.

"Look what she made for you!"

He pulled a bundle from his pocket. It was pink. Mimi cocked her head.

"See?" he said.

Mimi gasped.

He held a little pink satin doggie jacket. On its back was her name, spelled out in shiny, sparkly jewels.

"Ooooooooo," Mimi melted a bit then caught herself.

"Don't be so easy," she scolded herself.

She looked at Bob and held back her love.

"First, I meet her," she sniffed. "Then...maybe...I try it on."

"I'll tell you what," Bob said. "First, you'll meet her. You'll like her, I know it! She's waiting outside. Then...maybe, you'll try it on...?" he pleaded.

Mimi smiled and jumped back into his arms. He wrapped the jacket round her.

"Come on, Mimi," he murmured. "Let's go home!"

When Bob and Mimi made their exit from the Animal Control Center, a small crowd was waiting to greet them. When they saw the little Frenchie wrapped in pink satin, they burst into applause. They clapped for every one of the Night Dogs as each had made his exit with a new Friend. They had seen the Nephew's story on TV, the blog and the newspaper. They all had come down to the Center to claim one of the sad-storied dogs for themselves.

"Don't worry, folks," said the Officer. "We've got plenty more. Isn't that right, Spotty?"

Spotty sat up and waggled his front paws.

"Come on down," the Officer said.

Every dog and cat in the shelter was claimed that day.

The Nephew was there filming, blogging and posting the happy follow-up to the weekend's sad story.

On Sunday, he had covered Old Friend's impromptu funeral. It was fairly grand for an event thrown together on the fly. The young police officers had put money together to have his body cremated and the ashes placed in a handsome box. The Nephew had supplied a picture of Old Friend with Boss from Francine's video. The picture was pasted to the top of the box next to pictures of Sergeant Joe Whelan in uniform and a very young First Lieutenant Whelan in army fatigues. The young cops marched the box to the cemetery and buried it in the resting place for former policemen. Old Friend's real name was carved on the headstone. The policemen took off their hats and said silent prayers while a bagpiper played a final, sad tune. The nephew's blog got so many hits the server crashed and had to be re-booted.

Today, he filmed each dog's triumphant march from the Animal Center to the cars of their new owners. The crowd laughed and cried and applauded.

"I hope the server's fixed," the Nephew thought as he filmed

Bob and Mimi greeting the new girlfriend. Mimi licked her face and allowed her to fit the pink satin jacket around her shoulders. They got in their car and waved to the happy crowd. The Nephew looked at his watch.

"Uh-oh," he said. "Time for Court!"

He got in his car and sped off.

The courtroom was dark, the silence heavy. Machines whirred. Francine's face appeared on a projector screen.

"He was trying to find the owner of this one," Francine's voice trembled. She lifted Mimi up and their two sad faces filled the screen.

"He was on his way to the other park when he was attacked!"

The screen went dark.

The courtroom's lights switched on. The Smoker rubbed his eyes. The Suit next to him jumped to his feet.

"Your honor, I object!" said the Suit, his voice loud and indignant. "This video has no probative value and will be highly prejudicial to my client!"

"The lady never mentioned your client," said the Judge. "She didn't mention anyone specific, only that the man was attacked. Overruled. I'm going to allow it."

The Suit sighed and sat down. He looked at the Smoker. The Non-Smoker and his Suit leaned over to hear what he had to say.

"Plea bargain?" he said. They all looked down at their hands and gave this idea some thought.

Chapter Forty

New Beginnings

Angel thrived under Day Care Guy's loving eye and soon grew into a lithe and long-legged teenage charmer. He learned lots of tricks and happily performed them for potential new customers, of which there were many.

"Almost too many," Day Care Guy thought.

From time to time, the Nephew's blog re-visited their story. Every new post brought packs of new dogs to the Center.

"Soon, I'll have to expand," he thought. He scratched his head and wondered how he could possibly do that.

Angel's smiling puppy face and bouncing good humor engaged every new dog he met. His long, silky red-gold hair always drew compliments from the owners.

"He's gorgeous!" they would say to Francine. "What products do you use?"

"On him? Nothing," she said. "He's a natural."

"You know," she told Day Care Guy one evening. "Now that he's ...um...normal..." They smiled at the shared secret.

"The name doesn't suit him" she said. "Killer Too harsh for such an angel dog."

"That's what I'll call him, then," said Day Care Guy. "Angel."

He stroked his puppy's head.

"Sent to me from heaven," he said.

"Yes, I was," Angel nodded.

"I'll make a new pocket collar for him," said Day Care Guy, "with his new name stitched on the side. Come here, my Angel-cake," he picked the puppy up.

"Oof! Getting too big to be carried. Let's go make a new collar."

With the source of the slime now gone forever, Francine took her precious small sample to a chemical analysis lab. When the results were in, the chemist called and asked her to come to the lab for a chat.

"Where did you get this?" he asked.

"I......eee....found it!" Francine stammered, her eyes darting everywhere in the room. She stroked Angel's ears and the silky feel calmed her.

"I was out for a walk and found it," she lied with confidence. Some of this was true. They had walked to the boxcar where the two men held the puppies captive.

"It looked like pomade," she said. "I tried it on some of our dogs and it worked wonders."

The chemist's fixed stare was unsettling. She took a deep breath.

"I wanted to know what was in it so I could make more on my own," she said.

"That will be hard," said the chemist. His odd stare moved from her face to Angel's.

"This dog's coat is magnificent," he said. "Did you use it on him?"

"No," she relaxed a little. "He's a natural."

"Well, good for him," said the chemist. "About eighty percent of this is made of compounds and elements we could identify. The rest of it," his eyes narrowed, "is...just...not of this world."

She looked down at Angel. The chemist's eyes followed hers. Angel smiled back at them both.

"I'd make more for you if I could," he said. "But I can't."

"That's the best I can do, young lady," the chemist pushed his report across the table. "And here's your jar. There's a little bit left."

His skeptical eyes searched her face and found nothing. He sighed and stood up.

"Good luck making more," he said. "Let me know how it goes."

Doggedly, Francine mixed and stirred and blended and tested each new batch of pomade.

"Good lord," said Day Care Guy, looking at the results of the most recent blend. Some of Lester's hair poked out in points. Other parts shriveled together and knotted up in tight little balls.

"I hope that's water soluble," he said.

Her determined entrepreneurship inspired him. He resolved to put the same effort into his pocket collar. His design was complete and the basic product ready to go. He worked on composing lists of sizes, colors, custom stitching styles for the pet's name, and different types of pocket material. The basic collar would have a rough leather pocket. The pricier line, focused on smaller, fancier dogs, would have pockets of kid or suede.

The Nephew offered to film a short commercial and post it on his blog.

"Oh, no!" Francine exclaimed, looking down at Angel and fluttering her hands. "I don't have a bag!"

"But he does!" said Day Care Guy, smiling at the Nephew's phone camera.

"The Doggie-Do-Right Pocket Collar holds up to three bags, depending on their size!"

With a flourish, he pulled a bag out of Angel's collar pocket.

"You'll never be embarrassed again!" he told the camera. Angel flashed his winning smile.

The Pocket Collar was an instant hit. Orders came pouring in. Day Care Guy had to focus on manufacturing, leaving much of the Day Care Center work to Francine.

"I couldn't have done this without you," he said, packing up the thousandth collar for shipping.

"I know," she smiled. "It's been fun. And with the dogs all to myself, I've had time to test my new formula. I think I have a winner! Here, pups!" She snapped her fingers.

Ben and Lili, Jerry and Fifi, Lester, Rufahlo and Melinda all came forward.

"It's not as miraculous as the original but it seems to work on all kinds of dog hair!" She was very excited. She watched for his reaction.

Ben's fur was soft and shiny and appeared recently brushed. Lili's curls were soft and gracefully framed her face. Fifi's long hair swayed gently with every movement. Jerry and Rufahlo's short coats glowed with healthy shine. Melinda's long, copper-red hair swung as freely as Fifi's. Lester's 'do was perfect, each poof full and round and symmetrical.

"They're gorgeous!" Day Care Guy was awed. "I think you got it!"

He hugged Francine and looked at their charges.

"You didn't do Lucy?" he asked.

"Oh, no!" Lucy sniffed. "I'm no crash test dummy!"

"Now, Lucy," said Boss.

"What?" Lucy snapped.

"Nothing," he chuckled, "nothing at all."

"When it's perfect," she said, "then, she can try it on me!"

"It's perfect," said Day Care Guy. He held Francine very close. "You've done it!"

They kissed. Some of the dogs looked away, others stared openly, sharing their happiness.

"I told you," Melinda said to Lucy.

"Yes, you did," Lucy said. "You were right."

"Good lord!" said Melinda. "Let me remember this day!"

They introduced the pomade as a free gift with purchase.

"And with every pocket collar," the newly flamboyant Day Care Guy played to the Nephew's camera, "you'll receive a free jar of Angel Hair Pomade!"

He gestured to the row of sitting, panting dogs.

"Short, long," he touched each dog's head in turn. "Straight, curly, wiry or silky smooth, Angel Hair Pomade for Fabulous Dogs will make it glow with healthy shine."

"And manageability!" Francine said.

New orders flooded their web site and mailbox. Soon Angel Hair Pomade was selling on its own and did as well and better than the pocket collar. They had to hire staff to look after the dogs while they tended to their new businesses. New dogs arrived at the Center almost every day.

After one very long and busy day, Day Care Guy flopped down in his big TV chair.

"We have to expand" he said.

"Yes," she said.

He looked at Francine. He cocked his head to one side.

"I said 'we'," he said softly.

"I heard," she smiled.

He took her hands in his.

"Will you?" he asked. "Expand?"

She giggled.

"I mean, will we….You and I together…" he stopped.

"Yes," she said. "We will."

They kissed. This time all the dogs stared openly. Papillion twitched and fell into Rufahlo's side.

"Isn't it romantic?" she sighed.

"It is!" He bent and licked her ear.

"That pomade," he exclaimed. "It's great! It even tastes good!"

When Francine and Day Care Guy finally got married, they were able to afford a large and lavish party. They could invite everyone important in their lives and offer wonderful food, drink and entertainment for their guests. It was large and lavish but stopped short of being fancy. There was no point getting too fancy when half the guests were dogs.

Angel was their best dog. He wore a white satin collar with a pocket of soft kid leather. His name was spelled in rhinestones on the side. As he marched them up the aisle, his smile sparkled brighter than the collar's tiny jewels.

Boss wore Lester's blue bow on his collar.

Francine had braided a "Scenes" pattern into Lester's fur. His left side showed a warm sun shining on a house in a beautiful meadow. A dozen stick dogs romped in the sun. His right side showed a stick man in a top hat holding hands with a stick lady. A bow held a long, flowing veil in the stick lady's hair.

Lucy wore every piece of jewelry her Lady Friend could find. A tiara of sparkling hearts twinkled in her top knot. At the appointed time, Lucy took the long ribbon handle in her mouth and pranced up the aisle with the ring bearer's pillow. The crowd oohed aahed and applauded.

The Gentleman turned to his Lady.

"She's still got it, don't you think?" he asked. "I think she should try again."

He cocked his head to one side, puzzled. He hadn't felt the pain but here was a great idea.

"She should show again," he said.

"You're right," said the Lady.

As a precaution, the Gentleman reached for his forehead. There was no pain.

No one wanted to call it a night and the party went on 'til all hours. No one complained as the new Mr. and Mrs. Day Care Guy had invited every neighbor within the sound of the Three Dog Night Tribute band's party music. There would have been no one to respond, as all the young cops were at the party.

The Bus Driver regaled several young ladies with the story of Mimi's bravery.

"She ran right up to the thug, jumped at his leg and chomped down hard!" The ladies gasped.

"He kicked her away but his pants leg tore and she ran away with it in her mouth. It was that rag that put those bad boys away!" The women cooed over Mimi. Resplendent in a bright gold satin jacket, Mimi modestly down-played her heroic role.

"Anyone would have bit him," she said. "I just happened to be there."

Bob and his new girlfriend beamed with pride.

The Bus Driver's cousin, the kind man from the doughnut shop, asked his wife if, maybe, they could adopt a dog. Overwhelmed by the joy of the occasion, his wife finally broke down and said yes. Their excited children couldn't decide which one they wanted, so they went home with both Larry and Moe.

"Two down," Melinda smiled. "Four more to go!"

Lucy's Gentleman struck up a conversation with the Animal Control Officer. They agreed to take their dogs out hunting some weekend very soon. Lester and Spotty were overjoyed to have the chance to play together again.

"I want in on that action," said the Uncle. He'd worn his police dress uniform to the party.

"Great!" said the Gentleman. "Do you have a dog?"

"Not yet," said the Uncle.

"You'll take charge of Lester, then," said the Gentleman. "Boss is as much as I can handle."

They discussed possible weekends and favorite hunting locations.

The band announced a dance contest and eager couples filled the floor. It was very close between Lucy's Lady and Gentleman and Rufahlo's two daddies but, in the end, it was the bride and groom's Cajun two-step that won the day.

"You're such a good leader!" Francine laughed

"Partner," Day Care Guy said. "We're partners."

They kissed and everyone applauded.

Jerry and Fifi's two mommies had brought home made dog treats. They were quite fibrous and before long had the predictable effect. No one minded. Everyone laughed and Doggie-Do-Right Pocket Collars were in use all over the lawn.

The band called for a Doggie Fashion Show.

"I didn't know!" Rufahlo cried. "I would have worn something more...more..."

"Never mind," said Papillion, her top knot bow twitching off to one side. "Let's go up there anyway. We won't win but that will be good practice for you. You don't have to be first every time."

"Let's go!" Rufahlo said and they took their place in the line.

"Oh," sighed Papillion's mommy. She plucked at the sleeve of her long, gauzy dress.

"I wish I had known." She touched her flowered hair ornament, hoping it was still on straight.

"She looks lovely," said the Uncle. He rubbed his badge with his sleeve and wondered why he felt nervous. "Is that her boyfriend?"

Papillion, twitching with excitement fell into Rufahlo's side. He nosed her back up.

"They do seem to like each other," the lady said. She twisted a wave of her waist length hair. She turned to the Uncle.

"Such an odd couple," she said.

"May I get you a drink?" he asked.

Although his red leather pocket collar contrasted beautifully with his black and white coat, Randy decided to sit this one out.

"A working dog," he said, "doesn't do costume."

"Go on," said Bailiff. "You're just being snooty."

"Go on yourself," said Randy. "I'll stay with the child."

"No," said Bailiff. "I have more fun here."

He put his paws on the child's stroller tray.

"Are those the doggies?" He waggled his ears.

"Ha ha ha!" the child laughed and grabbed one ear in his hand.

"Are those the doggies?" Bailiff pointed his other ear at the costume line. "Are those the doggies?"

"Ha ha ha!" The child looked at his parents and pointed, never letting go of Bailiff's ear.

"Ha ha HA!" He shouted and pointed at the line.

"Doggies!" he shouted. "Ha ha HA!"

"His first word!" his mother whispered.

"Good man!" said the farmer. Cautiously, he reached down and stroked his child's head. For the first time, the child didn't pull away. With his one hand still clutching Bailiff's ear, he reached his other hand up and touched his father.

"Good dog," the farmer whispered and tried to hold back tears. The mother took his arm and rested her head on his shoulder.

On the basis of general excellence in concept and superiority of execution, no one could come close to Lucy's presentation. Since she already had a tiara, she was draped with a ribbon that read "Best Dog in Show."

"Ah," she said. "So this is what it feels like!"

"That's it!" said the Gentleman.

"Yes!" said the Lady. "She's going to show again!"

The Nephew filmed it all right down to the very end when the last stragglers said good night and good luck to the happy couple.

"I'll get another book contract out of this," he thought as he packed the bits of equipment into his Chrome bag.

Chapter Forty-one

Hunting

A few weeks later, three men and three dogs huddled together in a duck blind. They shivered in the pre-dawn chill but a rosy, rising sun promised a warm fresh day.

"There!" said Lucy's Gentleman. He aimed and shot.

"Darn," he said. "I wonder if I cleaned this one properly last night? A bit of grit can really put off your shot."

"Well, I know I cleaned mine," said the Animal Control Officer. "There!" he said. He aimed and shot.

"My hands are cold," he said. "A bit stiff on the trigger"

"What do we do if they get one?" Lester asked Spotty.

"Swim out to get it," Spotty said.

"Wooo!" Lester shivered. "Awfully cold for swimming…"

"There!" said the Uncle. He aimed and shot.

"Hmmm," he muttered, looking over his gun.

"I wouldn't worry about it," Spotty smirked.

"There!" said the Uncle again. "You guys ready?"

"No," said the Gentleman.

"You go," said Animal Control.

The Uncle aimed and shot.

"Hmmm," he said again and looked at his gun more closely.

"Too bad," said Boss. "I'd love a swim."

"We'll go later," Spotty said, "when it warms up."

"I say," the Gentleman said to the Uncle. "I mean, let's just face it. Grit or no grit, I'm not the best shot."

"Me, neither," chuckled Animal Control.

"But you," the Gentleman said to the Uncle. "You're a policeman. Don't they make you practice?"

"They do," said the Uncle. He looked out over the smooth,

shining lake. He looked down at his gun.

"I...," he started. He took a deep breath.

"I have a new lady friend," he mumbled. "Met her at the wedding. She's...." He looked down. "A vegetarian," he finished.

"Ah," said the Gentleman.

"Hmm," said Animal Control.

"She didn't mind me coming," said the Uncle. "But I know she'd be happier if I didn't hit anything...."

"Then why waste the ammunition?" The Gentleman laughed. "I'm not likely to hit anything."

"Me neither," said Animal Control.

"That's right," said Spotty.

"Let's build a fire and have some coffee," said the Gentleman. "I brought an excellent dark roast from Kenya!"

Men and dogs trooped happily back to their camp. They spent the rest of the morning gathering tinder and wood and built a fire. The fire warmed them up while they talked and joked and drank their coffee. The dogs lolled peacefully in the sun.

About mid-day, it seemed warm enough for a swim.

"Great!" Boss yelped and threw himself into the water. His huge wake splashed at the rest of them onshore.

"Ah!" the Gentleman squeaked. "Leave some in the lake, big boy!"

He threw himself into the water sending a wake almost as big as Boss's onto shore.

"Bracing!" he shouted. "Come on!"

The others splashed in and swam.

"Let's go," said Spotty, wading in.

Lester ran a few steps, launched himself, and belly-flopped in near the others.

"Good boy!" called the Uncle. "Quite the lad for such a fancy dog."

"He's got spunk," said the Gentleman, treading water. "And he's very smart."

He tsked tsked. "Wasted on those shows. My wife insisted on shows. She never let him come out with me before." He cocked his head. "She's focused more on Lucy now. That's good for everyone."

"Race you to the pier!" said Animal Control.

"You're on," said the Uncle.

They dove and swam and treaded water then finally heaved themselves back onto shore.

"Anyone hungry?" asked the Uncle.

"I could murder a duck," said Animal Control.

"If only," the Gentleman laughed. "What should we do?"

"Be right back." Boss dove back into the water. He was under a long time. Just as Lester was starting to worry, his head came out of the water. Flapping in his jaws was a large, unfortunate fish.

"That's my Big Boy!" the Gentleman cried. "Let's get that fire going again!"

They cleaned the fish, wrapped it in some tin foil the Uncle had in his gear and cooked it on the burning coals. Animal Control had some packets of salad dressing that made for an excellent sauce. They ate with their hands and shared bits with the dogs. They topped off the feast with more coffee and sat back satisfied.

Someone produced a deck of cards. While the dogs lay drying in the sun, the Gentleman won several hands of poker.

"Winner buys the drinks!" the Gentleman said.

They dressed and drove down to a local road house. They passed several pleasant hours with beer, games of darts, trivia contests and chat.

"Oh, heck," said the Uncle as the afternoon lengthened into evening. "Where's my wallet?"

"I only took your cash," said the Gentleman. "Not your wallet."

"Darn!" The Uncle slapped his forehead. "It must have dropped out of my pants when we were changing down at the lake!"

"Well, let's go before it gets too dark," said Animal Control.

By the time they reached the lake shore, dusk was gathering.

"Any idea where you might have dropped it?" asked the Gentleman.

"No," said the Uncle. "I never thought to check for it. I have no idea."

They looked at the large area they had covered and considered the advancing dark. A crescent moon glowed dimly in the sky.

"I don't know," said the Uncle. "Maybe...hey, boy! What? What's up?"

Lester was nuzzling and licking his pants.

"What?" the Uncle laughed. "What are you doing, goofball? Stop!"

"Let me try," Lester said. He launched himself through the car's open window. Spotty followed.

"Hey!" cried Animal Control. "Spotty!"

He looked at the Gentleman, concern in his eyes.

"He's never run off before," said Animal Control.

"If I didn't know better, I'd say Lester is trying to track the smell," said the Gentleman.

"Good thinking," said Boss.

"They both had their noses to the ground," said the Gentleman.

"Well, they're gone now," said the Uncle.

"I'll get my flash light ready," said Animal Control.

Just as Boss was starting to worry, Lester and Spotty burst out of the underbrush. Lester had something in his mouth.

"Good boy!" the Uncle exclaimed when Lester dropped the wallet at his feet.

"Amazing!" said Animal Control.

"Good man!" The Gentleman beamed with pride and gave Lester's ruined top knot a pat.

"Hey!" said the Uncle. "It's wet!"

He sniffed the stained leather.

"Ew!" he said. "Who peed on my wallet?"

The other men slapped their thighs and howled with laughter.

"You did!" gasped the Gentleman. "Most likely."

"I guess we know where you dropped it," choked Animal Control.

"Well, the cash is still dry," said the Uncle. "Who's up for a night cap?"

"Me!" said the other two and they drove back to the road house.

Over the one last beer, the Uncle spoke seriously to the Gentleman.

"I don't think he got lucky," said the Uncle. "He's got a very good nose."

The Gentleman sipped his last bit of coffee and waved to the bar man for more.

"Funny you should mention it," he said. "We play a game at home. I let him sniff a toy and then I hide it. He finds it every time."

"We could use a good dog on the force," said the Uncle. "Chase-downs, search and rescue, that sort of thing. A good nose is a big help," he said. "We used to have one," he bent and stroked Boss's big head. "But then this Big Boy retired."

"A police-poodle!" Animal Control laughed. "That would be something!"

Lester was beside himself. He jumped and twitched and threw his front paws on the Gentleman's lap.

"Please, please, please, please, please?" He wriggled and shivered and twitched harder than Papillion.

"Of course," said the Uncle. "He'd have to be more calm than

342

this. We'd have to…"

Lester sat down quickly and made himself as still as the stuffed moose head hanging over the bar.

"That's more like it. Look at him!" said the Uncle. "So much potential! May I train him?"

"Yes, yes, yes, yes, yes!" Lester growled through gritted teeth.

"Do what Lucy does!" said Boss. "Focus!"

Lester scrunched his face and did his best to sear psychic thought beams into his owner's forehead.

"Ow!" said the Gentleman softly. He rubbed his forehead between his brows. He shook his head and blinked.

"Yes!" he said brightly. "Certainly worth a try!"

Lester was so happy he had to try hard not to pee himself right there on the roadhouse floor.

"I told you!" Spotty said. "Yay!"

"You're gonna do great!" said Boss.

The men discussed the details over a very last beer and coffee. Overwhelmed with happiness, Lester tussled around with Spotty while Boss snoozed gently on the floor.

Chapter Forty-Two

First Show of the Season

Showtime! The Day Care Center crackled and buzzed. Everyone hustled and fussed and rushed to get ready for the First Big Show of the season.

"Do I have to wear this?" Day Care Guy struggled with his tie.

"Yes, you do," Francine yanked it into place. "You look fabulous. You'll see."

"Fabulous," he muttered. "That's new for me."

"I'm sorry," said Lester. "Wish I could be there to see it."

"I feel good," said Rufahlo. "I can do it!"

He nudged his friend's shoulder.

"Thank you for helping me for so long," he said. "Look! Here's your trainer."

The Uncle came in holding a leash in one hand. His other hand held the hand of Papillion's mommy.

"And here's mine," Rufahlo said fondly.

"Come on, boy," the Uncle said to Lester. "Big day ahead of us! Suspect chase-down. Hope you had a good breakfast."

As she put Papillion down, the lady's waist-length hair brushed the floor.

"I don't know how it happens in your mind," she was saying, "that the back seat of a new car becomes a doggie chew toy!"

"She didn't hurt it," said the Uncle. "It's a cop car. It's seen worse."

"Try to behave," said the lady to her dog. "We're going to take this up with your doggie psychic."

Papillion wasn't listening. "Are you ready?" she asked.

"Yes!" Rufahlo stood tall and confident. "But maybe we practice a little more in the car?"

Day Care Guy drove Melinda, Boss and Lucy. Francine took

Papillion, Rufahlo, Ben and Lili. Fifi's moms would meet them there.

"Now, remember," Papillion instructed. "You're doing opposites."

"Opposites," Rufahlo rehearsed. "I hear the command. I think of what I would do and then I do the opposite."

"Believe in yourself!" Papillion pounded her paws for emphasis. "Trust yourself!"

"You go, dude!" said Ben. "You'll be great!"

"Your first show," Lili smiled.

"I can't wait to see it," Ben grinned and gave himself a scratch.

In the other car, Lucy sat calm and silent between the two big dogs. Her eyes were glassy and stared at something no one else could see. Boss started to say something but Melinda waved him quiet.

"She's in the zone," she whispered. "Leave her there!"

They drove on in tense, excited silence.

"And now," the Announcer's voice boomed. "Let us welcome a newcomer to our ring! Only recently rescued from the streets, he's here to show us what he can do. A big welcome for…Gentleman Jerry!"

Jerry puffed his chest with pride and showed big, glittering teeth. The crowd's reaction was mixed. A Pit Bull in the show ring was a new and nervous experience. Jerry jumped up and landed on his hind legs. He waved his front paws and smiled at the crowd. A new collar with rows of golden topazes sparkled in the spot light. Fifi Mommy #1, dressed in a sternly tailored, almost military suit, shouted "Go!"

As they strutted proudly round the ring, the applause grew in warmth and volume.

"Yay!" Fifi cheered wildly.

"Whoo-hoo!" shouted Ben.

"Go, Jerry!" shouted Mommy #2.

Jerry took his place next to Rufahlo.

"You look great!" Rufahlo said. "But I can't look at you anymore! I must focus completely!"

"OK," Jerry said. "Me too! Focus!"

"And now," the Announcer's voice was low and dramatic.

"The first command!" He paused. Tension built.

"Trust yourself! Trust yourself! Trust yourself!" Papillion chanted quietly.

"Sit!" the Announcer boomed.

Rufahlo's muscles twitched to one side, then stopped. No dog moved.

"Opposites!" he thought, banishing the urge to roll over.

He sat. His posture was proud and perfect. All the other dogs sat.

"I was right! I guessed right!" his thoughts raced. "Or all the other dogs were wrong too...no! No! I guessed right! OK, stop thinking! Focus!"

"Sit ...up!" the Announcer boomed.

Again, his muscles twitched, this time to the other side. His head cocked slightly.

Papillion held her breath.

"Opposites!" He remembered Lester from a show long ago, waggling his front paws up for him to see.

He sat up. He flashed his Show Dog smile and waggled his front paws at the crowd. Thunderous applause filled the room. All the other dogs sat up.

"Yes!" Papillion screamed, banging her paws on her seat.

"Yes!" Rufahlo thought as he smiled and waved to the crowd.

To no one's surprise, Rufahlo won that day's trophy for Best

Performance in Command Obedience.

To almost everyone's surprise, Gentleman Jerry took second place.

"Good dog!" squealed Mommy #1. She hugged his neck and waving the trophy in the air.

"Yay!" Fifi screamed.

"Whooooo!" Ben howled.

"Congratulations!" said Jerry.

"And to you!" said Rufahlo. "And to me," he thought. He smiled and waved at Papillion.

Although the Best in Show award was seen as a spectacular upset, no one questioned the decision.

"And now," the Announcer's voice was reverent. "We have here, back in our ring, a dog we feared lost to us forever. Please welcome back...." He paused as dog and handler got into place.

"Queen Lucy of the Sky, in Diamonds!"

The spotlight snapped on. Day Care Guy stood tall and handsome. The tuxedo Francine insisted that he wear suddenly seemed right. His red glitter bow tie complimented the rubies round Lucy's neck. She sat up and waved her paws regally at the crowd. Her diamond heart tiara, matching ear pieces and paw bangles twinkled gently. Gasps of awe and wonder filled the room.

He looked down at her big, long-lashed eyes and perfect hair. She seemed a much bigger dog than the snooty little toy that terrorized the Center.

"Ready?" he asked.

"I was born ready, honey," she said. "Let's go!"

Slowly, with great control and pageantry, they pranced and high-stepped round the ring. The applause was deafening. People stomped the floor and pounded their seats.

"Whoooo!" Boss howled.

"You go, girl!" Melinda screamed.

Wrapped in her Best-in-Show blue ribbon and sash, her body curled tightly around the huge trophy, Lucy slept peacefully all the way home.

"Quite the come back," Melinda said softly.

"I'm so happy for you," Boss said. "And so proud."

Lucy smiled in her sleep, stretched her legs and wrapped them once again around her trophy.

Day Care Guy kept his tuxedo on while he posted pictures on their web-site. The Nephew picked up a few and re-posted them on his blog. Within minutes, flowers and congratulation telegrams arrived from the Lady and Gentleman. Once again traveling for business, they had watched the entire show's live streaming feed on their computer.

"So proud of you!" the telegrams said. "All hale, Queen Lucy!"

Lucy never moved. She slept soundly through the night in her tiara and jewels, her legs wrapped tightly round her trophy.

Chapter Forty-three

Muffins!

One evening a few months later, Francine curled up on the sofa with Angel. She switched on the TV in time for Antiques Roadshow.

The Center was quiet that night. Only a few dogs were boarding.

Lester and Boss were there.

"We're visiting a town on a different dog show circuit," the Lady had said. "I want to see how Lucy does there."

"We'll go camping," the Gentleman promised, "as soon as I get back. Be good, my boys." He patted both their heads and left.

Randy was there on a rare overnight.

"We're going to see a specialist for the child," the Farmer had said. "We have to take Bailiff with us. Stay here and be good, my boy." He gave Randy a good, long pet.

"We'll be back with the sheep in no time."

Tonight's Antiques Roadshow was a special edition featuring Art Deco jewelry. Francine sat enthralled. Angel rested quietly at her side.

Lester, worn out from a long day of search and rescue, snoozed quietly. Boss lay next to him, visualizing another triumphant win for Lucy. Randy chewed on a stuffed sheep toy.

The door banged open. Day Care Guy burst into the room.

"Francine! Francine!" He kicked the door shut with one leg. A large cardboard box filled his arms.

"Look what I found!" he put the box on the floor. "Look what I found at the Dog Park!"

He opened the lid. She looked in and gasped. Angel looked over her shoulder. His jaw dropped.

In the box were two little, long-haired, red-gold puppies with large limpid eyes, and long, slimy, ear-tubes.

"Like him!" Francine gasped. "Angels!"

"Yes, we were," said Busy.

"And now, we're here," said Old Friend.

"How...how..." Angel stammered.

"You know how!" Busy winked. "It was written."

"And then, we changed it," said Old Friend. "Really, this fascination He has with slugs is just too strange!"

"But easy to fix," said Busy. "Lucky for us."

His luminous eyes bored into Angel's.

"Ha ha," he said. "Now, you have to run after me!"

"They're beautiful," Francine cooed, picking up Busy in her arms.

"Earth-dog-space-alien mutants!" Randy shouted. "I knew it!"

Day Care Guy picked up Old Friend.

"No, they're not," said Boss. He cocked his head and stared at the puppy.

"Hello, my baby boy," Old Friend smiled.

"It IS you!" Boss jumped to his feet and wriggled with joy.

"But what about your ears?" Angel asked, still in shock. "How will they change?"

"Already happening," Busy smirked. "Listen to them."

"Get some jars!" Francine said. "I have to get more slime before their ears molt!"

Day Care Guy gently put Old Friend down on the floor and ran to get the jars. Old Friend toddled over to Boss and leaned against his side.

"And some food!" Francine called.

"Yeah!" said Busy. "Where's the food?"

"They must be starving," Francine said.

"Where's the food? Where's the food? Where's the food?" Busy ran in circles. Lester woke up.

"What the…look!" he said. "Little dudes with slime ears just like yours used to be!"

"Yes," said Angel, still unable to move.

"I wonder if they can shoot that stuff like you did," Lester said.

"Watch me," said Busy as Day Care Guy approached with the jars. He snapped his tubes up into a V, then shot them forward. His aim was a little off and Day Care Guy got sprayed in the pants before he moved the jar to meet the stream.

"Wow," said Day Care Guy.

"Me, too!" said Old Friend and sprayed into the other jar.

"Wow…" Francine said.

"Food!" said Busy when he stopped spraying. "Where's the food?"

Day Care Guy put two small bowls on the floor. The two pups buried their faces in the food. Within seconds, Busy was finished.

"More food!" he cried. "Where's the food? More food!"

He slammed his little body against the coffee table, dislodging a mini muffin from a pile that sat there on a plate.

"Muffins!" he shouted. He picked it up and ran across the room toward the pet door.

"Not that one!" Angel yelled. "It's chocolate!"

"Ha ha!" Busy's laugh was more little devil than angel.

"Now YOU have to take care of ME!" he shouted and slammed through the pet door.

"Come back with that muffin," yelled Angel and slammed through the pet door after him.

Francine stayed up all night feeding and watering the new pups. After every bowl of food, they dutifully shot their ear slime into her jars. In the coming months, long after the tubes had fallen away and new soft, red-gold ears had taken their place, she would mix a quarter teaspoon of the true slime into every batch of her own formula, "Angel Hair Pomade for Fabulous Dogs!" Customer response was unanimous: the new formula was out of this world.

The End

This book is dedicated to the memory of my beautiful Cammie-Dog, the Border Collie, and her boyfriend Rocky, the Red Doberman. Many thanks to Rocky's owners, Ted and Brischa Borchgrevink, for the picture!

Bonus Material

This story began its life as a musical for the stage. "Dogs! It's the Musical!" made its world premiere in a Silver Moon Theatre production in April, 2011, in Sonoma, California.
(Photo courtesy of Kevin R. Tobin)

Our Final Show with Silver Moon Theatre
(Photographer unknown)

Anne Petersen as Lucy with Sue Martin as Melinda
(Photo courtesy of Kevin R. Tobin)

Lucy and her son Lester, played by Anne Petersen
and Chris Wall
(Photo courtesy of Kevin R. Tobin)

Boss, Lester, Angel and the Night Dogs, featuring
Rich Pharo as Boss
(Photo Courtesy of Adrian R. Hyman)

The Day Dogs, with Lester in the middle, joined by
Angel, Jerry and Ben
(Photo courtesy of Adrian R. Hyman)

Rufahlo and Papillion, played by Rob Everett and Yoli Holman
(Photo courtesy of Kevin R. Tobin)

Mimi and Bob, played by Rhonda Guaraglia and Jim Kent
(Photo courtesy of Adrian R. Hyman)

Rose O'Connor started her story telling life at National Public Radio. On-air director of "Morning Edition", she also worked on "Folk Festival USA", "Jazz Alive", and contributed to "All Things Considered". This is her first novel.

www.ingramcontent.com/pod-product-compliance
Lightning Source LLC
Chambersburg PA
CBHW020222180626
46810CB00006B/2017